**W9-CNH-273**

A Regimental Affair

Also by Allan Mallinson

A Close Run Thing
Honorable Company

A
REGIMENTAL
AFFAIR

—

A Novel

—

ALLAN
MALLINSON

BANTAM BOOKS

A REGIMENTAL AFFAIR

A Bantam Book / March 2002

Library of Congress Cataloging-in-Publication Data
Mallinson, Allan.
A regimental affair / Allan Mallinson.
p.   cm.
ISBN 0-553-11154-X
I. Title.
PR6063.A36615 R4 2002
823'.914—dc21
2001035691

Published simultaneously in the United States and Canada

Bantam Books are published by Bantam Books, a division of
Random House, Inc. Its trademark, consisting of the words
"Bantam Books" and the portrayal of a rooster, is Registered in U.S.
Patent and Trademark Office and in other countries. Marca
Registrada. Bantam Books, 1540 Broadway, New York, New York
10036.

The King's Peace

I found myself obliged, by every tie of duty and affection to my people, to suppress in every part those rebellious insurrections and to provide for the public safety by the most effectual and immediate application of the force entrusted to me by Parliament.

His Majesty King George III,
Debate on the King's Speech from the Throne,
Parliament
June 1780

1815

At the commencement of the present reign, and indeed thirty or forty years ago, peace officers were seen keeping order among the crowd, but now not a court-day passes without a strong military force being stationed on the public highway.

Henry Brougham, MP,
future Whig lord chancellor

PART 1

THE BREVET

THE PRIVILEGE
OF RANK

The Horse Guards, March 12, 1817

Five major generals—so much scarlet and gold that the usually somber meeting room of the commander in chief's headquarters was for once a place of color—sat in comfortable upholstered chairs at a long baize-covered table, their chairman, Sir Loftus Wake, Bart., the vice adjutant general, at the head, while on upright chairs at the wall perched the Duke of York's military secretary and two clerks. The atmosphere was somnolent despite the morning hour. In front of each general officer lay a blue vellum portfolio tied with red silk, as well as paper, pencils, and a coffee cup of delicate pink Rockingham, rather out of place. Some of the cups were empty, and were being attended to by a footman in court livery. Major General the Lord Dunseath, a dyspeptic-looking man with a purple nose, waved him aside without a word, intent on some detail in his copy of *The Times*. The footman next proffered his coffeepot to Sir Archibald Barret, KG, a kind-faced man in spite of his eye patch, who merely sighed and declined with the same breath. Major General the Earl of Rotheram, noble browed, a picture of decency, lit a cigar instead, but Sir Francis Evans, Kt., crabbed and lacking any appreciable chin, with an ear that was turned forward like a tailor's tab, accepted more of the strong araba and took out his snuffbox. The footman hesitated by the next, empty, chair and then moved to replenish Sir Loftus's cup.

Sir Loftus Wake resembled a small garden bird in both looks and animation. His frame was spare indeed, and his eyes—his whole head—darted from papers to watch, from watch to door, and then back again with the speed and regularity with which small birds must search about constantly for predators. He stared again at the empty chair and then at his half-hunter. "It is a quarter past. Where *can* Sir Horace be?"

Lord Dunseath, his nose always a beacon of his disposition, put down his newspaper and made a loud huffing sound. "Well, if he's trying to come through the City he'll never get here. They're hanging that caitiff Cashman at Newgate this morning. *The Times* says a crowd's expected. A *mob* more like, I'll warrant! I trust you've a line of cavalry between them and Whitehall, Wake?"

"Oh, come!" said Sir Loftus, more agitated still. "That will be no occasion for trouble."

"Don't you imagine it," huffed Dunseath again. "I was 'ere last December when those damned Radicals at the Spa Fields marched on the Tower. As close to revolution as I ever saw!"

"Stuff and nonsense, sir!" said the Earl of Rotheram, blowing a cloud of smoke ceilingwards. "I was at St. James's the whole time. It was all wind and wine. Hunt and his like—rabble-rousers, yes, but I hardly fancy they have the stuff of a Robespierre in them!" The earl was ever a man in whom the moderation of the shires found a faithful voice.

"I wouldn't be so sure, Rotheram," warned Dunseath. "There's radicalism seething all about. In some places the machine breakers are as active as ever. And there's a deal too many discharged soldiers and sailors as well. All prey to jackanapes like Hunt."

"On this latter I would not dissent. And where might we seek to lay blame on *that* account? I think it truly ignoble that this government has discharged its fighting men in so mean a fashion. There are beggars in scarlet in every lane."

Lord Dunseath's nose seemed darker still. "What would you have had Liverpool do, then? Exalt Pitt's income tax another penny to provide sturdy beggars with pensions? We want done with it!"

Lord Dunseath's voice was rising in both pitch and volume, but the Earl of Rotheram remained unperturbed. "I very much doubt we shall see an end to the income tax now that it is so expeditiously collected.

And I should not have thought it too great a burden on men who stand to profit so much from peace—and, indeed, who have profited so much already from war. At least they might rid us of the wretched Corn Laws."

"Now, *that,* sir, is radical talk!" spluttered Dunseath.

"Gentlemen! Gentlemen!" pleaded Sir Loftus Wake. "I hardly think the Horse Guards is the place for politics."

The military secretary had moved towards the chairman, meanwhile, and he now whispered something in his ear.

Sir Loftus looked relieved. "Well, gentlemen, it seems that, since we are five, there is a quorum. So let us begin without Sir Horace; and if he does arrive—"

At this point Major General Sir Horace Shawcross, KCB, did indeed arrive, flushed and angry. "In God's name, what's become of this country!" he boomed. "Insolent devils holding up every carriage in the City, and not a constable in sight. It would've been the same along the Strand an' all had there not been regular horse there."

"See, Rotheram; *The Times* warned as much," said Lord Dunseath, his nose almost glowing with satisfaction at the news.

The Earl of Rotherham merely raised his eyebrows.

Sir Horace Shawcross ignored the exchange as he half flung his cloak at an orderly. "When in God's name is Parliament going to grasp the nettle? If we don't have proper police soon there'll be no peace for the keeping anywhere, and the army'll be ruined doing the work!"

Sir Loftus, though well acquainted with Sir Horace Shawcross's choleric disposition, was taken aback by his vehemence, and the strains of his pronounced Lancashire vowels were permitted, for the moment, to continue unchecked.

"Damme, I'd the very devil of a job in the Midlands with them Luddites." He pronounced "Ludd" to rhyme with "hood."

Sir Francis Evans smiled to himself.

Even had Sir Horace seen it, it would not have mattered, for his hero, Robert Peel, chief secretary for Ireland, pronounced the word in the same way. "Now, if we had a peace preservation force, as Peel has got himself in Ireland," he boomed again, "we could stop all this nonsense in a trice."

The Earl of Rotheram set aside his cigar. "Peelers? In England?"

"Rather them than us having to do the work," replied Sir Horace gruffly. "Rather would I be under an Albura saw again than chase round doing police business!" He pulled aside the chair with his right hand, his left having been the object of the surgeon's blade after that bloody battle, and slammed his hat on the table, setting the cups and saucers atremble.

For what seemed an age, Sir Loftus stared intently at the hat, for it was the old service shako of Sir Horace's beloved 47th—"Wolfe's Own"—rather than a major general's plumes. Sir Loftus, as vice adjutant general, was most punctilious in these matters. Indeed, he seemed quite oblivious now to the growing ruction about his committee.

"Said there'd be trouble," muttered the purple nose from behind *The Times*.

"*Everyone* 'as been saying there'd be trouble," growled Sir Horace. "But what's the good of that? If we had proper police we might do something about it."

The Earl of Rotheram sighed.

"Aye, Rotheram, well might y'sigh," complained the voice of Lancashire, "for it's your party that won't see sense."

The Earl of Rotheram had, indeed, spoken against the proposal for such a force when last it had been debated in the Lords. "I should sooner trust to the good sense of the magistrates than have some damnable system as they have on the Continent. We've not fought Bonaparte these past twenty years just to have a score of little Fouchés in every town."

Sir Horace looked startled until he recognized the French. He drank his coffee in one go and held out his cup for more. "Rotheram, you're as good a man as ever walked them broad acres o' yours, but you underestimate the seething there is, and the dissatisfaction of folk who are a prey to violence every day—in town and country alike. I grant you the odd poacher might disturb *your* peace, but that's nothing to having yer livelihood and property—aye, and yer very life itself—a hostage to the mob's whim."

The two men looked across the table at each other uncomprehendingly, as if it were the great divide of the Pennine range itself, for Sir Horace's family was cotton rich and Whig, whereas Lord Rotheram's was land rich and Tory. In their own counties the families were as well regarded by the poorest of their workers—be it in factory or farm—as any could be. And these two sons had served England dearly in its late trial, Sir Horace's hand being matched by the earl's right leg. Yet each saw the future as differently as might two horses see the same fence.

Sensing exhaustion on the subject of a professional constabulary, Sir

Loftus Wake sought to regain his authority. "Well, gentlemen, perhaps we should adjourn this debate and be about our proper affairs this day."

To his considerable relief there was a general murmur of agreement.

"We all want to be 'ome afore dark," added Sir Horace gruffly.

"Well, therefore, let us begin the proceedings of the twenty-third meeting of the Army Brevets Committee." He replaced his pince-nez firmly and turned over a page of his portfolio. "May I first respectfully remind you that the purpose of a brevet—"

"We all know what the purpose of a brevet is, Wake!" rasped Sir Horace. "Let's be having the business!"

Sir Loftus looked pained once more. "My dear general, I have no reason to suppose that you are anything but in the right. However, it has ever been my practice to proceed on the supposition that not everyone should be expected to retain each and every detail of Horse Guards administration. In that way we may be sure to avoid any profound error."

Sir Horace looked unconvinced. "As you please, then."

"Very well, gentlemen. The purpose of brevet rank is to advance those officers of exceptional merit and who might otherwise find their promotion retarded by lack of means to purchase the next higher rank, or indeed by a lack of regimental vacancy in such a rank." He paused. "It does not carry with it the additional pay, of course; neither is it recognized regimentally, but only in the army as a whole." He glanced about the table for confirmation that the purpose was understood.

No one seemed to be paying much attention, but Sir Loftus was pleased he had been able to read through his brief so far without further challenge.

"These the nominations?" asked Sir Horace, pulling at the ribbon on the portfolio in front of him.

"Yes," confirmed the chairman anxiously. "But do permit me to explain more fully."

Sir Horace raised his eyebrows a little petulantly and gave up fingering the silk.

"Our work this morning," continued Sir Loftus, quickly, "is in two parts. The most important is to recommend ten lieutenant colonels' brevets. But first there is the same number of majors' brevets. The Duke of York's military secretary would be obliged if all our recommendations were done by the dinner hour so that he might take them for the commander in chief's approval this evening."

"Well, let's be about it, then," demanded Sir Horace. "How many names are there for each brevet?"

"Two," replied the chairman. "And so, gentlemen, if you would please open now the portfolios before you, you will see the summaries of service and the letters of nomination for each of twenty captains. In the usual manner we shall each of us award a mark out of six, and when I ask you for that mark I should be obliged if you would all, at the same instant, indicate it to me by the dies which the military secretary is now distributing."

The lieutenant colonel placed an ebony die, half as big as a sword basket, in front of each member of the committee.

"And may I respectfully remind you, gentlemen, that the die has two blank faces, for any lesser score than three would be unseemly."

All nodded. And then, at Sir Loftus's bidding, they began the task of assessing the twenty claims to a coveted brevet.

An hour passed in varying degrees of silence. From time to time a clerk was sent scurrying away on some errand or other, but the seven major generals labored in the main with little need for clarification. When all were done—Sir Francis Evans the last to finish, but only by a minute or so—Sir Loftus motioned a footman to bring Madeira and seedcake to the table, and as smoke from assorted cigars began to fill the room once more, he invited the committee to declare their marks for each contender. "Let us begin, then, with number one: Captain Lord Arthur Fitzwarren, First Guards."

Five dies each showed six, except Sir Loftus's own and Sir Horace Shawcross's, which showed four. The clerks took note.

"Captain Sir Aylwin Onslow, Second Guards."

The scores were as before, except that Sir Horace's die showed three.

The chairman made a thoughtful "um" sound, before naming the third. "Captain the Lord Collingbourne, Royal Horse Guards."

The scores were as before, except that Sir Loftus's die now showed three as well as Sir Horace's. "We seem to be in a fractional degree of disparity," said the chairman, diffidently.

"Seems to me you're both marking meanly," said Sir Archibald Barret. "Even I can see that!" He adjusted his eye patch pointedly.

"Meanly be damned," huffed Sir Horace. "All I've seen so far are men with more than adequate means to buy their own advancement. None of them has seen campaigning service. All they've seen is the inside of St. James's and got themselves a good patron!"

"Sir Horace," began Sir Archibald, kindly; "it is not the good fortune of every officer to hear the sound of the guns every day. These are diligent young men with much to offer the staff. Especially now that peace is come."

"Perhaps," conceded Sir Horace. "But there is ever a need for men on the staff who know what it is to fight. If peace is indeed come then it's even more important that there are officers in positions of influence who know what is the true business of war. Peace will not be with us forever, and the devil in a long peace is that the army forgets how to fight!"

"Prettily said, Sir Horace," acknowledged Sir Archibald, "but let us not be overly fastidious. Let us just suppose that in ten brevets we shall turn up ten officers as can with honor serve their country best."

Sir Loftus Wake now showed something of the quality for which he had been entrusted with the committee's chairmanship, suggesting that the military secretary make a note of those nominations where there was a disparity of more than two points as members saw them. "And then, perhaps, we may look again at those names in light of our findings as a whole."

The members of the committee were content, and the next nine names passed without much comment.

"Captain John Daniells, Sixty-Ninth Foot," said Sir Loftus for the thirteenth.

Sir Horace's mark was six, Sir Loftus's five, the others threes and fours.

"Now, this I don't understand," sighed Sir Horace. "Daniells is described by Sir Charles Alten—who did, after all, command the division at Waterloo in which that regiment was—as the most able captain in his command, and certain to rise to general rank."

"But you see," replied Sir Archibald Barret, rubbing his eye patch a shade wearily, "he scarcely needs a brevet to secure that prediction. He'll fight his way there in the usual way—as you did and I did! *We* are trying to place men in positions of responsibility on the staff *now*. I am very much afraid that if a major general says he wants someone as his brigade major then that is greatly more to the point than one who simply predicts a man will reach high rank."

Once again Sir Loftus managed to stay Sir Horace's protest. "Gentlemen, what are we *meant* to be about is the advancement of officers who will serve their country with distinction. This, I believe, is what we are trying to do. We each, perhaps, perceive that service to be rendered differently, but not the ultimate effect. The process is not science, though. I do beg a little forbearance from members."

Calm returned to the table as three more names were marked—Broke of the Rifles, Lord Henry Lygon of the Bays, and Sir Idris Llewellyn of the 23rd Foot.

"Number seventeen," said Sir Loftus, sounding a little tired. "Captain Matthew Hervey, Sixth Light Dragoons."

Sir Horace displayed five, Sir Loftus six, the others fours and one three.

"Oh, come now!" Sir Horace complained. "Lord Uxbridge writes that this officer has one of the best cavalry eyes in the service, and Colquhoun Grant says he did sterling service lately in India for the duke. What more d'ye want?"

Sir Francis Evans answered this time, his chin for the moment out of sight below his collar, his tab ear, like Lord Dunseath's port-wine nose, reddening as it always did when he was perturbed by something. "We cannot go awarding brevets just because someone is a Waterloo hand. The rest of the army is becoming impatient of the duke's habit of favoring men so. Hervey has no experience of the staff, and he is not proposed for any special appointment."

"That, I grant you. But it's not merely Waterloo. The man, it seems, did extraordinarily well on his own in India."

"India!" muttered Lord Dunseath from his lately silent corner of the table.

"My noble lord," sighed Sir Horace, forcing himself to measure his words, "if we continue to think of India in that manner, we shall waste much experience of fighting that we can ill afford to. Mark my words: these Indiamen have things to teach us."

"I never heard such nonsense! Brown faces is all they see. How can a brown face teach an officer more than a Frenchman?" Lord Dunseath's own face had turned red, and his nose almost violet.

"*Please,* gentlemen," Sir Loftus appealed; "let us not disparage any of these candidates. They are all worthy men. Let us proceed to the remaining three."

"Very well," said Sir Horace, "but I must have the floor if Daniells and Hervey do not show when the count is made."

"Of course, of course: I have said already that it will be a member's prerogative," conceded the chairman.

When the declarations and the counting were all done, Sir Loftus announced the preliminary brevets. Daniells's name was not one of them; neither was Hervey's.

"Then I must protest most strongly," said Sir Horace, striking the table with the stump of his absent hand.

Sir Loftus was an officer who sought concordance in the committees of which he was chairman. But although he had risen by his skill on the staff rather than in battle, he shared Sir Horace's opinion of Daniells and Hervey. He did not know, however, if his staff skills would extend to converting the other members of the brevets committee to that view. He summoned the footman to bring more Madeira.

Earlier that morning, Captain Matthew Hervey had found himself once more at the Horse Guards, in the yard below the room where the major generals would discuss his fitness for a brevet.

"Shall we walk there directly, or take a chaise through the park?"

"Let's walk," said Hervey with a smile. "Let's see your guardsmen at drill."

Captain the Lord John Howard, in full dress—smart as a carrot new-scraped (the buckles of his shoes were gleaming so bright that Hervey knew they could not be pinchbeck)—returned the smile and picked up the step as they struck off towards the Horse Guards' parade and St. James's Park. A company of the Grenadiers, as they were now calling themselves (Howard's own regiment), was wheeling in slow time at the farthest corner of the parade ground by the judge advocate general's garden at the end of Downing Street, but they were too few, and it was too dull an evolution, to merit more than a passing observation, though their band made a pretty noise. The dismounted sentry at the arch, from the Oxford Blues, had brought his sword from the slope to the carry as they passed, and Hervey had returned the salute with a hand to his shako, thrilling more than a little to the compliment, for the Duke of York's headquarters was the place from which all the king's men, no matter how far-flung their post, had their fortunes ordered. It did not fall to every officer to walk thus.

"Shall you tell me what was said?" asked Howard, unable to contain himself any longer. "Did the Duke of York have laurels for you?"

"I didn't see him," said Hervey simply.

Howard looked at him with disbelief. "But that is why you were come here!"

"Yes," agreed Hervey absently, for the sight of the parade ground had brought to mind the last occasion he had walked here. Then, Howard had been his arresting officer, and the future had looked black indeed, until the confusion leading to his arrest was suddenly revealed. The revelation and the honors that had come with it seemed as yesterday. But he made himself rally. "You would scarce expect, though, that the Duke of York would be able to spare the time to see a mere captain of light dragoons."

"That is deliberately to demean yourself, to degrade your station as aide-de-camp to the Duke of Wellington!"

"*Lately* aide-de-camp. As I told you before, I was discharged by the duke."

Lord John Howard sighed. "Hervey, I am truly astonished. You are appointed aide-de-camp to the first soldier of Europe—of the *world* indeed—and you ask to be relieved!"

"There's no profit in doing a job which is better fitted to others."

"But you scarce served beside the duke. Might you not have given the prospect a chance, at least?"

"You are in the right there, my dear Lord John," said Hervey, looking straight ahead still. "I didn't serve directly on his staff. But India resalted my appetite to be with troops—and not just *any* troops."

Howard shook his head again. "You have a most uncommon attachment to your dragoons. No good to you may come of it if you persist."

"And you in the Guards have no such attachment?" Hervey's frown implied skepticism.

"I confess I was never able to recognize my company unless the serjeants had taken post. That is the way in the Guards. It would not do for an officer to know a private man's name."

"Stuff and nonsense! I never heard its like," laughed Hervey. "You are beginning to sound like d'Arcey Jessope. I know for a fact that you visit the Chelsea Hospital every week and have seen to pensions for half a dozen who were at Waterloo!"

The captain of Grenadiers stayed his argument abruptly. How Hervey knew of his charity, he could not imagine. But there was no doubting that his friend had detected his pretense at Guards insouciance. "I was not there, you see," he replied simply. "And if you weren't at Waterloo . . ."

The point had not occurred to Hervey quite so plainly before.

"I listen to Rees Gronow in White's. He never boasts, of course, or says anything that might promote his part in things, but I know that being at Waterloo has changed the entire way in which he thinks. Is that not so?"

The band had broken into quick time, encouraging both men to step out. Hervey was keen to leave the subject behind. He liked Lord John Howard a good deal, and thought he might even come to like him as much as he had d'Arcey Jessope—though he could never be a true intimate because, like Jessope, Howard did not wear a blue coat and a buff collar, and the roman VI on his shako.

"Howard," he announced, "I shall be pleased to breakfast with you." He took his arm. "Only let us avoid mention of things which are now properly in the past. There is more before us than behind: of that you can be sure."

After their breakfast and a change into plain clothes, the aide-de-camp and the former aide-de-camp took a chaise to the City, for Hervey was determined, now that there was no duty to detain him in London, to secure a seat on the first coach for Wiltshire. The last occasion he had had for one had been the better part of three years ago, when, with Bonaparte dispatched to Elba and peace seemingly come at last to Europe, he had been given his first leave in as many years to return to Horningsham and his people. And there he had met Henrietta again.

He would have a very great deal to speak about with Henrietta. He had rehearsed it the better part of his passage home from India, and the delight he was taking in the prospect of seeing her was now and again marred by the darker parts of those litanies. However, that she might throw him over—or that she might, indeed, have done so already—could not take away the pleasure in just *seeing* her again, for it had been all but two years since their hasty affiancing and his even hastier departure. But for the time being at least, Hervey had only practical concerns, and these were welcome as a distraction from those others.

On that last occasion for posting to Wiltshire, he had gone to the Saracen's Head in Skinner Street, the offices of the Universal Coach and Waggon Company, to pay over the odds for an inside seat on one of their mails, a balloon coach which had thence conveyed him at a full nine miles an hour to Salisbury, whence after a night's fitful sleep at the Red Lion, he had taken the Bath stage for Warminster. And although he hoped the demand for seats had slackened in the intervening two years, this was his intention again now.

Lord John Howard was minded to go with him to Horningsham, too, for Hervey's sister, Elizabeth, had become the object of his considerable admiration (but which fact he had not yet been quite able to tell his friend). Duty at the Horse Guards, however, would delay that pleasure a further while.

As the chaise got closer to Snow Hill, its progress was checked to an unusual degree, even allowing for the habitual congestion of the narrow thoroughfares of the City. Lord John Howard stuck his head out of the window and called to the driver for his opinion of the delay.

"Cashman, sir! They're hangin' 'im at noon outside Beckwith's gun-shop in Skinner Street. I doubts as I'll be able to get the carriage through to the Saracen's at this rate."

From both windows they could see men and women, in the main respectably dressed, walking with grim purpose in the same direction they were heading, though with more ease.

"I think it better if we alight," said Howard. "This will never do."

They stepped down from the chaise—not without difficulty—and Hervey paid the driver. "Straight on up here, then, sir, on across Gray's Inn Road and you'll be there soon enough. And mind, gentlemen; there'll be pick-pokes and nippers all over the place."

They thanked him and joined the flow of people eastwards. "Who is this Cashman?" asked Hervey, fastening tight his coat. "I heard speak of him at the United Services this morning."

"Ah," replied Howard, raising an eyebrow. "It's a very rum affair indeed. There was a big gathering of Radicals on the Spa Fields at Clerkenwell last December. The crowd was whipped up by agitators and the like, and then a couple of hundred of them marched into the City, breaking into some gun shops on the way."

"What happened when they got there?"

"Oh, the mayor had things properly seen to. They couldn't make any mischief at the Exchange, so they set off for the Tower instead."

"And then?"

"The mayor had sent for the cavalry, and they dispersed them without too much trouble."

"And Cashman was one of the ringleaders?"

"Heavens, no. He was just one of the poor sots to be taken in by the likes of Hunt."

"Hunt?" Hervey had been little enough in England these past five years to know anything much of the troubles, let alone the names of the ringleaders.

" 'Orator' Hunt they call him—a fearful rabble-rouser. Makes mischief all over the country at present, what with his calls for reform. He and others like him are the real villains of the piece. But it was Cashman who broke into Beckwith's, and he stands convicted of stealing arms for the purposes of insurrection. He's being hanged outside the very shop."

Hervey sighed a sigh of "cruel necessity."

Howard caught his meaning and was—to Hervey's surprise—not wholly in accord. "There are many who believe his former service was not taken in mitigation, and that he was ill-used."

"What service?" asked Hervey, now intrigued.

"He had, it seems, served bravely for some years in the navy, and they'd discharged him without arrears of pay or prize money. According to the *Morning Post,* he'd applied to the Admiralty for redress on several occasions, and he'd been there in person on the morning of the Spa Fields meeting. It's at the very least a possibility that his actions that day were more in anger and frustration than in any spirit of revolt—insofar as the quantity of gin he'd consumed allowed them to be in any way his own."

"What a devil of a business then," Hervey conceded. "The court hangs a man for mutiny who has proved his loyalty under more trying conditions."

"I tell you, Hervey," said Howard, lowering his voice and glancing to left and right, "it makes a fellow ashamed the way these men are treated by a supposedly grateful nation. There are men with stripes on their arm cleaning out gutters for a few pence—Waterloo stripes, too. I can scarce look them in the eye."

As they came to Snow Hill, they found the streets blocked by posts and chains, allowing only those on foot to pass, and in Skinner Street itself the pavements were railed off with sturdy wooden planks. A large press of people seemed set to topple the barriers at any moment, but somehow they were holding, the crowd brooding rather than clamorous—though there was no doubting the sympathy for the gallant tar about to be hanged. And the crowd was, indeed, a thorough mix of people, of both good appearance and bad, for to the clerking classes and the respectable poor of Hackney were added the sweepings of St. Giles's—the rookery of rookeries. The special constables from each of the City wards were here in force, though

Hervey thought them hardly sufficient to deal with a crowd turned ugly. In Whisken Street there were firemen on alert, ready to assist with subduing disorder if need be. In the yard of Newgate Prison were three-score militia-men, and in the streets adjacent to the route of Cashman's procession were yeomanry cavalry, while in a nearby courtyard, out of sight, a half troop of regular cavalry stood as the force of last resort.

"There are rumors." Howard's voice was hushed. "Plans to rescue him as he arrives, to bustle him away to Broad Street. There are so many Irish there he'd never be found."

"You didn't mention he was Irish."

"No, I didn't. That confounds things, too, does it not?"

Hervey sighed again.

A great roar went up from the crowd, followed by booing and cries of "Shame" as workmen drawing the wheeled gibbet arrived from Newgate. The special constables looked about anxiously, tapping their staves nervously on a shoulder or hand. "I don't fancy they might do aught but save themselves if this crowd makes ugly," said Hervey.

"It will be the cavalry that has to deal with it. And they'll get no thanks, no matter how bloodlessly they manage," Howard agreed.

"I hate the business with magistrates. I had enough of it in Ireland. The sooner there's a proper constabulary the better."

"My dear friend, I could not agree with you more. Our guardsmen are never so disquiet as when they're deployed for the civil power. A com-pany of Grenadiers who stood fast throughout at Waterloo were close to insolence when they were turned out during the Corn Law bill."

They pushed a little farther up the street in the press of people still ar-riving, making for the scaffolding which the Newgate men had trundled to the front of Beckwith's shop.

Howard stopped. "Look here, Hervey," he frowned. "I've never seen a man hanged before, and I don't think I care to."

"I've seen it not a great many times myself," Hervey assured him, "and though each time the man had committed the foulest murder I could take no satisfaction in it."

Howard shook his head.

"Let's away, then," said Hervey, putting a hand to Howard's shoulder.

The press was too great for any quick escape, however, so they de-cided to work their way along past Beckwith's shop, its windows stoutly boarded, and out towards the wider Essex Road beyond. But this they found not easy either, for many of the onlookers were resentful of what they presumed was an attempt to get closer to the gibbet. After a full half hour they had advanced scarcely fifty yards.

Suddenly there was a roar from the crowd behind them as the carriages carrying the sheriffs rounded the corner, and then the cart bearing Cashman himself. Hervey climbed onto a window ledge to see what was the cause. "I think it's our man," he said, unable to balance there for more than a few seconds. "And he's dressed in his sailor's best."

Cashman was, indeed, a sight offensive to every right instinct. He stood proud and erect, with not a sign of fear. He had on his blue jacket and white trousers, and a black silk handkerchief tied smartly about his neck, bareheaded as if mustered on deck for divine service. He was calling to the crowd, now muted by the appearance of their hero. "This is not for cowardice," Hervey heard him call defiantly. "I have done nothing against my king and country, but fought for them!"

The crowd roared its approval, putting to flight the roosting pigeons on St. Botolph's spire two streets away.

"I always fought for my king and country, and this is my end."

The noise grew louder, and the constables had the greatest trouble keeping a way clear for the procession.

"Huzza, my boys, I'll die like a man," shouted Cashman as he reached Beckwith's shop. "If I was at my quarters I would not be killed in the smoke; I'd be in the fire!"

The crowd was now as angry as ever Hervey had seen men away from the battlefield. The constables had to make free with their staves to get the sheriffs and clergy to the scaffold.

"Hurrah, my hearties in the cause!"

Hervey wondered for a moment in *which* cause, though he hardly expected that a man in Cashman's position could be expected to say anything of sound mind.

"Success! Cheer up!" The gallant tar scaled the scaffold ladder as surely as if he had been climbing to the yards, waving aside the minister who was attempting words of comfort and inviting him to repent. "Don't bother me. It's no use. I want no mercy but from God."

Hervey and Howard were now but twenty yards from the scaffold and could see everything perfectly.

"This fellow's a cool customer," Howard whispered. "Is it gin or rum speaking, do you think?"

"He treads the boards. But he does it bravely, for sure," replied Hervey, shaking his head in doubt.

The hangman put the rope around Cashman's neck. The crowd gasped and then groaned. Then he tried to put a nightcap over Cashman's head, but the sailor would have none of it. "No, thank you, Mr. Ketch. I'll see till the last!"

Here was courage indeed, thought Hervey. He had seen bravado turn to nothing when the moment came.

But Cashman's resentment seemed to get the better of him, and he began a tirade against Beckwith himself, whom he supposed was cowering behind the boarded windows of his shop. "I'll be with you there," he shouted. "My unquiet spirit'll walk your floors."

"Oh, God," sighed Howard. The hangman had come down the steps and was standing by the lever which would trip the hatch beneath Cashman's feet. "I cannot see this, deserving or no."

Hervey was about to turn away, too, when Cashman called out again. "I am the last of seven of them that fought for my king and country. My father was killed, too, in the Service. I could not get my own, and that has brought me here!"

"This is too much," Howard muttered. "And I who have never heard a shot fired in anger am stood gawking."

"Come, then," said Hervey, turning.

But Cashman called for the crowd to give him three cheers, making them both turn back once more. And then, in the language the sailor knew best, he called to the hangman to "let go the jib boom."

Suddenly his words were choked off. His body swung crazily in midair. He struggled only briefly, but it silenced the crowd. When his writhing was no more, several of the onlookers muttered "God rest his soul." Some made the sign of the cross. For a while, as the sheriffs' men took down the body, there was scarcely a word, but as quickly as the silence had come the clamor returned, and everywhere there were shouts of "Murder! Murder! Shame! Shame!"

The constables looked about anxiously as Hervey and Howard took the opportunity to push their way to the end of the street. There was the sound of splintering timber and then a terrific roar as some of the rougher elements mounted the scaffold and pulled down the gibbet. The pavement boards outside Beckwith's shop gave way and the crowd surged into the middle of the street, the constables quickly abandoning their attempts to hold them back and running to the west end where one of the City magistrates stood with an armed guard.

"We'd better leave them to it. This is no place for either of us," said

Hervey, having to fend off one of the ladies of the district (business always increased after a public execution).

The magistrate looked nervous, too. More people—and a sight less respectable looking than before—were coming from the rookeries. The crowd in Skinner Street was now in a distinct tumult. He clearly feared for property and life. Hervey saw him signal to one of his deputies at the end of the street, and then take out his pocketbook.

"Our Sovereign Lord the King," he began, though the tumult was so great that none beyond a dozen yards could have heard him, "chargeth and commandeth all persons being assembled immediately to disperse themselves and peaceably to depart . . ." A piece of rotten fruit struck the magistrate square in the face, but he faltered only for a second before continuing; "peaceably to depart to their habitations or to their lawful business, upon the pains contained in the Act made in the first year of King George for preventing tumultuous and riotous assemblies. God save the King!"

But this magistrate was not going to wait a full hour for the crowd to disperse, as the Riot Act required. In less than a minute there was a sudden roar and then the clatter of hooves above it, as the City officials' force of last resort appeared from around the corner.

"Great gods!" exclaimed Hervey. The facings were unmistakable. "It is the Sixth! And I recognize some of those dragoons!" What a place to see them, jeered by their own countrymen when only a year ago they had been cheered to the eaves. He balked at the prospect of what they had to do, but he wanted to be with them nevertheless. "Go to it, the Sixth!" he called, before he could think better of it.

Howard had turned the color of the Sixth's facings. His eyes were empty.

"My dear *fellow*," said Hervey, grasping his arm, "I think we'd better get you some brandy."

"No, no; it is all right. I want just to walk, that is all," he replied, shaking his head.

Hervey glanced back over his shoulder at the dragoons.

"Why don't you stay?" said Howard. "I'll make my way back to Whitehall: there's no chance of getting to the Saracen's Head by the looks of things."

Hervey was not of a mind to leave him, but Howard protested he was perfectly well enough to find a chaise.

"Very well, then," Hervey conceded. "But let's dine as we said. A little later, though—say, eight? At the United Services," and he reached for his hunter to see how long he had. It was gone—twisted from the chain, for it had no safety swivel. "Oh, in heaven's name!" he groaned.

Lord John Howard raised his eyebrows as if to apologize for his city.

"It saw me through Belgium and India, and now a wretch from—"

Howard stayed his protest with a hand on his arm. "I think I should remain here with you."

"No," said Hervey shaking his head. "They'll not have another thing from me. Go back to the Horse Guards. You have duties to be about."

Hervey turned back to see the dragoons already beginning to advance with sabers drawn.

"The flats, mind; the flats only!" called their cornet, a face new to Hervey.

He thought it odd that a half troop on duty such as this was under command of so junior an officer. He could see the serjeant—Noakes, a steady sort, but never a man for troop work—behind the rear rank. A fat lot of good he'd do there with a greenhead cornet in front! But Hervey was relieved to see that the right marker was sound. What a welcome sight was Collins, his old covering corporal. Collins had galloped for him in the Peninsula, and at Waterloo, *and* (eighteen months ago, now) to Boulogne, and from there to Le Havre with Henrietta on that ill-starred chase to reach his ship. Why Collins had but two chevrons still, Hervey couldn't imagine. He'd back *his* wits in an affair, any day, against those of Auntie Noakes.

The sight of drawn swords served notice to the crowd. To some it was a signal to be off, and Hervey was pleased that the cornet had sense, at least, to advance slowly enough to give them plenty of room. But to the roughs at the far end of the street the appearance of the cavalry was a signal to increase their mischief, and to open a steady fusillade of brickbats. These dropped well short of the dragoons however, onto the front of the crowd not yet managed to get away. Soon there were men—and women— fallen to the cobbles, some bleeding from gashes about the head. It would be an even uglier sight from astride a horse, thought Hervey—and bewildering, too, since the "innocents" were now in the way of any effort to quell the more violent rioters. But it was not a time for too much thinking. If the line of dragoons stood still they'd positively *encourage* trouble.

Another hail of stones fell, closer to the line this time. "Turn about, turn about!" Hervey shouted: the hindquarters of a troop horse would, he knew, be a powerful street sweeper—and would do no lasting damage. There was certainly no room now for the flat of the saber underhand. The cornet must have seen this, for he shouted to his dragoons to raise swords. This only made the roughs bellow defiantly, and increase their fusillade of stones. Some of the braver ones climbed to the roofs of the buildings either side of the street, and it was not long before they began hurling slates down at the dragoons.

One of the first casualties was the cornet himself. A piece of guttering hit the brow of his shako and then his charger's head. He managed at first to stay in the saddle, but before his coverman could close to support him the charger reared full upright, paddling with his forelegs as if at a prizefight. The cornet, half dazed already, had no chance. He fell heavily to the ground, hitting his head hard on the cobbles. The dragoons behind tried desperately not to trample him, but more than one iron struck.

"Christ!" cursed Hervey as he pushed roughly through the crowd to reach him.

Some dragoons had stopped, trying to shield the cornet where he lay. Some were still pushing forward at the crowd, and those behind were falling into confusion, not knowing what was happening in front. Serjeant Noakes looked at a loss, while Hervey could see Corporal Collins shouting something to the front rank, whose dragoons began returning sabers to the carry and kicking their horses' flanks to urge them forward.

Good, thought Hervey. Get the front rank forward five lengths to make space!

Corporal Collins was now a length ahead of the others. He turned his trooper sideways and put him into a trot close along the edge of the crowd. It seemed to do the trick. Panic for a second or so silenced the missile throwers and allowed Collins to re-dress the front rank so they could press forward knee-to-knee. "Keep them swords *sloped!*" he shouted the while.

"Well done, well done, Corporal Collins!" said Hervey. One of the crowd eyed him suspiciously. He had better be careful. This was not the place to be taken for an agent.

The solid line of horses pushed the crowd steadily back until the missile throwers on what remained of the scaffold suddenly realized they were within range of being captured, and started to scramble down the far side. Collins called to the corporal of the second rank to show a front to the Newgate end to discourage reinforcements, and in another ten minutes they had reached the Essex Road, and Skinner Street was clear. Serjeant Noakes now reasserted command (he could scarcely pretend any longer that the confusion prevented his getting to the front) and posted videttes to which the City constables could rally.

Cursing to himself, Hervey pushed through the looser knot of onlookers to the picket line of dragoons at the ingress to Sekforde Street, where the unconscious cornet and injured dragoons had been taken. He had a mind to take the command himself, but seeing order restored among the ranks pressed on down the street instead.

Several of the men recognized him and called out with the enthusiasm that always came with the end of a bloody affair. "Good day, Mr. Hervey, sir; we thought you was gone for good."

Hervey raised his hat and smiled as best he could, but did not stay to exchange banter. Round the corner in Sekforde Street a constable pointed to the Crown and Mitre. "They've taken the injuries in there, sir."

Hervey entered the low, gloomy taproom of the city alehouse, scarcely able to make out who was where.

"It's Mr. Wymondham, sir," said an NCO, indicating the motionless figure on a long table. "I've sent a dragoon to fetch that doctor from the 'anging."

Hervey did not know Cornet Wymondham. He supposed he must have joined in the past eighteen months. He nodded approving to the NCO, and put an ear to the cornet's mouth.

"Can I go and find another doctor, sir?" asked Wymondham's coverman, whom Hervey recognized as a handy dragoon from F Troop.

"Yes," he said, "though I very much fear it will be of no avail. His breathing is so shallow as to be unnoticeable."

He said it with sadness rather than certainty—and without thinking. A young cornet, green, probably his first time out—what an impious waste. Hervey was as angry with whoever it was that had sent him here as with the crowd which had done the mischief. "Find a doctor as fast as you can. It's his only hope!" he urged suddenly, cursing himself for conceding defeat in the dragoon's hearing, and hoping his agitation might make up for it.

Hervey put his ear to the cornet's mouth again, for there was no rise or fall in the chest. He was reluctant to believe this fine-looking youth could succumb to a stone hurled by a street rough. Something told him he ought to turn him on his side. He called to the NCO for help.

They turned him ever so carefully, but Hervey felt the blood and the pieces of splintered bone at the back of the skull, and it made him so qualmish he almost let go.

"Good day, Captain Hervey, sir," came a voice from the doorway. "We none of us knew you were back. I'm sorry you had such a poor show of us, sir. How is his lordship? Pride a bit bruised, sir?"

"Not good, Corporal Collins. Not good at all."

Collins looked abashed. "Sir, I am truly very sorry. I thought he'd just be thrown and winded."

"I don't think he'll live, frankly."

"Oh, Jesus Mary! If I had ridden next to him—"

"You looked to me exactly where the right marker *should* have been, Corporal Collins. There's no call to be chastising yourself."

"He's only been with us a couple of months," said Collins, shaking his head.

"Did you say 'his lordship'?"

"Yes, sir. Cornet the Marquess Wymondham, Duke of Huntingdon's son."

There was no doubting that it seemed to make matters worse.

At that moment the sheriffs' physician arrived in a sociable. Hervey showed him the wound, but the physician took only a brief look and shook his head. "I've no vulnerary skill, I'm afraid. We'd better have him to Guy's Hospital. They're used to dealing with steeplejacks falling, there."

They carried him outside on a door, and laid it on the floor of the sociable. "I'll go with him. My assistant will have to manage the others. Send any of them on to the hospital that you see fit. But only if you must. They'll be safer away."

"A dismal prognosis, that," said Hervey as the chaise drew away. "I suppose I had better write to the duke this evening. And the lieutenant colonel."

"I suppose you better had, sir. What a terrible thing to have to do—and so soon back."

"Lord George is still the lieutenant colonel?"

Corporal Collins shook his head. "The Earl of Towcester, sir."

Hervey looked puzzled. "His is not a name I've heard, Corporal Collins. Was he a heavy?"

"I don't rightly know, sir," replied Collins, gathering up Cornet Wymondham's sword belt. "I think his lordship has been on half-pay a little while, sir. I'm not sure what was his last active regiment."

"Ah," said Hervey; that explained it.

"With your leave, then, sir, I'll resume my duties. But may I ask if you are returning to us, or are you still with the staff?"

"Of course you may ask, Corporal Collins. I am no longer with the staff, but I don't yet know when there'll be a vacancy for me."

"Let's hope there's one soon, sir."

Hervey looked him straight in the eye. There was a note of something in Collins's reply which suggested it was more than the politeness of the ranks.

But Collins volunteered nothing.

"I wish we were meeting at a better time," sighed Hervey. "There's a lot we might talk about. Forgive me if I seem less than pleased to see you again, Corporal Collins. It is certainly not intended."

"No, sir," replied Collins simply.

"Tell me, though, before you go: are there heavy calls on the regiment at present?"

"No, sir." The rising cadence indicated that Collins had not guessed his mind.

"I mean, I was surprised to see a new cornet in so . . . *susceptive* a command."

Collins remained silent. Unlike Serjeant Armstrong or Private Johnson, he was always guarded with his opinions.

Hervey rephrased his inquiry so that it did not require so obvious an opinion. "Where is the rest of your troop?"

Before he could answer, a runner came up with an urgent request by the magistrate to be escorted back to Bow Street. "Very well, at once," Collins replied, and then glanced at Hervey. "With your leave, sir?"

Hervey nodded, his frustration obvious.

"I think all the other officers are engaged today, sir," he added, touching his shako peak discreetly as he turned for the escort.

CHAPTER 2

NOVELTIES

Albemarle Street, That Afternoon

When Hervey returned to the United Services Club there were two letters awaiting him. The first was brief and very much to the point:

Albany

The Most Hon. The Earl of Sussex
returns Captain Hervey's compliments,
and would be favored if he would call upon him
at ten A.M. tomorrow, 13 March.

Hervey had left his card at the London residence of the colonel of the
regiment the day before, as custom had it, but he had scarcely expected
that the colonel would receive him. It was as well he had not made it to
the Saracen's Head, for in seven years and more with the Sixth he had
still to meet its colonel, and by all accounts, the Earl of Sussex was a most
agreeable man. *And* such a meeting could not serve anything but well,
surely, to his getting a troop sooner rather than later?

The second letter was an altogether different proposition—a most intriguing affair. He smiled as he read its obsecrations.

Long's Hotel,
New Bond Street,
12 March

Esteemed Sir,
I have the honor to present myself as one who has with true
humility learned of your service at the late Battle of Waterloo,
and of your interest in all things that are *novel* and *advantageous* to the execution of His Majesty's business. And if you
will forgive the presumption of my writing to you then I feel
assured that I might be of *inestimable* service to you in your
most *distinguished* profession, for I have lately manufactured
a *repeating* carbine pistol such that will multiply the usefulness of its possessor a full *seven*fold.

Honored sir, if you will give word to my man by whom this
letter is brought then I may attend on you *at once* to demonstrate the ease and utility of this device—whose invention is
awaiting patent in conditions of *utmost secrecy*.

Believe me, sir, I am yours *most* faithfully,
Elisha Haydon Collier

This was an invitation he could not overlook. A repeating carbine—the
possibilities were great indeed.

At three o'clock, therefore, he found himself in the company of Elisha
Collier on the heath at Hampstead. On their way there Collier, who professed himself an American citizen but one who was as loyal to King
George as it was possible in his circumstances to be, spoke loquaciously
but omitted anything of substance—until Hervey began to think that the
engagement would prove futile. But once they arrived, Collier set about
his demonstration with such purpose that Hervey was soon able to imagine that he was indeed to see something singular. From the boot of the
chaise Collier's assistant removed a pallet, three feet by two, and six
inches thick, and attached it to a tree some thirty paces away, pinning a
roundel target to it. He then beat the cover beyond the tree for as far
again. When he was returned, Collier turned to Hervey. "I believe you
have, sir, faced many an enemy at such a range, and I hazard that many

was the time when you felt the want of handiness in your service weapon."

Hervey made no response. Both propositions were palpably certain for a soldier.

"Then, sir, you may have no fear ever of finding yourself in such a predicament again," Collier declaimed, raising his hat and bowing.

The gesture was so theatrical as to make Hervey smile. But at once Collier's expression turned almost demonic. He pulled open the portmanteau at his feet, pulled out a long single-barreled pistol, took rapid aim at the target, and with scarcely a pause to recock and close the pan cover between each, fired seven rounds. Hervey, though startled, watched the making of holes in the roundel and clapped his hands in admiration. "A very effective display of musketry indeed, Mr. Collier—not merely of pyrotechny!"

Collier's benign expression returned. He looked pleased by the acclamation. "I think I may safely wager, sir, that every round may be accounted for in that target. Do you wish to inspect it closely?"

"No, I do not think there is need for the present," replied Hervey, eyeing the weapon keenly. "I have read about such guns, Mr. Collier—they are hardly new—but the cylinders or barrels were always turned manually, and they were prone to jamming. Yours, very evidently, has some mechanical means of rotation. And a reliable one at that."

"Indeed, sir—just so! That is its ingenuity. You may readily suppose of its handiness to mounted men in particular."

Hervey was ready to acknowledge it, not least in the thought of how it might have served in Serjeant Strange's hands that day with the French lancers. Strange's sacrifice still visited him, and all too often. No one had managed to persuade him that his actions that day could not have been other than they had been. Perhaps it was simply that he had galloped away from the lancers, and Strange had stayed. That he had had to gallop away, he could not reasonably doubt. That Strange had had to stay, to delay the lancers, he could not doubt either. But still there was something that gnawed at him. "And impressive for its being a *flintlock*," he said finally, gathering up his thoughts again as if loose reins.

Collier eyed him curiously, and Hervey wished at once he had said nothing. But was there any reason why this American should have known of the percussion lock which had saved his life at Waterloo?

"May I explain that mechanism, sir?" Collier continued.

Hervey was now all attention.

"You have noted, of course, sir, the cylinder arm of seven chambers. It is driven to rotate by a coiled spring which is first put into tension by rotating the cylinder anticlockwise—the opposite direction from which the barrel turns in firing."

Hervey was not so overawed by the earlier spectacle as to be at such a loss with such mechanical principles, and he frowned a trifle impatiently.

"Forgive me, sir," said Collier hastily, "I did not wish to impute—"

"No matter," said Hervey. "It has been a long day. Please go on."

"The very essence of this action—as you will appreciate, sir—is to have absolute alignment of chamber and barrel breech after each rotation. It is this which has defeated all gun makers until now."

Hervey nodded again. There were a number of other things, too, but he was content now to acknowledge that the alignment was the most crucial.

"A cone—shall we call it a male—is formed at the breech and mated, as it were, successively with a female countersink cut in the mouth of each chamber, locking the chamber and barrel into alignment."

"But how is the chamber held fast against the barrel breech, since you have just shown me that you pull back the cylinder in order to rotate it into tension?"

Collier smiled. "Yes, yes, indeed, sir! A rare grasp of mechanical detail, if I may say so." He pulled back the cylinder again. "Two means there are. First a helical spring—not the same as for the rotation, mind—and second is this"—he indicated a small sliding bolt—"which is sent forward by the fall of the cock to butt against the rear of the cylinder. It locks it quite sound, and acts, too, as a safety device, since it prevents the cock from falling fully unless the barrel and cylinder are correctly engaged."

"That is, I declare, ingenious," nodded Hervey, trying it for himself. "And the rotation: how does the cocking advance the cylinder?"

"See this hook, sir, linked to the hammer?" said Collier, handing the arm to him. "It is engaged with a skirt on the rear of the cylinder—see? When the cock is drawn back, the hook pulls back the cylinder from the breech and the spring does its work. As soon as the next chamber comes into line the hook finds a notch in the skirt and is disengaged—and the helical spring forces the cylinder forward again."

Hervey smiled. It was very ingenious indeed, so ingenious that he almost forgot about the actual initiation of the charges. "Now that much I am assured of, Mr. Collier. But how are the chambers fired?"

"Let me demonstrate, sir," said the American, taking back the arm. "It is, if I may say so myself, a particularly tidy method. Each time the pan cover is shut down for discharge, this ratchet and pawl here puts successive deposits of priming powder into the flash pan by turning a feed plug—you can't quite see it with the arm assembled, sir—at the bottom of the steel."

Hervey shook his head and smiled in admiration again. "May I fire it myself?"

"Why, of course, Captain Hervey. Let my assistant load the chambers first and fill the priming magazine, and then you shall put the spring under tension and fire at will."

Collier's assistant handed him the loaded arm and asked if he wished the roundel to be replaced. Hervey replied that this should not be necessary since they were sure that there were seven hits there already.

"Shall I fit the butt to it, sir, so that you may fire it as a carbine?" asked Collier, holding up the extension.

"No, thank you. I should like to feel its balance as a pistol, for the barrel is uncommonly long. Do I presume it is rifled?"

"Indeed it is. With nine lands. That is what gives it its accuracy. I wager I could have placed five marks on that roundel at twice the distance."

Hervey was surprised by the ease with which he could hold the aim, for the barrel was in excess of two feet. He squeezed the trigger. The gun jumped back in his hand more than would the service pistol, but it was not excessive. He cocked again.

"Close the pan, sir," prompted Collier.

He fired again. There was not as much smoke as he expected, and he saw at once the second round had struck the target, too, on the outer ring again. He adjusted his aim and repeated the action—and then a fourth and a fifth time. It was extraordinarily handy. He could scarce believe it. The sixth and seventh rounds he fired with equal address. How perfect the weapon would be were they percussion fired, as his carbine was. What odds then might a dragoon accept!

"You are much impressed with it, yes, Captain Hervey?" asked Collier.

"Yes, yes indeed. But I must admit to one doubt, however. And that is the hardiness of the mechanism as a whole. For campaign service, I mean. I have doubts that it would stand up to a dragoon's rough handling. And might it not be susceptible to dirt, causing the rotation to jam?"

Collier's response was eager. "When clean, and with a little oil on the working parts, there is no reason for it to do so, though I concur that to allow a great ingress of dirt would be to risk such an outcome. I have fired forty-two rounds in rapid succession, pausing only to reload the cylinder, without interruption."

Hervey was to some extent reassured, but there was no doubting the danger in having a weapon which might fail in the exigencies of campaign service. Damp powder was a bad enough risk already with the service flintlocks.

"But you must not accept my word alone for it, sir. I would be most honored if you would take the arm for a month's trial, and at the end of that period I would beg the favor of your recommending it—if you were to feel inclined, as I'm sure you shall—to the Duke of Wellington."

So here, at last, was Collier's purpose revealed. But no matter, thought Hervey. If the weapon were to prove as capable as it now seemed then he would have every wish to recommend it. "Yes," he replied. "I should be most happy indeed. Though I must tell you that I am no longer on the duke's staff; neither might my opinion be of any moment with him."

"I am content with that, sir. I would send it myself to the Ordnance, but I believe it would be the better for having an advocate."

Hervey was enjoying his celebrity. "Very well, Mr. Collier. We shall see how it fairs on Salisbury Plain."

Next day Hervey woke early. Though the curtains were full-closed he could see it was not yet light, although there was already a noise of carting in the street. He thought to light a candle to see the time, but with a sick feeling he recalled that he no longer had a watch. He had ordered tea and shaving water to be brought at a quarter to seven, and a bath at a quarter past, so there seemed no great need for him to do anything but enjoy the remaining repose—such as might be with the noise of the carting traffic and the chorus of birdsong growing by the minute, dominated as the latter was by the far from melodious starlings. He lay musing at how queer it was that so unbecoming a bird should have so pretty an egg. What had happened to his collection of them, he wondered? He had amassed so many in Horningsham before going to Shrewsbury. There were only two more days to the Ides, now. Such a time it would be in Horningsham for natural history. The wood-pigeons would have begun their soaring and their clapping and diving. There would be redwings and fieldfares getting ready to go north again after winter. And very soon—perhaps already—they would be replaced by sand martins come from Africa. These would be feeding high still, above the Wylye and the lake at Longleat, before returning to the crags to dig out last year's nest holes. Might he get home in time to see the first swallows? The beginning of April was their habitual season. How dull might seem the village plumage after India, though.

Those garden birds would even now be courting a mate—and threatening their rivals—for tomorrow was a full month after St. Valentine's Day. It was the better part of two years since his own affiancing, and he had not been able to make even one Valentine gift to Henrietta. Since his arriving in Paris, on the second of the month, he had sent three expresses to Horningsham (or, rather, one to Horningsham and three to Longleat), the most recent only this last evening. But he had had none by return. There again, he had perforce changed his quarters so frequently and without notice that none could have found him. And in this latest express he had been able to say only that he fervently hoped to be in Wiltshire soon—and depending only on the Earl of Sussex's pleasure (not that he truly expected a significant delay). Beyond that, what could he do but trust in Henrietta's patience and say his prayers? And *think* of her, over and over again. Think of when they had enjoyed the woods and meadows of Longleat, first in childish innocence and then in faltering courtship. She had teased him when a child and tormented him when full-grown. Horningsham was Henrietta as much as it was his family.

Meanwhile the morning was fast advancing. His bath had not been as warm as he had hoped, and the fire—which he had tipped one of the club's servants handsomely to have banked up—was more smoke than flame, and certainly very little heat. Perhaps it was not really so chill, but his blood was still accustomed to the warmth of Madras, and a fresh March morning in London was not to be underestimated. He had shivered more than once. But a breakfast of kidneys and eggs and toasted bread (and coffee exemplary hot) had set him to rights, and he left for Albany feeling comfortable enough without a surtout.

The Earl of Sussex received him promptly. "My dear Captain Hervey, I am very glad we are met at last," he said, holding out his hand and, despite his years and a leg which a musket ball at the Helder had rendered half-useless, closing briskly with him. "Sit you down, sir; sit you down!"

A footman placed a chair adjacent to the earl's, and Hervey did as he was bid.

"I generally have sherbet at this time. My digestion is not what it was. But yours, I should imagine, is plenty robustious. Would you care for Madeira?"

Hervey most certainly did. It was a taste to which he had become happily accustomed in Captain Peto's company to and from the Indies.

"I am very glad you are come this morning. You will not have heard of Huntingdon's son. Killed in the streets yesterday with the regiment, trying to quell a riot. It has saddened me more than I can say."

"I did know, Colonel. Indeed, I saw the riot." He thought it of no purpose to add that he had gone to Guy's Hospital that evening, too.

"Shall you stay to luncheon and tell me of it?" said the earl, with evident sadness. "Young Wymondham was my godson."

Hervey accepted readily. It was a handsome invitation, even with so sorrowful a purpose.

"Let us postpone talk of it until then, and stay instead with pleasanter thoughts," the earl suggested. "We have not met before, and I much regret it. But it is not, perhaps, so curious—these last tumultuous years and all. I do, though, make it a rule to receive my officers on gazetting. In fact, *before* they are gazetted, preferably."

"Indeed, your lordship. It is well known." The Earl of Sussex was an assiduous colonel in this, as every other, respect. Only the exigencies of war had distanced him from his beloved Sixth.

"I remember your nomination for a cornetcy well, though. By Pembroke's hand. No little recommendation, that. If I remember rightly, he said words to the effect that he did not think Wilton House had ever had a better pupil!"

Hervey felt himself redden. "Lord Pembroke was very kind, sir. He allowed me much time in the company of his riding master."

"Foreign, I suppose?"

"Yes, sir—Austrian," smiled Hervey, noting the sigh in Sussex's question.

"Now, when did that occur? The cornetcy, I mean."

"Eighteen hundred and eight, sir. I was but seventeen."

The earl took a sip of his sherbet. "So you were at Corunna?"

"I was, sir."

"Did you see anything of Moore?"

"Oh, yes, sir. He was everywhere."

"So I heard tell. I wonder if Wellington would have got the army had he lived."

It was a question posed often enough, but not one Hervey felt able to address in his circumstances. "I saw rather more of General Crawford, sir, for we were with his division some of the way through the Astorgias."

"Black Bob? And was he as fearsome as his name?"

"I think his men were more terrified of him than of the French—the officers especially."

The Earl of Sussex seemed to be deep in thought. "And then you were at Ciudad Rodrigo, and saw the lines of Torres Vedras."

Hervey nodded. This much was what all of them in the Sixth had seen.

"And then at Albura, and you greatly distinguished yourself at Salamanca."

Hervey, proud to be so recognized, and by the colonel whom he had never before met, was nonetheless discomfited by the approbation.

But the Earl of Sussex had not finished. "And you showed great dash, and no little resolve, at Vitoria. At Toulouse you were commended for your action by the Duke of Wellington himself, and you crown all these at Waterloo with plaudits from Lord Uxbridge. Captain Hervey, this is a record to be proud of!"

"Thank you, sir," Hervey replied, wondering how the earl had been able to recall what were, in any scheme of things, trifling affairs.

"And then there was *Ireland*."

The word came as a cold douche. Hervey swallowed and opened his mouth to speak, but before he could the Earl of Sussex raised a hand.

"There is nothing for you to say on the matter, for I have it in every detail from Lord George Irvine."

"Sir, I—"

"Captain Hervey, there really is nothing for you to explain. And let me say this to you. The courage you displayed so many times in the field is that which I should *expect* every officer of mine to demonstrate, given the requirement. And the address with which you have dealt with matters of tactics is that which I would *hope* for in those same officers—though it is not given to all to be capable of exercising such percipient judgment."

Hervey felt somewhat at ease again. There seemed to be an agreeable purpose in the earl's words, and he wondered what it might be.

"But the course you followed in Ireland was an instance of rare valor. I have known many brave men—men who have defied shot and shell to go at the enemy when all seemed lost—who have seemed incapable of standing up for what they believed was the right course in the comfort and safety of an office. Indeed, they had rather face certain death than confront a superior with an unpalatable truth. Believe me, Captain Hervey, such courage, exercised soundly, is a diamond of considerable worth."

"Thank you, sir," said Hervey. It seemed quite evident, now, that the Earl of Sussex was not merely receiving him with the usual formularies, and he felt himself greatly flattered.

"All of which brings me to the ultimate purpose of my asking you to call this morning," said the earl, signaling his footman to withdraw. "Have you had any communication from the Horse Guards in the last twenty-four hours?"

Hervey was not sure precisely what constituted such a communication. "I had to call on the Duke of York's military secretary yesterday forenoon, sir. But since then—"

"Then you do not know that you have been given a brevet?"

Hervey had been promised a captain's brevet before India. It seemed strange that Lord Sussex should have heard of it only now.

"I mean a *majority*, Hervey. The brevets committee approved it yesterday."

Hervey was dumbstruck. Not only did he not know of it, he would never have thought it possible since, by his reckoning, his substantive rank was lieutenant, and promotion to field rank required at least one year in the lower rank to qualify.

"Have not your agents informed you?" the earl persisted. "You have been gazetted captain for almost eighteen months!"

"No, sir. In truth I have not yet been to see them."

"Well, then, make sure that when you do you collect what must be healthy arrears of pay!" The Earl of Sussex's eyes were kind, and the lines on his brow and about his mouth curved upwards, so that when he smiled, as he did now, his whole face was a beacon of his pleasure.

"Why, yes, sir. *Indeed.*" Hervey was almost lost in reflecting the smile, but he managed to keep a hard head for the particulars. "My first inquiry, though, shall be what vacancy there is in the regiment. But I confess that I am more than a little confused by what this brevet may mean with regards to it."

"In *that* I may certainly be of help." By now the earl was positively beaming. "Let me explain a little of what has transpired on this account."

Hervey was intrigued. Why should there be anything that amounted to an account?

"It was a near run thing, I'm told." The earl took another sip of his sherbet. "But you shouldn't let that dull the satisfaction of the brevet. It seems you had some strong supporters in that assembly of major generals, once they'd heard your record."

Hervey felt intensely gratified. A superior's approval was every soldier's pleasure.

"Particularly, it seems, Sir Horace Shawcross. A splendid man! As bluff as Harry. He's to go to India, and he's asked for you to be his deputy adjutant general. What say you to that?"

Hervey was almost speechless again. "Sir, I . . . I am conscious of the high honor the general does me . . ."

"But?"

"But I had very much set my heart on a troop."

Lord Sussex smiled again, this time almost paternally. "You don't know how glad I am to hear you say that, Hervey. It's not every man that would turn down advancement and valuable patronage to be at regimental duty. And you shall not be disadvantaged by it. I promise you."

Hervey was puzzled, and tried to conceal it. In terms of advancement he was bound to be disadvantaged by declining General Shawcross's offer.

"I'll explain," said Lord Sussex, settling back into his chair as if the explanation was to be a long one. "Great heavens, how it shall give me pleasure! Lord George Irvine, as you may know, relinquished command on promotion about a year ago. He has the East Coast District."

Hervey confirmed that he had recently learned of it.

"There was no major in the Sixth who could replace him," continued Lord Sussex. "For of the four on the regimental list Escrick had been on half-pay for innumerable years and was not inclined to leave his estates; and nor am I sure he would have been entirely suitable. Nasmyth would have been unable to find the purchase: his interests on the Baltic Exchange were cruelly ruined by the blockade. Sir Digby Willesey is, frankly, too old and infirm: he must spend half the year at least by the sea. And Joynson is hopelessly ill-fitted for command, though by all accounts he is an able administrator."

Hervey was astonished by the candor, but held his peace nonetheless.

"The agents had received bids of up to twenty-five thousands. The regulations forbid it, I know, but since the overprice would go, indirectly, to the widows' fund I was of a mind to nod to it."

Twenty-five thousands! Hervey was speechless. It was not only a prodigious sum but four times the regulation price. What chance might he ever have of commanding the Sixth by purchase?

"I had hoped, of course, that Joseph Edmonds would have command, but the prices have grown so much of late throughout the cavalry that even had he lived I doubt he would have had the means."

Having known something of Edmonds's situation, in the settling of the late major's estate, Hervey had no doubt that he could never have afforded it. It was doubtful that Edmonds's means were any greater, even, than his own. Peace had an odd price, he rued.

"The Earl of Towcester bid the highest, and indicated to me that he wished to make a generous investment—especially in horses. And, given the hard service the regiment had seen, I thought it welcome. Towcester has been on half-pay more years than I should have cared for, but he seemed anxious to return to the line. All this I discussed with Lord George, of course."

It was curious, to say the least, to be taken into the colonel's confidence so, and Hervey evidently showed it.

"Oh, come now, Captain Hervey. It will be no earthly good if you do not know what has been our mind."

The reply confounded Hervey even more, for why should he have to know what was the colonel's mind in the case of the succession of lieutenant colonels?

Lord Sussex then seemed to hesitate before pressing to an observation that intrigued Hervey even more. "I am of a mind that Towcester will wish to sell in but a year or so."

Hervey thought it would be highly improper to make any inquiry as to why, even though the earl had raised it.

"And at that point I should not wish to bring in another extract," added Lord Sussex, shaking his head.

Hervey could only applaud that sentiment. But was it a realistic one when there was no major to succeed?

"I have discussed this particular with Lord George at great length, too, and he and I are wholly in accord. *You* shall have command, Hervey!"

Hervey's mouth fell open. "Sir . . . I . . . how . . ."

The Earl of Sussex was smiling broadly again, much satisfied with the effect. "A step at a time. Your brevet was the first one—and I am very pleased to say that our efforts in that direction were successful. You will be aware that the regulations require that you complete twelve months' service on the active list in the rank of major before you may be promoted lieutenant colonel."

Hervey knew the regulations well enough.

"And then there would be the matter of the purchase price."

"Just so, sir," said Hervey, for he saw no cause to waste the colonel's time in this respect. "I have not the means to raise a fraction of that price."

"Yes, I know as much. If you *were* to find yourself somehow in possession of that sum, would you be desirous of the command?"

There was not the slightest hesitation. "Of course, sir!"

"Then let us trust that you shall find it. *Or*—and it would not be fitting that we speak of particulars—that the means shall otherwise be found. I hope I make my meaning clear?"

Hervey nodded.

"Make no mistake, Captain Hervey, I am determined that you shall have the regiment ere next year is out. Which means, as you very well know, that you must receive your recommendation for promotion to lieutenant colonel at the end of one year's service as brevet major. D'you think you might manage that?"

It was the fulfillment of any officer's ambition, and the means by which he could now with assurance present himself to Henrietta and her guardian as a man with prospects. He felt taller by several inches even as they spoke. "I shall do so to the very best of my ability, Colonel." And then he seemed to have doubts. Or, rather, he thought he *ought* to have doubts. "Your Lordship does not, then, consider that I have not the years?"

"Great heavens, no!" said the earl, frowning and shaking his head. "As I recall, Wellington had the Thirty-third in Holland when he was not five and twenty. Didn't do him—or them—much harm."

The comparison astounded him—as perhaps it was meant to, for the Earl of Sussex wanted no dissent.

"Now, I may tell you, at present in the regiment there is a captain's vacancy—two, indeed—and I have instructed the agents that one is to be yours. Your brevet remains extraregimental of course; you shall be *Captain* Hervey with your troop. Only remember this: the brevet is the means by which you shall have that accelerated advance to lieutenant colonel. Your commanding officer is the means by which you will have that recommendation—and, thereby, the promotion. I trust I make myself clear again, Hervey. One year; *one year*! You *can* manage that, can't you?"

"Oh, yes, sir!" said Hervey emphatically. "I believe I may assure you that you need have no fears on that account!"

"Then come and share my table," said Lord Sussex, rising and beckoning Hervey with boyish delight. "I don't think I could wish for more agreeable company."

CHAPTER 3

RETURNS

Horningsham, Ten Days Later

"I blame Mr. Keble," declared Hervey's mother roundly. "Never would your father have carried on so if *he* had not filled his head with such notions."

Elizabeth Hervey glanced across the breakfast table at her brother, with a look that requested sympathy for having to listen again to the vicar of Horningsham's wife on the subject.

"And now we shall all be dispossessed of the living, for your father will not be persuaded to moderate his habits. And who, then, shall give him any other? For there isn't a patron who would be disposed to a parson who had been so recalcitrant. No, no: we shall be forced to throw ourselves on the charity of your aunt Spencer, though heaven knows they could ill afford to have us in the deanery, for Hereford will be thick as thieves with Sarum. Mark my words!"

Hervey tried to avoid his mother's eye by gazing through the window on the pretense of distraction by two combative jays. He had used the same stratagem many times before in that small but comfortable dining room. Since the death of his elder brother he had shifted one place to the

left at table, so that he sat directly adjacent to his father now—a little farther from his mother, and offset from Elizabeth, whose place had *not*
moved in the reordering of things—but otherwise it seemed to him that
nothing had changed since his earliest recollection of that room. Except
that his mother now wore a lace cap and was a little fuller, and his sister
no longer had her ringlets. More was the pity, Hervey considered, for
Elizabeth's ringlets had given her a pertness which nicely offset a sometimes overearnest disposition.

"Do not be too downcast, Mama. We might always carry the Gospel
abroad, to Matthew's India, perhaps!"

Elizabeth's attempt at levity, misconstrued, perhaps, did not find favor
with her mother, who scowled back disapprovingly.

Her brother now sallied to her rescue, though with equally unhappy
results. "Mama, the bishop cannot dispossess Father from the living. Not
without recourse to law, surely? And Lord Bath would never have that."

Elizabeth, regretfully, explained their mother's gesture of hopelessness. "Lord Bath's is not the advowson. Horningsham is a diocesan
peculiar."

Since his return, some days ago, the subject had been put to one side
in the general rejoicing. Only now, the day of his father's summons to the
palace at Salisbury, was an open discussion entered on.

"What exactly are the bishop's objections, Mama?" asked Hervey.
"He surely cannot mind a little variation? We are hardly a parish that
many take note of."

"Oh, it is not the bishop himself who does this," said Mrs. Hervey,
waving her knife dismissively. "It is his archdeacon. We have all had excess of his zeal these past twelve months since his institution."

Hervey could not have known of the new appointment. Nor, indeed,
would it have been of any moment to him were it not for the mischief
it was making now. "Very well, then, Mama. What are the *archdeacon's*
objections?"

"That the choir is put in surplices."

"Is that all?" Hervey was bemused. "The choir has been surpliced
since I myself was in it."

"And your father has taken to preaching in his, instead of a Genevan
gown."

Hervey was even more astonished at the insignificance of the offense.

"There is a little more to it than that, is there not, Mama?" suggested
Elizabeth carefully.

"Oh, I do not suppose they will let him off lightly. There'll be other objections, I'll be bound."

Elizabeth raised her eyebrows the merest touch, but her brother was already alerted to the point. "What might these other objections be?" he asked her.

Elizabeth glanced at her mother to see if she wished to take up the question herself, but Mrs. Hervey evidently did not. "He has taken to celebrating the Lord's Supper during the week."

"But that is scarcely offensive to the bishop, is it? Father is anyway obliged by rubric to say morning and evening prayer. To what can there be objection in adding the Communion?"

"The Prayer Book forbids the celebration of Communion privately," said his mother, with another heavy sigh.

"But on this all may not be lost," said Elizabeth, with a breeziness intended to lift her mother's rapidly flagging spirits. "For we might yet find sufficient parishioners to attend."

"At least until the fire has died down," suggested Hervey.

"Quite." Elizabeth frowned. "If only he would not be so . . . *Romish*, as the archdeacon calls it, when he celebrates."

"Romish? How so?" Hervey was finally alerted to the true seriousness of his father's situation.

Elizabeth looked anxiously at her mother, who purposefully turned her gaze to the window. "He places candles on the communion table and stands eastwards. With his back to the congregation, that is."

"Though there isn't one," smiled Hervey. But he knew it was a practice—as well as the candles—that would bring strife. "Is any of this of a Sunday, too?"

"No, only the surplice for his sermon."

"That much is as well," opined Mrs. Hervey. "Though if he speaks any more with Mr. Keble, heaven knows where it will all end!"

"Mama," protested Elizabeth. "You cannot blame Mr. Keble. Father has held these opinions for many years before he visited with us. You may as well blame the Jesuit at Wardour, for Father has dined with him many more times than he has ever spoken with Mr. Keble." It was well known in the village—and therefore in the diocese—that the Reverend Thomas Hervey had for many years enjoyed monthly conversation with Father Hazelwood. It was even supposed by some that these were occasions for auricular confession, and yet this had never given offense (as far as the family was aware), for such was Mr. Hervey's genuine piety and devotion to his parish. It was true that he had some years ago written a monograph on the life of Archbishop Laud, but since it remained unpublished its support for Laudian excesses could only be imagined.

"Well, we may say good-bye to all hopes of preferment, at any rate," complained Mrs. Hervey. "We shall not see even a canon-residentiary now!" And with that she rose and left the room.

Elizabeth knew that her father had long considered himself past all preferment, but she was also aware that her mother still entertained some hope of easeful retirement in a cathedral close, and it had occurred to her more than once that her life might take a more lively turn were she to be translated thus. And much as Hervey would have been loath to quit the place in which he had been born, he, too, had hoped that his father might see out his days in such comfort, for there was little enough prospect that the modest family annuity would allow him to do so.

It appeared that John Keble had visited twice while he had been away, and Elizabeth had been to his priesting at Trinitytide the year before. Hervey imagined that to his father the young clergyman was a remembrance of his elder son. Hervey had also imagined some attachment forming with Elizabeth, for in John Keble's letter to him (a most welcome *poste restante* in Paris) there was mention of quitting Oxford—and therefore its rule of celibacy—for his curacy in the Cotswolds. But it was evidently not so. Devoted to her father though Elizabeth was, there were evangelical sentiments in her which might in any case militate against such an alliance. She read Hannah More copiously, and had only recently declined a position out of Clapham with the Society for Returning Young Women to Their Friends in the Country—not out of any qualmishness, but from a conviction that her father and mother had need of her.

With their mother gone, Hervey thought he might change the subject. "How are your good works in the town, Elizabeth?"

"Never in all our years at Horningsham has there been such distress," answered his sister solemnly. "The marquess has set in place a system of relief, but it does not extend beyond the estate, and so many were the calls on the parish last year that funds were exhausted before harvest-time. Warminster Common is become more than ever a refuge for beggars and every kind of felon."

Hervey could easily believe it. At the time of his going to the Sixth it was known to be a fencing crib for the three counties.

"Gangs now maraud from there. They take the game, sometimes quite openly, at Longleat. Daniel Coates sat three times each week with the other magistrates last month, and still there is no end to the lawlessness. Father will not allow me to visit, though."

"And how should your being allowed to visit the common prevent this?" Her brother frowned skeptically.

"I do not for one minute think that it would. My concern is for the children who are being raised in that depravity. And Daniel Coates believes there should be a mission there, too." Elizabeth knew this recommendation would turn her brother's opinion.

"I shall see Daniel this morning. He's coming to look over Jessye."

"Do you know he is the owner of three brewing houses now?"

"Which keep his bench well supplied with miscreants of a Monday, no doubt!" Hervey smiled.

Elizabeth smiled, too, for she was not so much an evangelical as to be an advocate of temperance.

Hervey was pleased, for with a smile her face became pretty, and he still entertained hopes of a husband in regimentals rather than clericals.

"He is the only farmer hereabouts who has managed to keep all his laborers in work these past two years." Elizabeth said it with real pride, as if Coates were family. "He has not dismissed a single one. Indeed, he has even engaged some of the wretched Imber shepherds, so much in need of relief were they."

"Well, I'll be very much interested to learn how he has been able," replied her brother. "For everything I read is of depression in that business."

She frowned. "It's an ill thought that with peace there comes a fall in demand for the county's wool. I hope we shall never come to be thankful for war as the means of providing for our workingmen."

"Let us hope not," he agreed. "Though I should sooner see sturdy men in a red coat—with the colors, that is—than have them without work. There are men in scarlet begging along every road from here to London."

"I can believe it, for there are several in Warminster, and a sorry sight it is, too. They would at least be provided for in the army. And they would be under discipline, too. I confess I am sometimes a little afraid of them in the town now. And that was never so before." She poured him more tea and then for herself. "By the bye, Matthew, do not take against Mr. Keble for this business of Father's. I truly believe there is not any guilt attached to him in this—if guilt, indeed, be the right notion."

"No," sighed Hervey. "I don't suppose I should have been inclined to think Mr. Keble guilty. How is he?"

Elizabeth frowned again. "I *think* he is well, though his eldest sister suffers ill health still. You did know, did you not, that a younger one died of consumption?"

Hervey did not. He had written to him from London but a fortnight ago: he hoped the letter did not intrude on any grief. "When did this happen?"

"Two summers past—the time, in fact, that he stayed here."

That was a mercy in its way, thought Hervey, though he had written to him several times from Ireland unconscious of his grief. "I had no way of knowing when I wrote to him later. And he said nothing by return."

"Then he will presume you still do not know."

"I shall write to him at once. I should very much like to see him again."

The younger Towle girl, elevated to parlormaid since last Hervey had been home, came with the news that Mrs. Pomeroy was returned. The household would no longer be reliant on extemporary measures in the kitchen, therefore. "Well, Matthew, shall you join us for a proper dinner this evening?" asked Elizabeth. "Or do you expect to dine at Longleat?"

"I really cannot say," he said, reddening a little. "I still don't know that Henrietta will return today. Tomorrow is the more likely."

Moreover, he was by no means certain that Henrietta's return would bring an invitation to dine. Indeed, nothing had discomposed him quite so much of late as the anxiety that his sweetheart might jilt him. And now his father's troubles with the bishop seemed to threaten his happiness even if she did not, for if the Reverend Thomas Hervey were dispossessed of the living, then his son would be obliged to support the family—with the very means he required to keep a wife.

Hervey looked long at Elizabeth as she gave Hannah Towle instructions. Might she not at least be able to set his mind at rest on the first question? He had never been able to fathom the true extent of his sister's intimacy with Henrietta, the two being so different that he could not imagine on what basis their familiarity proceeded. In truth, he invariably underestimated their connection, though it made little odds, since asking his sister about his fortunes in love would have been entirely ignoble to him.

Two years of absence suddenly seemed a long time. If Henrietta had changed, then perhaps Elizabeth had, too? Hervey's mother had told him that despite what she was sure had been the pressing attentions of three suitors—of whom Lord John Howard had been one—Elizabeth showed no signs of accepting any offer of marriage. He was sad of it, for his leaving Horningsham with Henrietta would be to make a lonely woman of his sister, now especially that their brother was dead. And, indeed, if the business with the bishop went ill for their father, who could tell what would become of the family?

"Did you hear what I said, Matthew?"

He was brought rudely back to the present. "No, er . . . I . . ."

"I said that there is one about whom you have not yet asked."

He looked puzzled.

"Mrs. Strange: I saw her yesterday. She asks to be remembered to you."

He had not forgotten. He had inquired of her of both his mother and father, but their replies had not yielded much beyond the here and now. "I had a letter from her in India, thanking me for the position."

"You may never do Horningsham a better favor. The school thrives and her charges are devoted to her," said Elizabeth, admiringly. "You may see her take them each afternoon on walks about the village. The children learn so much of natural history that I should be ashamed myself to be put to the test. I do believe she knows the name of every flower underfoot. And before they walk they have spent three hours and more with the slate—writing and numbers and all manner of things. I have even seen her teaching geometry!"

Hervey was gratified by Elizabeth's enthusiasm. "And the obligations of worship don't trouble her?"

Henrietta shook her head with the same look of admiration. "She is more punctilious in her observance than any but the wardens. And then afterwards she will go to her own chapel. She is the finest of women. You were very right and clever to see the opportunity in her bereavement."

"Has she formed any friendships, do you know?"

"She has dined with us on more than one occasion, but she keeps a distance. In truth, I'm sorry for it, but I cannot but respect her wishes. As for more intimate attachments, I know that one of the farmers who attends her chapel has made her an offer, but so far she has not been inclined to accept it."

"Has she spoken at all of her situation? How her husband came to be . . ."

"Killed? Yes."

Hervey felt uneasy. "What exactly did she say?"

"She told me that you somehow felt you bore a responsibility for his death."

"She said that? *I* never told her so!"

"Oh, Matthew! Sometimes I think you have not the slightest notion of what a woman can see. Why did you not tell me of it when you came home?"

It was a fair question. What was the purpose of close kin if not to share such doubts? Why did he suppose that, just because the death of Serjeant Strange was on the field of battle, a woman might have no understanding of the turmoils of conscience that followed? And yet perhaps a woman could only see so much. Indeed, a *man* who had not known the face of battle could only see a little. He looked at Elizabeth and saw a sensibility that could not—and should not—ever understand what the prospect of death in battle made of men. Sudden, violent death; by a hand that was in a frenzy to sever the spirit from its body. That, or else to make the body a cripple: to impale on the bayonet's point; to stab or slash or cut with the blade; to shatter with the musket's ball, the rifle's bullet; or disembowel with the cannon's shot. How could he even *look* at Elizabeth—close as she was to their Savior's commands as anyone could reasonably be—and not feel he had quitted a part of her company forever?

"Matthew?"

He hesitated, and then smiled. "We must allow that Mrs. Strange is a perceptive woman."

"Then why don't we walk together this afternoon, and we shall see her. We might call on her, even."

"Yes," said her brother, smiling still. "I should like that very much."

Jessye lifted her head from the early shoots of spring pasture and looked at her master without a sound. Hervey had been watching from the gate of the old glebe meadow for a full five minutes before she saw him. The mare was content, at her ease. Somehow, he supposed, she must know that she was back in the place where first she had stretched her legs to a trot—and then more—all those years ago. When was that? all of twelve years before. She had certainly seen and endured more than any village horse hereabouts ever had. Now, as March went out like the lamb, and before the summer swarms of flies had come up from the water meadows, there was no pleasanter place on earth for her to be. And, thought Hervey, Jessye deserved it. After what she had been through only this last year she deserved it. He had vowed months ago that never again would she have to attend the call of the trumpet, let alone the bugle, and now he was sure of it, even though she was the best age for a charger—beyond the worry of splints, her bones being stronger with each year. He would never find another like Jessye for agility and bottom, he told himself, and perhaps even for honesty. But if he cast her now from service she could take her ease without the broken wind and lameness that was the fate of many a trooper which had served too long. She could sate herself on the Wiltshire pasture instead of haphazard campaign fodder, enjoying good timothy from the Longleat hay meadows through the winter, and fresh water from the chalk streams of the downs.

"I'm going to put a stallion to her, Dan," he announced.

Daniel Coates smiled. "Now, there's the mark of the man full-grown!"

Hervey looked at him quizzically. The snow white hair and weathered face, deep grooved and sun dried, spoke of age, but for the rest there was nothing that revealed the passing of his many years. Such had been the reward—as well as riches—for Coates's soldierly virtue and sober living.

"I've observed it many times—the urge to see a foal when a man's taken from a horse a little too much."

Hervey made a sort of frown, enough to acknowledge the sentiment.

"Do you have a stallion in mind?"

Hervey shook his head. "More an idea of the horse I want from the foal. About Jessye's height—half a hand higher, perhaps, but no more."

"And a bit more blood?" suggested Coates, nodding his head as if he could see the reasoning. "Jessye not quite as fast as you'd care?"

"She was never outrun in the field," said Hervey quickly, as if to make amends for disloyalty.

"In which case," replied Coates, looking purposely bemused, "you want another Jessye!"

Hervey smiled.

"Have you seen Lord Bath's improvement stallion?"

"No, I've not. To tell you the truth, Dan, I've called on the marquess, but he's much occupied by affairs in Parliament. He went to London at the beginning of the week and I haven't been to the house since."

"When does Henrietta come—Friday you said?"

"Yes. That is what the express said. But Derbyshire is some way distant, and I don't suppose the roads at this time will have been much mended?"

Coates clapped an arm on his shoulder. "I would dare any odds that yon carriage will move like a fly coach. Besides that, the turnpikes've been macadamized while you've been away. In any case, that young lady would ride astride if she thought she could be here the sooner!"

Hervey smiled again. "How can you be so sure?"

Coates was not sporting with him, though. "I didn't tell, did I? She came to Drove Farm to ask me all I knew of the Indies, and how long I thought you might be gone."

"When was this?" pressed Hervey, gratified yet surprised that Henrietta could have shown so much eagerness.

"Just after she came back from France. Oh, a great occasion it was—a barouche with the Bath arms in my drive!"

Hervey made a little *"Oh"* of disappointment. "But that was the better part of two years ago."

"Matthew Hervey," sighed Coates, clapping his shoulder again. "I 'ave been on this earth long enough to recognize certain things when I see them. And, I may tell you, the look in that yon lady's eyes was not going to go absent in the space of two years. She made me promise to let her know the instant I'd any knowledge of you. *And* she reminded me of it when last I saw her—at the Michaelmas rents."

Hervey could have heard nothing so heartening. Michaelmas was only six months ago. "I gave the lodge keeper a half sovereign to let me know within a quarter hour of her carriage arriving—by whichever gate!"

"If I was you I'd sit at the picket post myself from midmorning o' Friday!" said Coates, his smile as wry as if he were still the young dragoon.

Hervey was stung. "Dan, don't suppose that's not my instinct, too. I'd be riding the Fosse Way this minute if I could be sure it's how she'd come. But it would be indecent—surely?—not to allow her a few moments to herself before receiving me."

To Hervey's further dismay, Coates laughed. "Oh, don't mistake me, Matthew. I stand in admiration of such propriety. It's just that our worlds have been so different. Margaret tramped from one end of Devon to the other when she got news that the regiment was back from America."

Hervey had never known Margaret Coates. But what he had heard over the years made the revelation less remarkable than it might have been. Nevertheless, Coates's point was well made, and he envied the freedom for so ardent an advance. "Dan, I confess I know little about putting a mare in foal. Might you tell me?"

Coates was content enough to let them both return to simpler matters. "Where do we begin, Matthew?"

"At the beginning," laughed Hervey, with a look of mock despair. "When must I put the stallion to her, and when shall she then foal?"

"By the end of May."

"Very well. Why?"

"Because when you put the stallion to a mare depends on when you want her to foal. A big cold blood—one of the Suffolks that ploughs the glebe, say—will carry a full year, or even longer. Ponies and smaller types can be as short as forty weeks. I reckon Jessye'd be in the middle somewhere: say, eleven months—calendar months, I mean. You don't want her dropping her foal before the beginning of April. The grass'll be too poor for best milk, and I like to see foals 'ave the sun on their backs for the first six months."

"Then May it shall be. When I find the stallion will you tell me what's what?"

"I will. But if you go for the marquess's improver then his stud groom'll tell you all you need. Jessye looks in good fettle. You'll keep feeding her barley, won't you? There isn't enough goodness even in this pasture just yet."

"Indeed I shall. She'll be as round as a barrel soon."

"Aye, well. Not *too* round. I don't hold with that notion. My ewes always carry better through the winter if I get them up to the rougher grazing by the end of July."

Hervey nodded.

"Come over to Drove Farm soon. You can help with the late lambs. And you can tell me some more about what you got up to in India—and this brevet. And I shall call you Major!"

Hervey smiled. How congenial was the pleasure Daniel Coates took in his triumphs. "I'd like that very much. Just as soon as Henrietta is come and I am back from Hounslow. It should only be a day or so, but I must pay my compliments to the colonel."

"Of course you must. What a thought it must be to be seeing a regiment you'll soon command. *Colonel* Hervey! What a fair prospect!"

"There are one or two bridges to cross first, Dan," said Hervey, with a cautionary frown. "And I am not to use even the majority while at duty with the regiment."

"Aye. Well, I'll say not a word to anybody. You may be sure of it." Coates began to dig out his pipe. Hervey still saw the man who had first helped him astride the woolpack, before even the old donkey was considered a safe enough ride. His old friend bore the signs of his years—that was a fact—but not in the mind, for sure.

At length the old dragoon spat, and rubbed his forehead with his sleeve. "Did I tell you I saw Bonaparte?" he asked, matter of fact.

Hervey was astonished. *"Bonaparte?"*

"Aye. The emperor himself."

"How in heaven's name . . ."

"In Torbay. Just after you was gone to Paris. He was aboard the *Bellerophon*. Now, *there's* a ship, Matthew. They held 'im there a week or so while they decided what best to do with 'im. When I heard, I posted down there at once. Prospect of a lifetime!"

"Indeed. I never saw him. Not ever."

"There were boat trips out to see 'im by the score. He used to come on deck."

"Well, he'll not trouble us again in this world," said Hervey resolutely.

"No," said Coates, nodding. "We should be able to count on a few years' peace at least." And then he smiled again. "Where do you think Colonel Hervey shall draw his saber then?"

Goodness, how becoming that title sounded! Hervey positively glowed. "Well, nowhere this side of the world. That's for sure."

Coates nodded. "India, d'ye mean? I wish I'd seen India. Just pray it's not Ireland you're sent to."

Hervey simply raised an eyebrow. Ireland had all but undone him two years before, and he had no wish to see the country again—not even for the hunting and the good friends he had made there.

"No," said Coates. "It's no job for a soldier, is Ireland. No good for him ever comes of it, that sort of work. But we shall have the same troubles here soon, the way things are going. Half the country's been in riot or distress this past year. I've never known things so bowstring-taut."

Hervey disclosed his experience of the Cashman hanging.

"The Spa Fields business?" Coates nodded knowingly. "That Orator Hunt as whips up the crowds farms over the plain at Upavon. I've known 'im years. At first he was just a nuisance. Now he's a danger true enough."

But it was too fine a morning to be speaking of such things. Then Hervey suddenly remembered. "Dan, I can't think how I've not told you before. I have a repeating carbine to show you."

Coates whistled. "Now, that *is* something! You're sure it repeats, though? It doesn't just carry more charges? I've seen some cutcha affairs in my time—as your Indians would say."

"Believe me, Dan: this is a repeater right enough. I watched it put seven balls into a target in quick succession. And then put *seven* in myself!"

"Then this I really do want to see. Will you bring it over soon?"

"Just as soon as I'm back from Hounslow—a week at most. Now come and see my mother. She is sorely in need of cheer this morning."

It was a quarter after noon the next day when Hervey got word that Henrietta had arrived at Longleat. The hour presented a problem, since he supposed the family would be at their table: he could scarcely intrude without an invitation. But Daniel Coates's admonition stung him still, and he was soon hurrying to the stable for his father's cob. Between the two of them, Abel Towle and he had Jessye's dam under saddle quicker than a dragoon at Alarm, and Hervey was kicking on even as his father's man was trying to pull the straw from her tail.

But slow, ever so slow, was the old mare. Hervey hadn't the heart to demand a trot when she refused his asking, even though the road was downhill for most of the way—and the last mile nothing but. From the gatehouse, on grass grazed short and springy by Lord Bath's blackfaces, she did manage a stumbling jog, though still, he rued, no more than a doubling pace for even a battalion company (a *light* company would have shown him their heels for certain).

At last he was at the steps of the great house. One o'clock: he had walked it quicker many a time, *and* arrived with not a bead of sweat. But this time his agitation was not from exertion. Here was the strange tightness in his vitals again—the analogue of peril, a gauge which showed that destruction was at hand unless he took immediate action. But what was he to do? What control over events might he seize? Henrietta's was surely the initiative, not his. Nothing he said now—no matter how ardent or profound—would change her heart if it were against him, for fickle she had never been. He had the necklace that the Rajah of Chintal had pressed upon him in his pocket—a favorite, the rajah had explained, of his late wife. It seemed so much a bauble now when he thought of how he had . . . *abandoned* Henrietta (could there be any other word?), first in London, then in France. And yet, surely, if she were so vexed with him— so vexed that their engagement was already broken for her part—she would have sent word that she would not receive him? He rallied a little, but then relapsed as quickly at the thought that she might merely wish to vent her anger on him.

He pulled the bell loop. Soon he would know the worst. Longleat Park had been at the center of his thoughts, one way or another, since first he was conscious of them. He heard the sheep on the hill and the rooks in the hanger: would he be allowed to hear them ever again?

The door opened. It was not a footman but the housekeeper who bid him enter, with a friendly "Good afternoon, Captain Hervey, sir."

The smile encouraged him, and he smiled in return. "Mrs. Cousens, I am very glad to be returned. Is Lady Henrietta at home?"

"She is," came another voice, from the great staircase.

For all the times Matthew Hervey had been in want of words, never had he greater want than now. He could find nothing to utter but "Oh." It sounded first like surprise—dismay, even.

But Henrietta was smiling, too—a warm, generous, open smile, for she had taken his "Oh" to be rapture. Though she stood above him on the stairs she still contrived that doelike look which had greeted him on his first return from France, the dark pools that were her eyes half raised to him, half turned from him. And there was a blush to her cheeks that no rouge had made.

He rushed to her eagerly, and they embraced with all the ease of seasoned lovers, kissing full and long, exchanging endearments with a happy passion, telling each other without words that all was now right and would never again be otherwise.

"I watched for you coming," Henrietta laughed, shaking her head. "You have no idea how my heart leaped when I saw you ride through the arch. I wanted to run to greet you, but you made your way so slowly I feared the worst."

"My father's cob," Hervey began, then said no more, for they kissed again.

The family being away, the lovers were able to enjoy a cold table together, each admitting to a curiously strong appetite. Afterwards they walked to the hanger and on to Heaven's Gate, the place from which best to admire the house's fine proportions and gardens. They had done so many a time before, but never alone. They sat on the same seat they had known since the schoolroom, and Hervey had never felt himself so content. Henrietta took off her hat, pushed her head back so that her face was full to the spring sunshine, and closed her eyes. The rajah's necklace sat sensually about her neck. Its emeralds and rubies—so at home in the palace at

Chintalpore—seemed the image of decadence in the Wiltshire country-side, but Henrietta reveled in its opulence, and Hervey loved her for it.

Perhaps it was her look of contentment that made him suddenly anxious again. A part of that contentment was surely her attachment to the place in which she had lived so happily and comfortably since her infant days?

Something of this communicated itself to Henrietta. "My dearest, what is the matter?"

Hervey measured his words. "You love this house, do you not?"

She answered at once. "Why, yes. There has never been a place so dear to me."

Hervey's look partly revealed his concern.

"But that is not to say there won't be in the future," she smiled, shaking her head a little. "Things are different now."

That was not quite what he'd meant, however. "Have you heard the trouble that my father has with his bishop?"

She put a hand on his and squeezed it reassuringly. "Tell me what news."

"He was summoned to the palace yesterday. The bishop—kindly, says my father—told him that he must observe strictly the rubrics of the Prayer Book, or that he might have to answer to the consistory court."

"And what shall he do?"

"I don't know, for I am not sure how dearly he holds his convictions. At worst, though, he might be deprived of the living, and though he says his annuity is sufficient for the family, I don't believe it to be so. In which case it will be my duty to support them."

Henrietta nodded her understanding, and sympathy.

Evidently the full implications were escaping her. Hervey made a despondent gesture with his hand, nodding in the direction of the house. "My dear, I have better prospects now within the regiment, but even so, how might I—"

"Matthew, *dearest*." Henrietta squeezed his hand. "That is of no matter to me. None at all."

"But—"

"Matthew, I do have a little money of my own," she smiled.

The extent of Henrietta Lindsay's fortune had never been the subject of speculation within Hervey's hearing. He knew her people to have been from the Borders, and that somehow their estates had become derelict, so that they had come south just after she had been born, and that soon afterwards both her parents had died, and distant kinship had brought her to Longleat to be the marquess's ward. More than that he did not know. "It is hardly a good beginning."

She smiled even more broadly. "Matthew, if fortune hunter you be, there can scarcely have been a less determined one!"

He blushed deeply at the memory of his early hesitancy. Now he knew that he would have done with it once and for all. "When shall we be married?"

She was only momentarily taken aback. "The first of May."

Hervey seemed a little surprised at the exactness.

"As soon as I knew you were come back I made a beginning."

"I see," he said, smiling with no little admiration. "Could it not be the week before, though?"

"No, Matthew, I'm afraid it could not."

"The first of May is a regimental review. It wouldn't be easy for people to get down. Are plans so *very* far advanced?"

"I did so want a May wedding. As Princess Charlotte had."

He understood that female desire. Might the nuptials be later, then? Heaven knows he had no wish himself for delay, but—

"Well," she said, solemnly. "We have to have a good moon, or else the carriages will never make the lanes safely."

That was reasonable, Hervey acknowledged. But there would be another good moon towards the month's end.

"*No,* Matthew, that will not do," said Henrietta, most emphatically, and more than a little flushed. "Do not have me spell it out. There are some things over which I can have no influence!"

They looked at each other. She was not going to turn away, whatever her instincts. Then it began to dawn on him, and he became as red as the sky would later be. He put his arms around her again. It was an embrace with a new intimacy, for they had crossed a threshold, if only in the mind.

"And so what do you think of the arrangements for your wedding, Matthew?" said Elizabeth as they waited for the family carriage to take them to dine at Longleat that evening (his arriving home late with the invitation had caused her no little confusion).

Her tone intrigued him. "Why do you say that?"

She smiled, wryly, but said nothing.

"Do you *know* of them, then?"

"Of course I know of them! Do you not think that Henrietta might have wished to discuss them? And you were not here to listen!"

And so for a week Elizabeth had had it in her power to set his mind at ease—if only she had had any cause to think it necessary. Why in God's name had he not asked her, he rued.

"What do you think of the notion of a wedding in Longleat House?" she pressed. "You are surely very flattered by it?"

"Oh, indeed; it is a very elegant notion," he agreed readily. It was true that he had thought little before, if at all, about the ceremonies themselves, supposing they would be conducted in the usual way in his father's church at Horningsham—or, if canon law required it, at Longbridge Deverel, for in that parish, strictly, lay the great house.

"Henrietta has thought of nothing else since Princess Charlotte's wedding," Elizabeth explained.

"Yes," said Hervey, pensively. "I read something of it in Madras. Prince Leopold . . . of Saxony?"

"Yes. Henrietta was a maid of honor to the queen."

Hervey was impressed.

"She would be the first to tell you there were eleven more."

A dozen virgins: in days not too far gone, the reward for saving a royal elephant, he recalled. How distant Chintal now seemed. He smiled.

"Oh, you must not joke of it, Matthew," Elizabeth warned. "Henrietta is very devoted to the princess."

This news spared him the need to excuse his smiling. "I did not know she even knew the princess."

"I don't think she does—not well, that is. But I should say that her affection for her is very great."

Hervey nodded, content.

"That is why she is so especially enamored of a May wedding, as Princess Charlotte's was. And why she is so intent on its being in Longleat House, for the royal ceremony took place in the Prince Regent's palace."

"What? In Carlton House?"

"Have you been there?" asked Elizabeth, with just a hint of awe.

He laughed. "Heavens no! But the talk in London was all of how racy that place is. Nero's Hotel, they call it. Hardly the place for solemn nuptials, I should've thought!"

Elizabeth looked a little shaken. "But Henrietta was there, and speaks of how graceful an occasion it was. Fifty or more sat down to dinner beforehand."

"Beforehand?"

"Apparently."

Hervey pulled a face suggesting he found the idea curious.

"And then the ceremony itself was in the crimson drawing room."

"Crimson?" said Hervey, teasing. "That must be very close to scarlet."

Elizabeth screwed up her face, too, exactly as she always had. There was not so much Hannah More in Elizabeth that she could not smile at the ribald. "Mystery, Babylon the Great?"

"You had better go no further," he warned, smiling, too.

CHAPTER 4

FIRST PARADE

Hounslow, Three Days Later

The cavalry barracks at Hounslow had not been sparingly built, especially not the high wall which surrounded the twenty acres of parade square, stables, and quarters. Hervey did not care for the look of the wall. It reminded him of Cork. No doubt its purpose was to keep out intruders of whatever description, as in Ireland. But this was England, and who would want to intrude on a cavalry barracks? Walls confined, and that went against the spirit of the Sixth. Something rather nobler than bricks had kept the regiment together when times were a good deal more troubled.

Entry was easily arranged, however. The picket corporal, a man from D Troop he didn't know but who recognized him, pointed the way to regimental headquarters. The man's uniform was as new—nothing of the patches and fading they had all become used to by Toulouse, and which had scarcely been better by Waterloo. A reward from a grateful government it should have been, sighed Hervey to himself, but likely as not it was from a rich commanding officer. How good it was, though, one way or another, to see the regiment back in proper fettle.

As he walked towards regimental headquarters, soberly dressed in dark green, and black silk hat, the band struck up on the far side of the square. Hervey had not heard them since Ireland, and then it had been a thin noise they made. Now they filled the barracks with a strong treble and bass alike, the trumpeters' triple-tonguing was admirably sharp, and the clarionets—still something of a novelty—were altogether less shrill than before. He walked round the square to take a closer look. There were three times the old number, and all as immaculately uniformed as the picket corporal, the four sable bandsmen brilliant in Turkish silks. The bandmaster was not old Mr. Merryweather, though. This one was much more active. And when he shouted to the bandsmen—he was shouting a good deal—it was with a heavy German accent.

Picket turned out as if on review, and a band forty strong with a German bandmaster—Hervey headed for the orderly room convinced he might be in a foot guards barracks. It was, indeed, an impression of efficiency that wholly belied the scene in Skinner Street.

The commanding officer received him unusually formally at orderly room. Hervey remained at attention, waiting in vain for the invitation to sit. "You will find that much is changed, Captain Hervey," said the Earl of Towcester, and with a note of challenge in his voice.

Hervey thought it best to say nothing beyond, "Very good, Colonel." Lord Towcester's pale blue eyes were the coldest he had ever seen, and his thin lips parted only a very little when he spoke—just enough to allow the words to slide past with a distinct sneer.

The adjutant, an extract from the Second whom he had never met, took a step forward. "The commanding officer is to be addressed as 'His Lordship,' Captain Hervey."

The tone was of reprimand, and doubly did Hervey resent it, for it was hardly a gentleman's way of correcting something so minor, quite besides the fact that it had always been the Sixth's custom that *all* ranks called their commanding officer "Colonel." He breathed deep. "As His Lordship pleases."

"Very well, Hervey," replied Lord Towcester, looking up only momentarily. "I take note that you shall join for duty at the end of August. And you are aware that your brevet rank is not recognized regimentally?"

"I am, your lordship."

"Very well. Do you stay to luncheon?"

"Yes, sir."

"Then I shall see you in the mess at that time. Until then, Captain Hervey."

Hervey bowed.

The commanding officer rose and bowed stiffly by return.

"And by the bye, Captain Hervey," said the Earl of Towcester, turning his back to look out of the window, "I had just better say that I want none of those Indian ways in my regiment. We are His Majesty's light dragoons, not Hindoo horse."

Hervey was so taken aback by Lord Towcester's manner, as well as his sentiment, that he could say nothing. Yet say something he must, for with the commanding officer's back turned he could not now take his leave. "Thank you for receiving me, your lordship," he managed at length. He knew it needed a supplementary, but he could think of nothing he might utter. He left the orderly room dispirited.

There was a full hour to luncheon. He wished he were not staying, now. And that thought made him the more dispirited, for the shared table of the mess was a precious memory. Perhaps he ought to walk the lines. But he was not in uniform, and it might be awkward. He looked at his new watch again—a poor thing, he mourned, after Jessope's hunter: watering parade would be finished and the stables quiet before the midday feed.

First Squadron's stables were indeed a restorative. There might not have been the complete quality of the Rajah of Chintalpore's establishment (he could still remember his disbelief on seeing so much blood), but the change here was every bit as striking as with the band. Every trooper looked as good as the chargers most officers were riding at the close of the Peninsula. Even after a year in Ireland, when the regiment had been able to readopt troop colors, they had only achieved uniformity at the cost of conformation and substance. But now A Troop had its bays again, and B its blacks (and, he would find later, E—the smartest—its chestnuts), and they were lookers in the best sense. And, he was pleased to see, the Sixth were still disdaining the regulations, for the trumpeters' mounts were grays. But, sadly, the regulation *was* applied in the one thing he hated most: every trooper's tail was docked. It was not just India that convinced him of the horse's right to a fly whisk. No officer in the Sixth who had seen any appreciable service in the Peninsula supported the practice. Hervey lifted a few tails: none had been nicked, thank heavens. *That* was a device that had never taken hold in the regiment, thanks largely to the Earl of Sussex's strictures, compelled by a riding master of uncompromising discipline ("The horse, sir, will carry its tail just as soon as *you* allow him to work through his back!" The words rang in his ears, and he remembered how they had stung him so when first he had joined).

First Squadron's lines were peaceful. There was the sound of hay-grinding here and there as the odd trooper had a little to finish, and here and there a jingling as a chain was pulled through its ring in the standing stalls. There was the odd stamp of iron on cobble as a horse shifted its weight, and the occasional snort and whicker. But otherwise he might have been in a cloister. *This,* he told himself, was what he was returning to—not a peevish colonel.

The Stables call summoned him from his musing, as it did the dragoons to the horse lines. Better that he were elsewhere than the bustle of haying-up, feeding, and watering to come, so he walked briskly to the mess. The place was as silent as the stables had been, with a half hour before the first officers might arrive. Earlier in the season, the anteroom would have been full of those who had had a half day with hounds, not yet ready to take out a second charger to hear the huntsman blow Home. But this late on, they would be out for a full day no doubt. Perhaps they would be few at luncheon.

Hervey looked about the walls. There were familiar pictures he had last seen in Cork, and some less so. There was an exceptionally fine portrait of the Earl of Sussex in the uniform of colonel, by the hand of Sir Thomas Lawrence, said an inscription. But he couldn't find the girlish Romney of Princess Caroline, and he supposed it must be elsewhere, in the headquarters, perhaps. *The Times* of three days before lay open in a chair, testimony to a recent, perhaps hurried, departure—or to the steward's indolence. There were copies of regimental orders in leather binders on a table, together with the regimental list. Hervey picked up the latter and settled in a low chair to study it. Half the names he did not recognize. The major's—Eustace Joynson—he did. "An able administrator, I think," the Earl of Sussex had said, but Hervey was certain, as the colonel had implied, that Joynson had no great instinct for the field, where the actions of the enemy, or even the mere chafing of events and the elements, soon put even well-laid plans to naught. Second Squadron bore not a single officer he recognized. Its captain, Lord Henry Manners, was one of the Marquess of Grantham's sons. That much was promising, for the marquess had been a much-regarded brigadier before a tirailleur had shot him down outside Badajoz. The other troop in the squadron was commanded by a Captain Addy, and the subalterns were likewise unknown to him. Cornet the Marquess Wymondham's name was there with Third Troop, still to be excised. Hervey sighed at the remembrance of the boy's broken head resting in his hands in that gloomy alehouse.

Third Squadron was a mix. Strickland, its captain (and E Troop leader), he knew well enough. Strickland had bought in from the Tenth just before Waterloo and quickly won the confidence of the ranks for his cool head under the heaviest fire that day. Hervey was glad at least of one veteran of the Sixth of Irvine and Edmonds. And there was "Saint" Lawrence, too—the junior cornet at Waterloo, whom Hervey had placed in charge of old Chantonnay and his ravished daughters on the road to Paris. F Troop—black, like B—was as unfamiliar as D. Its captain, Hugh Rose, by reputation a buck, had exchanged from the Thirteenth when they were warned for India. Hervey didn't suppose he would see him much with London only a chariot's gallop away.

But in what would be his own squadron—First—came the real surprise, for there, with B Troop, he read the name of Ezra Barrow. Barrow had been adjutant for half a dozen years or more, brought in on commissioning from serjeant major by Lord George Irvine, and so Hervey supposed that his getting a troop must be field promotion rather than purchase. Yet how that had been so, he couldn't imagine, for so rapidly were regiments being disbanded—all but the first two twenties had gone—that there could hardly be room for promotion without purchase. In any event, Barrow's was not the name he would have chosen for his second troop, though it was at least one he knew, and one that had known the regiment under Irvine and Edmonds. The Sixth hadn't had a troop leader from the ranks for a decade or more. It was always tricky. He'd seen one or two in other regiments, and good they'd been, too, but often as not it was the men themselves who disliked it most. He wondered how the lieutenant colonel was taking to it. But then he read one name that cheered him heartily—Seton Canning, now a lieutenant. At Waterloo, Seton Canning had been his only officer by the time he had had to step into command of First Squadron. "The boots" had brought out First Troop from the terrible melee after the Greys had run on, with all the skill of an old hand, though it had been his first time shot-over. Good, good, he thought: Seton Canning and Armstrong—a start, at least. How he had missed Serjeant Armstrong's straight talking, and powerful sword arm, in India. How grand—as Armstrong himself would have said—to see him again. Then just as he was about to turn the page to study the quartermasters' lists, a noise in the entrance hall announced the arrival of the first for luncheon. Hervey recognized none of them.

They were a dozen at table. And a good table it was, too, thought Hervey, even for a high day (which it was not)—plover's eggs, turbot, and a baron of Somerset beef, with hock and a Chambertin. The troop leaders were there, less Manners, as well as a couple of new cornets. There were two officers from the Rifles, guests of Addy, and the DAAG from the district headquarters. But there were no quartermasters and no riding master, no surgeon (medical or veterinary) nor paymaster. Perhaps, thought Hervey, they were all at duty elsewhere, but it still seemed strange.

Hervey sat between Joynson and Strickland, almost directly opposite Lord Towcester. The lieutenant colonel's manner was markedly different from that at orderly room. Hervey might have called it *exuberant,* even. Yet although Lord Towcester's mouth smiled, his eyes did not, and there was an edge to his manner, still, which Hervey could not quite fathom. Conversation seemed also less than free, dictated more by the colonel than flowing naturally, as he remembered it at its best.

"Might we have the cellars better found, Joynson?" said Lord Towcester, frowning at the Chambertin. "I can scarcely ask the Prince Regent to disturb his digestion with this."

It was well known to all at the table but Hervey that the colonel was intent on entertaining the regent as soon as he might. "Whatever your lordship wishes," replied Major Joynson obligingly.

There was the beginning of a silence that Hervey thought he might ease. "Where is the portrait of Princess Caroline, sir?" he asked Joynson.

The major turned red.

The adjutant answered for him. "His lordship has ordered its removal."

Hervey realized the danger too late, for the mess had long held a truce on the matter. Until the end of the Peninsula, Caroline had officially remained their colonel in chief (*unofficially,* they had been known as Princess Caroline's Own), and there had remained an affection for her, especially among the quartermasters and serjeants, with many old hands able to recall her warm if sometimes indelicate manners during her visits. There had been many an opinion in Cork that the regent had ill-used the princess.

"She is grown monstrous fat, I hear," said Lord Towcester abruptly.

Hervey was taken aback, and evidently visibly, for Ezra Barrow shook his head at him, warning him to let it go.

"What's that, Barrow? You know otherwise, do you?" challenged Towcester, his face reddening and his eyes narrowing.

"I know nothing of the princess, your lordship," replied Captain Barrow quickly. "Except that it would be a pity if Her Royal Highness were to tax her constitution as badly as does the regent."

The response did not please the commanding officer. "Do you say that the Prince Regent is obese, sir?"

Barrow remained more perfectly in control of matters than Hervey would have supposed possible. "*I* do not say so, your lordship. One more opinion would scarcely be of any point when there are so many already on the matter."

The adjutant now joined the colloquy, and piled the coals higher. "I hear tell she wore a gown so sheer in Naples last month it was as if she wore none at all!"

"Scarcely an alluring sight," scoffed the colonel.

This was really most unbecoming, thought Hervey, and his fault, too, for mentioning the picture.

"She seduced Murat there, y'know," continued the adjutant, blithely. "And now she's living openly with a Mussulman of all things—the Dey of Algiers!"

There was an anxious silence.

Strickland broke it. "And she is happy, as the Dey is long!"

It was a mercy, for there was laughter all round. Indeed, so keen was it that the chaplain must have laughed had he been there.

It even seemed to restore Lord Towcester's equilibrium. "Call for the port, someone," he said, taking a cigar from the box which the steward had brought. "Now's as good a time as any to announce our good fortune. Gentlemen," he beamed, "this autumn we are to furnish the escorts at Brighton!"

There was a general hubbub, during which Ezra Barrow leaned across to Hervey and shook his head again. "Time for me to go, this news. I can't afford the expense of that place. It ain't soldiering." The Birmingham vowels were as strong as ever.

Hervey wasn't so sure. There was nothing like ceremonial to fill a regiment with pride—except a famous victory. He thought it no bad thing at all that the Sixth be given this trial, for it would take effort, indeed, to be fit for the regent's eyes, as well as for those of the population of Brighton, doubtless become expert during the past decade. And what gentler way, too, to begin the marriage state than wintering by the English seaside? "Let's take a walk after this is done," he said to Barrow.

But spirits were high about the table. "Where is the betting book?" came a voice from the end.

A footman brought it to Captain Rose. "Very well. Cornet Finucane wagers Mr. Seton Canning the sum of five guineas that the measurement from stifle to hock of Eclipse did not exceed twenty-four inches!"

The wager provoked intense discussion all round. "And who is to adjudicate?" asked Captain Addy.

"The hippogrammarian," declared Lord Towcester, blowing a great deal of smoke across the table. "One of his horse-butcher friends dissected the animal if I'm not mistaken."

There was appreciative laughter.

Hervey felt himself back in the Sixth he knew—a place of raucous, even at times tasteless, good humor as well as of cultivation. There were always ups and downs. Better, then, to dwell only on the happy side. Perhaps things were more promising than he'd imagined.

It was past three before they were able to break away from the commanding officer's court, and so Hervey and Barrow had to content themselves with a stroll around the manège yard instead of outside the walls. Barrow was the longest-serving of the Sixth's mess after Joynson and Hervey. Coming from the Royals with Lord George Irvine after Corunna, he had never endeared himself to the regiment's officers in the way that his patron had (being as short on ceremony as he was long in experience). Nevertheless he had been respected as a diligent and efficient adjutant. He was a man of the Midlands, the industrial Midlands, perhaps the only one in the regiment, and he had never quite seemed one of the Sixth before. But now, Hervey was more than happy to walk with him as a comrade in arms. After all, they had first borne the battle's heat together, as well as the sun's, at Salamanca almost five years before.

"Things have changed, Hervey."

"The army never changes, so Joseph Edmonds used to say."

"I didn't say the *army's* changed. *Things* have. The regiment's not the same."

Hervey had little enough cause to be enamored of the new commanding officer after the business in the orderly room, but he had no wish to become further depressed by Barrow's spirits at the very time he was returning to all he loved best. "There are bound to be *some* differences with a new colonel. I have to say the regiment's looking smarter than I've seen it in many a year."

"Oh, that I grant you. And I'd be the first to own we'd grown rag-arsed, even in Ireland. But it's not the *only* thing. You don't have efficiency solely through smartness."

"And the horses are better than I've ever seen them, too," added Hervey, still unwilling to share Barrow's discouragement.

"That I grant you."

"Well, what is it, then? The NCOs do their duty as before, do they not?"

Barrow furrowed his brow.

Hervey knew that an ex-adjutant was perforce a professional skeptic when it came to subordinates and the performance of their duty. "Do not tell me Mr. Lincoln hasn't things right in that direction!"

"There've been some queer promotions," Barrow declared. "I've always believed as long service should be rewarded, but only when accompanied by merit. Some of the troops are sorely ill served in my view. At the last board, Mr. Lincoln was not even allowed to sit in."

Hervey recognized the integrity of the opinion. For the RSM not to have a say in promotions was strange indeed. "Why was that, d'ye think?"

Barrow shrugged his shoulders. "I don't know. I just don't know."

"No notion at all?"

"Well . . ." Barrow sighed heavily. "I do have a notion, and that is that Lord Towcester does not see the necessity of leavening seniority with aptness, because . . . he has seen so little service himself."

Corporal Collins had said as much as they stood beside Cornet Wymondham in the Skinner Street taproom. "What service *has* he seen, exactly?"

"Well, to be certain, nothing these past ten years, for he's had the Trent Yeomanry all that time."

"And before that?"

"I know not. I heard say he'd been in Flanders with the Duke of York."

"Then," sighed Hervey, "we'll have to pray that the residents of Brighton are not too hostile. And that you and I can make something of our troops in the way that Edward Lankester and the others did."

"Aye," nodded Barrow. "But by heaven, it tests a man. And after every-thing the regiment's been through these past ten years."

Hervey sighed again. "It was easy to be loyal to a man like Lord George. I suppose the real test is being loyal to a man less agreeable. But a colonel is owed loyalty as of right."

Barrow agreed. "Aye, he has to earn his respect—like all of us—but he's due his loyalty. That I grant you, too."

"It really may not be so bad, you know," said Hervey, smiling, trying to rally his own spirits as much as Barrow's. "It can never be easy for some-one come from the yeomanry. It will take a little time. I daresay he'll soon be satisfied once the regiment begins to answer."

Barrow said nothing.

When Hervey returned to Horningsham, at the end of the week, there were two letters waiting for him. The first was from the Reverend Mr. Keble. It was a long, warm, thoughtful letter replying to his from London, expressing his earnest wish that they should meet again soon. Hervey was especially pleased to receive it for a number of reasons, not least of which was his (and Henrietta's) wish that John Keble should jointly officiate at the wedding. Henrietta had formed a favorable impres-sion of the Oxford man that day at the great henge, almost three years ago, when she had done all she thought proper to declare her own feel-ings for Hervey, though he had not yet revealed any for her. And now that things did not stand harmoniously between Horningsham and the close at Salisbury, it was improbable that the bishop could preside at the ceremony, in which case it would have to be Mrs. Hervey's brother-in-law, the dean of Hereford, who would solemnize their vows. But though the dean was a fine man, he was no poet, and it seemed best, therefore, if it were Mr. Keble who gave the homily. So Keble's expression of keen-ness to see him again was a welcome portent.

Another reason, and this had really only occurred to Hervey a month or so ago, was that John Keble was the only man with whom he spoke, in any more than the everyday way, who did not wear uniform. Of course there was Daniel Coates, but with Coates he was not truly intimate, for their re-spective ages made their connection ever one of master and pupil. And besides, though Coates had left the colors twenty years ago, Hervey could still not quite think of him as anything but one of General Tarleton's dragoons—revere him, indeed, as Tarleton's trumpeter. India, with its brief excursion to the world beyond the barracks and the battlefield, and the acquaintances of exotic opinion and taste, was now far behind him. He was again, as the Gospel had it, "a man under authority, and having soldiers under him." The army was not a world so apart from the everyday as was John Keble's kingdom of God. But apart it was—not because Hervey wished it to be but because it *had* to be. How might a soldier face death if he were not made to act contrary to what the instincts of any mere mortal told him? John Keble was not only, therefore, a guide to matters spiritual; he might easily prove his best counselor in things temporal.

The second letter troubled him deeply.

Lynn Regis
Norfolk
25 March 1817

Dear Captain Hervey,
It was so very good of you to write. A grieving father is consoled by nothing so much as the thought that his son died doing his duty, as countless fathers' sons have died in these troubled times.

It was my younger son's dearest wish, from when he was but a boy, to see service against The Great Disturber, and he fretted all the while at Eton, even as the Army was assembling before Waterloo. And I confess to you that when I saw the casualty lists following that battle I gave thanks to The Almighty that he had spared my son from such a test. I do not dismay, though, as perhaps I might, that his death was at the hands of his fellow countrymen, for to do so might make in me a resentfulness that would be a canker. Neither do I need pain myself that there was any dereliction of duty on anyone's part that, if it had been otherwise, might have rendered the outcome different, for Lord Towcester has written to me saying that my son's squadron leader was the finest of officers and his serjeant the most experienced of men, so that nothing more might have been done to render him better support in that singular duty.

I am ever grateful to you, sir, for your kindness in writing,

and if this appears to be but a very inadequate expression of
it, then be assured that it is caused only by a heart that I fear
may be forever broken.

    I remain, sir,
    Huntingdon

The problem was the quite obvious untruth in the assurance that the
Duke of Huntingdon had received from the lieutenant colonel—although
Hervey could not be sure what the Earl of Towcester had actually written. He had no reason to doubt that Lord Henry Manners was "the finest
of officers," but Manners had not been in Skinner Street. And although
Serjeant Noakes could certainly be described as experienced, in that
twenty years' service was vastly more than most soldiers could lay claim
to, the greater part had been spent with the quartermasters. Had it been
one or the other, Hervey might have been inclined to think that the Duke
of Huntingdon—perhaps even fortuitously—had got hold of the wrong
end of the stick. But *two* misapprehensions was altogether different.

    Hervey turned it over again in his mind. Was it proper to ease the suf-
fering of the next of kin by such an artifice? Had he not, himself, spared
Margaret Edmonds the details of her husband's shocking death at
Waterloo? Had he not sought to spare Mrs. Strange the anguish of knowing that her husband had died in the way he had? *Yes*—but not in order
to conceal some neglect. Indeed, had he not been at pains to tell her of
the sacrifice Serjeant Strange had made, so that he—Hervey—might get
his dispatch to the Prussians?

    But it was a dreadful thing indeed to imagine one's lieutenant colonel
capable of so ignoble a deed as covering up a misjudgment in this way.
And this the man on whose favor his promotion rested. Was there not, as
ever, more to things than met the eye?

    Hervey laid both letters aside and looked out of the window at the de-
lightful corner of Creation that was his father's garden. He had enough
things with which to occupy himself at present—and pleasurably so. By
the time the regiment decamped to Brighton, Lord Towcester would be
content, and the regiment, too: was that not the Sixth's way? He really
shouldn't make it his business to worry, he told himself.

CHAPTER 5

AN HONORABLE
ESTATE

Salisbury Plain, St. George's Day

Hervey set his horse at the fence and kicked on. The big gelding took off long and pecked on landing. Hervey was so off his balance he was on the ground in a trice. It had been so quick he could do nothing to save himself, but not quick enough to spare him the exasperation of knowing it was happening. His hat fell onto the other side of the hedge, an iron missed his head by an inch, and the gelding galloped off across the vale. Winded and bruised, but no bones broken, furious with himself but not humiliated, for there was no one to see, he cursed everything—himself most. All the leaps for the king he'd made, or for his life, and a hedge in Warminster Bottom put him on his backside! Thank God it hadn't been a field day with the regiment, where "dismounting involuntarily" was an occasion for damage to both pride and pocket. He couldn't blame his horse, and he didn't. He'd put him at too big a fence for a youngster, a horse he didn't know well enough, and his mind had been elsewhere. But the sound of liberated hooves now pounding the chalk would turn every eye for miles. "Hell," he cursed again, this time moderating the oaths. "Hell, hell, hell." He rubbed his shoulder, which had taken his weight as he hit the ground.

There was so much Hervey liked about this gelding, though, not least because he was a gray, iron gray, and he had always liked that color, especially when the quarter dappling was as pretty as this one's. He sat up to see the quarters disappearing at a great pace in the direction of Drove Farm, where Daniel Coates had stabled him for a fortnight since the dealer had brought him from Trowbridge. It could have been worse: he might have been in the middle rather than on the edge of the downs. But, there again, had he been in the middle he wouldn't have found a hedge to jump. There was no point ruing his luck: the gelding had dumped him and that was that. Better to stride out for Coates's place while there was still light enough to see him back to Horningsham afterwards.

What he had intended to do was take back the repeating carbine, which Coates had been trying for the better part of the month, and with it the old soldier's opinion, too, for Hervey felt it time to make some report to its supplier. For his own part he was very much impressed with the weapon. A day or so after arriving home, he had taken three rabbits near the hanger above the glebe before the rest made it to their burrows—something he had never managed even with his percussion-lock. And though it had jammed on one occasion he had righted it easily enough. But Daniel Coates's opinion would be the long view, and that he must surely prize above his own? And soon he would be having it, for scarcely had he walked half a mile when he saw Coates trotting towards him on his old chestnut cob, the gray in hand.

"Good afternoon, Master Matthew!" hailed Coates as he neared.

It was the old greeting, the way Daniel Coates used to address him when they had been together all those years ago, Hervey on the leading rein. And many had been the time the young Master Hervey had failed to keep his pony between himself and the grass, and ever grateful had he been that it was as springy on the plain as bogmoss in Ireland.

"Good afternoon, Mr. Coates," Hervey replied, humoring the old dragoon. "Do you have a hobbyhorse I might try?" If anyone was to bring him his loose horse, better that it were Daniel Coates. But Hervey's equestrian pride had taken a fall, and though he might make a joke of it, that pride which remained was a sight more hurt than his bones. In truth, he would have been content to pick his way back to Horningsham at once.

At Drove Farm, however, Coates was keen to show him his usual hospitality, and the jug of purl was brought. "Sit you down, Matthew. I have something important to tell you."

Hervey sat in his usual chair; Coates's manner had a note of warning he had heeded with profit many a time before.

"Your carbine, Matthew. Before I give you my opinion, I should like very much to know what is *yours*."

Hervey gave it simply. "I should choose it for myself."

"Instead of a Paget?"

"At all times."

Coates nodded. "Instead of the percussion-lock?"

Hervey considered carefully. "It would depend on the circumstances."

"Aye," conceded Coates. "Might you elaborate?"

Hervey had not expected to be pressed to a view, but in principle the answer was straightforward. "In the wet I should prefer the percussion-lock. When dry, the repeater."

Coates nodded again. "Because the repeater's advantages are voided by damp?"

"Just so."

"But dry, it has the edge over the other?"

"Yes," said Hervey, quite assured. "It can fire at many times the rate of the other."

Coates thought for a moment. "And would you approve it for your dragoons?"

"Yes." Hervey did not feel *quite* so assured.

Coates made a thoughtful "um" sound.

"And *your* opinion, Dan?"

The old soldier sighed. "Can't be too careful with your flats and sharps, Matthew," he said, shaking his head side to side.

"So you have always said, Dan," replied Hervey, curious as to what was implied. "That's why I brought the carbine to you. What's your worry?"

"For a start, it's a might too tangled for a private man."

"You mean he might not master the mechanism?" said Hervey, with a touch of disbelief.

"No, not that. Any as can be taught to strip and assemble a bridle ought to be able to cope with this. The problem, as I see it, is that the mechanism jams. Just like the first ones I saw years ago. A bit of dirt and the chamber won't turn. And where there's a field day and a dragoon, there's dirt!"

Hervey was disappointed. And, though he concealed it, even a shade exasperated. "But Dan, where there's a field day there's damp, too—nine times out of ten. I've told you before that I've seen a whole troop's carbines misfire after a deep fording. And heaven knows you've seen it yourself. That was why I prized your percussion-lock so highly."

Coates nodded. "Just so, Matthew. And if this mechanism weren't a flintlock I should embrace it gladly. But here you have the chance that it will misfire *and* jam."

Perhaps his shoulder was hurting more than he pretended. Perhaps he was not attentive enough. But Hervey just could not see the logic. "But Dan, if it misfires with the first round, you're no worse off than if it had been the Paget in your hands. And if it jams on the second, then what have you lost?"

"Looked at that way, it's a fair bet, I grant you. But it seems to me you're doubling a man's doubt in his firearm."

Hervey was dismayed. Coates was sounding opposed to what was better because it was not as good as it might be. Indeed, he was sounding not unlike the very Luddites he so railed against, fearful of some notion because it were new. Had he aged so much in the past year and a half? It was a loathsome thought, he knew, but Hervey began to wonder if Daniel Coates were not on that cusp where a man turns from being an old soldier to an invalid, from a sage whose wisdom protects to a reactionary whose fear only stifles. He rubbed his shoulder hard, praying for patience. "You would not wish to persuade *me* against it, though, would you, Dan?"

"No, I wouldn't wish to persuade you against it. But I would counsel you to choose the percussion carbine any day."

It seemed to amount to the same. "And so you do not think I should recommend it to the Ordnance?"

Coates shook his head. "I should be very circumspect were I you, Matthew. Urge them to trials, certainly—but no more. Except perhaps to allude to Forsyth's percussion caps, and say that the two in combination might make a formidable weapon. Though you cannot say anything of the caps to your American, of course."

"No, of course." It wasn't necessary of Coates to remind him of that, but he could hardly blame him for being prudent.

They had a second glass of purl, then Hervey made his apologies and said he must be leaving: he could still get to Horningsham before last light, and the gelding was too green to be passing carts and cattle on a dark road. He realized it sounded rather lame, and hoped it didn't give offense. He might have stayed for some supper, but he was no longer in the best of sorts, what with the fall and the wary counsel.

Coates was obliging. He called for his man to fetch the gray.

As Hervey climbed into the saddle (he used the mounting block— better not to give the youngster any more surprises), he began to rue his impatience. How short his memory had been for all he owed. "Thank you, Dan," he said, with a smile that revealed his contrition. He held out his hand. "I'll be sure to write in very measured terms of that flintlock. For certain it would never have done for me at Waterloo—not in that sea of mud." He knew he ought never to forget it.

Coates smiled back, a smile of paternal pride, albeit adoptive, and he clapped him on the leg. "And one more piece of advice, Matthew . . ."

Hervey waited.

"Three more days to yon wedding. Don't go putting any more green horses at oxers!"

When he returned to Horningsham that evening, Hervey was much re-lieved to hear from Elizabeth that the archdeacon's visitation, which his ride on the plain was in large part designed to avoid, had gone more than tolerably well. The bishop's caution to the Reverend Mr. Hervey the pre-vious month had required him to submit to an inquisition, as Mr. Hervey put it, at the end of thirty days. And those thirty days had passed heavily, for Mr. Hervey had not shown any great inclination to abandon the prac-tices which the bishop apparently found so odious. When Hervey had left the vicarage that morning, therefore, it had been in the expectation of hearing on return that there would be proceedings of one sort or another against his father—a summons before the consistory, at least; or even, perhaps, his license suspended. Hervey had pleaded with his father to let him stay. He could not be of any help beyond the filial, but that was some comfort to a father was it not? But Mr. Hervey had insisted that this was a matter that he himself must bear.

It appeared, however, that the meeting had been one of respectful lis-tening and then accommodations, said Elizabeth. She had been there throughout, much to her surprise as well as the family's, for Mr. and Mrs. Hervey had imagined that the archdeacon would wish his visitation to be entirely private (Mrs. Hervey's loathing of the archdeacon had disposed her to believe that he would not welcome witnesses). At the last minute, Mr. Hervey's spirits had faltered somewhat, and therefore Elizabeth had found herself the supporter.

"And so what was agreed on?" asked Hervey, as Elizabeth stood watching him rub down the gelding.

"Well, Father was truly Christian—or, at least, he was very clever. He was at the greatest pains to explain each and every little thing to which the archdeacon had found objection. And he did so with such a humility that the archdeacon, who was disposed at first to be a little stiff, was quite warmed to Father by the end. And he stayed to luncheon."

"Did he indeed? Who would have thought it. So all along there has been much smoke and little fire?"

Elizabeth furrowed her brow. "I don't think we can say that. Did Father ever show you the letter of complaint? It was a long list, and it was written in attorneys' language."

"No, he didn't show me," Hervey replied, emptying a quarter of a bucketful of crushed barley into the stable manger. "But Mr. Keble told me that if the complaints were upheld, then any diocesan would be obliged to act. There's no doubt that Father might have been un-beneficed had the archdeacon still found fault today. As Mr. Keble pointed out—as *you* did, indeed—Father does not own the freehold." He pulled the bar across the stall gate and took up his coat.

Elizabeth noticed the streaks of dried mud across the shoulders. "Matthew, you haven't taken a tumble, have you?" There was a smile on her lips.

"Yes," he frowned.

"Oh, dear. He isn't going to do, then?"

Hervey was of a mind not to reply, but thought better of it. "He'll do very well." He smiled and shook his head. "It was I who didn't do! He took off half a stride before I was ready and—"

"Did anyone see? Are we to read of it in the *Warminster Miscellany?* 'Captain Hervey, lately returned from—' "

"Enough!" her brother protested, taking her arm and closing the bottom half of the stable door behind them. "Nobody saw. Daniel Coates brought him back soon afterwards and we had a laugh about it."

"I can imagine Daniel's laughing. Did he say more?"

"About what?"

"About your gun. That is what you said you were to see him about."

"Oh . . . we had a good talk."

They walked to the front of the house as the first pipistrelles were beginning their nightly acrobatics, which, now spring was truly come,
would soon be rivaled during the day by the house martins which returned every year to the vicarage. Hervey followed their swoops and
turns for a while, as if they might help his thoughts.

"Elizabeth," he began, after an interval, "do you think Dan is become old? I mean . . . I know he's not getting any younger, but today he
seemed . . . well, a little less . . . *reasonable*."

Elizabeth furrowed her brow again, and shook her head. "No, I have
not thought that—and not a week goes by that I don't see him in the
town. And Lord Bath was saying only the other day that he was the best
magistrate in the whole of west Wiltshire. Why do you ask?"

Hervey paused another while, and then smiled. "You'll think me
proud, but he would not see the advantages in my new carbine. He could
only see the faults. And that, I've observed, is the mark of someone become old."

Elizabeth frowned at him. "I should not wish you to be *my* judge in
anything, brother!"

"I have never known you to be other than an optimist—to a fault, indeed!" he replied at once, opening the door of the house for her as if it
were an end to the matter.

The door to their father's library was open, and the Reverend Thomas
Hervey was sitting by his fire—a fire was always lit there throughout
May—with glass in hand and contentment on his face. He turned as he
heard them come in. "Well, well, well. Here's a turn-up, eh? All those
weeks troubling over my books, and then the archdeacon is all sweetness
and light. I'm not sure I ever met a more reasonable fellow."

Elizabeth soon demonstrated that her brother's opinion of her was
more brotherly than exact. "Father, I should not be too quick to that sentiment were I you, for I did not observe any change in his mind, only a
desire to have things done with."

"Oh?" said Mr. Hervey, disappointed with her opinion, though
unsurprised—proud, in fact—that she should give it so freely. Elizabeth
had been his mainstay these past three years since the death of his elder
son.

She poured him more sherry. "Well, Father, on each and every complaint you assured him that you believed you were following the practice
of the early Church—'before Rome erred and strayed' were your very
words."

Mr. Hervey nodded, and her brother grew a little in awe of her, for here were affairs that he had never had occasion for mastering.

"And you gave him evidence, and cited authorities," Elizabeth continued. "And it seemed to me that the archdeacon was less inclined to concede your argument lest it reveal his own ignorance. So that, even now, he may be delving into his books in order to refute that argument should the time come."

"Oh, now, surely—" protested Mr. Hervey.

But Elizabeth persisted. "Because it appeared to me that the only issue on which he was certain that you stood in breach of any ordinance was that of facing east at the communion table. I notice that you forbore, for once, to call it an *altar*. And that was his chief concern."

Her brother thought it only right that he should make some contribution. "And how was this resolved, Father? The Prayer Book is quite explicit, is it not?"

"Explicit, yes, but not dogmatic. I didn't argue the point, though. I assured the archdeacon instead that he would hear of no further complaint in this regard."

"Oh, so you *did* concede in one matter at least!" tried Hervey.

"Matthew," his father replied, gravely: "I have said what I have said."

Hervey looked a little chastened. And then his father smiled. "Your friend from the wooden world is come, by the way."

"Captain Peto?"

"He stays at the Bath Arms, but he'll dine with us—in about an hour, indeed. We are all so late today."

Hervey was thoroughly enlivened by the news. "Oh, how I wish Henrietta were back to meet him! There'll be so little chance before Thursday. What did you think of him, Father? Is he not the very embodiment of a frigate captain?"

"I thought him a very fine fellow at once," he replied squarely.

Elizabeth smiled. "His voice was perhaps a *little* too great for such confined quarters, and he seemed to bump into the furniture rather a lot. But I liked him at once, too. Do you know, he says he believes this to be the farthest inland he has ever been?"

Hervey smiled more. "I can well believe it!" And then the clock struck the half hour. "Oh, have you seen Johnson? I must tell him about tomorrow."

Elizabeth frowned, but it was an approving sort of frown. Private Johnson had preceded Hervey to Horningsham by several days, and with him Jessye, and had been warmly welcomed by all. "Find Hannah Towle first, for he's been making eyes at her all day!"

In a village such as Horningsham, which owed its well-being to a great house like Longleat, it was by no means unusual for important affairs of state to be played out within the witness of the meanest of its inhabitants. But even Horningsham did not expect ever to be party to the news that broke next morning. It appalled and fascinated everyone alike, from day laborer to Lord Bath himself. The details were dreadful, and needed no embellishing in the retelling. The shock about the village was so apparent that even Private Johnson, a visitor with an undeveloped sensitivity, felt its strange effect during his progress from one end of Horningsham to the other on an errand for Hannah Towle.

One of the yeoman farmers, the same that had proposed to Mrs. Strange and whose property lay remote at the very edge of the parish bounds, had been found murdered in his own house, and his maidservant, the only other occupant, was likewise dead and her body disposed of in the garden well. Nothing more was known but that the house bore the signs of ransacking for money and valuables, and that the parish constable had hastened there at once. In no one's memory had there ever been such a thing—in the most distant past, even—and it was everywhere assumed that the culprits must be from Warminster Common, which all knew to be a sink of growing proportions. Except, as the Reverend Thomas Hervey pointed out, the farm lay the other side of the village from the common, so the murderers would have had to make a very great detour in order not to have been seen there. The farmer himself had no kin in the village, and his maidservant's family was from the neighboring parish, so Mr. Hervey had no immediate pastoral calling: the coroner's business would likely be slow, and the funeral many days off therefore—a mercy in not claiming his attention as the wedding approached.

At Longleat, Lord Bath was in a mood of some despair, for—the more personal effects of the crime apart—he believed it reflected ill on the stewardship of his demesne. Such things might happen in cities, or on estates where the owner took no careful interest in affairs other than its rents. But not here. Wiltshire wasn't Clare or Kerry, after all, and he was not an absentee landlord. And what might the parish constable discover? He was good enough when it came to the odd bit of mischief, but this was altogether too grave a crime for a man whose principal occupation was the maintenance of the Longleat fire engine. No, it would not do. Lord Bath would not wait for the trail to go stone cold while Constable Gedge completed his thorough but fruitless inquiries. He would send at once to London for Bow Street detectors.

When Hervey set out for Longleat in the midmorning he had a mind to call on Mrs. Strange to condole with her, for he imagined that an offer of marriage on the farmer's part supposed some degree of intimacy—or, at least, familiarity. But as he passed the school he heard the children singing a hymn—and by no means a somber one—so he presumed Mrs. Strange was not so indisposed as to put off her charges and draw the curtains at home. He therefore rode on to his appointment with Henrietta, who would be returned, he trusted, from that nearby fashionable spa where ladies could find everything that a lady needed. The appointment was not so much with Henrietta, however, as the two of them with Mr. Keble. John Keble had also dined at the vicarage the night before, and the meeting this morning, he had explained, was in order to discharge his obligation in certain matters respecting the Prayer Book.

The meeting began well. They sat in a small summer breakfast room, the late spring sunshine warm through windows full east, with orchids from the Longleat hothouses about them. Hervey's and Henrietta's chairs were drawn close enough together for them to place a hand on one another's from time to time, with Mr. Keble's chair somehow arranged so as not to be too formal, though not yet so intimate as to make for any additional awkwardness in his discourse with them. First he explained that, in order to preach as he intended, and so that the dean, who was to officiate, might omit the lengthy declaration of the duties of man and wife which the Prayer Book otherwise required, he felt obliged to "share with them certain things." And so the familiar injunctions of Saints Peter and Paul were rehearsed, and the parties were content. Then, with a certain delicacy of manner, he asked their leave to go a little further. He wished, with considerable authority as well as delicacy, to "lay their minds at rest," as he put it; to disabuse them of any doubts they might have as to "the worthiness of the desires of the flesh within wedlock." Henrietta smiled serenely, and her countenance gave no indication of whether the desires of the flesh were in any respect understood. Hervey shifted slightly in his chair, and feared somehow that his own understanding would be all too readily exposed.

"For it would be contrary to all Christian doctrine," explained John Keble, "to imagine—as did the Gnostics—that the body is the enemy of the spiritual life." Henrietta listened as before. She had not the slightest notion of who the Gnostics were, but her instincts were true enough. Hervey *had* known who the Gnostics were, and what their heresy was, but had forgotten, and he drifted off into recollection of his Shrewsbury divinity. Indeed, he would have languished there an age had not John Keble's discourse suddenly taken an unusually frank turn. Henrietta's eyes lit, at last, as the young priest began speaking with perfect candor of the growth in love that came with its physical consummation. Hervey did not see her eyes, for he was avoiding them intently, wondering how a man so recently ordained priest, so unworldly a man, could speak of this so assuredly.

"So let me conclude with Scripture," said Keble at length, and rather to Hervey's relief. "Not St. Paul, this time, but from the Old Testament—from the Song of Solomon."

Hervey glanced at Henrietta. She touched his hand for an instant, telling him at once she understood all, perfectly.

" 'As the lily among thorns, so is my love among the daughters,' " began John Keble.

Henrietta smiled so happily that he paused, very deliberately.

" 'As the apple among the trees of the wood, so is my beloved among the sons. I sat down under his shadow with great delight, and his fruit was sweet to my taste.' "

She smiled wide again. Her neck, where the demure single string of pearls circled it, became red in vivid patches, and her eyes grew larger.

" 'He brought me to the banqueting house, and his banner over me was love. His left hand is under my head, and his right hand doth embrace me.' "

Hervey at last turned full to Henrietta. She looked more desirable than at any time he had seen her, and he ceded his thoughts to all that the words aroused.

The day of the marriage between Captain Matthew Paulinus Hervey, bachelor of the parish of Horningsham, and of Lady Henrietta Charlotte Anne Wharton Lindsay, spinster of the parish of Longbridge Deverel (as the banns had lately declaimed them) passed slowly at first—all *too* slowly, they would both agree—until, from about three in the afternoon, the time began to pass twice as quickly as it ought. And so, though he had made his preparations with meticulous care, the bridegroom found himself hastening to fasten the knee buttons of his regimental court dress as Lord John Howard, his supporter, looked anxiously at his watch. They got into the carriage a full fifteen minutes later than Hervey had planned, risking being caught behind others in the darkening lanes, but the driver earned himself a sovereign by taking his team at a canter the length of Horningsham and the park drive, arriving three minutes before the time Hervey had first intended. The groom was therefore content once more as they stepped down.

It hadn't been his idea to wear uniform. A somber coat would have been his preference, but Prince Leopold had worn his uniform at Carlton House, and so Henrietta had wished her affianced to do the same. Lord John Howard wore the self-same uniform (albeit a brand-new set) in which he had first appeared at the vicarage two years before. The memory of that unhappy business—when the lieutenant of foot guards had come with the mistaken orders for his arrest—crowded Hervey for an instant when, as then, they had got into the carriage. But all that had been put from his mind by the gallop to Longleat, and they stood now as if friends of long years.

Longleat House was lit inside and out as he had never seen it before. The music of a string orchestra could be heard even above the talk of the seventy privileged guests who had just been treated to a dinner of immense refinement in the great dining room, and, indeed, of nearly the same number of only marginally less privileged guests who filled the Tudor hall—the yeomen and tenants of the village, those who had nursed bride or groom to adulthood, and the NCOs of the Sixth who would form their guard of honor. Roast pork filled their plates, and hops their glasses if burgundy was not to their liking. And both parties, separate and content, were now beginning to rise to make their way to the grand state room, where they would bear witness to the marriage vows.

At one end of that elegant room was a velvet-covered altar, just as at Carlton House, with chapel ornaments brought from Longbridge Deverel, including two handsome candlesticks six feet high. A little string orchestra played Purcell airs as the principal wedding guests began to find their places in the ranks of gilded chairs, and at the rear the yeomen and tenants assembled, though in a more respectful hush—fine worsteds and cottons to the silks and satins in front. Hervey, quite composed, took his seat with his family. He had managed to exchange a few words with the NCOs as they took post along the wall at the back of the state room, and he was much gratified that their turnout was as fine as he had seen, perhaps finer—testimony to his troop serjeant major's authority, or else (dare he imagine?) to that mutual respect which was the regiment at its best. Serjeant Armstrong's hessians were so mirrorlike that Hervey thought he must have shuffled every step of the way to prevent their cracking across the instep.

The dean of Hereford, flanked by John Keble, entered quietly through a side door, and together they took their sedilia. Shortly afterwards, the marquess's butler, the master of ceremonies, gave a discreet nod, and Hervey left his place and went out to meet his bride.

Hervey knew that a bride on her wedding day was transfigured. Legend had it so, as well as village lore. But Henrietta's transfiguration was beyond anything he had imagined, for beneath the veil her features had an ethereal quality—her eyes, hair, and complexion luminous. Her dress was exquisite, and he stood before her quite unable to express anything but utter admiration, and silently, at that.

"Sir! A button!" snapped Private Johnson suddenly, having stationed himself with his customary prescience. "Excuse me, ma'am," he said to Henrietta, pulling his captain aside into the little anteroom off the hall.

Henrietta smiled warmly at so faithful a servant, and turned to her bridesmaids. "Elizabeth," she said, with perfect composure, "I have never been sure of anything as at this moment." It was true that her bridegroom had perhaps never appeared to her more dashing in his regimentals than now, for levee dress set off everything in appearance about Matthew Hervey that a woman might admire. But more than that, she knew the uniform signified a strength and a constancy on which she might, with utmost certainty, rely. This ceremony might show Longleat at its finest, and witness to the great affection in which she was held by its lord, but she would quit it gladly for the complete affection with which Matthew Hervey would honor her, and would follow the trumpet for that love, no matter what its calls and privations. And she hoped he might soon trust in that.

"Is tha all right, Cap'n 'Ervey?" asked Johnson, pushing the needle once more into the stiffened cloth of the tunic collar to secure the idle button. "Tha looks like tha's seen a ghost."

Hervey looked at his groom incomprehendingly. "What?"

"Tha's miles away, sir!"

He had indeed been miles away. He had visited things years past, in his mind—all the way back to that first encounter with the little girl who had never been far from his thoughts ever since, deny them though he so often had. He smiled, the color now coming back to his face. "I saw quite a *few* ghosts, Johnson. But they don't trouble me anymore."

"Eh, sir?"

"Never mind. Is that button fast yet?"

"It is." Johnson knotted the thread, bit off the ends, and fastened the collar up again.

Hervey clapped him on the arm, grinned his thanks, and took his place at Henrietta's side.

"Are we ready, Matthew?" She smiled at him full again.

This time he returned the smile—and with interest. He nodded to the master of ceremonies, who signaled to a footman, and the little string orchestra began the march from *Alceste* to which Hervey, his bride, and her retinue would process to the altar.

The seamstresses of Bath, whom Henrietta had long thought superior to those of London, had made so faithful a replica of Princess Charlotte's wedding dress that it might have been supposed she wore the original. Except that Charlotte's figure stood in unhappy comparison with Henrietta's, and the removal of several yards of the silver cloth would not have been possible without destroying the overall effect. Layer upon layer of the costly fabric was sewn with silver thread, and embroidered at the borders with patterns of shells and bouquets. It was cut full below the high bodice, and while the original had—as many sadly observed—emphasized Charlotte's corpulence, this Bath replica served only to present Henrietta's figure in all its elegance. Somehow, too, its frills, lace trimmings and garlands of diamonds wholly became her, rather than drawing attention away from her fine eyes and captivating face (under its wreath of rosebuds, leaves, and brilliants). Princess Charlotte had graciously given Henrietta leave to imitate her—to flatter her, indeed, by such imitation. But there were several in the assembly that evening who said how providential it was that the royal pregnancy kept Charlotte from Longleat now.

" 'Dearly beloved, we are gathered together here in the sight of God,' " began the dean. He had said the words many times before, and yet always they seemed new and full of promise—" 'to join together this man and this woman in holy Matrimony; which is an honorable estate . . .' " He enunciated the purposes for which marriage was ordained. And no one alleged or declared any impediment, when called upon to do so, why Hervey and Henrietta should not be joined together in holy Matrimony. Bride and groom answered clearly and distinctly when the dean asked of them both if they would honor their obligations to each other. Each of them spoke clearly and distinctly as they gave their troth to each other, Henrietta's right hand in Hervey's and then Hervey's in Henrietta's. And Hervey put the ring on the fourth finger of Henrietta's left hand and vowed with it to worship her with his body, and to endow her with all his worldly goods. They knelt, and the dean asked God's blessing on them both, commanded that those whom God hath joined should no man put asunder, and then pronounced them man and wife together. And when Hervey lifted Henrietta's veil, he marveled equally at his fortune that this woman had indeed consented to be his wife.

There followed Psalm 128, *Beati omnes*—". . . O well is thee, and happy shalt thou be"—and the Lord's Prayer, and others for general blessings and for fruitfulness in the procreation of children. Then all were bidden to sit to hear the homily on the duties of Man and Wife.

"I do hope this is not to be a long affair," whispered the marquess audibly to Lady Bath. "These Oxford fellows can be mightily pleased with the sound of their own voice."

John Keble, as he rose and moved to the middle of the extemporary chancel, gave no clue as to how long he would detain his congregation, nor, indeed, how engagingly. "Dearly belovèd, in the preface to the form of solemnization of matrimony, the persons to be married are bidden to come into the body of the church 'with their friends and neighbours.' "

The words, his voice, and his sublime aspect at once commanded unusual attention in a congregation enlivened by the host's hospitality.

"And this, Matthew Hervey and, now, Henrietta Hervey have done, for you indeed are their friends and neighbors. We need not dwell on the reasons for requiring that they should not come privily, save that those whom they love best, and who love them best, should bear witness to the mutual love that these two persons have for each other. *Love,* the last best gift of heaven." He paused. "Above all, they witness before God to this love, this gift of heaven, this heavenly grace, and they and we ask God's blessing that, as Isaac and Rebecca lived faithfully together, so might they. Sustained by the prayers and society of you, their friends and neighbors, and by the grace of God, Matthew and Henrietta may hope fervently that they might live as Isaac and Rebecca, and that they might follow Christ's commandment to love one another. *Love,* the last best gift of heaven. *Love,* gentle, holy, pure. *Amen.*"

John Keble turned and knelt before the altar. Hervey took Henrietta's hand. Neither bride nor groom could possibly know the range of sentiment for them in that chapel room. For the most part it was that of friends and neighbors, young and old, who had watched or somehow shared their progress to adulthood and their consent now to be man and wife. In Hervey's case, although his society was limited in comparison with Henrietta's, the range of acquaintances which his profession admitted was much the greater. There were some in that congregation, like Mrs. Strange, with feelings of obligation for a past kindness out of the run of the ordinary. Some, like Private Johnson, would own that daily life was infinitely the better for the command of their captain; one or two might even claim their very being here, rather than in the grave, was because of him; and there were some (perhaps no more than a dozen) who hardly knew either of them—officers of the Sixth happy to accept the customary invitation to see a fellow wed, including his commanding officer, whose duty it was to be there. It was impossible that John Keble's address should touch each as strongly; but touch each in some way it did, if for nothing but its singular brevity and clarity—as well, perhaps, as for its challenge. The silence between its ending and the dean's blessing and dismissal was memorable.

The service ended, the little orchestra began to play the "Triumphing Dance" from *Dido and Aeneas*—the bride's choice both for its purport and liveliness—and the congregation, led by Captain Matthew and Lady Henrietta Hervey, walked from the chapel room between a file of carried sabers and into the great hall where the band of the 6th Light Dragoons, high in the minstrels' gallery, struck up the regiment's quick march, "Young May Moon," to the spontaneous applause of all the guests, who now mingled freely, or at least unseparated, to enjoy their host's generosity once more. And only now did Henrietta feel an inclination to rue her idea of imitating *all* Princess Charlotte's arrangements, for she realized how very detained they would be by so many well-wishers. Not that Hervey imagined any such feeling on his wife's part. How *might* he, yet? He could only submit to duty once more, content with the thought that for Henrietta this must be the happiest time of the whole day.

It would be two hours and more before he came at last to understand the truth, the whole truth, of John Keble's words of the day before.

It was indeed a glorious May moon that lit the guests' way home that night—by foot, horse, and carriage alike—and which shone a full three hours on Hervey and Henrietta in their marriage bed. And it was after midday that Hervey came down the great staircase of Longleat House, for the first time in his life. His slight feeling of awkwardness in his new status was made worse by the obvious cause of the lateness of the descent (Henrietta would be a full fifteen minutes behind him). He was doubly surprised, therefore, when the butler greeted him formally but with polite indifference, and astonished when he announced that Daniel Coates wished to see him as soon as might be possible.

Hervey sighed (on this, of all mornings, might not Daniel Coates allow him to be his own man—for right or for wrong?). "He surely does not expect me to ride to Upton Scudamore?"

"Oh, no, sir. He is here, waiting," replied the butler.

"In heaven's name, for how long?"

The butler's voice changed just a point to explain the propriety of Coates's request. "Mr. Coates has not been home this last evening, sir. At about one o'clock this morning—after you had retired, sir," (Hervey colored a little) "he came up to me in—may I say, sir—a degree of agitation, and asked if I knew what were your and her ladyship's plans in the coming days. I replied that I was not privy to them, sir. Mr. Coates then said that he had to go to Bristol for several days in his magisterial capacity, and that he could not risk your leaving without his speaking with you."

Hervey knew he would see him at once—of *course* he would. But he wanted to know all there was of it beforehand. "Did you not offer him paper, Thurlow?"

"Indeed I did, sir, but Mr. Coates said he could not possibly commit his business to paper."

Ten minutes later, when they met together in the library, Coates bore an expression of great anxiety which was not helped by his evident lack of sleep.

"My dear Dan, whatever is the matter?" said Hervey, now genuinely concerned for the man who was in both senses his oldest friend.

Daniel Coates shook his head several times. "Your commanding officer—Lord Towcester . . ."

Hervey looked puzzled. "Yes, Dan? You met him last night?"

"Not exactly; not as such," he replied, shaking his head again.

"Well, what is it then?" He laid a hand on Coates's forearm.

"He's not . . . not . . . not *right!*"

By now Hervey was becoming exasperated. "Dan, to be frank, he's to hardly anyone's liking in the Sixth. And it's only too clear to me why! As, doubtless, it was to you."

"No. It's not just that. I've met 'im before."

Hervey was about to try allaying what he judged to be a veteran's anxiety when the old soldier rallied. "In Holland. In '99, with the Duke of York and Abercromby. I was an orderly dragoon at General Poole's headquarters."

Hervey began to listen intently, for he knew that tone well enough.

"We'd landed on the Helder towards the end of August, and it was muddle as usual. But a few weeks later we were giving the French a trouncing at last, on the coast, at Bergen. There was a hell of a long skirmish with the French 'ussars, all along the dunes for half a dozen miles—pouring rain an' all. It was mainly the Fifteenth and Eighteenth, but then the Twenty-third was thrown in, new-come from England. They went at it well enough, but then the French counterattacked good and proper out of Egmont, and rolled over them like they wasn't there."

Hervey knew the battle well—a good light dragoon action, he had always understood. And Coates had spoken of it before. But now it was as if he were still there, so intent was his look. "Go on, Dan."

"Lord Towcester—well, he wasn't Lord Towcester then: he was Lord Charles Keys, *wasn't* he—Lord Towcester had a troop of the Twenty-third and he upped and left them—galloped off the field as if the hounds of hell were after him! In full view of his brigadier!"

Hervey's mouth fell open. "How in heaven's name could he become a captain, then, let alone a lieutenant colonel?"

Coates didn't answer directly. "The Eighteenth charged through and through—young Stewart at their head, him that is Lord Stewart now, privy councillor an' all. 'That's the way cavalry should be handled,' called General Poole. 'And as for that officer who bolted, I'll have his name disgraced forever!' "

"But it seems he didn't," sighed Hervey.

"That night, I was outside the general's office waiting on him to take his dispatch to Lord Abercromby's headquarters. Just a curtain for a door, it had. Lord Towcester was brought in under arrest, and I heard everything. The general'd been appalled when he'd learned who the officer was, because he knew his father as a very old friend. He'd wanted to have Lord Towcester court-martialed at first, but said he couldn't bear to think of the pain it would bring so noble a man as was his father. He made him swear upon his honor to resign his commission at once and never again to seek one. And then Lord Towcester went out into the night, and no one ever saw him again."

"But this was all done in front of witnesses, was it not?" pressed

Hervey, disbelieving that such a promise could not have been enforced, let alone dishonored. "And the whole brigade saw the flight, too?"

"The only man that I know of who would have heard the exchange was the brigade major, but he died that winter. And General Poole went peacefully in his bed many years ago now. He called me in to take the dispatch soon afterwards and asked me if I'd heard what'd passed. I said I had, and the general said he believed he may well live to rue the day he had been so weak-minded about it. I remember it as clearly as if it were yesterday, for a general would never share such a thought with a corporal if he were not truly dismayed."

Hervey could not but agree. "But what about those who saw him bolt?"

"That I can't say," said Coates, shaking his head. "It was nigh on twenty years ago. Who remembers anything when so much has happened in between? And who could say anything against their betters anyway? I don't even know if Stewart himself saw it."

What a dismal thing to hear on *any* morning, thought Hervey. "So I have a commanding officer who is not merely disliked for his manner by all, he was—and therefore almost certainly still is—a coward. And, what's worse, his word counts for nothing."

"Aye, Matthew," agreed Coates, shaking his head gravely. "You see now why I was in such haste to warn you of it. A regiment commanded by a knave like him will be a damned pitiable place. He'd give you the point from behind soon as look at you. Stay on guard, Matthew! Stay on guard!"

PART 2

SKIRMISHERS OUT

CHAPTER 6

FROM WHOM NO
SECRETS ARE HIDDEN

Hounslow, Six Weeks Later

"His Lordship is most insistent on it, Captain Hervey. He wishes that you will take command of your troop at once. The major general's inspection is at the end of the month." The adjutant's tone was emphatic.

Hervey could not complain. These were the petty exigencies of the service, after all. But why had July been declared the grass month only weeks before, and officers promised leave? He accepted Lord Towcester's wish as if it were an order—that went without saying—but it seemed not unreasonable for the adjutant to say why the change had been necessary. Did the annual inspection come as such a surprise?

The adjutant clearly believed he had a fight on his hands. "If you wish to protest any more then you shall have to put it in writing to his lordship," he said, defiantly.

"But I have not protested in the least! I have merely asked to be told the reason for the change. Things will go all the easier with the troop if they know why it is."

"I do not think his lordship would hold with that sentiment. An order is given and it is a subordinate's duty to obey!"

Hervey sighed to himself. Only an imbecile would think that this truism was the last word on the command of men. "Dauntsey, do not mistake me. I say again that I have not the slightest wish to question the order. But I have always observed that our men go the better for it if they are told as much as possible."

"Our" came properly enough, for they both wore the same badge.

The adjutant sneered. "In my former regiment I pride myself that we were greatly more punctilious in such matters, Captain Hervey. You shall have to put your objections in writing to the lieutenant colonel. He would not countenance it if this conversation continued."

"And I say for a third time that I make no objection!" Hervey managed to keep his voice quite even, to begin with, but then his patience failed him: "See here, Dauntsey, if you go blustering to the troop captains in this way you will soon have their resentment, and it is not a good thing for a commanding officer to have an adjutant who cannot manage the captains."

The adjutant made to protest.

"I am not finished, if you please, Mr. Dauntsey. When you speak, it is as if the lieutenant colonel himself were speaking, and it is as well that you remember that privilege, for if you use words that the colonel would not have wished, then your authority will be shot through once and for all."

The adjutant wore a look like thunder.

"Very well, then, Dauntsey. I shall return to Longleat now, and I shall be back, as his lordship wishes, in seven days' time. Be pleased to give my respects to him when he returns."

Hervey left the orderly room and walked to the officers' mess, fulminating at the adjutant's disdain and presumption. He was angry at having been driven to speak so sharply, but Dauntsey had had it coming to him. The fellow had been deuced rude on their first meeting two months ago, and since his own arrival yesterday—to do no more than make a few domestic arrangements—Dauntsey had scarce had a civil word for him.

It was not good, though, to be on poor terms with the adjutant. For although Hervey was confident enough of keeping the likes of Dauntsey on his guard, a mean-minded adjutant could always exact his vengeance in other ways—on the troop itself, perhaps. And in Hervey's experience, when that went on for some time, the men could turn their resentment towards their captain rather than their true persecutor. An unpropitious start then, but better, perhaps, than to let things run on and have a bigger quarrel later. Well, it was done now, said Hervey to himself. Better to get his things into the chaise and be away.

How satisfying it was to have his own chaise. The stage was a mean alternative, even though he could now take an inside seat without having to worry about the cost. Serjeant Armstrong had called it swanking when first he had seen the carriage, with the Bath arms and all on the sides, and Hervey had been quick to admit to its provenance—and its temporary proprietorship. But it would still give him no little satisfaction to leave the barracks in it at once, beholden not even to the mess drag to get him to the staging inn.

"Hallo! You are off already?" said Captain Strickland, coming on the rig outside the mess a half hour later.

"Aye. The colonel wants me back early, it seems. There are things to do in Wiltshire first."

Strickland raised an eyebrow and half smiled. "The major general's inspection?"

"Yes."

"What a t'do that is. You've heard about the muddle I suppose?"

"No?"

"My serjeant major had it from one of the clerks. It seems that the general wrote months ago to say he wanted to see the regiment before the grass month. Someone failed to take note."

Hervey frowned. "Then I should not like to be who it was that failed."

Strickland smiled, but thinly. "I mean, it lay on the colonel's desk for an inordinate time."

"Oh," said Hervey, cast even lower by the intelligence. "Had I known that but a half hour ago I should not have pressed the adjutant on it."

Strickland smiled again. "I shouldn't trouble yourself on that account. Dauntsey is so terrified of Towcester that he couldn't bring himself to press him to an order. Nor had he the wit to issue even a preliminary one of his own. He deserved whatever he got."

"Then heaven preserve us if ever we have to turn out on some alarm!"

"Aye, just so," nodded Strickland solemnly. "I'm glad you're come back, Hervey."

Hervey felt the sentiment a shade awkwardly, though. "I'm glad you should say so."

"But I believe I must tell you I'm thinking of exchanging," added Strickland sheepishly.

"I'm very sorry to hear that." Hervey spoke with feeling, for though they had not served together long, they had at least shared a campaign. He wondered if he might soon have *any* kindred spirits of the old Sixth to serve with. "Do you have to?"

"I believe I shall."

"It won't be easy to exchange now, unless you're prepared to go to a regiment warned for India. A troop is hard to come by as things stand, what with disbandments and so on."

"I know. I'd go to India, though the climate would serve me ill. I'd exchange into the infantry even, perhaps not taking the difference either."

This last he said almost defiantly. He must indeed be desperate, thought Hervey, for Strickland was not a rich man, and could ill afford to throw away the difference in price of a captaincy—perhaps a thousand pounds if auctioned well in Charles Street. Might anyone find his commanding officer *so* unbearable? He put his hand to Strickland's arm. "Do you want to speak of it?"

"No, not now—not here. When you're come back."

The words were so heavy that still Hervey could not break off. "My dear fellow . . ." A thought occurred to him. "Why don't you come down to Wiltshire with me for a few days? I'd welcome the company, and you could tell me of how things are here."

Strickland brightened a little. "That is exceedingly good of you, but I'm captain of the week."

"Then as soon as I'm back let us dine together in the town, and you may tell me of it."

"Yes . . . yes; I should like that."

When Hervey returned to Longleat, Henrietta seemed to greet him rather anxiously. "I had such a presentiment of your not returning," she said, taking his arm as they walked up the steps to the house. "Matthew, dearest, I do not want us to be apart again unless it is entirely necessary—not even for a night."

The proposal was scarcely disagreeable. "But of course, my darling. I should not have gone to Hounslow alone had I thought for one minute the journey would not have been tedious for you."

"But you did not ask."

He was puzzled. "Would you have agreed to come if it had been disagreeable to you?"

wasn't in a gelding. "Yes, Matthew," she interrupted, frowning. "I believe I can understand that much!"

He did not redden this time.

Johnson led Jessye in hand to the big yard used for the coverings. Straw was spread deep and for a moment the mare looked as though she had a mind to roll, but he managed to keep her up, and stood close to quiet her. The stud groom brought the stallion directly, and with scarcely a hand needed to help, the big horse went to her.

Hervey had left Henrietta at the saddle room, expecting her to return to the house. He didn't know she watched from a window—not until he went back afterwards and found her waiting for him. She looked him full in the face—an admiring look, a look that said she understood him a little more. "What a thing is nature," she said. It was a distinctly reverent statement, but also determined. Nature's blush suffused her own face, and she took his hand and led him from the room.

Later, they rode out together, up past the hanger towards the picket post and around Arn Hill. Hervey thought he could do this forever, and said so. Henrietta thought he could not, and said so, too. Indeed, she *hoped* he could not, "for I did not choose to marry a squire!" But for the moment, though, there was nothing that either of them would rather do than ride to the downs. There was something about two horses in a landscape. Two was a number like no other. Three, four, ten, twenty, or even one: it was all much of the same. But two was different, for it spoke of intimacy. They rode for a full half mile without saying anything, content to let nature speak—a sky with scarcely a cloud, the downs without the hand of man. And now they were joined by swallows—two dozen or more. They dived and turned and soared all about them, swooping so close and low as to seem certain to collide with the horses' legs, though neither Hervey's gray nor Henrietta's little bay mare took the slightest notice.

"I have never seen the like," said Henrietta. "Never seen them fly so. They are enchanting. Why do they accompany us, do you think?"

"Perhaps they just like it."

"Oh, I hope that is so, Matthew," she said, smiling and looking about her. "I should like to think that a bird is as capable of taking such simple pleasure. I have never looked down at a swallow before, only up. They

"Yes!"

"Then you see why I did not ask."

"But Matthew, how could it ever be disagreeable to me to be with you?"

What a simple statement of love that was. A lump came to his throat. "My dear, I . . ."

She threw her head back, grinning mischievously. A strand of hair fell across her cheek, but she merely brushed it behind an ear. "Then it is resolved on. Only if I am ordered by the Horse Guards itself shall I leave you—and a direct order at that!"

Hervey smiled, too, embracing her and taking the pins from her hair so that it fell about her shoulders. "Then when I am on maneuvers with my troop you shall come up at night with the bat-horses."

"And share your bivouac?" She giggled. "Would your colonel approve?"

"He would be jealous."

"I could dress as one of your dragoons, then."

Hervey smiled again. "If the disguise worked, then it might lead to my arrest!"

She giggled even more.

"Besides, the dolman's a might too tight-fitting to be any sort of deception." He colored up even as he was saying it.

She colored, too, but it was with the little telltale patches of red about her neck. "Come," she whispered, pulling his arm. "We're not to dine for another hour."

In the afternoon he took up the *Warminster Miscellany* to read the account of the trial and execution of the two murderers of farmer Fremantle and his maidservant. The Bow Street investigators had done their work with remarkable dispatch, it seemed. They had arrived at Longleat two days after the wedding, and within five more had made their arrests. Not on Warminster Common, as everyone had expected, but in a next-door parish, albeit across the county boundary. And this fact made for alarm in Horningsham, for it was much easier to live with the notion that an outlaw from the common had done this vile thing than a couple of roughs from a village not unlike theirs. Nevertheless, it was some consolation to know that justice would always be served, for this must be a great deterrent to further crime, albeit at the expense of bringing investigators from London.

Hervey had been much taken with the Bow Street men. Lord Bath had asked him if he would see to things while he himself went up to Parliament for the estimates, and so each day, of a morning, the detectors would give him a summary of the evidence they had gathered the previous day, and tell him of their next intentions. He did not suppose he had met two more intelligent men, in the most practical sense of that quality. The senior of the two had been twenty years in the king's service, an artificer of sappers and miners. His assistant, by contrast, had for a long time been a bookkeeper with the Lunatic Asylum Protector Insurance Company. Their methods were meticulous, ingenious, and complementary, their hours long. Nor did they make the mistake of thinking they were dealing with bumpkins because they were beyond the sound of the Bow bells. But one thing had impressed Hervey greatly: from the outset the detectors had had complete confidence that they would bring the perpetrators to justice, and doubtless this had conveyed itself to all whom they interviewed, speeding the ultimate detection.

When this had been accomplished, the three of them had enjoyed a good dinner at the Bell in Warminster (which boasted the best double mutton chops in the county), before the Bow Street men had taken the afternoon stage for Andover, and thereon the post back to London. As Hervey now read the account of the hanging, he thought himself lucky that he had had pressing business at Hounslow after all, for the companion gallows at the top of Arn Hill, and two young men scarcely out of their teens brought by their own wickedness to so violent an end, would have been a heavy sight, even with the knowledge of the awful butchery of the farmer and his maid. For he knew there were men in the Sixth who might, in other circumstances, be capable of such a thing. And he would for certain have had to be there, not least to be a support for his father who, with the vicar of Warminster, had had to officiate on the scaffold. "A vast multitude of spectators," the *Miscellany* said there had been. And the Wiltshire Yeomanry had been out to keep order, just as the regulars had been with Cashman—another man who for sure would have been kept from the gallows had he still been in the king's service. In any event, the Bow Street men were the toast of the *Miscellany*—"the heroes of the multitude" said the paper.

He was deeply absorbed with *The Times* when Henrietta joined him. "What engages you, my love?" she asked brightly, leaning over his head to kiss his forehead.

"Nothing agreeable, I'm afraid," he sighed.

"Tell me of it."

"Well, habeas corpus is still suspended, and Lord Sidmouth is castigated for the way he is dealing with the agitation over reform. They accuse him of using spies too freely, and agents provocateurs."

Henrietta looked troubled, rather in the way she had when he had returned from Hounslow. "It alarms me sometimes. I might tell you there have been nights here when I have lain awake expecting the house to be attacked, when the slightest noise has made me fear for my life."

Her tone chilled him. He stood up and took hold of her. "My dear, such things don't come like that. We should have word well before."

She seemed prepared to believe his assurance for the time being. "In any case, I have no cause for fear now you are with me."

It had been the briefest of departures from her habitually carefree manner, but it registered with her husband nonetheless. Hers was the vulnerability of a world suddenly not impregnable. Like as not in her delightful years in the shelter of the Longleat acres, she had never seen anything more violent than a carter's whip to a horse, nor heard a curse stronger than a blade's dealt a bad hand at cards. But why then should she seem so fearful? He knew little of her childhood before Longleat, of course, but he hardly supposed it had been an unhappy one.

"We're putting the improver to Jessye again today." He tried to give the change of subject as uncontrived an air as possible. "The stud groom thinks it should be well this time." Jessye had failed to come into foal, a month ago, but the stud groom had said he doubted she was truly in-season. "He's got her a teaser this time."

Henrietta was smiling again. "Do *I* tease you still, Matthew?"

"Aye," he grinned, "but different from how you did!"

They kissed, but the door opened and a footman informed him that Private Johnson had Jessye ready for the stallion.

"You had better go to your other love," sighed Henrietta, refastening the buttons on his coat.

"Have you *seen* the improvement stallion?" he asked, as he made to leave. "He is quite magnificent."

"No. May I come with you?"

"Of course. He's one of the handsomest things you'll ever see. He has a coat like polished ebony. There's something in a stallion that—"

He was going to tell her there was something in a stallion which there are so beautiful! I should much rather we stay watching them than go to Lady Hore's tonight."

She had once told him that a day without a party was not worth recording in her journal. What a change this was. Or had she simply concealed this side hereto? "Do you see how they spread their forktails as they turn?" He gestured with his whip. "It must help them veer so acutely."

"And they have flown all the way from Africa! It is almost too much to believe. So far that . . . *You* have not been to Africa, have you, Matthew?"

"No, not *to* Africa. Around Africa. I saw its shores once or twice, but very distantly."

"I should like to see Africa," said Henrietta, still watching the swallows with a look of semiwonder.

At no time had she ever expressed, within his hearing, any desire to travel beyond Italy or St. Petersburg. He had even had his doubts, in Paris two summers ago, that she could be persuaded to come with him to India. He made no reply.

She watched the swallows for a full five minutes without a sound. Then she sighed very contentedly and turned to him. "I am so very, very happy with you, Matthew. I hardly know myself. I see things I have never seen before."

"And I, too," he assured her. "I do not believe that I truly knew what life was before now—before daring to *admit* that I loved you, that is, for I believe I have loved you a very long time."

She smiled at him reassuringly. She knew what trials had attended that declaration. They rode on a while longer in happy silence. "But Matthew, there is one thing I have been meaning to ask. The morning after our wedding—why did Daniel Coates wish to see you so urgently?"

Hervey sighed. He had decided against telling her at the time because it seemed so ill matched to the occasion, and since then he had found the notion hard to share with her since it could only increase her anxiety for him, and nothing she might say could ameliorate his own.

"Tell me, Matthew. It evidently disquiets you," she insisted.

He told her what Coates had said about his commanding officer.

She looked puzzled. "Why didn't you tell me before?"

"I think that I did not want to distress you—especially at that time."

"But Matthew, if something distresses you, then you must permit me to ease that distress. And I cannot do so unless you tell me all." She turned and looked at him direct. "There can be no secrets between us now."

She had still the appearance of contentment, but her voice carried an insistence which left Hervey in no doubt that she intended them to be a couple in every sense, in duty and disappointment alike. Indeed, Henrietta intended taking her marriage vows with the utmost seriousness, even if she had already largely forgotten their actual words.

Hervey could only feel chastened, but then encouraged, for hers would be a brave course for a soldier's wife at the best of times—and these were not the best of times. He smiled, stood in his stirrups, leaned out and kissed her. It said all there was to say, and in a manner which entirely delighted her.

CHAPTER 7

MANEUVERS

Hounslow, Three Weeks Later

"I well see your dismay, gentlemen," said Major Joynson, "but we had expected nothing more than the usual administrative inspection. That is why there have been no field days."

The troop captains were complaining of the lack of drill they had had, in light of the major general's wishes, just received, that next Thursday's annual inspection should take the form of a survey of horses, clothing, and equipment in the barracks, and then a day's maneuvers on Chobham Common. All the captains but Hervey, that is, for he had not the slightest notion how handy his troop was in the field, nor for that matter how it and B Troop worked together as a squadron. He had been at its head only since Monday, and during that time he had been able to do nothing more than any captain did on taking over his troop, which was to see that everything for which he might be held accountable with his purse was as the regimental books said it should be. He had looked at the sixty or so horses with a most careful eye, and been more pleased than he could remember—a far cry, they, from the tits and screws, the weavers and windsuckers, the quidders and crib-biters that had been their remounts by the end of the Peninsula. The private men, too, were bright-eyed, smart, and quick about things to the trumpet, and he was slowly getting the measure of the noncommissioned officers. His serjeant major, Kendall, was a man he would not himself have chosen, but thought might just do, for he was spoken of well in his time with the quartermasters. Armstrong was first serjeant, and for that, at least, Hervey was grateful. But he was sad that Collins was no longer in the squadron, for he would have wished him for his covering corporal again—though Collins was chasing his third stripe, and so he would have had to find another coverman sooner or later anyway. At yesterday's parade he had liked the look of an active young dragoon called Troughton, a Norfolk man with a good seat, light hand, and supple wrist. Perhaps he would watch and see how he fared at the general's drill. His trumpeter, Medwell, whose nickname in the troop was Susan (and Hervey thought he could see why), was so flawless in his calls that Hervey supposed it would not be long before Susan was made colonel's man. But for the time being, at least, he knew he could count on his orders being relayed exactly.

"Does the colonel have any notion of what form the maneuvers will take?" asked Ezra Barrow, seeing that there was no point in grumbling anymore.

Major Joynson said he did not, or, if he had, he had not vouchsafed them.

"When is he back?" asked D Troop's captain.

"I don't know, for rights," said the major, growing more uncomfortable by the minute.

"Perhaps we might address the problem ourselves," suggested Strickland, who seemed in better spirits than when Hervey had taken leave of him a month before.

They all nodded.

The major wasn't sure, however. "I do not know his lordship's wishes in such things."

Hervey was baffled. It was a very fair presumption that any commanding officer would wish the best efforts to be made. He sighed to himself. This was going to be a deuced hard pull. For the moment, though, he held his peace.

Major Eustace Joynson had all but been on half-pay these past eight years, with no more responsibility than organizing supply for the yeomanry of Kent when they were mobilized for invasion duty—which, since 1805, they had never been. He was a kind man, by all accounts, he meant well, worked hard and was far from stupid. But he disliked upsets. When Hervey had first joined for duty as a cornet, the then Captain Joynson was called Daddy by his troop, and was soon shed by the colonel when they reached the Peninsula. His return to regimental duty was therefore as unexpected as it was undesirable. With a martinet, at best, for a commanding officer, and a toady for an adjutant, the last thing they needed was a major who wouldn't say bo to the proverbial goose.

Hervey sighed. Heavens, what a change there'd been. It was a matchless regiment that had crossed the Pyrenees that winter, the year before Waterloo: Lord George Irvine commanding, Joseph Edmonds the major, and Ezra Barrow (aye, for all his brusqueness) the adjutant. Now even Mr. Lincoln was being elbowed aside, an RSM of the like the army took thirty years in the forming and could never get enough of. Hervey thought he might easily despair of his own prospects of promotion if his fortunes depended on an orderly room like this—as, indeed, it did. He silently resolved that, when the time came, his own troop, at least, would have the bottom.

Henrietta had spent the day writing letters to those with whom she was on calling terms, to inform them of her new quarters. These were small but comfortable, in a terrace near the heath, with a coach house to the rear and a well-tended garden. She had been content, but now she was not at all pleased.

Hervey promised it was strict necessity. "I have to have the troop out for a night. None of them seems to remember when last they did anything in the dark, and with the major general threatening to put us all through some scheme or other instead of just a review next week, there's really no time to be lost."

"You will not be gone more than a night? I don't much care for this place on my own."

He assured her he would be back by the time she was breakfasting. "Have you taken against the house?"

"No, not the house," she said, shaking her head.

"Then what?"

"I just do not like our being parted so soon."

"My darling, you would not have me sit at home when I know that my troop is in need of turning out?" He pulled the bell rope.

She shook her head. "I told you at Longleat, Matthew. When you go away, I have a presentiment of your not coming back."

Their manservant was at the door. Hervey smiled at him. "That will be all for the evening, Hanks. I shall not be home tomorrow. Please be especially attentive to the shutters and locks."

When Hanks had gone, Henrietta poured more tea. "How important is Private Johnson to your nocturnals?"

Hervey looked at her curiously. If only he could tell her of Johnson in the Pyrenees, on Waterloo eve, or the night in the forest at Jhansikote. "He is indispensable!"

She frowned again, and Hervey saw her intention. "You mean you would feel more secure were Johnson in the house?"

"If he's indispensable then it is of no matter."

"You think you might hold him hostage to my return?"

"You would have no harsh choices to make if he were here! Although Jessye, of course, is some miles away." The smile was now fully returned, for Henrietta was pleased with her tease.

"Then you shall have him," Hervey replied, teasing her in turn with the impression of giving it careful thought. "And he would certainly prefer it to beating about the heath, especially if this rain continues."

"But you said he was indispensable!"

"Perhaps I should have said that I wouldn't be without him when the time came."

She furrowed her brow. "You are funny. You are so certain of things. I could never be afraid if you were at hand."

"You mistake me there, my love. I'm certain of just a very few things to do with soldiery—learned the hard way, I might add. But beyond that . . ."

"Shall you tell me of them?"

That surprised him. "Tell you of soldiery?"

"Why not?"

"Well, I . . ."

"You have *never* spoken of it!"

He had never spoken of it because it had never occurred to him to do so. It was one thing to like pretty uniforms and bands, quite another to be interested in their purpose. It was true that many a fashionable female would try to get a view of a battle, safe on a hilltop, but he had never met any who wished to speak of war. What a month it had been. What a change there came in things when lovers shared at last the secrets of the marriage bed. How differently they looked to each other, and others to them. How differently they spoke, and of what things (which sometimes the morning would blush to hear). And now Henrietta would have him speak of things so wholly beyond her comprehension that he feared she might loathe a part of what he did. But they daily became more intimate, whether by a look, a word, or a caress, and so he must trust now in what she had said about there being no secrets.

They sat late into the night talking. He began with thoughts, and then, secure in her estimation as he had never been before, he told her at last of deeds. He told her all that had ever troubled him—or as much as she would permit, for once or twice she stopped him and said with great tenderness that she did not have to know any more. They retired well after midnight, after some of the candles had given out, but they slept little.

It rained all next day. Hervey and Barrow were together in A Troop office ruing the weather, while outside, some distance away at the guardroom, the orderly trumpeter was struggling with the semiquavers below the staff for afternoon defaulters. A knock at the office door covered his final C, which cracked as he overblew, trying to be heard above the torrents.

"Come!" called Hervey, hoping it might be Johnson with something hot. But it was not—only the squadron subalterns come to ask if the scheme were still to be had, at which Hervey looked at his fellow captain and smiled. "Nothing so bad, d'ye suppose, as that day in"—he could have said any number of places in Spain, sluiced top to toe with water colder than ice, but instead he chose to include them all—"before Waterloo."

Barrow nodded, but could not quite forbear to humble the lieutenants and cornets by saying that neither would there be lance points pricking at them through the rain. They left sheepishly, no doubt to repeat the admonitions when they in turn received the inquiry from their juniors. When they had gone, Barrow declared that their concerns had been proper enough, for the weather would take its toll of the men's uniforms, and with the major general's inspection so close, it would mean more expense and trouble. In truth, Hervey had already been minded to abandon the scheme, but, on the other hand, so torrential a downpour—especially if it continued during the night—would test the squadron more than any general could. It would reveal what he must do in the short time before the inspection.

And so, in the middle of the following morning, they left the barracks, marched on parallel lines of advance to Chobham Common, throwing out scouts for five miles along the river Ash, finding fords and swimming points, and eventually occupied a vidette line on Oystershell Ridge at last light.

At midnight, Hervey and Barrow rode the line, finding varying degrees of vigilance, and at dawn they began a rearguard which took them back again to the river. There they picketed its bridges, "blowing" them and retiring in the face of the "enemy," and then galloped to seize them again. They proved their carbines soon after (the old hands largely with success, the young ones largely without), then Hervey and Barrow inspected every shoe, and were agreeably taken by the permanence of the farriery.

The rain had continued throughout the night with little respite, but it had stopped after first light, and the sun soon had men and horses steaming before even the final gallop, so that if spirits had been at their lowest ebb before the false dawn, they were restored by the time Hervey's trumpeter blew Cease Firing just after nine. And those restored spirits were lifted still further when, after a short trot to the Red Maid at Bedfont, the quartermaster serjeants turned out a warm bran mash for the troopers, and tea, rum, beef, and potatoes for the dragoons.

On the ride back to Hounslow, Hervey and Barrow gave each other their opinions of the work. For the most part, Hervey's estimation of B Troop was favorable, but Barrow's of A Troop was markedly less so. "You've some clewed-up corporals, and Armstrong's price's beyond reck'ning, but it's that serjeant major of yours. Kendall just hasn't the zeal for a troop, and it gets to the men. You need rid of him, and quickly."

There was much else besides, little of it agreeable, so that stables was a muted affair when they got back to Hounslow—though Hervey's dragoons seemed pleased enough, brightened by the exercise and the encouraging words he had managed to find to finish his otherwise critical peroration at stand-down.

He left the barracks an hour before watch-setting. He was late for dinner—very much later than he had anticipated—and he was discouraged by how unhandy the troop had become since Paris. If only the fourth piece of tape could be Armstrong's instead of Kendall's. He resolved to make it his first objective with Lord Towcester. And between now and the major general's inspection he would have to use every spare minute to lick his troop into shape. And all he would have to do it with was the sand table and his imagination.

Henrietta was already reconciled to the lateness of the hour, and she listened tolerantly to her husband as he scarcely drew breath while recounting the battle of Chobham Common, bidding her stay even as he took his bath, and then denying his hunger to explain how he intended arranging things better for Thursday's inspection. She had long since dismissed her servants, and arranged a sideboard that would not greatly deteriorate by the hour—braised crab, fig-peckers, cheese, strawberries, and claret.

"Come," she insisted, when Hervey had said he would take only a minute or so to dress. "Put on your gown and come to eat. I have something to tell you." She kissed him on the lips, smiling conspiratorially, and led him to the dining room.

He took in the sideboard with some delight, if also with dismay, for while the Champagne he had been sipping was an extravagance he might justify as a reward for his exertions, their supper seemed rather more than he deserved, or, indeed, could rightly afford.

"Well, what is it which prevents my dressing," he teased, as he spooned some crab onto her plate.

"Private Johnson is a very good sort," Henrietta began. "He spoke very freely, you know. He was not in the least bit ill at ease."

Hervey smiled. He could well imagine it.

"He told me that things are not at all happy in the barracks."

"But *I* told you that."

"But do you know that your Serjeant Armstrong's wife has been teaching in the regimental school? *Running* it by all accounts, since the regular teacher is ill."

Hervey knew that, too. "But how does this make for unhappiness?"

"Because Lord Towcester, when he learned of who she was, declared he would not have a papist—and an Irish papist at that—teaching the regiment's children. Except that he apparently used words altogether too coarse to repeat."

Hervey put down his knife and fork. Caithlin Armstrong was a well-read woman. He himself had introduced her to Greek. The regiment's

children would find no kinder or cleverer teacher—at least, for the modest outlay it was prepared to make. "I wonder that Serjeant Armstrong
has not spoken of it." He sighed, a little bruised.

"He has too strong a regard for you."

"What do you mean?"

"I mean that he would not wish you to risk Lord Towcester's wrath
when there is quite evidently little chance of his changing his mind."

Hervey looked at Henrietta for a few moments, contemplating the
suggestion. "What do *you* think? Is it so foul a thing that the children be
taught by a Catholic?"

Henrietta did not answer at once, having achieved her purpose in
alerting him to the news he would soon hear, while warning him against
precipitate action. "Your Duke of Wellington would say so."

Hervey was not so sure of that proposition; the duke's views were
sundry in the matter of Ireland. "How do you know?"

"My guardian dined with him last year, and he was root and branch
against removing the Penal Laws there."

Hervey realized he had strayed from the point. "But I first asked what
you thought, my dear."

"Matthew, she is Irish, of the meanest sort. How can you presume her
loyalty in all things?"

"But plenty of Irishmen have spilled their lifeblood for England these
past twenty years."

"And she is a Catholic. What sort of notions might she fill the children's heads with?"

"Oh, Henrietta—*dearest*! You don't suppose she would teach them
that their parents are all damned to hell?"

"I don't suppose anything, Matthew. All I suggest is that with two
such grounds for anxiety, Lord Towcester might be said to have just
cause to be cautious."

Hervey saw that yet again she had skillfully evaded his question. "You
have *still* not given me your opinion, truly!"

"Ah!" she smiled. "My opinion is that Caithlin O'Mahoney—Caithlin
Armstrong—is a very dangerous woman. Look at the trouble she caused
in Cork!"

He went bright red and almost stammered. "That is very unfair—on
all of us!"

"Matthew, sweetest, I only tease!" Her smile revealed it, too.

He picked up a crab claw to compose himself. "Then tell me what is your true opinion."

"Why do you wish to know? My opinion cannot count for anything in such an affair."

The crab claw shattered noisily, failing in the purpose for which Hervey had taken it up. "Why should a man not want his wife's opinion?" He was tired and Henrietta was trying him, for some reason or other. It was not the soldier's welcome he had hoped for. "Why should a wife wish to withhold it, indeed?"

"Because," Henrietta drew out the second syllable as if to emphasize her own dismay in his lack of perception, "she might be afraid of what her husband would do as a consequence. I mean, Matthew, that if I say I approve of Caithlin Armstrong you will feel obliged—*doubly* obliged—to take things up with Lord Towcester. And I doubt that this would be . . . felicitous. You think I do not understand your character sufficiently?"

"But you would surely want me to do what was right? You wouldn't want me to say nothing just in case I called down the wrath of the lieutenant colonel?"

Henrietta frowned. "Oh, Matthew, my darling, it is not so simple as that, is it? You of all people know that to fight a battle when there is no chance of success is . . ." She seemed to be wondering how to finish her challenge.

"Contra jus ad bellum?"

She smiled. "If it is so, then it strengthens my point."

He sighed heavily. "Very well, then. I shall say nothing. I shall speak with Serjeant Armstrong, though, and try to find out if there is more. It's my intention anyway to speak with Lord Towcester to get a fourth stripe for Armstrong."

"Then you must weigh things in the balance very keenly," said Henrietta, sounding wise. "For his promotion is surely worth more to them than the few shillings the schoolroom would bring. *Yes,* I know what you will say," she added quickly, seeing him make to protest, "but let the Armstrongs be able to *afford* their pride before standing on it."

CHAPTER 8

TAKING THE
FIELD

Hounslow Barracks, a Few Days Later

The major general commanding the London district was a shrewd man. He knew all there was to know about the interior economy of a regiment, and likewise its drill, but all of this knowledge he had gained in the brigades of Foot Guards. Of cavalry regiments he knew nothing beyond what they had in common with the infantry, which was not a very great deal. He knew what to look for in a horse, as did any general officer. But he was all too aware that Waterloo light dragoons would demand a careful eye. He had therefore assembled a small inspecting staff of officers from the cavalry and horse artillery, under the command of a Waterloo veteran lately promoted colonel. And a month or so before, he had set the colonel the task of devising a scheme by which the Sixth's handiness in the field might be tested.

On the day of the inspection, General Browning and his staff rode into the barracks promptly at ten o'clock.

"General salute; prese . . . nt *arms!*" Lord Towcester's voice carried easily across the closed parade square.

The officers' sabers lowered to the present just a fraction ahead of the lieutenant colonel's guidon, as was proper, and the trumpeters, dismounted, sounded the first five bars of the lieutenant general's salute, as was a major general's due.

The commanding officer trotted up to General Browning on his blood chestnut to inform him that 467 officers and men of the 6th Light Dragoons were ready and awaiting his inspection. The general nodded in acknowledgment and then reined his charger left to begin his ride down the double rank of dragoons, as the band struck up airs from *Figaro,* reported to be his favorite opera.

The real work of the administrative inspection had been completed the day before, when the staff had examined every ledger and given every private man the opportunity to raise any grievance. They had found the Sixth to be in good order, and there had been no notices of grievance. The deputy assistant adjutant general—a major of the Coldstream—had reported to the general that the regiment seemed somewhat sullen compared with when he had seen them last in Belgium, but added that there had been so many new recruits that perhaps it was not too surprising they should lack the old confidence. General Browning was alert to the point, however, and as he rode along the front rank he, too, thought the men's eyes lacked just that *something* he had seen so often in the eyes of light cavalry—a special sort of alertness, *eagerness* perhaps. Well, he was confident that Colonel Freke Smyth would find out right enough when he put them through their paces on Chobham Common. Then he would know whether he had a regiment he could rely on. For he could not rid himself of the doubt, one way or other, that nagged him still about the affair in Skinner Street: the death of a young cornet in his district (and the Duke of Huntingdon's son, too) was not something that went easily with him.

After he had gone up and down the ranks the general complimented the commanding officer on the fine appearance of his men. Then the regiment rode past their inspecting officer in troops, first at the walk and then at the trot, wheeling and giving eyes right as pleasingly as Browning would have wished to see in his Foot Guards.

"Be so good as to have the trumpet major sound 'Officers,' Lord Towcester, if you please," the general said when he had dismissed the parade.

"All officers, my lord?" asked the trumpet major, saluting as he drove his right foot down at the halt.

Lord Towcester looked at the general.

"Just the troop leaders and their subalterns."

The trumpet major saluted again, turned to his right, and marched off five paces to blow the officers' call.

The quartermasters and other noncombatants—the paymaster, surgeons, and veterinarians—looked relieved when the call ended with the G, for the next four bars would have summoned them as well as the squadron officers.

Ten minutes later the squadron officers were assembled in the mess anteroom. "Sit down, gentlemen," said General Browning as he came in. "I wished to see your faces before the real business of the day began. And to say that of one troop I hope to see very little, for I have told your colonel that I intend taking it to act as enemy for the entire scheme." He glanced at Lord Towcester.

"A Troop, General. Captain Hervey's."

Hervey bit his tongue. Someone quite evidently had to be the enemy, but it implied that his troop was the one whose services the lieutenant colonel was happiest to dispense with. He rose to identify himself.

"Very well, Captain Hervey. Report at once with your officers to Colonel Freke Smyth. He will inform you of your duties while I give my intention to the regiment."

"It should have been the junior troop, F," said Seton Canning when they were outside.

"I don't want to hear your opinion of the colonel's decisions," Hervey snapped, seething with anger, though not, in truth, at Seton Canning, for he had worked up his troop so well in the past week that he wanted to see them tested.

Hervey's discouragement was allayed to an extent, however, when he learned what Colonel Freke Smyth had in mind for them. They were not simply to send men here and there with false reports, or to hand the usual piece of paper to an officer: *There is an infantry picket on the high ground to your front.* Instead they were themselves to maneuver as a troop in the face of the rest of the regiment, which was to advance as if covering an infantry division on the march to first encounter.

"These are your boundaries, Captain Hervey," said the colonel, pointing out the roads and streams across Chobham Common, which he had come to know so well in the last week. "There will be officers from the Blues on either flank to ensure that neither your troop nor the regiment transgresses them, and Major Jago from the horse artillery will be my eyes and ears with you yourself throughout."

Hervey opened his sabretache to make notes.

"And, mind you," warned the colonel, looking him fiercely in the eye, "there is to be no faking—no giving way to the other troops just to make them seem crack."

The thought had not occurred to him, but Hervey knew it must at some stage, for it was only natural to want his regiment to show well.

"Major Ormonde from the Blues will ride with you, too," added the colonel. "You are to explain your intentions to him before any maneuver, and if he disapproves you are then to follow his express instructions. Is that quite clear?"

"Quite clear, Colonel."

"Good. Then let us now to the detail."

Hervey had assembled his officers and NCOs in the old tap house by Chobham Rise. He had left his troop in the hands of Serjeant Armstrong (managing to contrive some plausible reason for this instead of with the serjeant major) who would bring them to the rendezvous as soon as their marching order and supply was ready. When Hervey had taken command of the troop he had asked to see the field standing orders, and had been surprised to learn that there were none. So he had dug up an old copy of those that Joseph Edmonds had written before they left Cork for Waterloo, and issued them to his squadron for his own scheme. He hoped that these would gain him a march, for without regimental standing orders there were bound to be discrepancies between troops, entailing last-minute alterations as the commanding officer noticed the lack of uniformity. And Hervey knew that he would need that time, for his orders were for the troop to throw out a vidette line across the whole of the regiment's frontage.

"And so, gentlemen," he emphasized, coming to the end of his own orders, "my intention, repeated, is simply this: the first half troop, as the contact troop, will observe the advance of the regiment from the Great Park at Windsor, and will fall back along the lines I have indicated." He pointed to the excellent new map from the Ordnance Survey, from which the NCOs had made their own sketches. "On the flanks, and a full three furlongs behind the contact line, are to be videttes guarding against flanking marches. In the event of the enemy's attempting such a maneuver, the videttes are to give battle briskly and to make out as best they can until relief comes. I do not wish any of the remainder of the contact troop to exchange fire with the enemy unless it is *absolutely* unavoidable." He looked at each man to emphasize the instruction. "Let me remind you that in an action such as this, the great object is to *see*. Fighting is merely a means to this end. There are other means superior and less hazardous, as we demonstrated on our scheme. Barrels clean, then, gentlemen, and swords in their scabbards unless it is impossible to move within sight of the enemy." It was as well that he laid emphasis on this now, for the true instinct of a light dragoon, he knew all too well, was to draw his saber and make straight for his man. Outpost work was never so exciting when they were denied a skirmish.

"Now," Hervey continued. "The communicating troop shall be formed of the second division. You will establish your relays in the places marked. I shall remain—so far as is possible—on this center line." He pointed to the old Windsor road running north-south across the common. "From here I shall send orderlies with reports to the controlling staff at Chobham. With me shall be a corporal and a dozen men which you shall nominate." He looked directly at Cornet St. Oswald, who nodded in acknowledgment. "And these shall be held ready, at a moment's notice, as my reserve. So, having now repeated my intention, do any of you have a question?"

For some time no one spoke. That much was pleasing, thought Hervey. His plan must be straightforward and his explanation clear.

At length Seton Canning looked up from his map. "If I can cover the front and have a few men spare, is there any reason why I should not patrol forward of the Bourne, rather than simply awaiting the enemy's advance?"

"There is no reason that I am aware of from the staff's point of view," Hervey replied, glancing at the directing officers, Majors Ormonde and Jago. "And in ordinary I should urge you to do so, but by my calculation you will scarcely have a man to spare, let alone a patrol. See what comes, though. You know which is the priority. If you can do more, then so much the better. Are there any more questions, gentlemen?"

There were none.

"Well, let's go to it. And remember, the general's orders are that we face the *enemy*, not friends. Good luck!"

It was the better part of two hours before Lieutenant Seton Canning was able to report that his line of videttes was secure. Just after two, he galloped back to the old coach road where Hervey had planted his flag, and there with Cornet St. Oswald they made the necessary adjustments and arrangements for the relay points. It had been many years since the Sixth had carried guidons in the field, but Hervey's trumpeter carried a lance with a yellow pennant and the letter *A* in blue, so that his troop leader's position should be known at once. By night a lantern, with red and yellow glass, would indicate the same, for Hervey had many a recollection of delay and confusion searching out a headquarters in some Spanish village in the pitch dark.

"*Do* you have any men to spare to patrol forward of the Bourne?" he asked his lieutenant, more hopeful than expectant.

"No, sir. In truth I could do with twenty more for the vidette line, for the country is so trappy on the left flank I'm concerned the enemy might slip through."

Hervey looked at Cornet St. Oswald.

"I could spare half a dozen, though private men only."

"Good man! Send them to first division at once, then." He was gratified by St. Oswald's willingness to cede that number. The cornet's priorities were right enough.

As the assembly broke up, Hervey looked at his watch—almost half past three, a full hour ahead of the time they had been given to have the line set. He commended his two officers. "Yes, gentlemen, very satisfactory indeed! I shall ride forward and check some of the videttes and pickets, and then I shall take post back here by the appointed hour. We are in for a long, hard night. I trust there are fires burning now for a warm dinner?"

Seton Canning and St. Oswald smiled. Of that he could be certain, they said.

Hervey set off up the old coach road with his new covering corporal (Troughton had indeed shown well in the past fortnight, and had sewn on his chevron only the day before), along with his trumpeter Susan and Private Johnson. He found the picket well sited at the bottom of a shallow hill where the regiment's advance guards would most likely have to commit themselves to one of two routes through the woodland. The NCO in command told him that Lieutenant Seton Canning had ordered both lanes to be blocked, so that the action of the advance guards, in attempting to clear the blockage, would reveal the intended route of the main body. The dragoons had been busy, therefore. They had felled four trees across the sandy lanes, closing them very effectively, and had put up *chevaux de frise,* which would cover the picket's withdrawal nicely if the enemy's scouts pressed them too hard.

Corporal Sykes had always been a steady man, thought Hervey—his own groom, indeed, when he had first joined for duty. It was good to see him wearing his second stripe to such effect now. "Where is the vidette?" he asked cheerily.

"A furlong to the front, by the spinney, sir."

Hervey could see the spinney clearly enough, on the crest of the rising ground, but not the vidette. "I see no dragoon. Has he taken post yet?"

"There's a *couple* of men, sir. I've put a youngster with Broadhurst— a very promising lad he is, too. They won't show themselves except to signal."

"Well done, Corporal Sykes. I'll ride up there to see what they can see."

"Shall I come with you, sir?"

"No, that's not necessary. I'll ride straight there and straight back." He turned to his escort. "Stay here for the present. There's no call for kicking up more dust than necessary."

Lance Corporal Troughton looked alarmed. It was mock battle, but a covering man had his duty all the same. "I shouldn't by rights let you off by yourself, sir, even to a vidette."

Hervey had once taken a spontoon in his leg because he had got too far ahead of his coverman. Corporal Collins would have said the same as Troughton, and he was pleased he'd picked a man who could think for himself and was not afraid to speak up. "No, you're right. Johnson, Medwell, and Corporal Sykes to remain here, then. Corporal Troughton comes with me."

Hervey put his gelding into a canter towards the vidette. He had still not got used to the idea that Jessye was no longer his charger. Besides anything, Harkaway was so green. There again, he had rather abandoned Harkaway. The splint had put the horse off the road for the best part of a year, it was true, but Hervey felt he had not seen to his schooling properly since then. Indeed, Harkaway had done scarcely a thing for two years but gorge himself on the green grass of east Cork, and Hervey had been hard-pressed in the last month to get him to bend even a little and bring his quarters under. The gelding had a good mouth, though, and a good turn of speed, and—above all—he was honest. Hervey thought he could have him right by the time they went to Brighton. Gilbert, the gray, would take longer, however, for he was foaled a full two years later. If he could just keep Harkaway between himself and the ground for the duration of the major general's inspection, he would be well satisfied.

"Good afternoon, sir," said Private Broadhurst, coming out of the spinney and saluting from the saddle of his little bay trooper. He spoke confidently, with a trace of a smile, evidently taken by the captain's visiting his vidette.

"Good afternoon, Broadhurst," said Hervey, returning the salute and encouraging him to make the smile definite. "An English summer's day. What better thing could there be than a vidette!"

"Aye, sir. There's nowt better." And Broadhurst meant it. A more straightforward, uncomplicated dragoon had probably never drawn pay. His accent was that of Johnson's county, but from a little farther north, and not nearly so pronounced. Even so, the other dragoons had dubbed him "Johnson's nip" when he had first joined the troop.

"Have you seen home since returning from France?" Hervey swished the flies from Harkaway's ears. He would need the citronella soon.

"No, not yet, sir. I was hoping to have leave before the year's out, though. After Brighton, that is. I'm keen to see Brighton."

Hervey nodded. Harkaway was getting restless as the flies swarmed thicker. "Where is your coverman?"

Broadhurst smiled at the idea he should have a coverman. "Private Wick, sir? He's a good'n, and only eighteen. He's posted the other side of the spinney keeping watch on the road. Shall I lead you through?"

"Yes, please. I want to know his orders."

Private Wick heard them coming, but only turned to salute when they were beside him, so determined was he to have first sighting of the enemy. He had joined after Waterloo, and fretted that he had not yet seen action, especially of an evening in the wet canteen when the stories of that day were being retailed.

"Good afternoon, Wick," said Hervey, smiling encouragingly at him. "Do you see anything at all?"

"Nothing, sir. There's not even a rabbit moved since I was posted."

Hervey searched the ground with his telescope. It revealed nothing, too. He handed it to Wick. "See if things look different."

Private Wick had never looked through a telescope before. "No, sir; not different, just closer."

Hervey liked that, and smiled to himself. Of *course* things only looked closer. But a telescope was worth more to a dragoon on outpost duty than a carbine—yet the Ordnance had none for the issuing. "Right, then, Wick: tell me your orders."

The young dragoon began without hesitating an instant. "I am to watch the road and all to my front between the white house on the distant far hill, sir"—he pointed with his sword arm—"and the line of the stream to the right. And I am to tell Private Broadhurst as soon as I see anything at all."

"Anything?"

"Aye, *anything,* sir. Private Broadhurst says that the enemy might disguise himself as even an old Gypsy woman."

He said it with very serious purpose. And he was right, for Broadhurst had known ruses like that in Spain. "And what then shall Private Broadhurst do on report of a sighting?"

"He will signal to Corporal Sykes at the picket, sir."

Hervey turned to Broadhurst. "Your signal code?" He knew he hardly needed to ask.

"Might Wick give it, sir?"

Hervey nodded.

"Go on, then, Wick," smiled Broadhurst.

"I go to the back of the spinney, sir, where I can be seen by the corporal at the picket, and put my horse to walking in a circle. Clockwise if the enemy is a cavalry patrol, the other way if infantry. And I put 'im into a trot if there are a lot of 'em."

"Well done, Wick," said Hervey. "How shall you know if they are cavalry or infantry at the farthest distance?"

"Because the dust rises higher from cavalry, sir. And for infantry it is lower and thicker."

"Good! And what if it is artillery and wagons?"

"Then the dust isn't even: it's all over the place, sir."

Hervey was pleased. "And how might you judge the distance to the enemy?"

"At seven furlongs you can tell if the enemy is cavalry or infantry, sir. At three, sir, you can count 'eads. And between one and two you can see what uniform they is wearing."

Hervey turned to Private Broadhurst. "You've drilled him well. And I think you'll be the first to put the drills to the test, for this is the enemy's main route of advance, by my reckoning."

"Will he go on through the night, do you think, sir?"

Hervey tilted his head. "We have to be ready for the possibility. You are clear as to the signals then?"

"Aye, sir: unshaded red lantern for enemy approaching, carbine shot for alarm."

"And when do you make the alarm, Wick?" said Hervey, turning back to the young dragoon.

"If we're surprised—"

"Which we *shan't* be," said Broadhurst emphatically.

"Or if the red light isn't repeated back to us by the picket," added Wick.

"Just so, just so." There was nothing more for Hervey to test. He was sure that if the Duke of Wellington himself were to ride up he could not find fault with this vidette. He turned to leave, but then a notion came to him. "Are you a Shropshire man, by any chance, Wick?" Perhaps it was the way he pronounced "light," as C Troop's serjeant major did, and the town boys when Hervey had been at school.

"Aye, sir," replied Wick, with a proud smile both at the fact and at its interest to his officer. "From Shrewsbury, sir. Have you been there, sir?"

What Hervey liked about the Sixth—one of the many things he liked—was the way the private men would speak up. He had once tried to coax the most innocent opinion from one of d'Arcey Jessope's guardsmen, only to be met with incomprehending silence. And here was the youngest dragoon asking him a question. "I was at school there," he replied.

"At Shrewsbury School, sir? The big school?"

Private Wick's first syllable of Shrewsbury rhymed with "shoe," and Hervey was tempted to make a little sport, for many a time he had got close to blows with the town boys over the matter. He thought better of it, though. "Yes," he said, simply.

Wick positively beamed. "My father kept the gate there, sir."

"Indeed, yes, I remember now. 'Gaoler' Wick, as we called him."

"Yes, sir. I knew as that was 'is name among the gentlemen," replied the young dragoon, proudly.

Hervey shook his head. "Well, I may tell you, Private Wick, your father had a heart of gold. But you will know that already. Many was the time I thawed myself by his fire, and drank his tea."

Wick was beaming with pride now.

"Is he well still?"

A frown at once replaced the smile. "No, sir. He died two years ago."

"Oh, I am sorry," said Hervey. "Your mother is well provided for?"

"Oh, yes, sir. The school has given her rooms and everything. She does for one of the masters." The beam had returned.

Hervey was doubly pleased, for as well as making for a contented dragoon it was what he would have hoped from his old school. "Well, Wick, we can continue this at another time." He pushed his telescope into its saddle holster. "There are things pressing elsewhere, don't you think, Broadhurst? How long would you suppose it was after us that the regiment left barracks?"

Private Broadhurst thought hard for a moment. "Well, sir, knowing 'ow things is at present, they wouldn't 'ave left until everything were perfect. . . . At least three hours, I'd say."

Broadhurst didn't miss much, either, thought Hervey. "In which case we should expect them within the hour, and then there'll be two more of good daylight left. They could advance a fair distance before last light—well beyond the Bourne, indeed."

The estimate proved right. A little after six o'clock the warning sentries began reporting that the videttes were circling. The pickets stood-to, the relays brought the intelligence to Hervey's flag post, and a galloper set off to the notional army headquarters with a first sighting report at twenty-two minutes past the hour. Later, the inspecting staff would compare timings thoroughly, but Major Jago was already noting in his pocketbook that reports arrived with impressive speed and were handled with confidence and dispatch. Hervey's orders to the contact troop were that videttes should fall back on the warning sentries when the enemy came within carbine range (for to remain any longer risked a ball in the back on retiring), and there to form a second vidette line while the sentries fell back on the pickets. The pickets would engage the enemy's scouts, only withdrawing if the advance guards came up in force, by which time the videttes and warning sentries would have taken post on the new observing line behind. These lines he had carefully chosen from the map and confirmed from the saddle with his two troop officers, and, because they had practiced the maneuvers the week before, he was sure they would be able to keep close track of the regiment during its passage of the common, greatly outnumbered though his troop was.

It had taken the firmest resolve on Hervey's part not to be drawn forward himself. His every instinct was to get a sight of the enemy, and he had thought long about placing himself with Corporal Sykes's picket. But the best place for a commander, Joseph Edmonds had always said, was where he could best command from. And with videttes and pickets thrown across the most part of a mile of bosky heathland, that place was at the apex of a triangle which allowed reports to come almost as quickly from the flanks as from the center line. Heavens, it was frustrating, though, especially when shots began ringing out along the front. But he knew he could trust his corporals not to allow their pickets to be over-run. What about the flanks, though? Hervey knew that if this were real battle he could expect to count on squadrons abreast of him, but on this scheme there were none. This did not matter, the inspecting officer had said, because the regiment would not be allowed to stray outside its boundaries. What would happen at night, though, or with the dawn's mist? The enemy could stray, intentionally or not, and Hervey's flank pickets would have the devil of a job. At night or in mist, keeping station with the observing line two or three furlongs to the front, would take the greatest address, too (on his own scheme the week before, his flanks had been easily turned). He had therefore insisted on two of the most experienced NCOs being put to the task. But still he was unquiet.

Hervey now determined to employ observers *behind* the enemy's line, as the duke himself had employed them in Spain. The trouble was that he had scarcely men enough for the vidette and picket lines, so he decided to take a gamble by detailing Serjeant Armstrong to the task. This was a costly wager, for he had wanted to place Armstrong at the rally point instead, behind the notional line of infantry two leagues to the rear, where the troop would reunite and be revived, ready for what the inspecting officer might order them to do next. Serjeant Major Kendall, Hervey feared, was not up to seeing to a rally point by day, let alone by night, but Armstrong behind the enemy was a premium he felt unable to default on. There was nothing for it, then, but to trust the rally point to the troop serjeant major. That Kendall had botched it on last week's scheme was a worry, but was not that the purpose of the exercise—that shortcomings could be rectified before today?

At eleven it had been dark for three hours, and the action was still going well. The good moon was working in A Troop's favor, aiding both detection of the enemy and fast movement by the relays. Major Jago's own observers were reporting that the picket line continued to retire steadily but without penetration, while from Hervey's own dragoons there was a continual flow of intelligence on the enemy's progress. There had been a lull in the last quarter of an hour, though, and Hervey was beginning to get anxious that something was amiss. Major Jago had pressed him for his assessment, and he had had to admit the possibility that the enemy might have trickled through his line here and there: after all, they were hardly greenheads. But it was also true that by now the regiment had been advancing for six hours—tiring for both men and horses, perhaps more so than withdrawing in the face of that advance. Might it be the short halt, then, suggested Hervey—saddles fast, bridles off, and nose bags on, and water from the Runnymede ponds where the last reports said the advance guards had reached?

Major Jago had smiled appreciatively on hearing the assessment, and said he would leave him to his own devices for a while.

"*Sir,*" whispered Johnson as he came into the old pannage hut which now served as Hervey's command post.

Hervey thought it strange he should be whispering with quite so much effort.

"*Sir,*" he repeated, and with some insistence, gesturing towards the door.

The lantern was bright enough to read a map by, but it only cast shadows across Johnson's face, and Hervey could not make out what it was he wanted. The door scraped open, and Hervey shot to his feet at the sight of the general officer's cloak.

"You did say I might share your bivouac," said Henrietta, pulling off the Tarleton and smiling wide.

"What in heaven's name are you doing here?" gasped Hervey. "Where did you get that cloak? And those plumes! How did you *get* here?" He was about to ask a dozen more questions when she stopped him with a kiss. He glanced awkwardly at Johnson, who was making a show of looking the other way.

Henrietta, still smiling, began to rearrange her hair as if nothing were more normal.

Hervey glanced anxiously at the door. The last thing he needed was to have the inspecting officer find dalliance instead of alertness. "My dear, we are in the middle of a battle—"

"What are you doing in a hut, then?"

"Well, we are—" He realized the absurdity of trying to explain. "Johnson, would you—"

"Aye, sir," replied his groom. No need to spell it out—sentry duty, the other side of the door. He allowed himself a grin as he squeezed through, and Henrietta grinned back.

When the door was pulled shut she kissed him again, but longer. Hervey pulled open her cloak and slipped his arms around her. *"What—"*

She kissed him again. "I couldn't very well ride in a skirt!"

He was too nervous of discovery to be shocked. Whose breeches they were he simply could not imagine, and in truth he didn't much care, for she filled them very handsomely.

"Don't pretend you disapprove. Didn't the Queen of Scots ride like this?"

Hervey shook his head in half-despair.

"I am very tired." She smiled.

"I am not surprised!"

"Where shall you lie down tonight?"

He shook his head again. He would dearly like to lie down this very instant, to put out the lantern and trust to Johnson's vigilance. "I cannot lie down for a minute! The enemy could be close by us even now!"

"Well," said Henrietta. "A cavalry bivouac is a chaster place than ever I have heard of. And very dull!"

"Does anyone know you're here? Who brought you?"

She gave a little laugh. "The regiment was so taken up with getting itself to Chobham I just followed them. No one seemed to notice me."

How that could be so he simply couldn't conceive. "But how then did you find *me*?"

"When we got to Egham there were a great many spectators. And all the regiment were telling them what they were about to do."

Hervey shook his head. A dragoon loved to share his secrets.

"And I heard one of the officers saying that he was off to give you a surprise."

"What did he mean, I wonder?"

"I don't know, but about twenty of them left soon afterwards and so I followed them, hoping to see you."

"And then?"

"Well, at length they just turned into an inn yard, and the officer said they were to stay there until night."

"Where was this?" Hervey began to feel anxious again.

Henrietta look puzzled. "The Plough at Addlestone, I think it was. I rode on a little way, hoping to find you, but I became quite lost. And then an officer from another regiment happened by, and he seemed to know exactly where you were, and he brought me here."

"What was his name?"

"He didn't give it," she said blithely. "He had no idea who I was, and I thought it better not to say."

Quickly he found Addlestone on his map. "Johnson!"

His groom opened the door gingerly. "Sir?"

"Ask Mr. St. Oswald to come here at once."

"What is it, dearest?" Henrietta seemed puzzled that her scanty report should have caused such alarm.

"Addlestone is well outside the boundaries of the scheme. From there those dragoons will be able to slip behind my picket line, and they'll avoid even the flank picket if they strike a little farther south first. Who was the officer with the party that you followed?"

But Henrietta didn't know, for she had yet to meet them all.

"What color were the horses?"

She smiled. "Chestnuts, all."

"E Troop—*Strickland.*" He nodded. "He will have drilled them keenly. It could be Sandys or Binney with them, the troop officers. Both are capable enough."

The cornet came into the hut, squinting a little in the sudden, if dim, light. He saw Henrietta, and then looked at his troop leader curiously.

"Not a word, St. Oswald, not a word."

"No, sir, I . . . of course."

"I've just learned that about twenty men from E Troop, under Sandys or Binney, were lately assembled here"—he pointed to Addlestone on the map—"which makes them very well placed to slip behind our line, if, indeed, they are not already doing so."

Cornet St. Oswald glanced at Henrietta again. His admiration for his captain grew daily. Whoever would think of sending his wife as an observing officer!

"The flank pickets ought to pick them up, but if they ride south any farther then they'll be missed."

St. Oswald nodded. "Do you want me to go there?"

"Yes. It looks to me as though their best move would be to come in on this road here, about half a mile behind where our line now is." He pointed out the lateral road which cut right across the area of the scheme. It was one of his own reporting lines—a line which would serve to get his pickets back in hand if they were pushed too badly before it.

The more Hervey studied the map, the more it occurred to him that the slackening of pressure all along his front was more than just fatigue. The regiment had checked just sufficiently forward for E Troop's party to get in behind his own line without Colonel Freke Smyth's staff suspecting they had come from outside the boundaries, for he might be persuaded that they had found a gap in the picket line and slipped through. That was cunning, Hervey thought. No, on second thoughts it was devious; there was a difference. He looked at Henrietta. Thank God she had come that way. Armstrong had missed Strickland's men, but then he could not have been expected to be everywhere at once.

"Sir!" called one of the dragoons outside, excitedly. "A rocket!"

Hervey dashed from the hut. The firework was just beginning to fall, but its smoke trail was clear enough. It came from the right flank, from almost exactly where he made the lateral road to be.

"Armstrong! He's there after all!" cried Hervey, with a little note of triumph, and grabbing his cornet's arm. "Thomas, take your half dozen dragoons and make the biggest demonstration you can. Take my repeating carbine—you know how it works well enough. It will make your party sound twice the size. Let me get one of Major Jago's men first, though. The affair will need an umpire!"

Cornet St. Oswald was pleased no end with the plum.

Major Jago himself now appeared with his lantern. "What do you make of that rocket, Hervey?" he inquired suspiciously. "It isn't a Congreve, that's for sure."

"No, sir," admitted Hervey, noticing Henrietta concealing herself from Jago. "I bought it two weeks ago in London." And then he wondered why he was being so guarded. "It is the alarm signal from one of my videttes on the flank. I believe there is an incursion. I am sending Cornet St. Oswald and six men to intercept it. Would you send one of your staff with them?"

"Mm," went Jago. "I shall go myself. Come on, young man!" he called to St. Oswald.

"Matthew!" whispered Henrietta when he had gone. "That was the officer who brought me here when I lost my way."

"Oh!" groaned Hervey. Major Jago, he had suspected, was not a man to miss much. "The question now, though, my love, is how we are going to take you back again."

That question presented much less of a problem than he expected, for soon after Cornet St. Oswald's successful affair on the flank, Major Jago received word from Colonel Freke Smyth that the scheme was at an end, and that all of the regiment was to assemble at first light on the green at Addlestone so that the condition of the horses might be assessed by the veterinary surgeons and farriers of the Blues. Hervey had no doubts that the regiment would be adjudged exemplary in this, but he was surprised that the officers received a separate order to assemble at the Plough Inn, for it had been the invariable practice for them to attend at any such parade. But General Browning wished to breakfast with them, and that was that. Hervey was therefore able to ride with Henrietta as far as the crossroads short of the village, from where Johnson would escort her back to Hounslow.

Hervey felt a deep glow of satisfaction, as did his subalterns. After the order to Cease Fire, Major Jago had told him that not once had his picket line been penetrated by so much as a single scout, and that the affair on the flank had been the sharpest piece of work he had seen in many a year. He had not asked about Henrietta, but something in his remark about unorthodox tactics hinted that her identity and her part in things had not gone unnoticed. But it was Hervey's ploy with Serjeant Armstrong—and, indeed, with Armstrong's own conduct—that brought Jago's especial praise. Armstrong's orders had been to remain covert unless it were absolutely necessary to do otherwise. The rocket had been a desperate, and expensive, expedient to warn of the incursion. Now that the whole world knew of the wheeze, Hervey couldn't very well keep his stratagem secret. He would surely have to admit that he had set his serjeant to follow the regiment from the outset. He began to fear that Jago's praise was double-edged.

His fear soon proved not to be groundless. Lord Towcester was beside himself with rage when he learned of the rocket, and that it had been fired from *behind* the outflanking party (poor Strickland was mortified later to discover how his troop had been the cause). Neither did it help when General Browning complimented Hervey in front of the other officers on "his sharp action to counter the penetration" (at least he made no mention that the penetration was the result of someone's disregarding his instructions).

As soon as breakfast was finished and the major general and his staff were gone, Lord Towcester made to leave, and without a word. His adjutant, however, marched up to Hervey and addressed him sharply. "Captain Hervey, his lordship is very severely displeased that you should have sought throughout the inspection to thwart his ambition." He did not wait for a reply, turning on his heel instead and striding out after the commanding officer.

Hervey was speechless.

"You, too?" said Strickland. "I had the foulest tongue-lashing of my life as we came here. 'I should have known better than to trust a damned papist,' was what Lord Towcester said to me. The man's a mountebank!"

Hervey groaned. "I wonder how much a mountebank may do before he is called to account? I fear we're in for a very hard ride indeed."

CHAPTER 9

FOR THE SAKE
OF EXAMPLE

Hounslow Barracks, July 27

It was a black day indeed for the Sixth. Only the regimental serjeant major and the two senior troop serjeant majors had been serving when last there had been its like—and that had been in Flanders, when Pitt had been prime minister and Wellington had been but a lieutenant colonel. That campaign, two decades past, had been a wretched affair indeed, perhaps the depths to which the incompetence of the Horse Guards could reduce an army, and the basest to which human nature without discipline could descend. In such circumstances, it was widely believed that condine punishment was all that held a regiment from becoming a rabble. But here in Brighton, a fishing village made fashionable by the whim of the Prince Regent, the question of whether the flogging of a dragoon was necessary to maintain good order and military discipline was on the lips of every man in the regiment.

Lord Towcester had not the slightest doubt, however. Private Hopwood had struck an officer, and he had done so in front of his troop, entirely unprovoked. His reason for the assault was both cynical and at the same time naive. "His lordship is therefore determined to make such an example of the man that it will arrest any tendency to the striking of officers," said Adjutant Dauntsey, in reply to Hervey's intercession on the man's behalf.

"But there has *been* no tendency to the striking of officers. Indeed, there has not been a single case in my entire time with the regiment," Hervey pointed out.

"And a flogging shall ensure that the regiment's record is restored. You do know, Captain Hervey, that his lordship might have imposed a penalty of death?"

Hervey knew it perfectly well. Striking a superior officer, along with mutiny, desertion, plundering, burglary with violence, giving false alarms, sodomy, carnally abusing children, ravishing women, and riotously beginning to demolish a house, could bring a man before a firing squad or the hangman. And yet the details of the offense were so bizarre as to trouble the sternest of disciplinarians. "I should like one final attempt to persuade his lordship to further clemency," said Hervey, careful to make acknowledgment of the concession so far.

"I shall convey your request to his lordship, Captain Hervey. Is there anything else?"

"No, there is nothing else," Hervey replied. In his heart he knew that Lord Towcester was not for turning, but that could not bar his trying.

It soon became clear, too, that Major Joynson wanted no confrontation with the lieutenant colonel. The major sat in his office surrounded by ledgers and sheaves of paper, and evidently regarded the question of Hopwood's punishment as a distraction to his work. "Hervey, there hasn't been a flogging in years—that, I grant you—but then, there hasn't been a case of violent insubordination either."

"It wasn't 'violent insubordination,'" insisted Hervey, shaking his head in despair. "It was no more insubordination than—"

"Than?"

Hervey sighed. "Do you know all the details, sir?"

"I know that a dragoon called Hopwood struck Mr. Seton Canning in the face with his glove, in front of the whole troop. Do I need to know more?"

"You were not at the court-martial, sir. Do you know why he did it?"

"Is it of any consequence?"

In one sense the major was entirely correct: a private man striking an officer was an unallowable occurrence. But the major's manner suggested to Hervey that his submission in the business was entirely pragmatic. If there was nothing he could do about it, then why provoke trouble?

"Hopwood struck Seton Canning because a man from the fusiliers had told him that striking an officer brought deportation. He has a wife in Australia whom he abandoned three years ago, believing her to be untrue to him, and he has learned that she was accused falsely, and he is in despair of seeing her again."

"And yet I am unmoved."

"Sir, I relate the story not to excite sympathy for him but to show how unmalevolent was his intent. I know that may sound strange at first, but it was no more an act of rebellion than—"

The major sighed and took off his spectacles, rubbing his eyes wearily, though it was not past nine. "Hervey, has it ever occurred to you that the threat, the *possibility* of the lash—no matter that it has not been used in twenty years—may hold some of the regiment's meaner sorts in check? That this flogging, irrespective of the offense, may keep others from transgression in the future? Not insubordination, I mean, but generally."

There was undoubted logic in the major's argument, and Hervey was conscious of beginning to sound like those evangelicals who went round calling for the prisons to be made comfortable and the poor laws bountiful. But flogging had not been the Sixth's way, and the regiment had pulled through the severest times without it. "With respect, sir, I do not believe that many in either the officers' nor the serjeants' messes share that view."

The major put his spectacles back on and looked at him severely. "You have not been discussing the matter with them, I hope, Hervey?"

"No, sir." Hervey tried to conceal his mounting exasperation. "I should not dream of it. There is talk of nothing but the matter in the canteens."

"The canteens? How do you know that, Captain Hervey?"

"Oh, sir!" This time he was not going to trouble to conceal his dismay, nor even to answer directly. "The talk can't be anything other than injurious to discipline, for it implies that striking an officer is the most heinous of crimes in the lieutenant colonel's judgment. Unless, that is, he intends restoring the lash for any number of offenses."

"Hervey, I should be very careful were I you. We do not wish any more trouble than we have already."

"With respect again, sir, that is my intention also. That is why I am come before you."

The major took off his spectacles once more. "Are you sure you are not drawn into this too far, because the dragoon is from your troop?"

Hervey could not follow his reasoning. His obligation to act was precisely because Hopwood *was* one of his troop.

"I mean," Joynson explained, "that you may be seeing in this an affront, given that the lieutenant colonel has been so obviously displeased with you since the general's inspection."

This was a terrible prospect indeed. Had Lord Towcester ordered the flogging to humiliate him and his troop? Would a lieutenant colonel order a dragoon to be flogged solely to humble his officer? No, surely not! Surely not even a man who had run from battle. Hervey breathed deeply and shook his head to dispel the notion. "What is Mr. Lincoln's opinion?"

"Hervey," sighed the major, beginning to polish his spectacles, "I do not think that that is anything to do with you."

The major was right, of course. Outside Hervey's own squadron, matters were the preserve of the regimental staff. "No, indeed, sir," Hervey conceded. "I will take my leave, then. I have requested a hearing of the lieutenant colonel. I thought one last attempt at—"

"Yes, Hervey," the major interrupted, his voice seeming almost to tremble. "Do not think that I do not admire your dedication to principle, and indeed to your men."

But the last thing Hervey wanted now was Major Joynson's shrift. "Thank you, sir. I'm very much obliged for your time and counsel. We can only pray that it turns out well." He put his cap back on, saluted, and left the major's office, with a truly heavy heart.

"We can only pray," echoed Joynson softly, alone now. *One* hundred lashes? The law allowed three times that. It should not be impossible to bear.

Prayer was indeed all that remained, for Hervey was unable to gain a hearing of the lieutenant colonel. Lord Towcester remained out of barracks until the hour appointed for the punishment, and Hervey knew that any appeal in public would not only be to no avail but might prejudice the peace generally.

At midday the regiment turned out for foot parade in full dress, with sidearms, the officers in front of their troops. It was a solemn affair, without the usual banter from the ranks. Only the words of command, and these muted, broke the heavy silence from time to time. Private Hopwood was marched on to parade under close escort, and with him the half dozen other prisoners in confinement at the time, so that they, too, might experience the benefit of his example. When he reached the center of the front of the regiment he was halted, and the adjutant, stepping up to the commanding officer and saluting, received a sheet of paper, which he proceeded to read aloud. It detailed the finding of the court-martial and the sentence awarded. Hopwood stood erect throughout, so that only the guard at his side was able to detect the involuntary trembling which he struggled hard to control. Hopwood had not been at Waterloo, but it was not hard to suppose that his conduct would have been thus. Hervey felt anger welling as he wondered, by contrast, how the Earl of Towcester would have stood. Seton Canning, five paces behind, had been at Waterloo, and he would rather have been there this day. He it was who had received Hopwood's blow; it had not been much of one, and it had certainly not drawn blood. Canning had also been the first to ask the court-martial for clemency on the man's behalf, yet still he could not but feel that what he was about to witness was in some measure his fault.

The reading finished, the regiment received the order "Fours right" from Major Joynson, in a faltering voice, and the band struck up "Seventeen Come Sunday." It was so curious a choice that it had the reverse effect from that doubtless intended, for as the squadrons marched to the riding school by its merry tune, the resentment was almost palpable. At the doors, the squadrons halted and fell out to line the sides, four deep. At the farthest end, opposite the door, stood a wooden triangle five feet at the apex, and next to it the farrier major and two brawny farrier serjeants, jackets off, sleeves rolled up, and each holding a cat-o'-nine-tails. Beside them stood the trumpet major in full dress.

Hopwood was marched up and halted. He placed a piece of silver in the trumpet major's hand—a custom which not even the adjutant had recalled until Lord Towcester reminded him (the regulations said the trumpet major was responsible for training with the cat). The trumpet major then marched to the door to take up his post, and when he was out of sight of the lieutenant colonel he threw the coin as far as he could, and with unconcealed contempt. Hervey saw it, but he could take no satisfaction in having told Major Joynson the affair would have that effect.

Lord Towcester, in a clear voice, gave the order "Proceed." The farrier serjeants seized the prisoner and tied him to the triangle. Hopwood made no struggle. It seemed he was trying the while to meet his punishment squarely. But although he had stood without support he could not now control his bladder, and the wretched dragoon's incontinence became at once apparent to all. Hervey felt tears come.

Soon Hopwood was firmly triced up, his shirt stripped from his back and a leather gag placed between his teeth. The farrier serjeants took post either side of the triangle at attention. Lord Towcester was allowing the moment to have its full effect, but the chaplain, hitherto silent—and who, indeed, had made little impression on the regiment since his joining six months before—stepped forward and bowed to him.

"My lord," he begged. "Have mercy now on this miserable offender, as Our Lord Himself shall have in the dreadful Day of Judgment."

Lord Towcester went a deep shade of red. "When I wish to hear you, reverend sir, you may be sure that I will let you know. *Proceed,* Farrier Major!"

"*Sir!*"

There was not another sound in the school.

The farrier major raised his right arm. Its muscles tightened, the veins swelled. Down swung the lash with a sickening crack on Hopwood's bare flesh. "*One!*" called the farrier serjeant.

Hopwood writhed as no one had ever seen, as if the lash flayed his spirit from one side of his body to the other. Blood oozed from where the thongs cut deep into his side, his back vivid with great weals. Two dragoons fainted behind Hervey. He heard them fall, and saw three more across the school. One or two men were already pushing their way outside to throw up. Hervey had prayed hard that Hopwood would not cry out, but the sheer force of the lash drove the air from his lungs, his mouth already open in shock, the gag expelled. Hervey looked across at Lord Towcester. He could not be sure, but his face had a look of triumph at the sound. One of the farrier serjeants picked up the gag, brushed off the dust and jammed it hard into Hopwood's mouth—a rough but necessary kindness.

"*Two!*" cried the farrier major, laying the cat a little higher this time, opening new wounds and making more weals. But Hopwood had clamped his mouth hard this time, and there was nothing but the noise of the lash. Despite everything, Hervey felt pride swelling in him: there were other ways to demonstrate courage than on the battlefield.

"*Three!*" Hopwood's back was now a livid mass of raw flesh. Blood dripped to the sand.

"*Four!*" . . . "*Five!*" . . . "*Six!*"

Methodically the farrier major continued the count, the strokes falling regularly—ten to the minute.

Past twenty, and still the odd dragoon fell in a dead faint.

"*Twenty-five!*" Yet Hopwood made not a sound.

The farrier major stood back, and the surgeon stepped forward to feel the prisoner's pulse, as the regulations demanded. "He is fit to continue, my lord," he declared, shaking his head sadly, and then he signed for the punishment to proceed.

Hervey thought to appeal now, on account of Hopwood's fortitude. But he reasoned that the lieutenant colonel would surely see that for himself, and might indeed be inclined to order the full punishment to run if he interfered. The farrier serjeant now relieved his senior, and the farrier major took up the count. At the fortieth lash Hopwood suddenly gave a convulsive jerk, and then hung limp. The surgeon raised his hands and the falling blow was diverted. He felt Hopwood's pulse again, pulled up an eyelid to examine the pupil, then stepped forward to the lieutenant colonel. "My lord, he can bear no more."

A sigh of relief went up from all, officers and men alike.

Without a word Lord Towcester strode from the riding school.

The farrier major threw a bucket of salt water over Hopwood's back, untriced him, and handed him over to the hospital orderlies. Seton Canning made to go to him, but Hervey caught his arm. "Not now, not now," he said, kindly but emphatically.

As they left the school, Ezra Barrow came up to Hervey's side. "A word if you please. Shall you come to my rooms?"

In Barrow's quarters in the mess (he was not married) the captain from the ranks produced a brandy bottle and two glasses. "I can send for water, if you prefer."

"Don't trouble," said Hervey. "I think my stomach could do with it undiluted."

Barrow poured until the glasses were full, sat heavily in an armchair, and took a large gulp of his. "I've a mind to send in my papers, Hervey. I've never been opposed on principle to touching over—as the regiment is supposed to be—but neither 'ave I seen any occasion when I thought it was truly necessary. Perhaps once, when I were a young trooper—two men 'ad got horrible drunk and spoiled another man's wife. But never since then . . ." The strange Brummagem vowels had returned as strong as ever.

Hervey, too, had taken a large measure of the brandy, and was beginning to feel its powers. "I've heard it said there is something of a man's spirit that's forever broken when he's been flogged, that however his body mends, he's never the same again."

Barrow nodded. "I've heard that as well. All men are different, mind."

"Do you know what was Mr. Lincoln's opinion of the matter?" The RSM's opinion was always inscrutable outside the orderly room.

Barrow took another gulp of brandy. "I do. Even an RSM must confide in someone, and it's only natural to confide in one who's been in that seat himself."

"And?"

"I said 'confide,' Hervey."

Hervey would dearly have known the RSM's opinion, for it was so rarely given, and Mr. Lincoln had served the longest of any man in the Sixth. "I hope you *won't* send in your papers, Barrow. It seems that Strickland will, and soon enough there'll be no one but Towcester's lackeys. Besides aught else, your dragoons wouldn't thank you."

The glasses were by now full again.

"*Cod's,* Hervey! My troop's well found—it's true. But they'd no more miss me than . . . They like a gentleman, not one as is like them under the skin. You know that as well as I."

As a rule, Hervey knew it to be right. But though there was little actual love for Barrow in the ranks, there was respect nevertheless. "Barrow, your troop would follow you. That's the important thing, is it not?"

"Of course they'd follow. There are serjeants behind them!"

Hervey frowned. "Would follow *willingly.*"

Barrow huffed and drank more brandy. "Brighton'll be one turnout after another. Towcester will be lashing the whole regiment before a week. I haven't the stomach for it."

"It may not be so bad. We might see inside the Prince Regent's pavilion," tried Hervey, with a sort of smile.

"Hervey, I don't like saying this. It goes against everything I've held to in two and a half score years in the service. But yon Earl of Towcester is a bad lot. He'll fall foul of the Horse Guards sooner or later. They all do. But he'll lead the regiment a pretty dance ere then. And a lot of men shall pay a heavy price—Hopwood, me, *you* even. . . ."

"I've been trying to tell myself that it won't be so bad once we have real work to do."

"Maybe," Barrow conceded, though not sounding convinced. "But if I had the means . . ."

"For what?"

"To let them in authority know what is his true nature!"

Hervey understood. The financial stake for Barrow was too high. And perhaps, in its way, it was for him, too. He shuddered at the notion. It must never be so, he told himself: he must act disinterestedly, always. And if a man like Barrow was driven to thoughts of defiance, then was it not time that he himself made such a stand?

When Hervey returned home that evening, a little before eight, the brandy was no more than a dull headache, for he had turned out his troop for sword drill in the afternoon to sweat the flogging out of them. It had been a woeful affair to begin with, for Serjeant Major Kendall seemed wholly incapable of exercising any mastery over a body of men, and had it not been for the most judicious, and surprisingly tactful, intervention of Serjeant Armstrong, the parade might have become like a shambles of a busy morning. He had wondered when he could be rid of Kendall, when he might raise the matter with Lord Towcester. He had even discovered lately that the serjeant major had managed to get himself and the commissary wagons thoroughly lost during the general's inspection, where but for the early finish to the scheme there would have followed certain disarray in the troop. But Hervey could not yet broach the subject with the adjutant, even, for such was the strong detestation in that quarter that a request to have the man moved would only be met with accusations that he was trying to deflect the blame for his own shortcomings. There seemed no end to his problems.

The heavy silk curtains in the drawing room were closed, and candles burned brightly, although it was still light outside. The house was a picture of elegant comfort rather than of luxury, a good place for a soldier to withdraw to. Henrietta greeted him warmly. "Johnson has just this minute left," she said, holding her cheek to his lips. "He told me about the affair at the barracks. I am sorry, my darling."

It pleased and touched him that she should understand so perfectly. "A hideous business." He sighed deeply. "I should have been home before now, but—"

"There is a bath drawn for you. Why don't you wash away the day and then come to me as if it were a fresh one. I've news that should interest you."

"From Wiltshire?"

She gave him a puzzled smile. "Yes."

"Is my father to be made bishop?"

"Wait and see, dearest," smiled Henrietta. "I shall expect you down in half an hour, and then I shall tell you all."

His bath was a restoring exercise, but when Hanks poured water over his head he had a moment's vision of the salt water and Private Hopwood's back. He made an effort to put that from his mind, though, for Henrietta did not deserve to have to share the Sixth's troubles. He dressed quickly and returned to her side, hopeful of diverting news from Wiltshire.

Henrietta was holding a glass of Champagne, which she loved better than anything. He might not himself have chosen it in the circumstances, but the regiment's trials were not to be hers, and so he took the glass which Hanks proffered.

"Well?" he said, smiling. "What is it in Wiltshire that will interest me?"

Henrietta waited until Hanks had closed the door behind him, and then gave her husband another kiss. "My dearest, Princess Charlotte is with child!"

Hervey tried hard to conceal his disappointment at news that was of such little moment to him. Had he not heard it before, too? "My darling, what is—"

"And so am I!"

Sensations of every kind came over him. He was dumbstruck.

Henrietta, reddening a little, smiled wide at him. "Matthew, I am wondering why you seem so surprised. There has scarcely been a day when . . ."

This was certainly true, even on the night of the general's inspection. He took her in his arms, shaking his head with a sort of unbelieving pride.

"But I do believe it was the day when Jessye went to the stallion." She giggled.

He reddened, and then became anxious. "Shouldn't you be sitting? Resting? Have you seen a doctor? Is there—"

"*Matthew.*" She put a finger to his mouth.

He kissed her with the greatest tenderness. "Whoever could have thought that the day might end as well as this?"

"It is not ended yet, my dear," she whispered. "And I am not suddenly become as a piece of china."

Hervey was ready for the rude rebuff, the curse, profanity, obscenity— whatever it was to be—for he was the man's troop leader, the officer in whose charge Private Hopwood now was, punishment having been carried out. Joseph Edmonds had told him, when first he had joined the

Sixth, that it was unfair for an officer ever to confront a man when his senses were dulled by alcohol, or fired by another spirit, for if the man then acted violently—by word or worse—he, the officer, was in truth guilty of provoking it. Hervey knew that Private Hopwood was scarcely able to rise from his bed and assault him, but what if his verbal abusing was loud enough to be heard by all the others in the sick bay? What if the abuse were directed not at him but at the commanding officer, the adjutant, the farrier major—at anybody, indeed, who might then prefer a charge of insubordination? Would he, Hervey, have the right to overlook such a thing—as he was prepared to do now should the invective be directed at him personally?

But Hopwood's reply was silence.

At first Hervey thought Hopwood might not have heard him, being still drowsy, perhaps, from the laudanum. "Private Hopwood," he said again, thinking at least to give him back a little dignity in addressing him by his rank. "Is there anything I can do?"

Still Hopwood made no reply. Hervey was now caught between anger at the refusal to speak, for the man was still under discipline, even prone in his sickbed, and compassion for his evident wish to be shut of officers. He would not leave, though, without first making Hopwood meet his eye. But as he moved closer to the bed, he wished with all his heart that he hadn't, for Hopwood's eyes were streaming—a continuous flow of tears, as if all will to stem them were gone, and every drop of that soldier's spirit which had made him face his punishment so bravely the day before was being washed away. Hopwood was no longer a man in age three or four years his captain's senior; he was not even a child.

Hervey turned to leave, but as he did so came the extraordinary sound of hymn singing. Not the doleful stuff of Corporal Sandbache's prayer meetings, which even Lord Towcester had not thought worth suppressing, nor even the regimented chorus of a Sunday church parade, but a full-throated rendering of "He Who Would Valiant Be." By how many, Hervey wondered? It sounded like half the regiment! He quickened outside to find his troop and the chaplain, hats off, heads high.

The sound would be carrying throughout the barracks, and easily across the square. Hervey glanced towards the orderly room, where the lieutenant colonel's pennant was run up the pole; Lord Towcester was certainly at orderly room. The windows were closing one by one. All, that is, but Mr. Lincoln's.

Henrietta was on her day bed, and did not hear him come in.

"My *dear*," Hervey stammered as he saw her. "Are you unwell?"

She turned to see his anxious face, and laughed. "No. I am tired!"

It was not yet ten in the morning. "But—"

"Matthew . . ." she protested coyly.

He saw her tease at once, smiled, and kissed her forehead.

"Why are you home so soon? Is anything wrong?"

Hervey shook his head, then shrugged. "Oh . . . I just didn't want to be about the barracks."

"Whyever not? Ordinarily it claims you stronger than I can."

"That is not true!"

"Matthew, I am not complaining. You might not be quite so much the man if I had you all to myself!"

He frowned, then realized she was teasing him again.

"What has sent you home, then?"

He sat at the edge of her bed. "I went to see Hopwood—the dragoon who was flogged yesterday."

"Oh," she said, her face becoming less animated. "Do you want to tell me of it?"

"Would you mind?"

She sat up and took his hand. "Of *course* I should not mind. Why should I mind your speaking of anything which is making you unhappy? Did you not listen to *anything* that Mr. Keble said when we were married?"

He smiled sheepishly. "You carry the evidence, my love."

They kissed, but she broke off and pressed him to what had made him return.

"It was as if we had thrashed the very manhood out of him," said Hervey, shaking his head. "I can't think that is right, even for his offense—even for twice the offense."

She raised her eyebrows—a look that implied she might agree with him. "If *I* were a soldier I should want an officer who felt as you did. What do you suppose would be my chances of getting one?"

It was a curious way of putting the question. He wondered if she thought him alone in his sentiments. "My darling," he said, smiling gently at her, "you flatter me, but you must not suppose that mine is a lonely opinion. Since before I joined the Sixth they were known to be a regiment that did not flog. It was—if you like—a point of honor with the officers that we did not need recourse to it to prevent riot or desertion. No doubt there were some men who took advantage of it, but the regiment was never found wanting on campaign. And we were by no means unique. I'm sure that not one in four regiments of cavalry used the lash in the Peninsula. The point is, this business may have driven something of a wedge between the men and their officers. They assembled this morning to sing hymns outside the infirmary—*hymns,* of all things. And they sang most defiantly. It does not bode well."

She nodded, and took his hand again. "What shall you do?"

He sighed. "I had a word with Strickland after seeing Hopwood. Do you know he is on the point of leaving? He's continually subjected to insults for his religion by Lord Towcester."

Henrietta said that she did not know. Barracks gossip had yet to establish its conduit to her, other than by Johnson, who so far seemed inclined to allow only a trickle. "And what did you say?"

"I told him I had a mind to go and see Lord Sussex. That the colonel ought to know about the unhappy state of affairs generally. But he begged me not to."

Henrietta looked hesitant. "I am very glad that he did. Do you really suppose it would do any good?"

"It is Lord Sussex's regiment."

"Yes," she conceded, frowning. "But a man such as Towcester will not be without wiles. And how do you suppose things will turn out if Lord Sussex is unable to take your word against his? Lord Towcester has put a deal of money into the regiment. You said so yourself."

"I don't think that would affect Lord Sussex's judgment."

"Not his judgment, Matthew. I am sure Lord Sussex would know that what you said was the truth. But his judgment might be that the greater evil could come of taking action against Lord Towcester."

Hervey saw her point, and sighed again. "In any case, I had already decided against it."

"What have you decided instead? Or have you not?"

He paused, as if thinking how to explain. "I spoke with Serjeant Armstrong. We are going to try to get Hopwood's wife to come here from Australia."

"And that will repair things?" she asked, doubtfully.

"The troop want to buy his discharge for him. But that won't restore his pride. *That* we shall have to do by degrees when he returns to duty."

She nodded again, agreeing with his reasoning. "Has Serjeant Armstrong said anything else?"

"About Hopwood?"

"No. About Caithlin."

"No. He's reconciled to her leaving the school. She's to find some other work, I think. Something in the town, perhaps."

Henrietta knew that already. She had shared a dish of tea with her in the Prince Rupert only yesterday. "I mean that *she* is with child, too!"

"No! He said not a word!"

"She is only surprised it has not happened before now."

Hervey *almost* observed that a serjeant's quarters did not provide the same opportunity that they enjoyed. "Do you know, my love," he said instead, smiling. "Armstrong a father—it is a very serious thing. He may never be inclined to a headlong charge ever again!"

CHAPTER 10

THE LANDING

The Sussex Coast, September 1

The downpour was so heavy that Hervey's reins kept slipping through his fingers, and he had to wedge his insteps in firmly to save losing his stirrups. Driven almost horizontal by the wind, the rain lashed his face viciously, and no matter how he bent his head, water found its way down his neck and inside his tunic shirt. How the carbine locks were faring he could only hope. The men had bound them with oilskin before leaving the billets, but that had never been entirely proof against damp, and this storm on the downs was as bad as any he could remember in the Astorgias. And he *had* to keep his head up because the night was so black he could see next to nothing beyond his charger's ears. He would have dismounted and led, had the gelding not somehow been able to maintain a better pace on the rough road above the cliffs—perhaps because the chalk gave him a trail, perhaps because the sides rose two feet.

Behind Hervey were thirty dragoons—or, rather, he trusted that they were there, for he couldn't see them and he certainly couldn't hear them. He could trust, though, because Serjeant Armstrong was at the rear. Had the other half troop not been at Lewes for the assizes he would have taken them as well, and then at least he would have had two officers. If, that is, the lieutenant colonel had let him.

Lord Towcester had raged like a wounded beast when the revenue men had come to his orderly room. "Coast duty? Coast duty! I've not paid thousands for new jackets and shakos to have them ruined chasing smugglers! I shall protest to the Prince Regent himself!"

But the chief officer of His Majesty's Excise had been unmoved. "I regret the inconvenience to your lordship, but it is not every day that intelligence such as this comes into my riding officers' hands. We stand to apprehend contraband and owlers at one and the same time."

Lord Towcester had not been in the slightest degree animated by the prospect, however; only by the cost in appearance of his regiment. The latter was not something to which Hervey himself was insensitive—nor the other officers—but it seemed to him to be a cost that could be recovered, whereas the revenue's opportunity was not.

By now, Hervey knew the downs quite well, having ridden out most mornings, first on Harkaway and then Gilbert, and he had been glad to do so, for the lieutenant colonel had been in a bait since they arrived a fortnight before. Lord Towcester had expected to be attending daily at the pavilion, but the Prince Regent had not yet come, sending word that Princess Charlotte was not able to travel, and that he felt it his paternal duty to remain in London until she was able. But now, a full two hours after nightfall, Hervey was becoming worried. They were supposed, by his reckoning, to take a right fork at the top of Beacon Ridge, and by his same reckoning they had made that distance easily already—yet without finding the fork. Indeed, if anything they seemed to be going downhill. He was regretting not waiting just a little longer for the revenue guide, but they had stood, horses saddled, for more than an hour in the expectation of his arriving, and he had despaired of making the rendezvous if they stood any longer. He knew the old windmill well. It could be seen for miles. It should not have been difficult to find, were it not for this storm.

Now they were most certainly going downhill; his stirrups told him so. Where in heaven's name were they? He couldn't see the moon, three-quarters though it was, let alone a star. The wind was still in his face, perhaps a shade round to the right side, but no more than it might have veered. The sea must therefore be to their right still, but had they overshot Beacon Ridge, or had they turned fuller west and not made the crest at all?

It was no good asking anyone behind him. They had scarcely stepped off the well-lit streets of Brighton since arriving. One of the dragoons might somehow have seen the fork, however. But how long would it take him to go down the line anyway? And it would hardly inspire confidence. He reined about and halted by Private Johnson, just behind. "I can't find the turning to the windmill. We haven't passed it, have we?"

Johnson had only ridden this way a couple of times. He didn't know the fork, but he seemed certain they hadn't passed one. "As certain as anybody can be in this lot, sir."

With such a proviso, the reassurance was of no practical value. "Thank you, Johnson," said Hervey disconsolately. And then he cursed. "Go and get Serjeant Armstrong. We may as well see if he's certain of anything, too."

"I only said as I found!" Johnson protested.

Hervey knew his problems were already too many to go upsetting his groom. "Any tea?"

"I'm not bloody Merlin, Cap'n 'Ervey!"

He could imagine the grimace of a smile, even if he couldn't see it. "Go and get Serjeant Armstrong, then."

The column stood patiently, even the horses, as if submitting to the rain's whip was just a little more bearable than struggling and catching its sting awkwardly. Hervey wondered how dry was his map, though what use it would serve he couldn't imagine. It would be a sodden thing in seconds if he tried to read it, even under his oilskin cape. And there was no more chance of lighting a lantern than of unwrapping a carbine and expecting it to fire. He swore even worse, not bothering now to keep it below his breath, for the noise of the wind and rain would have masked it beyond two lengths even if he had bellowed.

Serjeant Armstrong came forward, cursing the dragoons to make way. "What's up, sir?"

"I must've missed the fork to the windmill."

"Well, I've seen none. But things are so black I'm not sure I would've seen it anyway. Where are we, do you think?"

Hervey was trying to keep his voice no higher than needs be to speak above the storm, but it still felt like shouting words of command on the square. "I *think* we're towards Ovingdean. All we can do is push on down this way and hope we find some landmark."

Hope wasn't a principle of war. Hervey had said it so many times that Johnson had even quoted it back at him once. Well, this wasn't war, and in any case he couldn't think of any alternative. If they retraced their steps there was no guarantee they would do any better than before—except that they might just meet the revenue guide.

He called for the corporal. Up came Sykes, a good man, Hervey considered him, but no Collins. He would spell out the orders. "Ride back down the route out, Corporal Sykes, and if you come across the revenue guide, bring him on at once after us. I'll leave a vidette if the road forks."

That done, they resumed the march. Hervey was soon praying that he'd done the right thing, for in a further half hour they had found nothing. By his estimate they must have gone another mile and a half—perhaps two—and they ought surely to be coming off the downs and across *some* signs of habitation, whether they were marching east or due north? Where in God's name *were* they?

Just as Hervey was beginning to contemplate desperate measures (splitting the troop, perhaps, and sending them to the four points of the compass), he caught a glimpse of a light ahead—just a flicker, but a light unmistakably. He pressed his legs to the girth and Harkaway lengthened obligingly. He wondered how he should close with the light, though. This was hardly enemy territory, but the revenue men had said they were up against villainizers who would not hesitate to fight, *and* with the means to do so. But he had lost so much time already. They should have been at the rendezvous an hour or more ago. Well, it was a rule of patrol work, and one which had never served him ill in the Peninsula, to take the risks early. He therefore decided to risk now, and instead of deploying in order to overwhelm any opposition, he decided to hold the troop where it was and send two scouts forward. He himself would be one of them.

"Serjeant Armstrong, please," he called back to Johnson.

"Serjeant Armstrong!" called Johnson to the man behind, and so on down the line.

Up came Armstrong within the minute at a fast trot. "Yes, I see it, sir!"

"I'm going forward to look." Hervey didn't need to say more. Armstrong knew his business. "Johnson!"

At twenty yards the light revealed itself to be a lamp in a window. But it was another ten before they were sure the window was the turnpike lodge's. "How in God's name have we come so far?" said Hervey aloud, for he reckoned they must have been riding due north, and this the Lewes high road ahead.

Johnson closed alongside. "Eh, sir?"

"Christ!" spluttered Hervey, sliding from the saddle and handing the reins to his groom.

Hervey doubled to the lodge and knocked loudly on the door. Moments later he heard a bolt being drawn, and then the spy port slid open.

"Who be it?"

"Captain Hervey of the Sixth Light Dragoons quartered at Brighton. I need your light to see my map."

More bolts were drawn, and after what seemed an age the door opened. Hervey entered at once, taking off his shako and cape, and pulling out his map in its oilskin. "I'm much obliged to you, keeper."

The lodge keeper was an oldish man, solid, easy in his manner. Hervey looked him up and down carefully, for it was always possible the man might be an accessory to the smugglers. But what clue might give away the association he didn't know. He spread the map (dry as a bone, thank God) on the table, and pulled an oil lamp closer. "Where exactly are we?"

Maps were not something the keeper was familiar with, though he could read. "Ovingdean's but a mile down the road to the right, sir."

The answer was enough. Hervey located the lodge on the Ordnance sheet and took out his hunter. "Great gods—a quarter to midnight!" It was later by an hour than he had thought. But the map showed a lane to the windmill from the turnpike just a few hundred yards on, a lane no doubt decent enough to take corn wagons one way and flour the other. If they kicked on they could be there in half an hour. "Who has passed through since nightfall?" he asked, giving the keeper half a sovereign.

"The Dover coach, sir. Nothing else—not on a night like this."

Hervey folded up his map and wrapped it back in its oilskin. "Is the road to the windmill easy to find?"

"It is, sir," replied the keeper, helping him on with his cape. "A furlong almost exactly. There's a milestone there."

Hervey thanked him and put on his shako. "I shall leave one of my dragoons here. I may need him to give directions."

The keeper said he would be happy for the company.

Outside it was still raining as hard, and seemed worse to Hervey for his having been sheltered from it for ten minutes. The night, too, seemed blacker, but he knew his eyes would soon become used to the darkness again. If only the cloud would break and let through some moonlight: how on earth were they going to see their quarry, let alone arrest them?

Hervey remounted and trotted back to the troop. Armstrong had made the dragoons dismount, despite the oaths and cursing that the saddles would get sodden. "Broadhurst, please, Serjeant Armstrong."

Private Broadhurst, the next for a chevron, doubled up the line and stood to attention almost peak to knee with his captain. "Sir!"

"Broadhurst, that light's a turnpike lodge. There's one keeper there. I think he's straight, but I want you to watch him—inside. And if Corporal Sykes and the revenue guide arrive, tell them that we've gone on to the windmill. The keeper will tell you by which way. Just have your wits about you generally, and wait till relieved."

"Sir!" Broadhurst saluted and doubled back to fetch his trooper.

"How long is it to the windmill, sir?" asked Armstrong, already mounted and gathering his reins.

"Half an hour if we can get a move on. There's a good track to it a furlong down the turnpike." He turned and called to Johnson.

"Aye, sir?"

"Your eyes are better used to this. Kick on to the milestone and find the cart track off to the right. We'll come up as fast as we can."

Hervey was happier now he could feel some momentum again. How much their late arriving at the rendezvous would prejudice the revenue operation he had no idea, for its details had yet to be given him. As they rounded the lodge and gained the turnpike he pressed his gelding to a careful trot: he didn't want to come down on slippery metal at *this* stage. But two minutes was all it took to find Johnson. And now at last he was confident of finding the windmill—a mile and a half to the right up a well-made track, the ground rising all the way.

Minutes later Harkaway checked, else they would have collided. A horse was square-on to them, standing stock-still in the middle of the cross-tracks. Hervey had barely turned alongside when he realized it had no rider and there were more horses to front and rear.

"Christ!" he cursed as he wheeled and reached for his saber. But a blow on the shoulder blade almost made him miss his grip. He ducked to Harkaway's neck to escape the next one, spurring him to turn on the spot to meet the assault. "Alarm!" he shouted, "Alarm!" and lunged forward in the saddle to make an upper cut into the darkness. His sword failed to make contact.

"Alarm" ran the length of the column, though what in God's name they could do in this light Hervey didn't know. "Trumpeter! Trumpeter!" he called repeatedly, until Johnson found him, and then Armstrong and finally Susan Medwell. "I think we've run on the owlers' train," shouted Hervey. "Serjeant Armstrong, take half a dozen men left along the crossing track, and I'll go right. Johnson, stand with two men to picket the track ahead about fifty yards, and detail another two as videttes here." Then he told off the same number, and struck along the drove determined to take one prisoner at least.

But the packhorses were gone, and though Hervey rode for a furlong and more he could find nothing. He dare not leave the drove for fear of losing himself. What would the owlers be trying to do now? They wouldn't still be making for the shore, not with dragoons—and, for all they knew, the revenue men—on their heels? They would double back, seeking safety inland, surely?

He turned and led his men back the way they'd come. It was no easier a business than leading them out, and he almost missed the cross-tracks, even with its vidette. If only the rain would cease: they'd at least have an extra couple of yards to see.

There was no sign of Armstrong. Had his serjeant had more luck? "Sound Rally," he called to Susan.

Hervey's trumpeter managed it very well, considering the gale, cracking the octave descent only once in three repeats.

In the ten minutes it took Armstrong to return, Hervey thought over his options. He could abandon the mission altogether: the owlers would surely be abandoning theirs and, now alerted to the presence of troops, the contrabanders would hardly risk a landing? But that decision ought rightly to be the revenue's. Or he could throw out a cordon in the hope of intercepting the owlers: at first light he might well catch them still trying to come off the downs. Or he could give up the owlers as lost and make for the rendezvous with the revenue. Could he throw out a cordon *and* tackle the contrabanders? Only with another two dozen men. Yet he was reluctant to let either opportunity go.

"Johnson, I want you to gallop for me." Johnson was knee to knee with him, but still Hervey was having to raise his voice against the wind.

"Aye, sir. Back to Brighton?"

"Yes, to Captain Strickland. His troop's the nearest. Give him my compliments, and ask if he will send as many men as he can spare—twenty at least—to the road back there. Tell him what's happened and ask him to lay up along the turnpike to catch the owlers as they beat back. I'll go on with Serjeant Armstrong and the rest to try to meet with the revenue. Do you have all that?"

"Aye, sir. Shall I follow you up once I'm done?"

"No. It'll be best that no one comes east of the turnpike. That way we should avoid mistakes. And you'd better remind them the password is 'Wellington.'"

Strickland's cordon was a very long shot indeed, and his own chance with the contrabanders was perhaps no greater. If only the guide had shown! If only he hadn't missed the fork!

It took them three quarters of an hour to cover the remaining mile to the windmill, for the going in that pitch darkness was as hard as any he could remember in Spain, and he was especially wary of running into the owlers again. As they broached the windmill rise he saw the reassuring flicker of a storm lantern, and then by its light the same revenue riding officer of the afternoon.

"Good God, Captain Hervey, we were within an ace of opening fire," he called. "Why in heaven's name are you come from that direction?"

Hervey didn't give their flash powder much of a chance in this weather, even inside the windmill. But you could never be sure, and even one ball might have struck flesh at that range, point-blank. "The guide didn't show in over an hour, so we set out as best we could. We came on the owlers a mile back and they've scattered to the winds. I've sent word back to Brighton for reinforcements to picket the Lewes road. And then we came on here as fast as we could."

The riding officer looked dismayed. "You'd better come inside."

By lantern light, sacking shielding the windows, Hervey was at last made privy to the revenue's information and intention. An Ordnance map like his own was spread on a table, and the officer—his face a chiseled image of incorruptibility—pointed to the route which he believed the owlers to have come. "They're seasoned hands, Captain Hervey. The wool isn't theirs, so their first instinct will be to save their own skins—though they won't abandon the packs unless they have to. My estimate is that they'll lie up on the downs until they can be sure of their escape route. Your men on the Lewes road will frighten them, that's for sure, but it would take two more lines—each from the road to the sea—to be sure of netting them."

"Will they alert the contrabanders?"

"It's a good question," said the riding officer, taking out pipe and tinderbox. "I should say not, though, for they owe nothing to the wetfeet, as they call them. The two ply their own trade independently. It's only the economy of using the same vessel that attracts them. There's no honor among their like."

Hervey peered closely at the map. "Where is it you expect the landing?"

"Here," said the riding officer confidently. "We have our sources, you know."

Hervey continued to study the Ordnance sheet. "But how, on a night like this, will any vessel be able to find the cove, let alone heave to and send out boats?"

The riding officer smiled. "It's a very fair question. Yet the answer is simple: there are lights placed on the headlands in such a way as to guide the craft to the very place from which to launch its boats."

"Lights which we can't see from land?"

"Exactly, Captain Hervey, but there are other methods, you know."

Hervey looked abashed.

"I have a cutter stationed offshore watching for those very lights," said the riding officer proudly. "Her instructions are to signal me with her observations."

"But if she signals, will that not alert the smugglers and those with the lights?"

The riding officer smiled. "Indeed so. That is why she will signal only if there are *no* lights, after midnight."

The danger of signaling a negative had been drummed into him as a cornet, yet he could see there was no alternative in the revenue's business. "And how do the contrabanders do their landings?"

The riding officer looked grave. "Usually they first land a dozen men, maybe two dozen, to secure the place where the contraband is to come ashore. I've known as many as fifty picket a cove for a rich cargo."

Hervey was puzzled. "I should have thought it far easier to have men secure a place from landward."

"True," said the riding officer with another wry smile. "And that's how it used to be. But with so many troops watching for Bonaparte these past twenty years it became too hot to assemble on the coast. Now that things have quietened, we'll see a return to the old ways no doubt."

Hervey nodded. "So, do we speak of Englishmen or French who will come ashore?"

"Frenchmen, for the most part. There are plenty of the old Grande Armée keen to earn some gold. And by God, they'll fight. They won't scruple in the slightest to use their firearms."

Hervey was not especially troubled by this, but the relative numbers were not good. If the French were to put fifty men ashore they would outnumber him more than two to one, taking account of the horseholders. Ordinarily that wouldn't trouble him either, but in this darkness, with this rain, and with mutual support so difficult . . . "Is this a rich cargo? Do you expect the landing to be in any strength?"

The officer looked grave again. "Indeed I do. That is why I asked for a whole troop of regulars."

Hervey raised his eyebrows.

"Is something amiss?"

"I have fewer than thirty men."

For an instant the riding officer's bile was roused, but his self-control had been too many years in the making. "I confide that the deficiency will be no fault of yours, Captain Hervey, but this makes things damned tricky. I'd intended that we should take the vessel and everyone about the business. But this weather was already making that a forlorn hope, and with insufficient men we stand little chance of taking the landing party. All we can safely do is seize the contraband and the porters, and the light men, for they'll have information of use to us."

"It will have to be with the saber, too, for we couldn't trust to pistols and carbines in this rain."

The riding officer agreed. "Let us talk of the details, then."

Hervey found the riding officer to be a practical man. That he wanted keenly to close with the contrabanders was beyond doubt, but he was not so reckless as to expose Hervey's dragoons to unnecessary danger, for, as he explained, they would succeed at the very least in putting the porters to flight without their uncustomed cargo. The design they worked out was therefore to send a party to the beach a half mile or so from where the landing was expected, to work along under the cliffs until they were in a position to mount an attack which would separate the porters from the contraband. A second party would, meanwhile, work along the clifftops until they came across the light men—the light on the other side of the cove would have to be left, for they hadn't enough men to mount two simultaneous approaches.

Hervey was able to tell each and every one of his dragoons what was the design, crowding them into the mill in their two parties, cheered by the fervor of the sweats who were only too happy to have another go at Johnny Crapeau, and by the eagerness of the greenheads to claim their first laurels with the old enemy. He was at pains to disabuse them of any notion that it would be an easy affair, however. And the revenue riding officer, likewise, warned that these were men who would fight hard for their money, as well as for their lives.

At one o'clock—more than three hours later than the riding officer had hoped—Hervey's dragoons began their final approach march. The rain had eased considerably, the wind had dropped, so that speech no longer had to be in a raised voice, and it seemed just a fraction less dark than before. The going was easier anyway with a guide, and they quickly found the path to the beach. Hervey, with Serjeant Armstrong, led twelve of his most experienced men down its precipitous length, slipping and sliding and cursing, but with nothing worse at the bottom than a dragoon with a twisted ankle. He had put the other party, of eight, in the charge of one of the revenue men, for he dared not risk fewer than seven horseholders, and even that would be a trial for so indefinite a period. The two parties had no way of signaling to each other, so which of them was to begin its work first would have to be left to circumstance. Ideally, the light men should be apprehended first, before they could extinguish their beacon, or else any commotion on the beach would have them flee. If only the revenue could see exactly where the beacons *were*—but so cunningly shielded to landward were they, that only by coming right up on them could they be fixed.

Down on the beach it was distinctly lighter. The chalk cliffs and the sea seemed to be reflecting the faint moonlight piercing the breaking cloud, and Hervey could now make out his men at three paces—though it was still not enough to exercise any degree of control if it came to a fight. The wind was little more than a breeze now, and the rain had been stopped for a full ten minutes. Now was the time to unwrap the firelocks and load. It took only a minute with these dragoons, yet even that was one minute more than it took Armstrong to slip a bulleted cartridge into Hervey's percussion-lock. Hervey himself carried his repeater. He carefully unwrapped the primed cylinder and fitted it to the carbine, surprised how quickly the real test of its handiness had come.

In single file, with Armstrong at Hervey's side, and the riding officer at the other, they advanced at a brisk pace to close the half mile. Hervey counted the paces, shorter slightly than he would have managed on firm ground, but three for every two yards nevertheless by his reckoning. After his fifth hundred they saw lights ahead, one well to the left—evidently on the contrabanders' ship—the others almost directly to their front, dimmer and moving. How *far* ahead, it was not possible to tell.

"They've begun to bring the stuff ashore," said the riding officer. "Their pickets will be posted, therefore. We'd better be ready."

It struck Hervey at once: if the lights were visible from here, they must already be at the picket. "I think we should—"

Two blinding flashes and two reports made louder by the cliffs' echo came an instant later. The riding officer fell back clutching his stomach.

"Wick, Tansey," shouted Hervey. "See to Mr. Poole. Remainder, extended line, at the double, advance!"

A shingle beach, at the double—this was a trial even for a rifleman. "Number from the left, *begin!*" shouted Armstrong, his voice carrying as it always did. The dragoons numbered off breathlessly.

After two hundred yards they were struggling to keep in line, from the cliff bottom to the water's edge, and beginning to blow as hard as their horses after a good canter. But they knew that if they didn't get to the lights quickly they'd face more determined resistance.

Another hundred yards. Hervey could see Armstrong was with him on the left, and another dragoon close in on his right. There were more flashes and earsplitting reports, point-blank. He leveled his carbine as he ran, and fired—once, twice, three times, all by instinct, for there was no target to see. Armstrong fired, too, as did the dragoon on his other side.

Hervey could now make out figures by the lantern light at the water's edge. A *welter* of fire came his way from front, flanks, above, and behind even—then screams, shouts, curses, oaths.

Hervey fired four rounds in rapid succession in an arc to his front, threw down the carbine, and drew his sword. "From the left, number!" he bellowed.

"One, two . . . five, six . . . nine, ten," came the numbers. Then "Armstrong, sir!"

Four men down, but Armstrong still there—thank God, gasped Hervey. Another fusillade brought fresh screams from his left. "Lie down! Reload!" he shouted. But he knew that with momentum gone, and the cover of darkness, he would never get his men forward now, even were Armstrong to drive them. All he could do was hold his position and harry the French with fire as they withdrew, for they surely couldn't continue the work with the threat of dragoons so close?

He was wrong. Just as the riding officer had said, these men would fight. In a few minutes more, fire opened again in their direction, and he saw movement, too. "Keep up a steady return, Serjeant Armstrong. Let's try to fool them we're more than we are."

"From the left, count to five, fire!" shouted Armstrong.

Hervey ran from man to man to reassure him with the hand. The far-thest dragoon to the left was bleeding badly from his leg—Finch, the old-est sweat—but he was still reloading as if at musketry practice. Hervey called him by his nickname as he bound up the wound with a silk square. "Choky, don't let those waves get to your powder. We can't abandon this place now."

The appeal was direct, and Finch knew it must be desperate. "I know, sir. But don't leave me to them French if you 'as to pull back. I can limp, with an 'and."

"I promise," said Hervey, gripping his shoulder. "But it's as bad a scrape as ever I saw."

The volleying to their front increased, and Hervey knew they must soon be overrun, for the French would have gauged their numbers from the puny return of fire.

"Captain 'Ervey! Captain 'Ervey!"

Hervey swung round and saw Johnson and the horseholders—eight more carbines and sabers! "Rally here! Rally here!" he shouted, standing and waving his sword. "Extended line. *Fire!*"

There was firing to his right, too, from atop the cliffs. They might just be able to hold their ground! It must surely force the French to with-draw? But that wasn't why they were there, just to hold a line on the beach. "Stand up, Light Dragoons! Draw swords! Prepare to advance! *Advance!*"

How many were with him, Hervey couldn't say. But he could hear Serjeant Armstrong shouting "By the center!" How magnificently futile an order! Clever, though, for the dragoons would be trying to dress in-stead of worrying what lay ahead.

"Double march!" Hervey bellowed.

Then it was crunching of shingle, cursing, and blowing. And then a terrific explosion in front, the discharge high, grape whistling over their heads, the rush of it felt in the face, even.

"Down!" screamed Hervey. What in God's name had they there? He pushed his shako back, and shouted again. "Serjeant Armstrong!"

Another explosion, just as loud, with grape feeling as if it were raking their backs. Armstrong crawled to his side, swearing terribly. "Let's give 'em a volley from 'ere in case they rush us."

Hervey prayed they'd managed to reload. "Stay prone, Light Dragoons. One round, fire!"

It was a ragged volley, but he counted eight shots, perhaps more—enough, please God, to dissuade the French from charging.

"They've swivel guns in them boats—that's what it is!" spat Armstrong.

Hervey could see nothing, still. "Then we'll be swept away if we press them any more."

"We've got to take one prisoner at least, sir! I can work along the cliff bottom and try and snatch one in the dark."

"I'll come with you." Hervey shouted for Johnson.

"No, sir. You've got to stay here, else these buggers'll take fright. Just keep up a fire to distract them French. Here's your carbine back. I'll only need a pistol butt."

Armstrong, the father-to-be, had lost nothing of his instinct for the charge. Hervey rued what the assignment had become—a desperate, confused contest, hand to hand. Would he always have such a man as Armstrong when it came to this?

CHAPTER 11

THE PEN AND
THE SWORD

Brighton, Next Day

"What the fornicating hell do you *mean*, Captain Hervey? A half troop's horses gone, Strickland's troop's uniforms in tatters, dragoons killed!"

Hervey bit his tongue hard. The preposterous sequence betrayed Lord Towcester's priorities very plainly, the horses and uniforms touching on his pocket, the dragoons of no financial consequence to him. And the death of a revenue officer would not disturb his lordship's thoughts in the slightest. Unless, that is, it might reflect on his own efficiency. But what was his commanding officer's sincerity to Hervey, who stood before him with the blood of that officer and four dragoons on his hands?

"And nothing to show for it—*nothing*! Smugglers escaped with not so much as a flesh wound, *and* with their contraband. So-called owlers disappeared into thin air with their wool—*if* there were any owlers in the first place!"

Hervey had begun to doubt this himself, though he resented intensely the sneer with which it was intimated, the words hissing from Lord Towcester's slitted lips like steam from a kettle's lid.

"Your lordship, I have said that I acted as I saw best."

"Indeed, sir; indeed. You take things upon yourself too freely. It is your Indian ways again. My regiment is at Brighton to guard the Prince Regent. It is not here to chase about after miscreants and Frenchmen. You hanker after the French war, do you, sir? Then why do not you exchange into some Indian regiment and sate your lust for battle there!"

The lieutenant colonel's tirade continued a full five minutes more. Throughout, Hervey remained rigidly at attention, his left hand holding his saber scabbard, his shako under his right arm. Never—*ever*—had he been bareheaded on parade before. In all the times as a cornet and lieutenant that he had found himself answering for some indiscretion or misjudgment, he had never suffered the indignity of being ordered to remove his headdress. Truly it was an effective device for belittling a man—for *humiliating* him, indeed—for it took away his surety, his sense of being an *entire* soldier. Hervey listened to the acid stream of denunciation, self-pity, and threat with a growing feeling of hopelessness. Nothing he had done before, and certainly nothing he might say, could mitigate his delinquency in the eyes of the Earl of Towcester. What *power* did a commanding officer of cavalry possess, for good or evil. It was a power that Hervey believed he would never now possess for himself, whatever the Earl of Sussex's aspirations. How right Henrietta had been to urge caution on him, though last night's events made that caution seem at once worthless.

"Well, Captain Hervey," concluded Lord Towcester, waving a hand in airy dismissal. "There shall be an inquiry, and thereafter, I have no doubt, a court-martial. And, if you are fortunate enough to escape a cashiering, I myself shall require you to resign your commission at once. And so you may as well begin now to find an Indian regiment with fewer scruples than it has officers. You will hand your sword to the adjutant and you will dismiss, sir."

As bad as the lieutenant colonel's invective had been, Hervey had not expected this last. His mouth fell open, and his fingers could hardly work to unfasten the sword belt. When the surrender was done, he bowed, turned to his right, made himself count "Two, three," slowly so as not to be thought of as bolting, and marched from the room.

Outside he replaced his shako and pulled his gloves tight. He saw, or thought he saw, the clerks and orderlies glance his way, to where his sword had hung. What was their regard of him now? Was he the cause of death of their fellow dragoons, or was he merely a curiosity—an officer, an Olympian, cut down, reduced, perhaps to a level below even their own? He walked from the headquarters—a hotel improvised in the manner

Lord Towcester considered fitting for the Prince Regent's escort—not knowing whether he would turn right or left. It did not matter now, for he neither commanded a troop nor had leave to be about the regimental lines. He ought to confine himself to the mess by rights, but he did not suppose that even Lord Towcester would insist on this punctilio. All he could do was go to his own quarters, the little rented villa off North Street, and explain things as best he could to Henrietta when she returned from London that evening. And then he must trust to the due process of military law.

A hand grasped his forearm. "Come on, sir," said Serjeant Armstrong. Hervey made no reply, content to follow.

He walked as if in a dream, past the regent's pavilion and on towards the maze of streets beyond. He saw faces, rich and poor alike, that seemed different from only a day before—the faces of men and women for whom the future might look bleak, but which was nevertheless a future without dishonor. And how he envied the poorest of them that.

"Serjeant Armstrong," he sighed as they turned in to a street of alehouses, "I don't think that drink—"

"No, sir. Not one of these. Just gan on a wee bit farther."

Hervey had come to find Armstrong's Tyneside as reassuring as he used to think of Serjeant Strange's Suffolk, though more years must pass before ever he could trust to judgment as wise as Serjeant Strange's.

Armstrong now stopped by a coffeehouse, and nodded to inside.

"Aye, it'll do very well," said Hervey gratefully, just managing a smile.

It seemed an unusual sort of place for Armstrong, but once inside, the connection was revealed. "Caithlin! Mrs. Armstrong!" Hervey had not seen her in a month and more. "What do you do here?"

"She came from Hounslow last week," explained her husband. "We've a room upstairs in exchange."

Hervey was suddenly agitated on account of her condition, but could not find the words even to congratulate her on it.

"Take a seat, Captain Hervey," she said with a smile that had lost nothing of its warmth, for all the incivilities she had abided these past months.

As Hervey and his serjeant settled at a table in the seclusion of a window bay, Caithlin Armstrong went to bring them coffee. It was a respectable enough occupation for a serjeant's wife, for the habitués of this place were solid citizenry, but Hervey could not help thinking of all that learning put to naught. She had more than half the fashionables who promenaded about the Regent's pavilion possessed, yet it would remain closeted because of *its* origin and hers, for her learning was of the hedgerow schools, and her Latin of the Vulgate rather than the *Aeneid*.

"Does Caithlin know of last night?"

"She does not."

"Then you shall have to tell her soon."

"I could just wait for the news to pass by the usual means."

Hervey sighed. "I fancy this is not an event to be retailed by the canteen route."

Armstrong lit his pipe. "I wouldn't be too sure. The canteen often as not gets things in a proper light. It gets the truth from below as well as above—if you know what I mean."

"I know exactly what you mean." Hervey thought for a moment. "And I counsel you to have a great care. This business will bring down many more than just me."

"You ain't done yet, sir!" said Armstrong with a shrug.

"Perhaps I deserve to be, Serjeant Armstrong. Perhaps if I'd waited for the guide—"

"Aw, come on, sir. That's not how we were taught. Major Edmonds would've tongue-lashed anybody if they'd ever said they were waiting for *orders,* let alone a guide!"

It was true enough. "But I went at the beach too baldheaded."

"We'd lost too much time. We couldn't've stalked it."

Armstrong's eye was what every officer wanted in his serjeant—and more. "But the lights, Serjeant Armstrong, the lights."

Armstrong made to spit, and then thought better of it. "What about the lights?"

"Where would any sentry be posted?"

Armstrong didn't have to be pressed. "That was unlucky. A few seconds more and we'd have had the advantage. And that first ball to fell the revenue man like that—it was the devil's own."

"I was still too slow."

"Look, sir, yon was a cannily posted sentry. In any case, we stood our ground and they had to abandon theirs."

Hervey knew it. But in the end, as Lord Towcester had contemptuously pointed out, all they had succeeded in doing was scattering the woolpacks and sending the French back into the Channel. They were not in possession of a single bit of contraband, wet or dry, nor any of its handlers, two of his dragoons were dead, and another three might join them by the day's end.

"Finch'll live, sir, never fear."

Hervey smiled at the prospect. "You know, I believe he was more afraid of being left on that beach than he was at Corunna."

Armstrong relit his pipe. "Dying in the dark like that—they're all afeard of it. What's it they say? There're no atheists at night with a muzzle jammed their way!"

"Thank God that Hill and Greenwood were single men."

"But they'd mothers, like as not."

It seemed perverse to wish instead that, like Johnson, they were sons of the orphanage. Yet Johnson had told him many times that he could never be a soldier with a mother anguishing for him.

Caithlin placed a pot of coffee in front of them. "Who had mothers?"

"None of *our* troop!" replied her husband, with a smirk.

"Jack Armstrong!" She put her hand to her breast.

"Just a manner of speaking, love." He looked, indeed, a shade chastened. "Sit down a minute, lass."

"Only a minute, mind."

They drew up a chair for her.

Hervey lost no time recounting events. By the end, he felt immeasurably better, for the honest company of the Armstrongs was the best of antidotes to Lord Towcester's spite.

Henrietta returned some hours earlier than expected. She looked troubled as her husband came into her sitting room, and she did not rise to greet him. "Princess Charlotte is unwell," she sighed, inclining her cheek to him as he bent to kiss her.

Hervey was sorry to hear it, of course, but it seemed strange that this should bring such gloom. "What is the cause?"

Henrietta looked at him, surprised. "Matthew, she is eight months with child!"

"But how is she troubled?"

"She has had two miscarriages, you know."

Hervey did not know.

"And she grew very large in the summer, so that Sir Richard Croft had to restrict her diet severely, and draw off blood each day. And I think this has greatly depressed her spirits, for she spoke very freely of her fears."

"You saw her?"

"Only briefly. She had asked me to take tea, along with several others, but then Sir Richard insisted on bleeding her again."

Henrietta had herself engaged Sir Richard Croft to obstetricate, for he was acknowledged as preeminent in that field, as indeed should the physician be who was to deliver the king's first great-grandchild.

"The princess is in the best of hands," Hervey pointed out.

"But ultimately she is in God's hands," sighed Henrietta. "And He may have designs that are unfathomable."

Hervey could not gainsay it, but he saw no profit in contemplating the melancholy fact. He moved his chair closer and took her hand. She smiled at him a little thinly, but even her anxiety could not dull the blush that had come in this third month of her own pregnancy. She had not yet any swelling that he observed, except he fancied in her bosom, and her hair shone like a stallion's coat. He had never imagined that her attraction to him could increase so.

They kissed long, and in doing so she seemed to forget her disquiet, and he his own troubles. Why might they not forget them a little longer? He rang for Hanks and said they would not dine, and that her ladyship's maid might be dismissed for the evening.

The next morning, Henrietta's spirits seemed largely restored, so Hervey hazarded to tell her of the events of the beach, and Lord Towcester's reaction. She comprehended everything at once—the extent and implications, the limitations and possibilities—and at once she resolved to act. She had extricated Hervey from arrest, in Ireland when his excess of conscience and zeal had provoked a jealous authority, and she saw no reason why she should not do the same now. To Henrietta, indeed, the exercise of influence was but a normal part of life. She had friends and she had artfulness, and the deployment of both for the good of her husband was entirely proper to her. True, she had been expecting to use her connections for his advancement rather than for his rescuing, but it was of no matter: the methods were essentially the same.

Hervey was brightened by her spirits. They had, indeed, been restored in the intimacy of their embraces the night before, but that she should be so buoyant now after hearing of his miserable condition seemed remarkable. Princess Charlotte was not mentioned once throughout their breakfast.

"Shall you rest today, or do we go for a drive?" he asked, quite care-free, indeed. "I have no duties to detain me." A dragoon without his sword—he did not count for anything.

"A drive? Perhaps. Later, though, for I've letters to write, and I should not put them off."

He poured himself more coffee, and then Hanks brought in the *Morning Herald,* and a letter for Henrietta from Longleat. While she looked over its contents—local news of a general kind from Lady Bath—he turned the *Herald*'s pages. One report caught his eye at once:

We learn of a very serious Breach of the King's Peace in the County of Sussex two nights last, wherein there took place a desperate clash of arms between His Majesty's forces and a *descente* of French smugglers, of whom some sources have it that their numbers were close on a hundred. A running fight with as many of His Majesty's dragoons has left a score of dead on both sides.

Hervey sighed. The scribbler's art could ennoble the meanest affair.

"What is it, my love?" asked Henrietta, the first two pages of her own news not detaining her long.

He read it to her.

"It sounds . . . heroic."

He smiled ruefully. "There were neither a hundred Frenchmen nor a hundred dragoons—though there should have been."

She smiled by return. "Matthew, my love, if someone wants to say there were a hundred Frenchmen opposed to you, then I should not be in any great hurry to disabuse them!"

He smiled again. "No, perhaps not."

"What does *The Times* say?"

"We do not appear to have it."

"Then we shall have to wait to see if they have any advance on a hundred!"

Henrietta's self-possession seemed remarkable. She seemed not the least anxious of her own situation in connection with her husband's. Hervey was about to make some endearment when Hanks entered again and announced that Private Johnson wished urgently to see him. Henrietta nodded, and Hervey bid him show him in.

Johnson was in best dress (he would explain that it was the surest way of being allowed to pass by the town patrols, who assumed him to be on official business). "Good morning, your ladyship, ma'am. Good morning,

Cap'n 'Ervey, sir. I thought you'd be wanting t'know that we've got all t'orses back, 'Arkaway an' all!"

Hervey was astonished. "How in heaven's name—"

"They'd all run east, and down into that valley that 'as that river."

"The Winterbourne?"

"Aye, sir. That's why Cap'n Strickland's troop couldn't see 'ide nor 'air of 'em from t'turnpike."

"And who found them?"

Johnson smiled even broader. "They all came in to Ovingdean trottin' behind t'Dover stage yesterday morning—still saddled. T'livery there caught 'em all."

This was good news indeed. And it would draw the sting as far as Lord Towcester was concerned—somewhat, at least. "Where's Harkaway now?"

"Back in 'is stall, right as a trivet."

"But with one more leg?"

Johnson smiled. "I'm glad yer not too out of sorts, then, Cap'n 'Ervey!"

Henrietta smiled, too. "I shall go to my sitting room to finish my letter, and you may talk all morning of corralling horses. I shall ask Hanks to bring more coffee."

When she had gone, Hervey bid Johnson sit at the table and tell him what other news there was.

"Not a lot, sir. Cap'n Strickland is in arrest, too, though."

"Not a *lot*? Just another troop leader arrested?"

Johnson frowned. "I thought you meant news in t'troop."

It was always well to remember the difference. A private man thought little beyond his own troop. "*Any* news, man!"

"Crowner's quest on Greenwood an 'Ill today."

"Is it, indeed? That is very prompt. Where?"

"I think they said it were at t'assembly rooms."

"At what time?"

"Twelve, I think. Are you going to go, sir?"

"Most certainly! I can't think why I've not been called to give evidence."

Johnson looked thoughtful. "Are you sure y'*ought* to be gooin'?"

"Just pretend you never heard me say it. What other news?"

"There's been a man from t'*Times* sniffin' round since yesterday mornin', but nobody's said owt as far as I know. But 'e's buying drink and offering money. It won't be long before some blabberer falls for it."

"And what might he say, Johnson?" Hervey had the distinct sense that his groom felt there was something to withhold.

"Anything 'e wants to 'ear. That there were two hundred Frenchies, led by Bonaparte himself!"

"So you don't mean that some might say we were wandering about the downs like lost Jews?" Hervey's concern for the good opinion of the canteen was genuine, as well as for the mischief the opposite opinion could make.

Johnson shrugged. "I've been lost in worse places. Isn't that what 'appens in t'dark?"

"Not if you're an officer," smiled Hervey wryly.

"But at least y'knew where y'was gooin'. I've known some officers as didn't even know that!"

Johnson was ever frank. It was one of the reasons he was still a private—and one of the reasons he was still Hervey's groom. "And is there anything else?"

"Oh, aye, there is: t'RM asks if you'd like to 'elp 'im wi' a new 'orse 'e's just bought. Up on t'downs, away from things."

Hervey was touched, for the riding master's invitation to schooling sounded like a message of support. "Please tell Mr. Broad that I should like to very much. And do you think you might look out some clothes for the inquest meanwhile?"

"Aye, right you are, then, sir."

Johnson left through the door that Henrietta opened. She smiled at him, as she always did, and then turned to her husband with a look of some distress. "Matthew, have you not received any word from Wiltshire of late?"

"No. Is there something wrong?"

"Lady Bath writes that your father is to be summoned before the consistory court."

Hervey's heart sank again. "But all that was finished. He made his peace with the archdeacon months ago."

She raised an eyebrow. "Evidently it was not a lasting peace."

"There is no mistake? I've heard nothing from Elizabeth, and she for certain would have written."

"There is no mistake, Matthew. Lady Bath gives dates and places—here, read it."

He took the sheet. It read plainly enough. "I'll apply for leave to travel to Horningsham at once." Then he frowned. "I'll not be granted it, of course. I'd better write at once."

The inquest into the deaths of Privates Hill and Greenwood was pleasingly brisk. The coroner was a no-nonsense sort of man who seemed not in the least dismayed by the attention the proceedings had generated, especially the reporters from the London broadsheets who with others of the provincial press filled one of the galleries in the assembly rooms. At the end of a brief deposition by the surviving revenue riding officer, he directed the jury to bring in a verdict of unlawful killing in the case of both dragoons, and adjourned the proceedings without elaboration. In an instant the London and provincial hacks besieged the uniformed observers for some titbit to enliven their day's copy: for once, Hervey was glad to be in plain clothes and apart from his fellows. All the hacks, that is, but *The Times*'s man, who raced from the court to a waiting chaise and made off with great haste to the capital.

Dawn the next morning saw Hervey and his groom on the downs above Brighton. The air had a taste of salt, but he found it invigorating, and with no one as far as the eye could see but the riding master, Lieutenant Broad, and Broad's groom, Hervey could forget his woeful condition for the time being.

Mr. Broad was another extract, but Hervey had taken to him from their first meeting. Broad had been in the ranks of the 1st Dragoons—Lord George Irvine's former regiment—for fifteen years before Lord George had arranged his commissioning into the Sixth after Waterloo. His predecessor as riding master, who had been a rough rider under three RMs, had been diligent but somewhat rigid. And though he had been generally respected, there were some (including Hervey) who thought he had become too averse to new ideas, so that the regiment's equitation, though sound enough, did not rise beyond the commonplace.

Mr. Broad, however, was both his own and a Woodbridge man in the question of the riding school. He had surprised some in the Sixth by his assertion that each horse and each rider was an individual, and that it was his duty as RM to bring on both *as* individuals, yet for the common task of the regiment. These were progressive views indeed, and Hervey had wondered at first how well the RM's own staff took to them. The answer, he had soon learned, was *well*, for when he had first visited riding school on returning to the regiment, it was evident how quickly the recruits absorbed their instruction. Broad must therefore have been as sympathetic with his rough riders as he was with his other charges, for they it was who had the close care of "the babies."

But Broad was not without his detractors. The adjutant, especially, abhorred his system, calling it too comfortable. And since the RM was directly subordinate to the adjutant, there had been many turn-ups.

"You see what I mean, Hervey?" he called from the chestnut blood circling at the trot. "He's just a fraction unlevel. And I can't tell if it's bridle lameness or the real sort."

Hervey watched keenly as the RM schooled the troublesome chestnut. Broad had the lightest hands he had seen in many a year: bridle lameness seemed unlikely with hands such as these, although, there again, it was a very indefinite condition at the best of times.

In five more minutes, Broad rode up to him and dismounted. "I'd like to see him from the ground, if you will. Drive him forwards in a long, low outline. Get him to step under more with his hind limbs to get more impulsion from them, and his back to swing more freely. Then I should be able to tell."

Hervey lengthened the stirrups two holes and, with Johnson's help, lowered himself carefully into the saddle, wishing to judge the horse's temperament by degrees rather than risk shocking him with a spring.

He began with shallow serpentines, changing the diagonal each time for Broad to judge the soundness of the leg. But ten minutes of this revealed nothing.

"Good!" called Broad. "I got nothing either. What do you think?"

"I think there's some resistance in going forwards properly. . . ."

"So did I. Can you start driving him, then?"

It was hard, but Hervey did so for a quarter of an hour, until both he and the horse were sweating prodigiously. Then he brought him back to a walk to let him down. "I really don't think there's chronic unsoundness in this animal. I rather like him, indeed. I just think he's been badly schooled."

"Bravo, Hervey. My sentiments, too. He'll have got butcher's hands at a Tattersalls doer's: they won't give a young horse *time*."

Hervey jumped from the saddle and patted the gelding's neck. "And so?"

"I shall buy him, then. A fortnight of this and he'll have a proper rhythm back. I'll lunge him in a Chambon tomorrow. Would you like to come again the day after?"

"Thank you, Broad," said Hervey warmly as the RM's groom took the reins. "Thank you very much indeed." In the hour he had been there he had not thought of their commanding officer once.

"It's a bad business, Hervey," said Broad abruptly, offering him a cheroot.

Hervey declined it. "*What* is a bad business?"

"Everything. The serjeants aren't happy, nor the corporals."

It was a rude return to regimental matters. Hervey sighed. "An officer is owed loyalty," he replied rather flatly. It was the principle on which they had all been nurtured as cornets. But then it had been easy enough. Hervey's first troop leader had been Joseph Edmonds, his last Sir Edward Lankester. And for the most part the lieutenant colonel had been Lord George Irvine. It was not difficult to be loyal to men like these. "We have to remain faithful, Broad, if for no other reason but that matters will be worse for our dragoons if we do not."

"I know," said the RM, speaking with more than a little experience. "I've seen from below the trouble that's stirred when the officers are unhappy."

"Happy officers, happy regiment?"

"Exactly."

Hervey stopped and turned to him. "What is it you are saying, then?"

"That there has to be some prospect of improvement, else nothing will reverse the ill spirits."

The RM's discretion did him proud, thought Hervey. He—more than the quartermasters, even—would know the minds of the senior ranks. Not that that was supposed to be difficult. Joseph Edmonds used to say that you always knew what your dragoons were saying, and usually what your NCOs were thinking—but the officers, rarely. "You know, Broad, I think we're missing Mr. Lincoln rather more than we might think."

The RSM's long leave of absence was the single most aggravating factor, some were saying. "It would be as well to promote another now," said Broad decidedly.

Hervey frowned. "I can't see how—"

"You don't imagine he'll return to duty, do you?"

"Why on earth would he not? Besides aught else, he surely has hopes of being promoted."

Now the RM frowned. "*Commissioned,* Hervey, not promoted!"

Hervey reddened. No officer commissioned from that August rank ever considered he was *promoted.* "Very well. But I for one would be dismayed if Mr. Lincoln were not back at his post before the year is out. Unless, that is, you know otherwise."

"What I know is that Hopwood's flogging tested his loyalty to the utmost. Lincoln was more opposed to flogging than you could have supposed. The orderly room serjeant overheard the RSM in with the colonel. And all I'll say is that his lordship left him in no doubt that his opinion was of little value."

"Then it was very wrong of the orderly room serjeant to speak of it."

"You're right of course, Hervey. But only up to a point. Who can the orderly room serjeant turn to when he believes his loyalty to the RSM demands some action? You might say that he showed more courage in coming to me than in remaining silent—for he didn't know what my answer was going to be."

Hervey conceded the point. "And what was your answer?"

"I told him he'd discharged his duty to the RSM in telling me, and that he must now discharge his duty to the colonel by telling no one else."

Hervey hoped that he himself would have had the presence of mind to put it thus. "And so you are now telling me."

"Yes, and I shall consider my duty completed in that, too."

Hervey nodded. "But one more thing. Why didn't you speak to the adjutant? He is your proper superior, and it's his duty to advise the colonel."

"Hervey, you ought to know full well that it would have been to no avail whatever—a hollow gesture. I exercised my judgment. Isn't that what an officer's meant to do—use his judgment rather than just carry out orders? Even officers from the ranks."

Hervey thought it devilish unfair that an extract—and from the ranks, at that—should have to make such a judgment. "You didn't consider approaching the major?"

The RM frowned again. "*You,* Hervey, are the senior squadron leader. *And* you've a brevet."

Hervey remained silent for a few moments. "What would you have me do?"

"Nothing, for sure, that would make things worse."

Hervey smiled despairingly. "I think almost anything would make things worse. And what you have quite forgotten is that as long as I'm in arrest my motive in doing anything will be questioned."

The RM did not reply at once, seeming to search for his words. "Hervey, if it comes to a court-martial, you must defend yourself with every ounce of guile you can summon. You must not think of it as a game of cricket."

"My dear Broad, do you truly think that—"

But the RM was in no mood for nicety. "And if things go against you, you must make appeal to Lord Sussex."

The very words "court-martial" chilled Hervey to the marrow. But the threat of it could play no part in his actions respecting Lord Towcester. The RM's counsel was brave. Many in his position would have kept it to themselves. But in the end it gave Hervey no true line to take. He would just have to pray that he could determine what duty demanded—for he knew well enough where it lay.

When Hervey returned to breakfast, he found Henrietta smiling, and with just a suggestion of triumph.

"Do we have good news at last?"

"I think it may be so," she said, smiling even wider. "You will not have seen *The Times,* I think?"

She handed him the paper, folded open to reveal the leading piece.

THREAT TO THE REGENT'S PAVILION

Brighton

We are most reliably informed that Tuesday's affair with the Frenchmen bent on depriving His Majesty's Revenue of their just receipts, and which occasioned the deaths of an officer of the Revenue and two private men of His Majesty's Sixth Light Dragoons, as well as a number more most grievously wounded, was a most desperate contest between the dragoons and upwards of one hundred heavily armed smugglers who greatly outnumbered our brave fellows. The Dragoons, led by their noble and gallant lieutenant colonel, the Earl of Towcester, had ridden through the foulest of weather and the blackest of nights to answer the Revenue's urgent request for assistance. And had it not been for the extraordinary address shown by His Lordship and his gallant officers and men, it is thought that the French might even have despoiled that part of the town of Brighton nearest their landing. We need scarcely add that His Royal Highness's own pavilion residence is within but a short distance, and, though it shall not be our business to provide intelligence of His Royal Highness's comings and goings so as to be of use to malefactors of any nationality, we may say with safety that it is not beyond the bounds of possibility that a most exalted personage might have been taken captive in such an expedition had it not been for the prompt action of the Regiment. We may further say, with the same assurance, that not even in their late campaigning in the Peninsula and at the Battle of Waterloo, have the Sixth Light Dragoons rendered His Majesty and the Nation greater Service, and that we expect confidently to report in due course the honors which must surely be bestowed on the regiment.

"How in heaven's name did such a piece come to be written?" Hervey's tone could not have been more incredulous. "I've never seen such a concoction of falsehoods! 'Inaccuracies' would be too charitable a word. And such speculation!"

"But it serves very well does it not?"

"It serves to make of Lord Towcester a hero, for sure."

"But does it not serve to absolve *you*, Matthew?"

"It may be so, but that is an incidental which hardly makes the fiction worthy."

"Oh, I don't know," said Henrietta, picking up a teapot as an excuse to look away. "But why do you say 'incidental'?" She turned back and lifted her eyelids just enough to catch his gaze.

He was stunned. Surely she could not have had anything to do with such a report?

"Do you really not think it settles things, my darling?" she pressed, looking away to the window again. "Lord Towcester is a hero. He could scarcely make one of his captains a case for court-martial!"

He smiled, very wryly. "I think, very probably . . . *yes*. It does settle things!"

She took back the newspaper, and kissed him.

"You are naught, you are naught," he declared.

She giggled in the wicked way he had provoked. "And you are very poetic. And you have no duties for a little while longer, I imagine. . . ."

CHAPTER 12

TO THE AID OF THE
CIVIL POWERS

Brighton, Three Days Later

Major Eustace Joynson had a sick headache. He had sick headaches often, and his doctor's prescription was always the same. He emptied a small envelope of calomel into a glass of water, watched it dissolve, and then drank it in one go. As a purgative it was admirable. As a counter to pain he could not tell, for although it had no immediate effect, the pain always passed, and so he could never be sure whether it was the white powder or simply time that was efficacious. He recoiled from taking laudanum, since that had rendered his wife to all intents and purposes an invalid—at least, she was no longer fit to be about society. One of his doctors said they might try the new morphium from Leipzig, but he was as yet wary of that. His sick headaches were invariably coincident with periods of demanding activity of the cerebral kind. Indeed, if the major were faced with a disagreeable decision, a sick headache could come on almost at once.

The past three days had not required of him any decision, but they had required unprecedented cerebral activity. First there were the courts-martial. Strickland's was a relatively straightforward affair to arrange, for the evidence was before them all in the shape, or rather the absence of shape—and color—of his troop's best jackets. But in the case of Hervey's court-martial there was the report of the revenue commissioner to await, and so the arrangements could only be tentative. And then had come *The Times*'s resounding praise, and with it a sea change in the lieutenant colonel's disposition, so that all the arrangements for the courts-martial had had to be undone, and hastily. The invitation from the Prince Regent for Lord Towcester to attend on him at once at Carlton House, which had followed within a day of *The Times*'s report, had further lifted the lieutenant colonel's spirits, but it also placed the major in a position of temporary command, and this was not conducive to absence of headaches. So when, this very morning, orders arrived from the Horse Guards to proceed to the north within twenty-four hours, the cerebral consequences for Joynson were unhappy.

"Hervey, I must go and rest—a darkened room. Please would you be so good as to see these orders are put in hand?" He gave him a sheaf of foolscap.

Hervey sat in the major's chair once he was gone, and read over the orders quickly to gain a feel for their substance: "General insurrection is feared in Nottinghamshire and south Yorkshire . . . seditious meetings . . . serious outbreak of violence against machines and property . . . threats made to magistrates and constables . . . Informers suggest traitorous conspiracy. . . . Six troops to reinforce Northern District . . . under direct command of Major General Sir Francis Evans."

He could hardly be surprised, for there had been reports in the broadsheets for the past month, though heavily censored. And, as Daniel Coates had said in his last letter, with habeas corpus still suspended, not even the bountiful harvest they were enjoying was likely to quell the discontent. Six months ago, the yeomanry had been issued with a general order to respond to calls for assistance from the civil authorities, and so Hervey supposed that the yeomen must be exhausted, for to order the "pavilion regiment" north was no small a thing.

He turned to the sheet headed "Regimental Orders." It was blank. What the major had meant when he said "See these orders are put in hand" was "*write* the orders and *then* put them in hand." He sighed. "Where is the adjutant, Serjeant Short?"

The orderly room serjeant said he was in Lewes for the assize dinner.

"Please bring me the standing orders for forced marching, then," said Hervey briskly, beginning to read over the papers again.

"There are none, sir."

"What?"

"None, sir."

"What about the orders that Major Edmonds wrote as we left for Belgium? They were printed and bound when we got to France, were they not?"

"Yes, sir, but his lordship ordered them all destroyed a month ago and said that there was to be a new edition."

"Indeed?"

"Yes, sir. In red morocco."

"Red morocco?" Hervey was about to ask why the old orders should be destroyed before the new ones were ready, but then realized it was not the orderly room serjeant's place to answer. "Very well, then, Serjeant Short—pen and ink please. And a large pot of coffee."

Hervey issued a preliminary order at once, but it took him the better part of two hours to complete those for the march itself. "The rate of progress shall be fifty miles per diem." (It was a fair compromise between speed and handiness on arriving, he reckoned, for they would have to cover a little short of a hundred and fifty miles.) "The first ten miles shall be at the walk, led, a full half hour, then at a steady trot. There shall be a halt of 15 mins. . . . Each horse shall be given water to wash the mouth only and wisp of hay. . . . The next six miles shall be at a fast trot and afterwards a halt of half an hour . . . horses to be unsaddled and rubbed down, and one peck of corn given, and water. . . . A second ten miles, first walk, led, then brisk trot . . . with halt as after first. . . . After next six miles at fast trot shall be a rest of two hours . . . horses to be given hay and feed of corn." (They carried this themselves, and Hervey knew he hardly need detail that the men should eat their haversack rations.) . . . "Then proceed ten miles and halt as the first, followed by last eight without halt. . . . At night billets a warm mash, with beans if weather foul, before evening feed . . . allowance per diem fourteen pounds of hay and twelve of oats, barley, or Indian corn. . . ." He made a separate schedule for the order of march, the times of departure, and the night stops—Uxbridge, Northampton, Nottingham itself. And then he made a start on the directions for carrying camp equipment. . . .

At length, pleased with his improvisation, he gave the sheaf of papers to the orderly room serjeant for copying and went to find his groom. It was now close on midday and the stables were quiet, Harkaway and Gilbert contentedly grinding corn in their loose boxes, but there was no sign of Private Johnson. His troop lieutenant's groom emerged from the hayloft. "Oh, good morning, Lingard," said Hervey, a little surprised, for he knew Seton Canning to be away to Lewes with the assizes still. "Have you seen Johnson?"

Private Lingard looked puzzled. "He's not here, sir."

"Yes," scowled Hervey. "I can see that. Do you know where he is?"

Lingard now looked distinctly uncomfortable. "I don't, rightly, sir."

Hervey sighed. "Lingard, what is the matter?"

"Nothing, sir."

This was evasion, by any measure. "Come, man! I've known you long enough to tell when you're not saying all."

Lingard had no option but to comply. "Sir, he's at riding school."

"Riding school?" Johnson had dismissed riding school for many a year. "Would you explain, Lingard? This is becoming a *little* tedious."

Lingard seemed embarrassed. "Sir, he's learning how to ride side-saddle."

Hervey made a chortling noise.

"Exactly, sir."

Johnson's devotion to Henrietta had plainly taken an unusual turn. "Very well, Lingard," sighed Hervey, struggling hard not to laugh. "Perhaps you would be so good as to ask Private Johnson to come to my quarters after evening stables—if by then he is still of a mind for soldiery. There are things to do. You've heard we're for the North?"

"No, I hadn't, sir. I'm only just back from Lewes. You mean *you* are going north, sir?"

"The whole regiment."

"We're leaving Brighton, sir?" Lingard sounded pleased.

"For a while, yes." Hervey gave Harkaway another favor, and then Gilbert. "Isn't Brighton to your liking?"

"Too much spit and polishing, sir. The best of it was the other night against the French. I wish I'd been there."

It was a strange thing with dragoons, Hervey marveled. They were like their horses. They spent their hours in the stable wishing to be out, and then once they were out they were only too keen to make straight back in. He only hoped the news would be greeted as well in the officers' mess, though in truth he knew it would not. George "Beau" Brummell may have been striking a pose when, the Tenth having been ordered to Manchester all those years ago, he protested that he had not enlisted for foreign service, but Brummell's sentiments were prevalent in the cavalry still.

Outside the stables he found Serjeant Armstrong in heated contest with the farrier corporal, except that the corporal was now silent. "I don't care which one of your men did this," came the raw Tyneside. "If ever I find a dumped foot in this troop again, I'll charge *you*—with negligence."

Armstrong was evidently relishing his duty as serjeant major during Kendall's convalescence (Kendall's dyspeptic ulcer was almost as troublesome as Joynson's sick headaches). And why should he not, thought Hervey, for Armstrong had been fitted enough for it innumerable times in the Peninsula? "Do you know where Johnson is?" he asked, when the farrier corporal had gone.

"He wasn't at watering parade, so I thought he was with you."

"No."

Armstrong's eyes narrowed, suggesting a frown beneath his shako. "That's rum. He's never slipped his collar before now."

"It's nothing to worry about." Hervey suddenly thought better of revealing Johnson's change of seat. "What do you make of the orders?"

"Glad of 'em. This place is getting stale. But I'm not much taken with police work, especially after the other night. I just hope we're not going to be buggered about by a lot of fuzzled justices!"

"I know, I know." Hervey paused to return the orderly corporal's salute, on his way to guard mounting. "How are things going?"

"Fine. We'll be ready all right. Just another half dozen to shoe."

"Any news of the serjeant major?"

"Still on gruel. Not even light duties for another week." Armstrong sounded content enough.

Hervey huffed, and looked embarrassed. "It's an ill wind. . . ."

"I didn't join the Sixth for foreign service either, Hervey!" Captain Rose blew cigar smoke ceilingwards. There were muttered "Here, heres" all about the anteroom.

"Leicestershire is adjoining country, Rose; look at it that way!"

"The place is full of mine shafts, isn't it? And forest? Trappy country to follow hounds in, I'd say."

The slight inclination of F Troop leader's eyebrows told Hervey that his objections were not entirely flippant. "It might make for interesting sport, though," he countered, warming to the imagery. "We should see hounds working, rather than just galloping with a big field."

Rose shook his head doubtfully. "But these northern foxes'll bolt straight back to the woods, or wherever. You'll lose hounds left, right, and center going in after 'em."

"I grant you we'll not have anything like the runs we'd have in Leicestershire, but we'll just have to go at our fox a different way."

"Meaning?"

"Stop up the earths, for sure. And terriers for if they do manage to run to earth. Perhaps we'll have to hunt as we do for cubs—drive Charles *back* onto hounds."

Rose smiled, still skeptical. "We'll see, Hervey. But I still say I haven't paid good money to hunt poor country!"

During this somewhat elliptical exchange, Hervey had begun to realize that his authority as the senior troop leader, although a matter only of days and pounds, was being accepted with some grace by the other officers. Hervey had already learned that no one expected the report from the revenue officer, when it came, to point a single finger of blame at his handling of events. In the passage of remarkably little time he had gone from dejection to . . . if hardly triumph, then certainly encouragement. The vexation was that the bubble reputation was not to be had in the cannon's mouth any longer but in the columns of *The Times*—and not by his own feats but by the guile of his wife.

Henrietta was surprised to see him return so early, and dismayed to learn the reason why. "I will not stay here in Brighton," she declared.

"My love, the very last thing I would wish is to be parted from you another night, but my father would welcome some encouragement at this time, and—"

She looked even more unhappy. "Matthew, if you say that I am to go to Wiltshire, then I will. Of course I will. But my thought was to come with you."

He could not have been happier with any notion. "But how shall you stand the journey? And it is not London. What lodgings shall we be able to find?"

"Oh," she laughed, "I can stand the journey perfectly well. And we can stay at Chatsworth. William Devonshire has said often enough that he hoped to meet you again."

"I shan't be able to stay there, not with my troop elsewhere," he cautioned. Then he brightened. "But I'm sure there will be opportunities to visit. It can't be many miles."

"May we travel together, then?"

The prospect of her company, and one of the best-sprung chaises he had known, was a great temptation. "I can't, I'm afraid, my love. Nor is it just the troop. Joynson will have a sick headache, like as not, and Lord Towcester won't join until Nottingham. The responsibility will be mine to see the regiment there."

"But I may travel *with* you, may I not?"

"Yes, of course. Though we shall be a little slow. You are sure you are up to so long a drive?"

"*Yes,* Matthew. I should be able to *ride* to Chatsworth if I really wanted to!"

It minded him to tease her about Johnson, but he was so full of admiration for her spirit that he could only sit and enjoy her delighted expression. He knew how much the trials of Princess Charlotte's confinement were troubling her, for the newspaper reports were more lurid by the day; she must inevitably make comparisons with her own condition, however inapt that might be.

Three days later, they were in Nottingham, and the troop returns were better than any of the captains could remember after such a distance—testimony to a sound march plan, good discipline on the part of the NCOs, and the quality of the regiment's horses. This latter was freely acknowledged by all ranks, and Lord Towcester's name was heard spoken of with increasing respect again. They had gone 157 miles in three days at a cost of only two horses dead—both from colic on the first night—and nine lame. As remarkably, there were no horses off the road with sore backs, an admirable pointer to both discipline and skill. The price was a fair number of limping dragoons, but, as their corporals were only too happy to point out, blisters on the feet were no hindrance in the saddle.

And still the regiment was Hervey's, for Major Joynson would not be fit to travel for some days yet, it seemed, and Lord Towcester had yet to arrive. They had had word from Carlton House that he would set out as soon as the Prince Regent decided to detain him no longer. Meanwhile, therefore, Hervey had to present himself to the general officer commanding.

Major General Sir Francis Evans, GOC Northern District, had established his temporary headquarters in Nottingham Castle. Of all the country's military districts, the northern was the most exigent. It had been so indeed since Trafalgar, after which there had been no longer any threat of invasion. The district ran from the Scottish border, through the northeastern coalfields, taking in the counties of Yorkshire, Lancashire, Nottinghamshire, and Leicestershire. The headquarters were at York as a rule, but the hotbed of trouble in his district at this time was undoubtedly Nottinghamshire, and General Evans was not a man to sit distant and aloof. But he was as crabbed as his reputation had it, and this morning he was belaboring a clerk for the scratchy signatures the man's pen was making, as Hervey entered his office. His right ear, turned forward so much that the troops called him General Tab, was almost as red as his tunic, and the redness of Sir Francis Evans's ear, Hervey had been warned, was a sure indicator of his temper.

"Captain Hervey, Sir Francis," said the DAAG, beckoning the clerk away. "Sixth Light Dragoons."

Hervey stepped quickly to the general's desk, halted, and saluted. "Good morning, sir."

"Are you the adjutant? When does the regiment arrive?" said Sir Francis gruffly.

"I am not the adjutant, sir. I am the senior troop leader, and I am pleased to report the arrival of six troops: three hundred and eighty-one effectives."

Sir Francis's ear grew even redder. "Where in hell's name is your colonel?"

Hervey was pleased to have been warned of Sir Francis's choler, though the warning did not entirely ease its sting. "He was summoned by the Prince Regent, Sir Francis. I am given to understand that he will be making his way here at any time." He hoped this was not too blatant a distortion of his latest intelligence.

"And where is the major, then?"

"He is sick, sir. He will follow from Brighton in a very few days, I am sure."

"Mm. I see. This is not a very satisfactory beginning."

"The troops are all well found and officered, sir." Hervey felt he was speaking up as much for the Sixth as for his colonel.

"Yes, but that is all very well, Captain Hervey. I must have a field officer here in Nottingham. The troops themselves I intend disposing throughout the county at the immediate call of the bench."

"Very well, sir. I shall take the orders from your DAAG, and hold myself here until Lord Towcester arrives. I trust that he will not be long." He braced up for the dismissal. It did not come.

Sir Francis Evans seemed to be eyeing him suspiciously. "*Hervey* . . . I have some recollection of that name."

Hervey could not think how, for they had never, so far as he knew, seen the same campaign. "I have always been with the Sixth, sir, except last year in India."

Sir Francis nodded. "I thought as much. You are brevet major, are you not?"

Hervey was as flattered by the recognition as he was astounded, and tried hard to hide both. "Yes, sir."

"Mm. Sit yourself down." He turned to his DAAG. "Bring us some coffee, Harry, there's a good fellow." Sir Francis's ear had regained its normal color. He leaned back in his chair, studying his temporary commander of cavalry, his chin disappearing beneath the standing collar of his tunic. "The duke thinks highly of you, as I recall."

Hervey was not sure if this was meant to be rhetorical, but the silence demanded some response. "Thank you, sir. I was in India on his bidding."

There was just the suggestion of a smile on Sir Francis's lips. "Then I fancy I might repose in you myself."

Hervey was not going to presume to sport with the general, even with such an invitation. The arrival of coffee was opportune. "Sir."

"To begin with, Hervey—and let it be rightly understood—there is no glory for you or your dragoons in aid of the civil power. There'll be no charging hither and thither, no flashy sword work."

Hervey had little enough experience of the application of that duty, beyond the squalid business of west Cork, yet he knew enough to be in no doubt as to its nature. "Indeed, sir. And I know I may speak for the whole regiment in this. The dragoons are glad of the change from Hounslow and Brighton, but they have a great repugnance for riot duty. We lost an officer killed last March in London."

Sir Francis nodded. "It is the most terrible thing to fire on one's own countrymen, however grave the provocation."

Hervey assented silently.

Sir Francis narrowed his eyes and looked keenly at him. "Yet there can be no shirking from duty, Captain Hervey. It shall have to be done at all hazards."

"I know it, sir," replied Hervey, with a tone of both regret and resolve which together seemed to reassure the GOC.

Sir Francis now appeared to take his ease entirely. He poured himself and Hervey more coffee, offered him a cheroot, which Hervey declined, though he would ordinarily have enjoyed its taste with his araba, and lit one for himself. It seemed that Sir Francis rather liked this young cavalryman: perhaps because Hervey had shown no trepidation in facing him (he knew his own reputation well enough), and for his general air of assurance. It was not every captain, in his experience, who would look forward to his duties—overmatched as they were for his rank—and with such equanimity. Sir Francis now recalled the brevet committee better. He had opposed Hervey's cause in the first instance, thinking him nothing more than another Waterloo hand. He recalled how Sir Horace Shawcross had pressed his case admirably, believing him to have special merit, and it was looking as though Sir Horace had been right. It was not the pleasure of a GOC to be able to talk confidingly with many men—sadly—and Sir Francis Evans did not intend letting an opportunity pass. "Let me tell you something of the genesis of all this, Hervey, and then you might be set more favorably to do the king's business. What do you know of the secret parliamentary committees—the January committees?"

Hervey was perplexed. If they were secret, how should he know *any-thing* of them? "I was not in England in January, sir, and I have not heard of them since."

"Too many have," tutted Sir Francis. "*And* what they reported. You know, of course, that habeas corpus is suspended?"

"Yes, sir."

"And that special legislation has been enacted to prevent the holding of what are deemed seditious meetings?"

He did not know.

"The committees found there to be overwhelming evidence of a traitorous conspiracy to overthrow the government—a general insurrection, indeed. And these two measures are the fruits of that inquiry. Bitter fruits they are, too."

Hervey intended making the most of the intimacy. "Do the magistrates exercise the powers aptly, sir?" His memory of the Cork magistracy was still painful.

"Depends whether they're Whig or Tory, or, for that matter, town or county. The Tory bench is a violent one on the whole—uncompromising . . . and damned irritating. But I will say they are bold. The Whigs on the other hand are a sneaking, base lot—always quick to call for troops, yet trucking with the mob. The county magistrates are a miserable set generally. They insult the people and grow frightened at every alarm. Those of the towns have a little more pluck, but the county ones bully them, inoculate them with their own fears, and then they pour in calls for troops. You'll have no very great love of them. But remember this: when you have gone back to Brighton, they must remain here, and with no protection but the parish constable and the shutters on their windows."

"No, of course, sir." Hervey had never envied the magistrates. He only was dismayed at their want of understanding and, it might be said, often enough their coldheartedness.

"Well, now, understand that my object in all this is to tranquilize the situation as much as possible. It has been my habit to meet with the magistrates weekly in the most troubled areas to impress on them, more than anything, that they must not interfere with the basic rights of the crowds to assemble, for not every such assembly is by any means seditious. If, of course, the orator is preaching arson, murder, or treason then he must be arrested as soon as the crowd is dispersed. But galling though it may be, I am very much afraid that it is better to let him finish his tirade than try to get to arrest him by pushing through the crowd, for that way spells only misadventure."

Hervey nodded. The affair of Skinner Street had been a salutary lesson.

"I am myself, as a rule, chary of using cavalry, for they cannot do much other than bully a crowd—though I'd rather have a crowd chopped a little than destroyed with firearms. The trouble is, in a town they're too easily assailed from above, and with impunity. Slates, coping stones—they'll hurl anything. You shall have to drill your dragoons to dismount as infantry, Hervey, else they'll be no use in some of these places. They'll have to be able to get aloft."

Hervey understood.

"Now, billeting. It's the very devil of a business always. You must keep your troops together. These towns have big enough places of one sort or another. In one or two there are barracks, even, or else farms nearby."

Hervey took careful note.

"And the yeomanry: have a care. To my mind they're overzealous for cutting and slashing. And they're tired, too. They've been out the best part of the spring and summer. As for the militia, I pray God we never become so desperate as to have to call *them* out, for I could never count on them. They'd throw in their lot with the mob too easily. You won't remember Devizes—it was hushed up right and proper."

"I am from those parts, sir. I heard of it."

"Well and good, then. The last thing we need is a battalion of militia mutinying."

Hervey made a note in his pocketbook to learn the whereabouts of the militia armories.

The DAAG came in. "Excuse me, Sir Francis, but you have your call on the lord lieutenant at eleven-thirty."

The GOC looked at his watch and made to leave. "Very well, Captain Hervey, you have my general intention. My staff will give you the details. Be so good as to inform your colonel of it when he resumes command, and ask him to call on me at the first opportunity." He held out his hand. "I have enjoyed making your acquaintance, sir. Good day to you."

Hervey took his hand before replacing his forage cap and saluting. The general's company had been an uncommon stimulant.

It was agreed that the regiment would rest for the day and that night in Nottingham before dispersing to their appointed towns. B Troop would march thence to Newark, fifteen miles to the northeast, C to Mansfield, about the same distance to the north, D to Worksop, ten miles farther on, E to Retford, some eight miles to the east of Worksop, and F would be the reserve at Ollerton, centrally placed between the others. A would remain in Nottingham, so that Hervey might have its command as well as the regiment's for the day or so before he expected Lord Towcester to arrive. This was not an easy decision. Hervey had no qualms about continuing to stand duty for the lieutenant colonel, and, indeed, without his lordship's intemperance the regiment would be very much the happier, but it meant that he would then remain in his closest proximity, and that could only bring greater distress. But Hervey had also to hope for Lord Towcester's early return, for Sir Francis Evans's notorious temper would be sorely provoked by the prolonged absence of the Sixth's commanding officer. He called a meeting of the troop leaders at three o'clock in the White Hart Hotel, where the officers would mess for the night, and then went to see how were his chargers.

Gilbert had been warranted a good doer by the Trowbridge coper, and so he had proved to be in the weeks at Hounslow and Brighton. All the same, Hervey was surprised by how well he looked—better than many a horse he'd seen after a day's hard hunting. The big gray turned from the hay rack as Hervey came into the White Hart's stables, and began to stale. The urine's color was no different from usual, and Hervey's nose smarted at the pungent smell, the same sal ammoniac as his old governess's reviving salts. He could leave the gelding to himself in that big stall, where, no doubt, he would be stretched out on the fine straw bed before the hour was out.

Harkaway, however, had lost condition. He stood tucked up, ignoring the hay—a sorry sight, indeed. Perhaps he had not had enough time to become fit again after being turned away for so long, although he had had slow, progressive work of late, and had seemed as fit as any trooper before the march. "What do you think, Johnson?" asked Hervey.

Johnson evidently had already been thinking. "I reckon we'd better physic 'im."

Hervey sighed. He was probably right, and yet Selden, their former veterinarian, whose opinions were held in high regard still, had foresworn routine physicking as much as bleeding. "Leave him another hour or so, but keep a sharp eye out, and if he's any worse get Mr. Gascoyne to look at him, and call me."

"Right, sir. I'll try and tempt 'im with a mash meantime."

Hervey nodded, as Johnson put the blanket back on Harkaway. The gelding scarcely moved as he fastened the surcingle.

"We can't be very far from your parts now, can we?" said Hervey, as Johnson ducked under the stall bar. "A day's march?"

"Aye, easy."

"Would you like leave to go there if things quieten down?"

Johnson shook his head. "I've no crave to go to Sheffield again, Cap'n 'Ervey. It's a mucky place."

"You wouldn't want to see anyone?"

"Who? They were decent enough folk, them as ran t'work'ouse, but they'd be long gone. An' I can't very well walk t'streets all day on t'off chance o' seein' somebody."

Hervey thought it better to let the matter rest.

At three o'clock the troop leaders assembled in the dining room of the White Hart. It was a room of some refinement, with a woven carpet and little oak, but the White Hart was undoubtedly a provincial hotel, only a fraction more elegant than a posting inn. It was, however, as serviceable a headquarters as they might find. The orderly room serjeant began distributing maps—a good start, they all agreed, for the absence of maps was the normal feature of the commencement of a campaign. And what maps these *were*: not the old county charts, or the coach cards which showed only the landmarks along a road, but the new inch-to-a-mile Ordnance Survey—detailed, accurate, and with the novel system of contour lines which gave a picture of the lie of the land. Hervey had asked for enough to give each troop a full set for the county, and a local sheet for every officer. From these he expected the NCOs to make sketches so they could familiarize themselves with the neighborhoods as quickly as possible. It was a promising start indeed.

At the end of the conference, too, there seemed to be a very fair degree of contentment. Barrow went so far as to say that if this were foreign service he wished they might see it more often, though Rose declared that, for his part, the weather in these latitudes was already taking its toll of his humors. But it was happy banter, and the captains fell out to their troops in good spirits, and looking forward to their meeting together again to dine that evening.

Shortly before midnight, when the contented diners were dispersed, if not actually retired, Lord Towcester arrived from London. The adjutant told him of the plans that had been put in hand, and the lieutenant colonel at once exploded with rage. Why was his regiment broken up in this way, he demanded? Why had the dispositions been made so? Who had presumed to choose which troop would go where? He sent for Hervey.

"What in the name of God do you think you do, sir?" bawled Lord Towcester as Hervey came to his quarters—so loud indeed that the whole of the White Hart must have heard.

Hervey explained, in as composed a manner imaginable, that the GOC had stated his intention, and that the consequent troop dispositions were all approved by him.

"Then you should have represented to the general officer commanding, in the strongest terms, that the dispersal of cavalry is contrary to the practice of war!"

Hervey was now thoroughly on the alert, for the lieutenant colonel's response was as irrational as it was hostile. They were no more at war than they had been in Ireland. "Your lordship, the general believes that the deployment of a troop to each town will of itself discourage trouble, and at the same time permit rapid reinforcement."

"Well, I do not, sir! It will inflame the population, that is all. And then we shall have trouble everywhere. Who decided which troop should go where?"

"I did, sir. There is little to choose between the towns, so far as the general is aware."

"And you placed yourself here in Nottingham?"

"Yes, your lordship." The inflection suggested he was puzzled.

"You chose to remain close to the general, when the other troops are expected to face the trouble alone? And with your wife here, too!"

Hervey boiled inside. He wanted to treat the insult as a matter of honor, to have it out once and for all, with pistols, swords—whatever the Earl of Towcester chose. He fought the urge for all he was worth, however, for the voices in his head—Henrietta's, Armstrong's, Strickland's— all begged him not to call out Lord Towcester.

He told himself that the hour was late, and the lieutenant colonel's journey had been long and tiring. In any case, the adjutant as the sole witness was not worth the trouble. "Your lordship, in your absence I was required to—"

"I think you take upon yourself a very great deal, Captain Hervey! You must have known that I was to arrive this evening."

"No, sir, I did not. I received no communication whatever." He managed, he hoped, to keep the simple statement from sounding like a complaint.

"Well, I tell you, sir," (Lord Towcester's voice had risen substantially in both volume and pitch) "that *I* command this regiment, and *I* say where the troops shall go. The adjutant shall countermand the orders at once and shall issue new ones at first parade. You may dismiss."

Hervey replaced his cap, saluted, and left. He was tired, confounded, and above all, he was angry at the additional labor which would now fall to the troops—and the inevitable delay and confusion it must cause, so that what might have been the appearance of a regiment under good order would like as not be quite the opposite. Perhaps he overestimated the difficulties they faced with these Luddites; perhaps Lord Towcester's arrogant disregard of them was more apt. But that was not Sir Francis Evans's opinion. Hervey stood for several minutes in the White Hart's empty smoking room wondering how much longer he could tolerate a martinet whose actions seemed calculated to bring the regiment to calamity.

There seemed no point sending any orders to his troop at that hour. Without knowing what was to be done, nothing could be gained by even a preliminary order canceling the previous one. He had to know first what was nugatory before he might halt it. The smoking-room clock showed that it was well past watch setting; his dragoons would be asleep. He decided to let them sleep on.

The night light was still burning when he went back to his room. Henrietta was sleeping peacefully, her tresses spread on the pillow as if just arranged by her lady's maid. He stood long looking at her, contemplating—marveling, indeed—the changes which nature was working within. Henrietta was changed forever from the girl he had known. She was changed the night of their marriage, as was he, though in different measure. And the quality of his love for her was changed now by what nature was working. Perhaps he began only now to comprehend truly what John Keble had meant when he spoke of their becoming one flesh.

He looked about the room. It was a mean lodging compared with Longleat—compared with the vicarage at Horningsham, even. He had brought her to a place no better than a corn merchant might use, although she did not complain. She had made light, indeed, of his concern at the meager furnishings, and his disdain of the boiled fowl that passed for partridge at the supper brought to her. Caithlin Armstrong might find contentment in such surroundings when she arrived with the sutler's wagons, and Serjeant Armstrong could have the satisfaction of knowing that his outlay gave her unaccustomed comfort, but *he,* Captain Matthew Hervey, had failed to honor his wife as her guardian would have expected, and he himself wanted. Would it ever be thus if she followed the trumpet?

CHAPTER 13

DUKERIES

Mansfield, Next Day

A Troop reached Mansfield towards the middle of the morning. Hervey had taken his amusement at this substitution silently, for Lord Towcester evidently had great satisfaction in sending him from Nottingham, not realizing that he would be a full three hours closer thereby to Chatsworth, whence Henrietta was driving even now. Indeed, he was a little surprised that the lieutenant colonel had not sent him even farther afield, to Worksop for instance, though he supposed that Towcester feared having him at too distant an arm's length.

Mansfield seemed a pleasant enough town, its population not especially hostile as the troop rode in. The town had a fine church—Norman towers were not a common sight in Hervey's part of England—and a handsome moot hall. There were curious dwellings carved out of the sandstone cliffs along the Southwell road, where, he was informed by his guide, there were many families still, and there were extensive Roman remains, though only partially excavated. A more peaceful place than Mansfield, in the heart of the once great Sherwood Forest, it would have been difficult to imagine. Yet only two weeks ago, an armed mob had attacked one of the new steam-loom factories on the edge of the town, the owner and his night watch only managing to drive off the assailants after killing five of their number and wounding a dozen more. The mob had returned the following night and, after a gun battle in which there were more casualties, succeeded in demolishing the factory. The scarred remains now stood as a stark reminder to the authorities that beneath the tranquil canopy of Sherwood Forest there lurked, as there had so many years ago, predatory bands.

Who were they, Hervey wondered, and who were the ringleaders? The bench, it seemed, had no idea, and the constable seemed afraid to ask. Hervey soon discovered that his troop was not so much *assisting* the civil power as obliged to *be* the power. No sooner had they arrived but Mansfield's most prominent citizens besieged him in the moot hall to inquire how he intended to pacify the neighborhood. Hervey had no idea, and could only assure his audience that he stood ready to answer—and promptly—calls for assistance from the magistrates. The predicament of a number of those living in isolated houses outside the town was brought to his notice, and he had to agree that passivity would save neither life nor property in their case. He asked what measures they themselves had taken, and was surprised by the degree of fortification which some of the houses had undergone, and the extent to which firearms were kept at hand for their domestic staff. But the steam-loom factory had been barricaded and defended, too, they pointed out, and that had not stopped its destruction. Hervey promised he would consult with the senior magistrates at once. And so, Lieutenant Seton Canning having taken the troop out to the grange on the Southwell road, just beyond the town, which was to be their quarters, Hervey rode with just his trumpeter and coverman to Clipstone Hall to meet the chairman of the Mansfield bench.

After the major general's dire warnings of the inadequacy of the magistracy, Hervey was very pleasantly surprised by whom he found at Clipstone. Sir Abraham Cole seemed neither a scheming Whig nor a baying Tory. He was instead a rather bookish man in his late fifties, with a ready, if slightly anxious, smile, and a civilized way with his words. His father had bought the baronetcy half a century before with his stocking-making wealth, afterwards buying and extending the hall, and Sir Abraham had since combined the running of the family business with his other passions—astronomy, collecting Chinese porcelain, and making a new translation of the Old Testament. Hervey sat in the library, admiring the shelves and sipping a fine Montilla sherry.

"Would you tell me please, Captain Hervey, if you are permitted to do so, what are your orders?"

Hervey smiled. There was something most engaging in Sir Abraham Cole's courtesy. "Of course, Sir Abraham. Put very simply, I am to answer any call for assistance from a properly constituted authority—the bench, the constables—and to act on my own cognizance as may be lawful for the maintenance of the king's peace."

Sir Abraham nodded. "And this means that you may take an active part?"

"It does," replied Hervey. "But the general officer commanding the district is anxious to avoid prolonged engagement or any appearance of martial law."

"That is understood," said Sir Abraham equably. "Have you heard of posse comitatus? It is the means, in common law, by which a sheriff—or now, indeed, the lord lieutenant—may call upon all male members of the county above the age of fifteen years to assist in preventing riot or enforcing process."

"I do remember now," said Hervey, recollecting his Shrewsbury history. "And I seem to recall, too, my father's being amused that the clergy were exempt."

Sir Abraham smiled again. "Indeed, yes. And peers, too—I shall return to them. Well, then, now that we have a force of regular cavalry to fortify the weaker spirits, I intend applying to the lord lieutenant under those powers to raise a body locally for the preservation of the peace. My desire these many years past has been that we should have a stipendiary constabulary. But that will be a long time in the coming yet, and so we must rely on the posse to provide us with special constables."

That was as well, thought Hervey, for the GOC had said that he was considering withholding assistance if a town or village had not taken its own measures to preserve the peace. "You were going to say something of peers, Sir Abraham?"

Sir Abraham Cole paused for a moment. "You are no doubt aware that we are on the edge of the Dukeries? I am sorry to say that Their Graces and Lord Manvers take a contrary opinion in respect of law enforcement. They are not troubled in their parks, you understand, and news of any outrage reaches them late, so that the sting is too far drawn. I truly believe they are of the view that broken machinery is a price willingly to be paid to avoid a greater insurrection."

"And does this make keeping the peace more difficult?"

Sir Abraham shook his head. "Well, it certainly doesn't make it easier. Their support would greatly assist us raising a special constabulary, for instance."

Hervey waited for him to say more, but it was some time before Sir Abraham seemed ready to confide in him.

"I have it on good authority that the Dukeries at night are something of a haven for drilling men. The keepers turn a blind eye."

"I am astonished," said Hervey, frowning deeply. "I find it hard to credit that peers of the realm could connive at ... *treason* in this way."

Sir Abraham nodded. "Looked at like that, you are in the right. But what if they did not believe it all amounted to a real threat of insurrection? I've heard it related that the Duke of Portland says the business of the Blanketeers proves that fears are too exaggerated."

Hervey sighed. "Let us pray they are right."

Sir Abraham asked if he would take luncheon with him, and although Hervey regretfully declined, he accepted a second glass of sherry, for he wanted to be clear on the bench's view of the situation, and he still had questions. "There are two distinct threats, are there not, Sir Abraham? There is that to the government—the Crown, indeed—and there is that to the peace hereabouts, in the form of machine breaking and food riots."

Sir Abraham agreed.

"The one might well sustain the other, however, and we have to proceed on that surmise. Their Graces might well be in the right about the real threat to the Crown, but if general lawlessness goes unchecked it may generate a greater malevolence. That, indeed, is what some of the political speakers are hoping, is it not?"

Sir Abraham seemed delighted. "Captain Hervey, I very much approve of all that you have said! I confess to having been in two minds about the arrival of the military, for my experience of military officers is solely that of the militia and the yeomanry, and I am afraid that it has not always been felicitous."

Hervey's own experience of both had been limited but equally infelicitous. "I thank you, sir. I trust you will find us handy." He finished his glass. "I believe we should meet later this week to speak of the employment of your special constables."

"Yes, yes, indeed. But before you go, Captain Hervey, allow me to show you—briefly, of course—my collection of Chinese porcelain, and my observatory."

Sir Abraham's invitation was so unaffected in its enthusiasm that Hervey could not but accept. And glad he was, too, for when they went to the observatory on the roof he was put in mind of a simple scheme which had long served the nation well in its darkest times, and which would do the same for the manufacturers.

The telescope, turned terrestrial, commanded a great tract of country. "Sir Abraham, do you think it likely that the machine owners can see each other's houses—from the roofs I mean?"

Sir Abraham thought a while, going through the names in his mind. "You wouldn't be able to see Barlow's place; it's past the Worksop road. It was his factory that was burned to the ground the day after mine. But the rest? Aye, you might see them."

"You would see a beacon, then?"

"On the roof? Aye, you should be able to see a beacon, especially at night."

"There have been no attacks in broad daylight, have there?"

"That is true."

"So if you were to arrange a chain of beacons, with a watch, then we could send assistance very promptly. I don't imagine, frankly, that Mr. Barlow's house is in danger any longer."

"Captain Hervey, that is a capital idea! I am full of regard for your address. I shall begin on it at once." Sir Abraham had his fist clenched as if determined to do something disagreeable.

Hervey hoped his resolution would spread to his fellow owners. "Then I shall send my lieutenant here tomorrow, and he can make the finer arrangements." He thought for a second, and then judged the moment right. "You know, Sir Abraham, it might be worthwhile setting new hounds on the scent of Barlow's ruiners—terriers, indeed, since they appear to have gone deep to earth. I have had occasion to see investigators from Bow Street in a case of murder, and from a most unpromising cold trail, they were able to dig out the murderers. The outlay would not be small, but—"

"Hang the outlay, Captain Hervey. I have such a strong presentiment of your succeeding in something here that I shall foot the bill myself for the time being!"

"How is Harkaway?" asked Hervey as soon as he reached Ransom Grange from Clipstone.

Johnson took Gilbert's reins and shook his head. " 'E was forging badly on t'way from Mansfield."

"Was it just tiredness?"

"There's summat up wi'im. Some o' t'others were knocked up when we got to Nottingham, but they were right by morning."

Hervey ducked under the bar of Harkaway's stall. "Did you see any blood at his nostrils at any stage?"

"No, sir, not once."

Hervey had no doubt that Johnson would have noticed the slightest bleeding. "What did the veterinary officer say?"

"Just to physic 'im, which I'd done anyway."

"Well, let's give him another mash tonight, with some niter."

Johnson pulled the bar back across the stall as Hervey stepped out. "I'm sorry, sir. I just didn't see anything. 'E's been in as good a fettle as any o' t'others up to now."

Hervey smiled and clapped him on the shoulder. "We'll have him to rights soon enough."

They left the stable and began walking to the officers' house. A dozen or so jackdaws were picking at the droppings in the yard. "*They*'re pleased we've come, at least," said Johnson.

Hervey smiled again as he watched them carefully selecting the un-crushed grains. "Oh, there are others, too. I had rather a nice meeting with the chairman of the bench earlier on."

"What d'ye reckon, then, sir? It's a lot quieter than I thought it'd be. We'd all thought we'd be on riot duty t'first night."

Hervey confided that he'd expected the same, though he was grateful to have been wrong. "Maybe it's just our numbers. Or maybe the ring-leaders are biding their time. There's more machinery being brought from Birmingham in the next week or two, and that might be a cause for trouble."

Johnson nodded. "We were wondering if we'd be allowed into Mansfield."

Armstrong would be asking him that, too, no doubt. It would be safer not to let his men associate with the citizenry, for besides the usual fights, it did not do to have the very force sent to coerce the populace drinking with them the day before. But Mansfield was hardly seething, and it was not the populace as a whole that was to be coerced. Hervey imagined there would be more peace caught from the dragoons than sedition caught from the townspeople.

"I'll have a word with Serjeant Armstrong. In any event, it should help the posse the magistrates are getting up."

"A pussy?"

"Oh, for heaven's sake, man!"

"You just said—"

"I said '*posse.*'"

Johnson looked genuinely baffled, and then began to smirk, a thing he did infrequently enough to induce a similar reaction in Hervey. "And what are they going to do with the pussy?"

Dragoons about the yard were now glancing their way. "They're organizing a watch," said Hervey, managing to regain a reasonable composure. He told him about the Bow Street men, too, but confided that he didn't expect to see them inside of five days. The letter to London had gone express, by Sir Abraham's pocket, together with a letter of credit so that the detectors might post to Nottingham with all speed. But they would have other business in the capital, no doubt, and he couldn't expect them to abandon those duties at once.

Meanwhile, he concluded that his best course was a vigorous show of force throughout the district, by day and by night.

Hervey was fast asleep when Johnson banged on his door two nights later.

"It's 'Arkaway, sir. 'E's down."

Hervey sprang out of bed, pulled on his overalls and boots, and snatched up his field coat. They ran to the stables, where the picket corporal was lighting oil lamps as fast as he could. "How long has he been down?"

"I don't know for sure, sir," said Corporal Sykes. "But he was up at midnight when I did the rounds."

As a rule, no one patrolled the lines themselves during the silent hours, for horses needed their peace as much as dragoons, but some of the barley feed that day had been fusty, and there were fears for the odd case of colic. But Harkaway had not had the barley. He lay quite still, his breathing shallow, with no sweating. The veterinary officer was twenty miles away, and Hervey was at a loss to know what to try.

Serjeant Armstrong arrived. He watched, silent, until Hervey pressed him for an opinion. "I just don't know, sir. I don't think I've ever seen a horse down and as still as this."

"He can't have picked up any poison. He's been all but in tandem with Gilbert the past two weeks. Mr. Gascoyne thought he was just off his form, tired after the march."

"We've all seen horses drop dead with fatigue, but not like this. Could his gut have twisted—or got a block?"

Hervey knelt by Harkaway's head and listened closely to the shallow but regular breathing. "Perhaps. But look at him: he's not sweating, and he's not trying to nip at the pain." Hervey looked up as the farrier corporal entered the stall. "What do you make of him, Corporal Perrot?"

The farrier corporal got down by the gelding's side and felt along his flank and belly. There was nothing unusual—just as Hervey had found. "It's queer, sir. He's not sweating, or showing any pain. He looks like an old horse snuffing." The farrier corporal's gentle Dorset was an emollient, even if his words were not. "It can't be colic?"

Hervey shook his head, unsure.

Perrot sighed. "Has he had colic before, sir?"

Hervey and Harkaway hadn't been together all that much: the Irish splint was the only thing he knew of to have bothered the veterinary officer. "I believe not at all. Do you think we should dose him with saltwater?"

The farrier corporal looked undecided. "Might it be *impacted* colic, sir?"

Hervey shook his head again. "I'm at a loss to know what it might be, Corporal Perrot. I don't want to dose him if we don't have to, not lying like this—and we'd never get him on his feet."

"I'd best have a look—if you don't mind, sir?"

Daniel Coates had once shown Hervey how to examine for impacted colic, but he had never had cause to. "Yes, I'd be very obliged if you would, Corporal Perrot. And I'll send for Mr. Gascoyne meanwhile."

The farrier corporal asked for some whale oil, took off his tunic and shirt, then rubbed the oil over his right arm. "Pull his tail clear for me, Johnson," he said, rubbing a little oil on the anus. The picket corporal brought a lantern closer. "What bloody good's that going to do, Sykes?" rasped Corporal Perrot, sliding a hand inside the rectum.

Corporal Sykes colored up, and even Hervey managed a smile. Harkaway barely moved a muscle at the intrusion. Corporal Perrot pushed on gently until his forearm had disappeared, and then began carefully probing the abdomen to locate any blockage.

A full five minutes passed before Perrot pronounced that there was no obvious obstruction. Hervey was disappointed, for although an impacted colic was a deuce of a thing to treat, they would at least know how to start. All they could do now was wait for the veterinary officer to arrive, and they knew he couldn't do so before morning.

"I'll stay with him, then, Johnson."

When Johnson was gone, Hervey looked long at the gelding, and with a growing sense of despair. Never before had he been at such a loss to know what to do. All he *could* do, indeed, was watch.

A little before first light, Harkaway gave up breathing. Hervey did not see the actual moment, for the gelding's respiration had become so shallow by the end, it was almost imperceptible. One minute Hervey knew he was alive, and the next he knew he was gone. And it was an end with re-lief as well as melancholy, for Hervey had known for several hours that nothing could put life back into so weak an animal. He did not get up at once, apprehending a forceful command to remain at Harkaway's side—an awe, numinal, powerful, which he had known once or twice in the Peninsula. It had not been something he had inquired into, nor later de-nied. He waited reverently for several minutes, until, quite distinctly, he felt his restraints slip away. Then he rose, took a blanket, and laid it over Harkaway's head, and went out into the morning.

Johnson was as grieved as Hervey, in some ways more so. He had seen enough horses die from wounds and malnourishment, strangles and staggers—from any number of causes, indeed—but never once reflecting on his own husbandry. It was as much to assuage his groom's dismay, therefore, that Hervey asked the veterinary surgeon, when he arrived shortly after nine, to carry out a critical dissection.

Hervey didn't care to watch it, and neither did Johnson. As he said to Mr. Gascoyne, the knife to a dead horse was a thing for the *boucherie chevaline,* or for Mr. Sanbel's new veterinary college, or even for Mr. Stubbs and his palette, but he himself had no stomach for it.

The knife revealed a sad story. "The pathognomonic was extraordi-nary, Hervey," said Gascoyne when he had done. "I looked at once at the lungs, for since you described respiratory failure those were quite obvi-ously the organs to start with. They were very morbid, indeed—chronic abscessing in the upper posterior part. I've never seen worse. There must have been hemorrhagia over a very long period."

Hervey was puzzled. "And yet neither I nor Johnson saw any blood about the nostrils—not once."

"By no means impossible," opined Gascoyne in his gentle Devon burr.

Hervey always respected the veterinarian's willingness to concede that there was much still to be understood.

"In any case," Gascoyne assured him, "a pulmonary hemorrhage of this magnitude is not something for which anyone might be blamed. There must have been some defect at birth."

Hervey expressed himself grateful, declaring, as cheerfully as he could, that it was now but a matter for the Rufford hounds.

After his meeting later that morning with Sir Abraham Cole, who was just come from the building site that was his erstwhile factory, and who expressed himself very content with the peace about the borough these past forty-eight hours, Hervey began contemplating a ride to see Henrietta. It was less than twenty miles to Chatsworth. If he set out after first parade next morning, he would be there comfortably by noon. They could at least enjoy a walk together before he returned for evening stables. And Johnson could come, too. It would be a tonic for them both, for Harkaway's death had cast a dismal spell over the grange.

But Henrietta had already saved them the ride. The Bath chaise was standing at the front of the grange as he came from watering parade, and only a moment's anxiety that something might be amiss dulled his thrill at seeing it. He took the steps two at a time to embrace her. "I can't *tell* you how good this is, now of all times."

Inside the grange she condoled with him, and said how she hoped to be able to say something of comfort to Private Johnson, too, for besides Hervey's own notice of his distress she knew from the evening in Hounslow that Johnson had developed a special feeling for the gelding. But in the end, she herself seemed in lower spirits than the news required, and this was betrayed by a rather distant look in her eyes.

"Is everything well?" asked Hervey, trying not to sound too anxious again.

She sighed. "There is no one at Chatsworth, for William is gone south. I felt the need of company very keenly."

It seemed strange that the need of company should depress the spirits quite so much, but he presumed it was the result of her condition. "I was to have come to Chatsworth myself, tomorrow," he said to rally her.

She smiled back appreciatively, knowing that his going there was a conscious decision to leave his dragoons, albeit for only a day. But her distant look remained.

"Tell me what is the matter, my love," Hervey tried again, taking her hand in a way that said he would not release it until she told him all.

"The news from London, of Princess Charlotte. I confess it troubles me greatly. Needlessly perhaps . . . but Sir Richard Croft is bleeding her every day, and allows her so little food. I read that she is become very disheartened, and speaks of the future being joyless."

He squeezed her hand and spoke softly. "Do you wish to engage a different physician? Is that your concern?"

Henrietta shook her head. "No. Dr. Croft is spoken of everywhere in the highest terms."

He put his arms round her. "My darling, there is no reason to suppose that your confinement will be as troubled."

"I should like to stay with you here, Matthew. I should feel better then."

"You could not be comfortable here, my love. And I should not wish you to stay in Mansfield, for everyone would know you were there, and if there were any disturbance—"

"I can stay at Welbeck. The Portlands are cousins of William's, I believe."

There could be no more objection to one dukery than another. And, though Hervey felt a little ashamed of the thought, it would do no harm to have an advocate at Welbeck if Sir Abraham's picture of ducal detachment were a true one. "I should be very happy indeed if you did. We could meet every day." Another thought occurred to him. "First you will want to send word, will you not?"

Henrietta nodded.

"Then while that is done, will you take Johnson for a drive? You could call on Sir Abraham Cole. He's chairman of the bench, and a very engaging man. And he has a very extensive collection of Chinese porcelain— which I confess I found rather too extensive for my taste. He lives alone a few miles out of the town, and Johnson could take some papers which he must sign."

The prospect entirely delighted her. Her spirits seemed already to be rising.

And now, explained Hervey, he must go and write to Daniel Coates, for Harkaway was his gift, and had been very much his pride. He was overdue writing in any case, and his last had been a gloomy affair, composed when he was at the low ebb of arrest. He would have more agreeable things to tell him on that account which would, perhaps, counterbalance the news of Harkaway. The old soldier liked nothing more than news from the field, and a troop dispatch, even allowing for the objectionable nature of a commanding officer such as Lord Towcester, was a thing to be savored, wherever the campaign.

CHAPTER 14

GOOD DEEDS
AND BAD

Clipstone Hall, That Night

Clipstone Hall was a fine gentlemanly residence. Its stone was good and solid, its lawns well laid. It was a place to which a man might retire of an evening, content in his day's work, whatever it might be, and enjoy his diversion and repose. As the sun began to set, the stones turned a mellow amber color, and the big oaks, which had stood in Sherwood since before the Conqueror, cast long shadows across the lawns, in which a rabbit or a pheasant sometimes braved the remaining daylight, before darkness gave them license to browse the mow. Rooks returning to their high nests cawed a general retreat, and Jacobs in the park bleated the same to their imagined lambs. To varying degrees, the picture was the same for the several owners whose pleasure it was to be close to their manufactures while enjoying a tranquil country living. But once night fell, especially when there was no moon, as this night, and when so much violence stalked the lanes, their country seats became places of anxiety, sometimes of fear, and occasionally of terror.

In this dim darkness, the clock of Sir Abraham Cole's parish church, just the other side of the park wall, struck two. Sir Abraham himself was asleep, but on the roof was an undergardener earning a handy extra shilling. He was wide awake despite the hour, for the ruination of Sir Abraham might well be his own ruination, too, and consequently of his wife and five children. But diligent though the gardener was, he neither saw nor heard the intruder. The Jacobs hadn't stirred, nor the geese at the back of the house; neither had the two King Charleses in Sir Abraham's bedroom.

The intruder, his face blackened, stole across the gravel drive as if he were weightless, and reached the doors of Clipstone Hall without a soul knowing. But although he had a pistol in his belt, it was not his intention to use it. Indeed, he intended neither the house nor its occupants any mischief—that night at least. Instead, he took from his pocket a letter, and pinned it to the front doors with a facing needle. Then he slipped away as silently, so that the discovery of the letter when it was daylight might be all the more menacing. At a dozen and more houses in the borough, the same was happening.

Sir Abraham was so alarmed when his man brought him the letter just before eight in the morning that he drove at once to the grange. He arrived as first parade was being dismissed, but the speed of his carriage and manner of his getting out arrested the dismissal. His meeting with Hervey was conducted with the entire troop standing, horses in hand, necks craning and ears straining.

"Captain Hervey, this was pinned to my door in the night. And it was the same at Taylor's and Arkwright's, too—probably everyone of the hosiers' association has them, and the bench, too."

Hervey took the letter and read the well-formed hand:

> Shirewood Camp
> To those whom it may concern—
> In consequences of the great suffering of the poor whose grievances seem not to be taken into the least consideration by government or the hirers of labor, General Ludd shall be forced to call out the brave Sons of Shirewood, who are determined and sworn to be true and faithful avengers of their country's wrongs.
>
> *And by night when all is still,*
> *And the moon is hid behind the hill,*
> *We forward march to do our will*
> *With hatchet, pike, and gun!*

Great Enoch still shall lead the van.
Stop him who dare! Stop him who can!
Press forward every gallant man
With hatchet, pike, and gun!

General Ludd

"The meter is very ill," Hervey pronounced. "I'll warrant they're tedious company."

The artifice was as reassuring for the dragoons as it was for Sir Abraham, who sighed in some relief. Nevertheless, Hervey lost no time in ordering NCOs' patrols to the hosiers on the watch list. Sir Abraham had not specifically requested it, but it was clear that prompt action was needed lest fear turned to panic.

"It is not for me to suggest it," Hervey said to him when the last of the patrols was gone, "but now is the time your posse would be of greatest value. I can't think that undrilled men can have much effect once real trouble has begun, but a large enough picket at each house and workshop might well deter attack."

Sir Abraham agreed, and, after a restorative, set off as quickly as he had arrived for the moot hall.

It was now that Hervey began to feel keenly the lack of any intelligence as to what was happening outside the borough. Doubtless he would know more by the end of the day, when the "usual channels" conveyed intelligence to the moot hall, but what he really wanted to know was what was happening with the other troops, especially Barrow's in Worksop and Strickland's in Ollerton on which he would have to rely for immediate support. He therefore ordered Lieutenant Seton Canning and Cornet St. Oswald to ride to the other troops to find out what they could, and then he returned to his map board.

Private Hopwood had made an enlargement of the Ordnance map by ten times, with color and lettering so careful that it looked as if it were a piece of fine engraving. His skill with pen, ink, and brush had come to light only by Caithlin Armstrong's diligence in visiting the infirmary with comforts (indeed, Caithlin's attentiveness had done much to hasten the healing of Hopwood's wounds, moral and physical). Hopwood's was a skill that not only aided the recovery of his self-respect but was of real value to Hervey, for after each patrol, the officer or NCO had come to the map to add the human detail gained in reconnaissance. And so by this, the seventh morning, Hopwood had drawn a remarkable representation of the borough, more complete, Hervey supposed, than at any time since Domesday.

"Would you like some tea, sir?" asked the draftsman.

Hervey looked him in the eye. Hopwood held the gaze until Hervey smiled and said yes. It had only been for a few seconds, but Hopwood could look his officer in the eye again. And he had asked if he would like tea—not waited to be asked but offered it, and not out of servility, or fawning, but because that was what a dragoon should do. He was ready to *rejoin* the Sixth instead of just mustering with the ranks.

It took him a full ten minutes to make the tea, however. Hervey didn't notice, for he was rapt in study of the map. Hopwood at last brought in a tray, and poured. "Milk, sir?"

"A little, yes."

He added the milk, and then turned to leave.

"Shall you not have any, Hopwood?" asked Hervey, still peering at the map with a magnifying glass.

Hopwood looked hesitant. "Can I, sir?"

"Of course. Go and get a cup and sit here while I continue to admire your work."

Hopwood did as he was bidden, but said not a word.

In a few minutes Hervey put down the glass. "Where did you acquire such skill?"

"When I left the workhouse, sir, I was apprenticed to a printmaker. I'd always liked drawing, but I could only do it on the slate before."

"If you were going to get a trade, why did you enlist?"

Hopwood smiled. "We made a lot of recruiting posters, sir."

"And you ended up believing them!"

"Aye, sir." He smiled.

"Go on."

"To tell the truth, I kept seeing soldiers in the town—it were Maidstone—and in the end I kept thinking that . . ."

"Yes?"

"Well, I just kept thinking."

"That you'd think the worse of yourself if you didn't put on regimentals?"

"Aye, sir, just that."

Hervey took another sip of the Honorable Company's pekoe. "This tea's good, Hopwood. I should be careful, or someone will claim you as a groom!"

Hopwood smiled. It wasn't much of a joke, but he knew Hervey was trying.

"You were in America, first, with the Fourteenth, weren't you?"

"I was, sir. But we didn't see a lot of fighting."

"No. But I've learned you saved a man from drowning."

Hopwood looked abashed.

"And from a river with sharp teeth in it."

"I couldn't very well leave him, sir."

Hervey looked at him with admiration as well as pity. "When your time with the colors is up, Hopwood, the thing to remember is that you saved a man's life, when no one would have called you coward if you hadn't. Nothing else is worth thinking of, you understand—nothing. It will be the only thing that matters."

"Thank you, sir."

"No more thank-yous, Hopwood. It's just time to kick on now."

"Aye, sir. That's what I'd like to do."

"Good!" He drained the cup. "Then look at your map and tell me what you observe."

"More green than I thought I had ink for, sir!" he smiled.

"Yes. Green all over the place, and a few roads."

"Is that a good thing, sir?"

"Not at the moment, but I'm trying to think of how it might be. It seems the hosiers and magistrates have all been threatened during the night. And either these Luddites are all like Robin Hood's merry men and live in the forest—which I don't believe for one minute, or why would they be so intent on breaking machinery which has nothing to do with them?—or else they're traveling along these roads at night. And if they're doing that then there must be a way to intercept them."

"It's a big place, sir."

"I know, Hopwood; I know. That's why we're going to need exact intelligence rather than just beating around in the dark. I'm praying that the Bow Street men will not be too long."

Later that morning, without notice, Lord Towcester arrived at the grange. Hervey's heart, lifted by the independence of his situation, fell at once as it became clear that the lieutenant colonel was not come for any supportive purpose—rather, indeed, the opposite. He had spent the past three days at Welbeck and then Clumber, where Their Graces had left him in no doubt of their disapproval of the intervention of regulars. They were strongly of the opinion that events should be allowed to take their course, with the yeomanry called out only when the trouble threatened the peace of the country as a whole. "As, indeed, am I, Captain Hervey. I understand you have had patrols all over the north of the county."

"We have been patrolling the jurisdiction of the magistrates, your lordship—to discover the lie of the land and to show a deterrent force. I have been in close liaison with the chairman of the bench, Sir Abraham Cole."

"*Liaison,* Captain Hervey? Liaison? Your business is to respond to a properly constituted request for assistance. Nothing more. Where is your troop?"

Hervey explained.

"And did a magistrate request this?"

"Not exactly, your lordship."

"What do you mean 'not exactly,' sir? There has to be exactitude in this business or else it will be the assizes for you!"

"I mean, your lordship, that the association members received threats during the night, and I thought it best—"

"Association be damned, Captain Hervey! Upstart tradesmen and Jews! I'll not have my regiment ruin its appearance and name by chasing round after half-wits who put a torch to a few hosiers' shops and their pretentious *residences!*"

Hervey boiled inside. He had seen more learning and good manners in one week from Sir Abraham than he had seen from Lord Towcester in six months—and he longed to say so. "My lord, these are honest men deserving of our protection. Sir Francis Evans said just that."

"Do not presume to tell me what is my duty, sir!" hissed Lord Towcester. "Do not presume that you know what is the district commander's mind better than I do!"

Hervey clenched his fists, bringing them instinctively to the stripes of his overalls so that, at the position of attention, he might better master his rage. He knew he had overstepped the mark, but he did not want to concede the fact. The trouble was, it was perfectly evident that Lord Towcester's sole object was to get back to Brighton at the first opportunity, and with his regiment in as pretty a condition as possible. He cared not one jot for the peace of the boroughs or the safety of the manufacturers. "Your lordship, it was certainly not my intention to presume anything. But Sir Abraham Cole has told me in great detail of the fearful eruptions of violence in the borough not five years ago. If the Luddites got the upper hand, there is no knowing where they would stop, for the opinion is that their grievances go beyond frame breaking. There is talk of general insurrection. And Their Graces in the Dukeries are members of Parliament—the nearest ones at hand. They might well be the first objects of the mob."

Lord Towcester remained silent.

Hervey pressed his point carefully. "And the militia, sir—they have not been embodied these last two years. You could scarcely count on them. The yeomanry is true, but—"

The lieutenant colonel seemed to calm himself a little. "I see." He turned towards the big colored map. "What is this?"

Hervey explained. "It was drawn by Private Hopwood, sir."

Lord Towcester looked at the dragoon standing to attention next to the board. "Indeed, indeed. It is very good, my man."

"Thank you, my lord."

"Have you been with the regiment long?"

Hervey rolled his eyes in disbelief. Hopwood remained steadfastly eyes-front. "Three years, my lord."

"Good. Good. Now, Captain Hervey," he said, turning back, "let it be strictly understood: I want no heroics. You are to withdraw your troop to these lines and await the properly constituted request of a magistrate. And it shall be for *limited* assistance, mind. The appearance of regular troops about the area is bound to fuel violent feeling. These hosiers must get up proper watches, dig into their Jewy pockets and pay for constables. I will not have the hosiers of Nottingham kept at my expense!"

"I'm obliged, your lordship."

"A Tory of the most boneheaded sort," wrote Hervey that night in his journal, though he could not claim the words as his own, for they had been Barrow's one evening in Brighton. "The sort who believes the Garden of Eden was inferior to any English estate," Barrow had scoffed, in his cups—and Barrow was a man known for his forthright contempt for the Whigs, too. Thus could Lord Towcester unite opposites, rued Hervey.

Fortunately, Lord Towcester had not specified *when* exactly the troops were to be withdrawn to the lines, though it was perfectly obvious he intended it to be at once, Hervey confided to the page. He had therefore calculated that he could get away with sending orders for recall at first light next day, which would at least reassure the hosiers and magistrates during this crucial first night. Thereafter, the paid watches and the posse, properly stood-to, ought to be able to give some measure of reassurance and—he prayed it would never come to it—*protection*. Each house had at least three firearms, Sir Abraham had told him, and as long as the others in the beacon chain were prompt and brave in relaying the alarm, it ought to be possible for each householder to ward off an attack long enough for Hervey's men to arrive.

Three days went by without any further threats made to the association or the bench. Indeed, they were a very agreeable three days, for the autumn sunshine was warm, there was no rain, and the tradesmen of the town appeared welcoming of the dragoons' custom, especially the innkeepers and owners of the public houses.

The Bow Street men had arrived—the same as had come to Longleat— and had begun their investigations at once. First they questioned the known witnesses to the attack on the steam-frame workshops, discovered there were more, took statements, compared them, began questioning the proprietors of the drinking places, and their taverners, and slowly, but resolutely, like an industrious spider, they extended the range of their investigation until they reached the town limits. In this way, they explained, they hoped to establish what method there was in the Luddite activity, and the degree of support, active or passive, which they enjoyed in the various parts. They would then go into the villages of the borough depending upon the results of this preliminary work.

But their work, methodical though it was, had not been proving easy. They had encountered, they told Hervey the second evening, a shyness in speaking of the subject, which quite baffled them—a shyness far beyond that which they encountered in London in the investigation of crime. They had not had a single piece of information "on the usual terms," although the senior of the two, the former artificer of engineers, was hopeful still of one of the pothouse owners. They went unmolested in their work, however, requiring no escort, although both of them carried pistols and looked well able to have a care of themselves. Mansfield was not one of the rookeries, they said, smiling.

Henrietta had driven from Welbeck each day to see her husband. She had not been at the abbey when Lord Towcester had visited, staying instead at nearby Woodhouse with the dowager, and though the duke had been kindness itself, she declared she felt unsettled by the distance, and when the Portlands left for London a few days later, she determined to lodge at the grange, no matter what the objections were.

She and Hervey had dined at Sir Abraham Cole's the evening before, and he had delighted them for an hour afterwards with his celestial globe, and professed himself much disappointed when they insisted they were unable to stay to see the heavenly bodies in their reality. They had driven back to the grange late, for a wheel pin sheared soon after leaving Clipstone, and finding the other officers had retired by the time they returned, they were able to retire, too, and enjoy an intimacy denied to them for a whole week.

Towards watering parade next day, Hervey found himself searching for Private Johnson. "Where in heaven's name is he, Serjeant Armstrong?"

"I saw him at reveille, and he was there on first parade, but I haven't seen him since. Do you want something doing?"

"No, not especially now. I just wanted to tell him I was intending to drive to Clipstone."

"I'll send someone to find him," said Armstrong. "Lingard!"

Seton Canning's groom came doubling. "Sir!"

"Have you seen Johnson since first parade?"

Lingard looked sheepish.

"What's happening, Lingard?" growled Armstrong.

"Sir, I . . . Johnson's in the feed store."

Hervey took over the interrogation. "What's amiss, Lingard?"

Lingard shifted awkwardly, evading Hervey's eye.

"Answer up, man!" barked Armstrong.

"Sir, Johnson is very upset."

"About what?"

"Sir, if you please, I think it's better that he tells you."

"Lingard!" barked Armstrong again.

"It's his mother, sir."

Hervey looked at Armstrong, puzzled. "But he doesn't have a mother."

"No, sir," said Lingard. "Sir, it'd be much better if it came from him."

Hervey sensed he was right. "Very well, I'll go and see him."

"I'll keep the store clear," said Armstrong quietly.

Hervey found Johnson sitting on a bag of barley, head in hands. He sat down next to him and took off his forage cap. "Do you want to tell me what this is about?"

Johnson sat up. There were telltale streaks on his face. "M'mother."

"Yes, Lingard said. I thought—"

"No, sir, that's what I'd always thought an'all." He wiped his nose with his sleeve. "I al's thought she were dead. That's what I were told, I'm sure it were. But she's 'ere, in t'town."

Hervey tried to keep a rein on his disbelief. "But how have you found this out? She wouldn't have known any of the troop's names."

Johnson merely shook his head.

Only then did it occur to Hervey that tears were a strange reaction to such a discovery. "Have you seen her?"

"No I 'aven't. I don't want to. I were 'appy enough as I were."

Hervey stayed silent for several minutes. "But Johnson, even now, to know your mother is . . ." He stopped when he saw the tears in his groom's eyes, and on his cheeks.

Johnson gave a deep sigh and seemed to brace himself. "Sir, some o' t'men met 'er in one o' t'pothouses."

"Yes?"

"Sir, she's been gooin' wi'em for over a week!"

Hervey felt a knot in his own stomach. Even the idea appalled. He put his arm round him. "I'm so very sorry."

After a while, he got up and told Johnson to stay where he was for as long as he liked. "I'll tell Serjeant Armstrong, and we'll try to sort something out. Is there anything you want me to do?"

"No, sir," replied Johnson, sniffing. "I'll stay by meself for a bit longer, and then I'll go and do Gilbert."

"All right, then, but only when you're ready."

As he left, Johnson stood up and turned his head after him. "Thanks, sir. I'm sorry."

Hervey told Serjeant Armstrong at once. "But how in heaven's name he came to find out, I can't begin to think."

Armstrong had already questioned Lingard robustly. "He sang like a little linnet, did our Lingard. Seems they've all been lifting a leg in that part of town since we came. Anyway, one of these women gets talking and says how she's got a son in the army but she's never seen 'im since he was a bairn. She put 'im in a workhouse in Sheffield twenty years ago, and never saw 'im since."

Hervey frowned. "But that's not very convincing evidence of mother-hood."

"She knew he was called Johnson, and she's got half a page from a Bible that's the testificate, or whatever it's called."

Hervey had heard Johnson speak of that before. "But even so . . ."

"Even so, sir. What she needs to do is get that page matched up with the bit they keeps at the workhouse, and quickly."

Hervey agreed.

"Meanwhile, I'll put this busy little doxy out of bounds. There'll be no more ascension days for the troop with her!"

Henrietta learned of Johnson's unhappiness soon after, and was very grieved for him. She knew at once what must be done, and reported as much to her husband.

"But you cannot possibly go to that place and see her!" Hervey protested.

"I doubt she'll be about her business in the morning. You said she lived in a cave. I shall go and see her there."

"Going to a hovel dug out of stone? To visit a? . . . It is insupportable!" He admired her pluck, though he hesitated to tell her so.

"Matthew, I have moved in society a very great deal, and in principle I should be doing nothing that I have not done before!"

It was a riposte so disarming that Hervey at once gave up any further protest.

Henrietta returned an hour later with the carriage blinds drawn, and told her husband that she was driving to Sheffield.

"Why? Why must you go to Sheffield?" demanded Hervey, so incredulous as to sound angry to her.

"Because the sooner the testificate is verified, the sooner Private

Johnson will know what to do. Mrs. Stallybrass—his so-called mother—
is inside the carriage." Her tone defied further protest, for the second
time that morning.

When Hervey told Serjeant Armstrong at watering parade later, both
men found themselves smiling. "Apparently Mrs. Stallybrass would not
give up the piece of paper, and so my wife had to take her with her. Then
she went to tell Johnson, and he insisted on going, too, because he said
he couldn't allow her to travel with a woman like that!"

"What a merry party they will be," said Armstrong, shaking his head.
"How far is it to Sheffield?"

"Twice as far as Nottingham."

"They'll not be back before night!"

Hervey raised his eyebrows. "She spoke of returning via Chatsworth!"

Armstrong shook his head in equal dismay. "I'm not even sure as my
Caithlin would have taken a fence like that!"

Hervey smiled again. "Oh, I think she would, Serjeant Armstrong. I
think she would. When's Caithlin coming, by the way?"

"Tomorrow, all being well. I've found clean lodgings five minutes
away, by the Southwell road."

"I'm glad of it. The latest from Nottingham is that the Prince Regent's
pavilion has closed for the winter already. So there'll be no pull from the
prince to get us back to Brighton. We might well see out the winter in
Nottingham garrison."

"Well, there'll be plenty of firewood, at least," said Armstrong, smiling. "I've never seen so many trees in all my life!" Then he frowned. "If
ever it comes to a chase, though, we'll lose every time."

"But what a place it is for *ambushing*!" enthused Hervey.

Armstrong nodded. There was no doubting *that*.

"Come and have a look at Hopwood's map. It's given me an idea."

CHAPTER 15

ATTACK

Mansfield, October 1

"Sir! Sir! Beacon's lit!"

Hervey woke more slowly than usual. He heard the banging on the door rather than the report. "Come in!"

The orderly serjeant held his lantern high. "Corporal Evans, sir. We've just seen the north beacon light."

"Have you roused the out-picket?"

"Aye, sir, and Mr. Canning."

Serjeant Armstrong was at the door a few seconds later. "I'd just begun my rounds. I've told Lingard to saddle up for you."

Hervey pulled on his boots and overalls, cursed as he broke the bar of a spur ramming it into the housing, fastened his jacket, wedged his shako on tight, took his gloves, seized up his sword belt and carbine—almost forgetting the ready cylinder—and took the stairs at a run. In the grange yard dragoons were already leading out horses under saddle (both outlying and inlying pickets slept dressed), and the lance corporal was numbering them off.

"Mr. Seton Canning!"

The lieutenant hurried across the yard. "Ready, Hervey."

"Stand-to second division, and follow on as soon as you can. Have St. Oswald stand by third. I'll take the picket with Serjeant Armstrong."

"Sir!"

"Trumpeter!"

Susan Medwell came doubling, followed by Hervey's coverman.

"I think this is it, Corporal Troughton. Stick close. Medwell, I'll want 'Charge' when we're near. It could scatter them without a shot."

"Sir!"

"Well done, Lingard. Put this in the bucket." He passed the carbine to his stand-in groom as he took Gilbert's reins and checked the girth.

"Picket ready, sir," called Armstrong from the saddle of his big dapple bay.

"Very well. Threes advance, at the trot!"

In fewer than ten minutes from first alarm, fifteen dragoons, their captain, coverman, trumpeter, and serjeant were leaving the billet for the besieged house.

Hervey's beacon system was in two lines, one for the houses north of the town, and one for those south. When a house was attacked, the watchmen on the roof were to light the beacon, and the watches on the other houses would relay the alarm by lighting theirs. Videttes, set at last light, observed the center house of each line, and galloped the alarm back to the grange. The center house had two beacons, so that if a house on the left of the line were attacked, and later one on the right, it could signal the subsequent attack. But the picket would not know whether the attack were left or right until reaching the center house.

There was a three-quarter moon, giving enough light to the road to allow the picket a good canter for most of the mile and a half to Warren Hall, center house of the north beacon line. There were men with torches at the gates as Hervey came up.

"It's down the line towards Pleasley, sir!" they called. Hervey left one man as post and took the rest straight on, increasing the pace once his eyes had recovered from the torches. At each house it was the same: they had relayed the farther beacon. As Hervey passed the last house but one he became suspicious of the Luddites' chance attack on the farthest point of the line.

"Do you want me to blow the Charge yet, sir?" called Susan Medwell.

"No. Let's wait and see."

Hervey's instinct soon proved right. They galloped up the drive of Pleasley Grange to see torches all over the place, but no Luddites. The roof watch came down the escape ladders in haste, and confusion.

"What's happening?" shouted Hervey.

"It's queer, sir," said the chief watchman. "We was attacked for all of ten minutes—shots and all—and then they just went. As if they heard you coming. But that was half an hour ago."

"Did you fire the beacon at once?"

"Aye, sir. I think it were that that frightened 'em off."

"Is anyone hurt?"

"No, sir."

"Very well. I'll leave two dragoons till morning. Threes about, Serjeant Armstrong!"

They galloped back down the drive as fast as they could. "Do you think what I think?" shouted Armstrong, closing up.

"I've been humbugged?"

"I wouldn't have taken it personal like that, but yes."

"How in God's name did they know?"

They checked to a trot to take the turn back onto the road.

"Well, they'd easily have known about the beacons. You could hardly keep them a secret. All they have to do is attack one house and then stand back to see how long it takes us to get here. Sons of Sherwood, they call themselves? Bloody Robin Hoods!" Armstrong spat into the hedge at an imagined outlaw.

"So they've watched us all the way here?"

"Probably."

"Shit!" Hervey felt like spitting, too. "Surely it's too much of a coincidence to be all the way this end of the line, though. What if they draw us to one end and then attack the other?"

"That's why you've got a second beacon."

"And what if the other line's now lit, the south line?"

"Well, we always knew we couldn't be everywhere at once. And neither can they!"

"No. That's why we had to be at the right place, because *they* choose the point of attack. What if they've decoyed us here, and then St. Oswald's picket to the other line. Canning's already galloping down here. I bet that second beacon at Warren Hall won't be lit till he's passed."

"You mean it'll be lit any minute now if they're having a go at Clipstone?"

"Exactly! Come on!" They pressed back into a canter.

It took the best part of an hour to get within reach of Clipstone. They had turned round Seton Canning's division within half a mile of Pleasley Grange, which meant to Hervey that the second beacon at Warren Hall could not have been alight a quarter of an hour before. But both beacons were well ablaze when they'd passed the house again, and now they could hear firing towards Clipstone from a mile off. Hervey ordered Medwell to blow for all he was worth as they galloped the last stretch, praying there were no trip ropes across the road.

From the top of the rise they could see the house plainly—more flames than just the beacon. Hervey barely checked to take the graceful curve of the park drive through the gates, his blood boiling at the sight of the flames as well as at his own deception. He shouted no orders, as there could be no plan. Luddites bolted in all directions before him, like rats fleeing a terrier. He chased after one towards the Jacobs' meadow, knowing he'd run him up against the park wall. A report and powder flash from the beech hedge to his right made him swing his carbine and fire instinctively.

"Oh, sir! Oh, God!"

He looked round. Susan Medwell was clutching his stomach.

"Hold up, man," he called, circling and seizing him round the shoulders to support him in the saddle. "Corporal Troughton!"

His coverman was already on the other side. "I've got 'im, sir."

Hervey let go and turned to the beech hedge. "Come out at once with your hands up!" He barely counted to five before firing into the hedge again, four times. A few seconds later a man stumbled out and fell to the ground.

"Leave 'im, sir," shouted Armstrong, jumping from the saddle and running towards the motionless figure, pistol cocked. He turned him over roughly, saw he was dead, and spat with the utmost force at the ground. "Where's that other bastard run to, sir?"

"The field, there, with the sheep. But the park wall will stop him."

Armstrong changed hands with the pistol, drew his saber, and took off after him.

"Go and cover him, Stancliff," called Hervey to the nearest dragoon. "Come on, Susan, my brave lad, let's get you down and bandaged."

But Medwell was dead in the saddle, and his little gray mare was anxious.

"Sir, he's gripping my arm so tight I can't—"

"Oh, Christ! All right, Corporal Troughton. I'll take his bridle. Morris!"

Another dragoon hurried over. "Sir?"

"Help Corporal Troughton get Medwell down. He's shot dead."

It was a struggle, but between the three of them they managed to lay Private Medwell on the ground with a degree of dignity.

Hervey tried now to hold back his disgust—his anger he was past caring about. He was never fool enough to believe that all dragoons were the same to him, and Susan Medwell he loved because he was a matchless trumpeter and as smart a man as ever he'd seen in uniform. And Medwell had loved being his trumpeter and never sought to hide it. "Jesus Christ!" cursed Hervey. "Shot down in his own country!"

Seton Canning came running. "Hervey, the house's well ablaze. We'll need help from the village."

"Send for it, then. And tell whoever not to take no for an answer! Is Sir Abraham safe?"

"Aye, they all are—except one of the watch has a flesh wound."

"I'll come in a minute." He took Medwell's cloak from the saddle arch and laid it over him. "Stand with him, Stancliff. I don't want anyone riding over him."

"Aye, sir," said the dragoon, taking the gray's reins.

Hervey and his coverman ran to the front of the house, where Sir Abraham and the watch were huddled. By the light of the flames he could see the dismay in the magistrate's face. "Sir Abraham, I'm so very sorry we were not here quicker."

"We held them off a full half hour. Kept firing above their heads. But they were determined to break in. They managed to prize off the shutters at the east side, though we threw bricks down at them the while. And then they fired the place—without a thought for who was inside, or how we might get down from the roof."

Hervey glanced at the line of gardeners and indoor servants passing buckets to the house. It seemed to him a forlorn hope. "Is there a fire engine in Clipstone, Sir Abraham?"

"There is. I paid for it myself."

"Then we shall have it soon."

Sir Abraham seemed reassured.

Hervey glanced over to the house again. "Corporal Troughton, get as many men as you can to the front doors. We can at least get some of Sir Abraham's things out."

"No, Hervey, no," Sir Abraham shouted. "I shan't have the deaths of any more men on my hands. Leave it. Leave it all."

Hervey motioned Troughton to do his bidding anyway. "With your leave, sir," he said quietly, and then ran towards the house, calling to Seton Canning to follow him.

The doors were wide open, and the gardeners were managing to play a stirrup pump to some effect over the stairs. The fire was still in the right wing, and there was as yet no smoke in the left, where Sir Abraham's porcelain collection was displayed. The study adjoined the main drawing room, which was well alight, so Hervey took Seton Canning and some of the servants straight to the china. In a very little time they had a chain bringing it out. The study was another matter. It took him several minutes to find the right doors—it was surprisingly dark—and when he had, the smoke issuing from beneath them suggested the study was gone. But Hervey couldn't turn his back on years of scholarship, not without trying. He felt the door panels: they were cool enough. He touched the gilt handles: they didn't burn him. He took a deep breath and opened one of the double doors a little way. The smoke swirled backwards with the draft from outside, giving him a clear enough view of Sir Abraham's desk. He knew the folios were in its drawers, only two dozen feet from him, but with so much smoke he needed a clew to be safe. Curtain ties provided the means.

He made three forays into the study. With the last he was forced to the floor as smoke swirled back with the shattering of one of the clerestories. Coughing badly, he managed to close the doors, however, and get Seton Canning's chain to pass out the ledgers—all of them. The Clipstone engine and its crew fought the flames tenaciously, but the battle was uneven. By dawn the house was burned out. On the lawns were a good many of Sir Abraham's pictures and furniture, all his Chinese porcelain, and his Old Testament scholarship. The man shot dead by Hervey was recognized at once by Sir Abraham when daylight came—one of his own workshop foremen. Serjeant Armstrong had taken the other fugitive alive after a savage fight which had left both of them bruised about the face.

And Corporal Harris had taken two more in Clipstone churchyard as he went for the fire engine.

Sir Abraham's first thought on seeing the extent of his loss was the condition of his servants. He gathered them together, indoor and out-door alike, asked the housemaids very politely to stop crying, and as-sured them all that they would not lose a single penny of their wages while the house was rebuilt, and that they would have a roof over their heads, somehow, by that very evening.

"A man that men would follow willingly," said Serjeant Armstrong, hearing it. "Some of these folks don't know they're born!"

There was an emergency meeting of the bench at midday. "Sir Abraham Cole presided with remarkable composure," Hervey told Seton Canning as they rode back to the grange afterwards. "The other magistrates looked decidedly shaky. They took a lot of persuading that their duties must continue as before."

"I would that they'd make a start with those two we caught in the churchyard."

"They'll be remanded to the assizes this afternoon," Hervey assured him. "Besides aught else, Sir Abraham wants them out of the borough as soon as possible."

Seton Canning nodded. "I'm surprised the bench assembled at all. I imagined they'd have barricaded themselves in after last night."

"I think it was the Bow Street men who put the resolve in them. They've a string of agents now, and it seems their questioning of the churchyard men this morning rendered very serviceable intelligence."

"What about the one that Serjeant Armstrong took?"

"Oh, they've even higher hopes there. He was found with a pistol on him, which means he could be charged with at least one capital offense. They believe he'll turn king's evidence."

Just as they were approaching the grange, there was a noise of gallop-ing on the road behind them. They turned to see Sir Francis Evans at full stretch. "Good Lord," said Hervey, reining his horse about. "What alarm's this?"

Sir Francis's horse was in as great a lather as Hervey had seen, but the general looked invigorated. "Heard about the night's trouble via the *Mercury* offices this morning," he called, springing from the saddle like a man half his age. "Came at once. Just seen Sir Abraham Cole and his justices. Promised 'em more troops as long as they maintain the posse in being. Urged 'em not to swing to repressive measures. I don't want my cavalry drawn into controlling crowds. I don't want them dissipating their strength when it's needed to fight the hard core of these Luddites!"

Grooms rushed to take the reins of the dozen or so horses now snorting and blowing by the gates of the grange.

"Come, then," said Sir Francis, clapping a hand on Hervey's shoulder. "A full and frank account of the past week, if you will."

Hervey began at once as they made their way across the courtyard to the grange house.

Serjeant Armstrong had hastily arranged for coffee. Coffee could allay a great many general officers' complaints, in Armstrong's experience, and the state of the quarter guard, which had turned out for him in cloaks because their tunics were still sodden from firefighting, would be bound to provoke a general's displeasure.

But no, Sir Francis appeared to have no cause for complaint. He took the coffee gladly, sank into a chair, and bid Hervey to do the same. "Tell me of those Bow Street men, Hervey. When did they come?"

Hervey explained the background a little warily, still, for the general's tone could have implied disapproval as well as curiosity.

He need not have worried on this account either, however. Sir Francis thought it the very model of assistance to the civil powers. "I truly believe that it's the fear of being taken in their own homes, with evidence for conviction, which will stop this criminality—for that's what it is, no more, no less. It's the same with the insurrectionists. It's not the plotters and ringleaders that get chopped down by the yeomanry. We can hang and transport all we like, but rooting out them that's scheming should be the priority. I met with the sheriff again yesterday, and he is ruing the dearth of intelligence from his own sources. I congratulate you, therefore, Hervey!"

"Thank you, sir," said Hervey. How easy it was to serve a man like this, a man to place one's trust in. "But I have to say I take no delight in last evening. I was humbugged, and I should have seen it before I did."

Sir Francis looked at him skeptically. "Captain Hervey, a word of advice. Do not be too ready to volunteer your failings to authority. You may find it too convenient, sometimes, for superiors to accept them in lieu of their own."

Hervey nodded. "I'm sorry, sir. I confess to feeling the loss of my trumpeter rather more than I should if this were France."

"Indeed, indeed. It is bound to go heavy with you. And you are aware, of course, that you will have to answer to the courts for the man you killed?"

"I know it, Sir Francis. Sir Abraham Cole said that I should engage an attorney at once, though he supposed it would amount to no great affair."

"I should damn well hope not!" Sir Francis drained his coffee cup, and then a thought seemed to occur to him. "Where is Lord Towcester? I haven't seen him in days."

Hervey explained that the lieutenant colonel had visited only recently, having been paying his respects to the greater landowners of the district.

"That's only right," said Sir Francis, nodding. "Then you shall have to send for more dragoons yourself," he added, emphatically. "It's quiet in Worksop by all accounts. They should be able to spare you a half troop. Well, Hervey, I consider myself very well instructed by all that I've heard. Now, explain to me once more what precisely is this scheme of ambush of yours. You can cover all the roads north of the town, you say—and at one and the same time?"

A letter arrived from Horningsham in the afternoon. Hervey opened it with some trepidation, for it was in Elizabeth's hand, and that could mean only one thing—ill news of the archdeaconry feud, for his father would surely have written if the affair had been resolved happily.

Horningsham
23 September 1817

Dearest Matthew,
I fear I send you discouraging news. Father has been summoned before the consistory on the quarter day next. He is greatly supported by Mr. Keble and others, in London, but it goes very badly with Mama, who is fearful that we shall be promptly dispossessed. I know that your duties in the North must prevent your being with us for many weeks more, and I would not wish you to have any cares on our account, but our mother and father would be greatly comforted by your visiting, especially if the consistory goes ill for us.
  Daniel Coates called yesterday and, on learning that I was to write to you, bade me ask if your instruction to him with

reference to Lord Towcester remained as before. I do not
understand the inquiry, and so I repeat the words exactly as
Daniel spoke them to me, and trust that their meaning is plain
to you.

Please give my very greatest love to Henrietta and say that I
shall write as soon as events permit. Forgive, please, the haste
in which this is written, but I have a short time only before a
postboy is to come.

Your ever affectionate sister,
Elizabeth

Henrietta's carriage returned to the grange a little before five. "Where
is my husband, Mr. Seton Canning?"

"I believe he has gone to take exercise, ma'am," said the lieutenant,
smiling. "Though why he should need it after last night's exertions is a
little beyond me, I'm afraid."

"You must tell me of them later," sighed Henrietta rather dismissively,
but taking his hand to step from the chaise.

Private Johnson had already jumped down from the box where, despite Henrietta's request otherwise, he had insisted on traveling since
Chatsworth, and Seton Canning now craned his neck to see the third
passenger, of whom he had heard so much.

"No, Mr. Canning, there is no Mrs. Johnson, or Mrs. Stallybrass,
rather."

The lieutenant looked puzzled.

Johnson saluted. "Excuse me, ma'am; Mr. Canning, sir. I'll report to
Serjeant Armstrong if there's nothing more."

Seton Canning looked at Henrietta, who smiled and shook her head.
"Very well, Johnson," he said, returning the salute with a touch to his
cap. "Dismiss."

Johnson said "Thank you, ma'am" to Henrietta (twice) and scurried
off to the horse lines.

"What a transformation!" said Seton Canning, taking Henrietta's traveling case. "I had no idea Sheffield could be so restorative of the spirits."

Henrietta smiled again. "He is very happy."

"He's reconciled to his mother, then?"

"No. He still does not have a mother. It was Ezra rather than Ezekiel."

"Ma'am?"

She set off up the steps of the grange house. "The testificate was a page from the Book of Ezra. Johnson's was from Ezekiel."

He looked no wiser yet.

"It seems the practice at the Sheffield foundling hospital—or the workhouse, as Johnson will insist on demonizing it—is to tear a page in half from a special Bible they have, and in the part remaining they record the details of the foundling, and they give the other half to the mother or whoever brings in the child."

"As a *receipt*?" Seton Canning sounded astonished.

"You have lived too long with gentlefolk by the sound of it, Mr. Canning." It gave Henrietta surprising satisfaction to say so.

"Ma'am, that is most unfair. I—"

"Oh, come, Mr. Canning: you don't suppose that *I* make a habit of walking in gutters!"

"No, of course. Would you like some tea?"

"Yes, very much."

He called for fresh water. "But the *name*—'Johnson.' That was an extraordinary coincidence, was it not?"

"No," she said, taking off her gloves. "All the foundlings that month were named Johnson."

"How on earth—"

"That is the custom—like naming hounds with the same letter in a year."

"Great heavens! How perfectly . . ."

Henrietta was warming to her newfound social sensibility. "If he had been left at Lincoln's Inn, he would have been named Lincoln no matter what the month. Just like your serjeant major."

Canning had again learned something new. "Where is Mrs. . . . Stallybrass now?"

"She is with the Bow Street men. I believe the phrase is 'assisting them with their inquiries.' Have you heard of 'twisting in'?"

He hadn't.

"Well, it is the secret rite by which someone is admitted to company of General Ludd. I shall say no more. It is not women's business."

Seton Canning could not imagine Henrietta conceding that there was anything of the kind, but he thought prudently to let it go. They chatted for not many minutes more before Hervey returned from his solitary ride. He managed a sort of smile, which alerted her to some distress while not suggesting the same to his lieutenant. He bent to kiss her, said how pleased he was to see the journey had not fatigued her, and then asked Seton Canning if he would leave them alone for a time. When he was gone, he asked how things had been with Johnson. She told him briefly of the particulars, saying that she would explain more about Mrs. Stallybrass when he had told her what was troubling him.

Hervey pulled a chair up close to Henrietta and gave her the news of Trumpeter Medwell's death.

Tears came to her eyes at once, for Medwell had been a regular visitor at their quarters. "What a terrible thing to be shot down by a fellow countryman," she said, dabbing at her eyes with a silk square.

"Everyone's been saying the same. It seems so much worse than falling to a French ball."

"Just like the poor Duke of Huntingdon's son in London."

"Exactly so."

Hervey took her hand, and sighed. "And there is ill news from Wiltshire. My father is to be arraigned before a diocesan court. Elizabeth believes he will lose the living."

"I think I had better go back to Longleat," she said, sorrowfully.

He took up her hand again. "My darling, I would very much prefer if you didn't."

Never had she heard him sound quite so dejected. She smiled, encouragingly, and kissed his forehead. "No, I shan't go. We stay together now, be what may."

CHAPTER 16

REVOLUTION STALKS OUR COUNTY!

Leading Article, The **Nottingham Mercury,** *October 3, 1817*

The insurrectional state to which this county has been reduced for the last month has no parallel in history, since the troubled days of Charles I. Even the depredations of Luddism in these parts only five years ago did not carry the attendant threats upon the Sovereign, his Regent or Government which have been uttered these last weeks in the name of Justice.

The rioters appear suddenly in armed parties, under regular commanders. The chief commander, whoever he may be, is styled *General Ludd.* They march to their objective with military discipline, ten abreast, and as soon as the work of destruction is completed, the Leader draws up his men, calls the roll, each man answering to a particular number instead of a name; they then fire off their pistols, give a great shout and march off in regular military order.

In spite of curfews and a *posse comitatus,* the Authorities seem powerless to halt the wave of machine breaking which nightly threatens the prosperity of these parts, and so thorough is that destruction, so indiscriminate in its abuse of employers who are spoken of by their workers as bad and good alike, that We are of the opinion that the specter of *Jacobinism* which stalked the Continent these past twenty years is come to our shores, and that only by the most vigorous action shall it be extinguished!

A week passed in which, despite the worst fears of the *Mercury,* the bor-ough of Mansfield—and, indeed, most of the county—remained peace-able, and Hervey and Henrietta were able to enjoy an interlude of domesticity at the grange.

One afternoon, an orderly dragoon brought a letter from regimental headquarters in Nottingham. Hervey read it, twice, and then put it down. "I can scarcely believe it. The man must be an imbecile!"

"Lord Towcester, I suppose?" sighed Henrietta, laying aside her novel. "Tell me of it."

"He says that the uniforms of my troop are now in the worst condition of any in the regiment and that I must put in hand their replacement at once."

"And are they?"

He looked at her in some surprise. "How can I know? For I have seen none but my own troop for three weeks! Barrow's was here for only a couple of days before Lord Towcester sent them back."

She simply raised her eyebrows.

"In any case, we've scarcely been chafing them for our own amuse-ment!"

"How shall you have them replaced?"

"The men must pay for them themselves, or else I must. We'll make claims on the borough, and the insurance companies for the fires we've put out, but I'll warrant the money'll be slow in the paying."

She picked up her book again, and grinned. "Perhaps the clothiers of Mansfield can knit you all new tunics!"

"Henrietta!"

"But it is, I grant you, a strange preoccupation in the middle of all this skirmishing."

"Nothing I do seems to please Lord Towcester. Sir Abraham sent him a letter of appreciation and you'd think it had been a protest by the Prince Regent. It's only when General Evans rides him that his stu-pidity's at all curbed."

"And where is the general gone to, that Lord Towcester is let out of his asylum?"

"London. To see Lord Sidmouth at the Home Office."

She merely raised an eyebrow.

All this was really most dispiriting. Hervey was tired of talking about his commanding officer. "What do you read there?"

"Miss Austen's last novel. It is called *Emma.*"

"Oh. A pretty name."

"Yes," she said, turning a page.

"I wonder if Emma Lucie is married to Mr. Somervile yet?"

"I hope so. They sound very suited from what you spoke of him. But I have had no word from her in response to mine."

"Another two months at least, even by the Egyptian route."

She raised another eyebrow.

He poured more tea. "Why did you say her *last* novel? Has Miss Austen declared she will write no more?"

"Oh, Matthew! She died but two months ago. Did you not read of it?"

"Evidently not. I am sorry of it. Was she very old?"

"She was not three and forty! And, I confess, her passing made me most alert to my own mortality, for I had spoken with her in Bath only the month before you returned."

"My darling!"

She shook her head. "Did you ever read the book of hers I gave you?"

He had to own that he had not. "I confess it never engaged me."

"Matthew, do you *ever* read novels?"

"Yes."

"Which last did you read?"

The answer came *almost* at once. "It was called *Waverley*."

"Was it of soldiery?"

He frowned. "There were some very romantic episodes."

"It *was* about soldiery! And how recently was it that you read?"

"On board ship."

Now she frowned. "The return or the outward passage?"

He sighed. "I prefer poetry."

She laughed. "I know you do. Then I shall read to you tonight, when we are in bed! John Keats."

He looked blank.

"Don't you remember? Mr. Keble spoke of him when we were at the henge those three years ago, but I don't think he'd been much heard of then. I have his first volume, published only this spring."

He smiled in pleasant anticipation. "You know, I *do* very much like it here."

She laughed again. "Of course you do, Matthew Hervey! You are surrounded by your dragoons, the lieutenant colonel is twenty miles away, and you have me with you!"

"In that order?"

"I think, probably, yes!"

They kissed, and would have moved closer, but a knock at the door reclaimed them. Private Johnson announced the Bow Street men.

"Come in, gentlemen, come in," said Hervey, holding out his hand and smiling with real pleasure. "You have been elusive this past week or so."

"Indeed we have, sir; indeed we have. Good afternoon, your ladyship."

Henrietta smiled as warmly, and asked Johnson to bring more cups.

"Sit down, gentlemen, please," said Hervey, helping them to chairs. "What brings you?"

"I think we may be very close to a deciding bout," said the senior of the two. It seemed an apt metaphor, for he had always looked to Hervey like a man at home in the ring.

"Indeed, Mr. Wilks? Then I am all attention."

The other investigator, the former insurance man, took out his pocketbook and sat poised to make notes. There was no look of the pugilist to Mr. Bartle. Rather had he the appearance of an apothecary.

Wilks drained his teacup, drew forward in his chair, and began to speak in a more confidential tone. "I do believe we know the identities of the leaders of the so-called Shirewood Brigade. It's they that have been organizing the violence in the north of the county."

Hervey nodded. "You know who is this 'Enoch'?"

Wilks smiled. "That much was easy, sir. Enoch is a hammer."

Hervey did not comprehend.

"The hammers they use for machine breaking. They're called Enochs after the ironworks that makes them."

Hervey felt a little foolish. "Do continue, please, Mr. Wilks."

"We had a meeting with General Evans last night in the castle when he got back from London." At this point Wilks looked rather uncomfortable. "I'm sorry, sir, but though I know we are in the borough's pay, and you asked us here, we had a duty to the GOC."

"Of course, of course," said Hervey, who had never for once supposed that Bow Street men worked to as rigid a system of command as his.

"Well, then, the Home Office, it seems, is of the opinion that although there is plotting against the government all over the place, it is haphazard. There's no method in it. All their spies and informers suggest the same, that these Luddites are only associated with the conspirators by opportunity—by suggestion, even, for the most part. And the likes of

Hunt and the Spa Fielders have no more connection with the trouble here than Bonaparte."

Hervey was glad to hear it, but didn't immediately see the implication.

"If we can give one knockout blow to one of these *brigades*"—Wilks's dislike of using an otherwise honorable term was quite evident—"then there's a very good chance the others will be cowed into surrender—or, rather, inactivity. They'll fear we've penetrated their secrecy entirely, and the threat of the gallows should do the rest."

"And we are now in a position to do this, to deliver this knockout blow?"

Wilks smiled, and the suggestion of the same came to the lips of his assistant. "We are, sir!"

"Would you like more tea before you tell us how, Mr. Wilks?" asked Henrietta.

"Indeed I should, ma'am!"

"And you, Mr. Bartle?"

"Very much, your ladyship."

She filled their cups and asked if they would prefer that she left.

Before Hervey could say anything, Wilks protested that indeed he would not. "For it was your information with regard to Mrs. Stallybrass that began the trail to this evening, your ladyship."

Henrietta seemed very gratified by this.

"Well, sir, it seems that your ambushing scheme has them running very scared. They can't assemble in the numbers they need, especially since the posse is now so effective."

It was now Hervey's turn to feel gratified.

"And your dragoons are so quick about the place that our night owls fear being counterattacked if they do manage to concentrate. It's the same at Worksop."

Hervey was pleased to hear that Barrow was having equal success, though hardly surprised.

"They've called a meeting tonight at the Crow's Nest in Cuckney."

Hervey knew the place. "About the remotest spot they could have chosen."

Wilks agreed. "If they can get there, there'll be every twisted-in commander in the North of the county—and one or two from as far afield as Derby and Yorkshire."

"How many?"

"Upwards of twenty. And they'll have their guards with them."

Hervey blew out his breath. "Twenty! That would be a devil of a fight with twice the number of dragoons."

Henrietta began to look anxious.

"With *three times* the number!" Wilks interjected. "These'll be desperate men when they're cornered. All of them'll face the gallows."

"I shall have to send for help from Ollerton or Worksop."

"I'd rather you didn't, sir," said Wilks. "It would be better that there was no extra movement of troops. They'll be jittery, these men, and I wouldn't want them frightened off. They'll know your dragoons by sight by now, and they'd recognize reinforcements from a different troop."

"Then I shan't be able to lay my ambushes tonight."

"No, sir. I wouldn't want you to, for that might discourage a few as well. No, we want the birds to flock to the Crow's Nest, like regular black crows of an evening."

"Rookeries, again, Mr. Wilks?" smiled Hervey.

"Rookeries indeed, sir. How many birds does it take to make a rook pie, d'ye think?"

"As many as will?"

Henrietta rose, a little pale, and excused herself. Hervey made to follow, but she bade him stay. "Just a little air, that is all. I was never partial to the dish."

"Very well, gentlemen," said Hervey, sitting down again. "But I'm afraid I shall have to have a written request from a magistrate—either that or an order from my commanding officer."

Wilks looked uncomfortable for the second time. "How can I put this, sir?" He cleared his throat. "The GOC said, most emphatically, that we were to treat direct with you, and on no account to speak of it . . . in Nottingham itself. The general will be here himself by five, he said."

Hervey made no comment. "So we shall ask Sir Abraham Cole?"

"That would be best, sir," agreed Wilks. "Also, the general's DAAG will come to apprise you of the position as regards the new act."

Hervey went to a writing table, wrote a few lines to Sir Abraham, and called Private Johnson to have them delivered straightaway to the moot hall, where the chairman of the bench had taken up residence. "Well, then, gentlemen," he said, taking the stopper from a decanter of Madeira. "I imagine we have rather a lot of details to discuss?"

———

Sir Francis Evans arrived shortly before five. His ears were bright red as he stepped from the stirrups to the mounting block, and Hervey took note of the danger signal. His look was more fearsome than merely angry, however, for there was a glint in his eye like a hungry bird of prey—a hawk which had spotted its quarry and was savoring the swoop. "Everything set, Hervey?"

"Yes, General," Hervey replied surely. "There is just the bidding from the magistrate to come."

"Good. Better tell me your intention, then." Sir Francis pulled off his gloves and set about the dust on his sleeves with the utmost aggression.

Hervey took him to his map board, where Johnson had already placed a steaming pot of coffee. "You don't miss tricks much, do you, Hervey?"

"Indeed, sir." Hervey assumed he meant the coffee.

"Nor do I, Hervey. Nor do I!"

"No, sir." Hervey was becoming a little lost, and thought he would press on with what he knew. "There is Cuckney, sir," he began, pointing out the little cluster of houses where the old Worksop and Chesterfield turnpikes crossed. "It's eight or nine miles from here, and the roads are good. The Crow's Nest was once a posthouse, and it has good-size stables, with a few liveries still." He showed the general a sketch plan drawn from the recollection of the half dozen dragoons who had visited there once or twice in the first days. "The Bow Street men say the Luddites will assemble over the space of an hour or so, under cover of regular taverners, and when all are come—by nine, they reckon—they will meet in the stables loft for about an hour and then disperse in time for the curfew."

"The trick will be judging the moment to take them. Has Barnaby instructed you?"

"Yes, General. He arrived an hour ago. As I understand it, the new act makes assembly for a seditious purpose illegal."

"Just so. It's meant to stop jackanapes like Hunt from drawing the crowds and hotting 'em up, but it could serve our purpose, too, for if there isn't enough evidence for charges under the common law for unlawful assembly, then we ought still to be able to net them for sedition. Either way it'll be the rope."

"Mr. Wilks says there will be an informer at the meeting, and that it will be his evidence that will convict."

The general looked very satisfied.

"But in the event that the man is not there, Mr. Bartle will already be secreted in the loft to witness it."

"And how shall he get there without being seen?"

Hervey smiled. "It's very ingenious, sir. He'll take a—"

"No," said the general, sharply. "I don't need to know."

"Very good, sir. So, we shall have our patrols about the roads before dark so as to give every appearance of the usual, and then they'll make a proper show of retiring from the district, but they'll assemble in the forest in subdivisions here." He pointed to half a dozen patches of green in a broad circle around Cuckney. "By the clock, they'll leave their hides and make a cordon about the Crow's Nest at a depth of about a furlong."

"That much is easy enough, Captain Hervey," the general agreed.

"It will bring Spain back to mind, for sure, sir."

The general saw that, too. "And then what?"

"Major Barnaby says that we stand to have things go badly against us if we do not call upon them to throw down their arms—assuming they will be armed, that is."

"It's a very fair presumption, Hervey."

"And in truth, sir, I don't wish to go in with fire against men who have not offered resistance."

The general made a wry smile. "*Tirez les premiers,* Captain Hervey?"

Hervey sighed. "You yourself said it was a most objectionable business firing on one's own countrymen, General."

"Indeed I did, Hervey. Your forbearance does you credit. And, in truth, there'll be more example in the gallows and the transport than dead meat."

"Quite, sir," he agreed, though a shade caught by the tone.

"But see here, those are decent sentiments, and never should I wish the day to come when we had insufficient officers of that mind. But these will all be twisted-in men, looking the gallows in the face. You're not to take any chances."

Sir Francis's robust support was very welcome. "No, sir. I intend that we shock them so greatly they will throw all in."

"Very well. And you shall have my best support."

Hervey was not sure of his entire meaning. "Sir?"

"I mean that I shall ride with you. I do not send men on such hazards while I warm myself by a fire!"

"No, Sir Francis, indeed not," said Hervey, with a slightly anxious note. "But—"

"If things go badly it'll be me to answer for it, and I'm an infinitely harder fish to swallow than a captain of dragoons."

"I am *very* much obliged, sir." Hervey supposed that the disadvantages of the general's interfering were outweighed by the safety he provided.

"Well, then: do we eat before we go?" said Sir Francis, with a proper smile at last.

"Yes, General—in half an hour, when my cornet is back with the bidding from Sir Abraham Cole."

"Good. I'll take a little Madeira with you until then."

Johnson brought a new decanter.

"There is one thing, Sir Francis," said Hervey cautiously as he took his glass.

"Aye?"

He cleared his throat. "I am uneasy that I have not . . . not had the opportunity to speak with my commanding officer on this affair."

Sir Francis Evans turned a gimlet eye on him, and his ear reddened. "Do not *sport* with me, Captain Hervey!"

Lieutenant Seton Canning moved like a seasoned woodsman along the forest track to where the last of the subdivisions stood waiting, the moon being up early and throwing all the light he needed. Corporal Clarkson was ready for him: "Subdivision fed and watered, carbines and pistols primed, nothing to report, sir." It had been the same with the others—all in their places, in good heart and eager for the chase.

"Another half hour, Corporal, and then we'll break cover. Stand easy!" Seton Canning lit a cigar.

Cuckney was about a mile to the south—the other subdivisions were a little closer—and timing was of the essence. The cordon had to be set by nine, so that if anything went wrong at the Crow's Nest they would be able to net the assembly as they bolted. But there could be no movement from the coverts until the very last minute in case a latecomer detected them and alerted the rest. They would even run the risk of bumping into honest travelers, but that was a risk they would simply have to take, in which case they would detain the wayfarers until the affair was over. When the time came, Seton Canning's dragoons would trot for half the distance to the hamlet along a green bridleway, which would take them four minutes; then, taking about the same time again, they would walk for the next quarter of a mile so as to make less noise, and then they would dismount and lead the horses the last furlong, posting dragoons at intervals until they met up with the other subdivisions and the whole village was encircled (this would probably take another ten minutes). They would therefore leave the covert at eighteen minutes to nine, a few minutes before the others.

"It is just gone ten past eight, Sir Francis," said Hervey, closing his hunter.

"Very well, then." The general's orderly held down the offside stirrup as his principal mounted the handy little mouse dun, which he seemed excessively attached to, and beckoned to his ADC. "If that mare of yours is still horsing, and squeals so much as once, I'll send the pair of you packing at once!"

"Sir!" The ADC was from the First Guards, and therefore wont to answer any inquiry or command with the simple affirmative, relying solely on its infinite tonal possibilities to convey meaning.

Hervey gave Henrietta a parting kiss, sprang into the saddle, and gathered up the reins. Gilbert crabbed right and rear, backing into the ADC's horse, who squealed and set her teeth at the gray's rump.

"For God's sake, Harry!" The general seemed much preoccupied with the behavior of his ADC's mare.

"My fault, Sir Francis," owned Hervey. "He's still a bit green about carriage lights."

The chaise's lights made a sweep of the party as it turned full circle in the yard.

"All set, Serjeant Armstrong?" called Hervey.

"Aye, sir," came Armstrong's voice from the window. "It's a press, but we're in."

"Very well, Mr. St. Oswald, lead on, if you please."

The general obliged Hervey greatly as they rode to Cuckney by saying nothing, except the occasional reproof to his long-suffering ADC. The moon gave the evening an almost merry feel, as if they were off to a levee or a ball. The first mile they did at a walk, and only a milk cart passed in the other direction (on the whole, Sherwood was not a place to be about after dark). Then they made a good trot on the macadamized turnpike—eight miles an hour—with something still in reserve.

Plans were all made, orders had been given; there was nothing for Hervey to do now but enjoy the ride—and relish, perhaps, what was to come. He found himself humming "Rule, Britannia," until he supposed it not quite apt, and then remembered another of Thomson's ballads.

> *"Pour all your speed into the rapid game;*
> *For happy he who tops the wheeling chase;*
> *Has every maze evolved, and every guile disclosed;"*

He had to search his memory hard for the rest, repeating the last line two or three times so that more than once Johnson glanced his way.

> *"Who knows the merits of the pack;*
> *Who saw the villain seized, and dying hard,*
> *Without complaint, though by a hundred mouths*
> *Relentless torn: O glorious he, beyond*
> *His daring peers!"*

"Is tha all right, Cap'n 'Ervey, sir?" asked Johnson in the nearest thing to a whisper he could manage.

"Yes," Hervey assured him. "Never better!"

All Saints' Church clock struck the half hour as they trotted through Clipstone. The village was ill lit and the street empty, but dogs began barking and soon there were faces at the windows, and braver ones at doors.

"Five minutes!" called Lieutenant Seton Canning sometime later in the northernmost covert. Men began stowing canteens and tightening girths. Soon the other subdivisions would be doing the same, taking the time by the flickering light of a candle (what a to-do it had been to find enough watches).

The road party sped on, up a long incline to where an old beacon tower kept lonely sentinel, the driver checking his team at the top for a steady descent.

"Mount!" Seton Canning's order was hushed but clear, and eight dragoons, their corporal, and lieutenant put left foot into stirrup, pushed up with the right and swung into the saddle. They formed twos on the track at the edge of the covert, and in a few minutes were trotting across the Worksop road and onto the green bridleway for Cuckney.

There was no clock to strike the three-quarter hour for Hervey and his men, for they were in the middle of the broad oaks which had built the nation's wooden walls. There was nothing but the odd forester's hut between here and Cuckney, not a light to tell the time by, either. But the pace had been steady and even: he knew they could be neither late nor early by more than a very few minutes. In another mile or so, when they reached the old ford on the Meden, he would close up and read his hunter by the carriage lights.

Cuckney church had no carillon, but Seton Canning was confident of his timing as he led his mare the last furlong before deploying in their cordon position, the other three subdivisions doing the same time on the farther points of the compass. The horses were quiet, to Seton Canning's and all the corporals' relief: it was going well.

The longcase clock in the parlor of the grange struck the hour. Henrietta glanced up. Nine o'clock—was that not the time when . . . She turned back to her novel, trying to remember what she had just read. And still she felt sick.

A pheasant started noisily from under Corporal Cook's feet, its alarm call sounding loud enough to carry to Nottingham. His subdivision froze. They remained stock-still for a full five minutes, until a vixen's bark nearby gave them their alibi.

The road party was late by a mere four minutes at the ford, and these they made up easily on the straight incline to Warsop Hill next, where Hervey halted the party at twelve minutes past nine.

"We're at the rallying point, Sir Francis," he said. "You can see our object quite clearly, yonder." There were only one or two lights a quarter of a mile distant, but they stood out distinctly on the open heath about the crossroads. "I'll leave Cornet St. Oswald, and he'll come at the signal."

"Very well, Captain Hervey. Do you recognize it if I say 'Bestir yourself, and then call on the gods'?" He held out his hand.

Hervey took it and smiled. "I do indeed, sir. And thank you for it. With your leave, then?" He saluted, took off his shako, reined about and kicked on.

A minute later the chaise rolled up to the hamlet at a steady trot, the driver expecting a signal to halt at any second. It came just short of the old turnpike lodge, a lantern swinging in the middle of the road. "What's yer business?" The challenge was in the rough accent of the county.

"Master Cutler on 'is way back to Sheffield!"

The sentry held up his lantern and moved towards the nearside door. Serjeant Armstrong had already slipped from the offside one.

"Show yerself, please, Master Cutler," called the sentry.

Armstrong sprang on him from behind. His forearm was round the man's throat in an instant, stifling any sound. "Not a word, lad, or you'll feel my saber in your side!"

Private Scriven was out, too, a regular pocket Atlas. They bound the man up tight with horse bandages.

"Pistol to 'is 'head, Scriven," rasped Armstrong. "Wait on Mr. Oswald's men to take him off!" He leaped back inside as the wheels began to turn.

"Well done, Geordie Armstrong!" said Hervey to himself. He would tell Caithlin of it, with the greatest satisfaction.

They slowed to a walk to turn into the Crow's Nest yard. "Who goes there?" came another challenge, this time from the shadows, and no lamp.

"Master Cutler, homebound. We've a lame wheeler. Have you a livery?"

"No liveries!"

"We pay handsomely," called Hervey from behind, seeing a window open partially in the loft and then close again.

"Why don't you put t'other 'oss on, then?"

"Because he's shy of the traces!"

The inquisitor stepped from the shadows. "The Master Cutler, d'ye say? I saw 'im meself only a fortnight back at t'Goose Fair." He put his hand to the door.

Armstrong had it open before he could turn the handle, driving his fist in the man's face with all his strength. There was a muffled cry, which had Hervey turning for the loft with his pistol. But no window opened.

"Come on, then!" Hervey called, jumping from the saddle and ramming his shako back on his head.

Out from the chaise sprang Armstrong, five dragoons, and Wilks, all now with shakos on, including the Bow Street man, for that was the surest way of recognition in the half-light and, God forbid, the smoke.

Up the outside steps they went, Wilks porting the sledgehammer. A footboard broke under Hervey's boot. "Who's there?" came from inside.

"Christ," gasped Hervey.

"Enoch!" boomed Wilks, and swung the hammer with all his force.

The door jumped from its hinges. In they burst. *Bedlam!* Shots—swords—clubs—fists—screams—oaths—threats—pleas.

On the road, St. Oswald, the general, and a dozen dragoons spurred to a gallop, and on the heath the cordon began walking in, sabers drawn, pistols ready, reins crooked on the arm.

"Remember—no shooting without challenging first," bellowed Seton Canning. "And outside the cordon only! Outside only!"

A minute later St. Oswald's party was at the inn, seizing Luddites as they fled the yard in terror, and then running up the steps to the fight in the loft. But it was all over. There were half a dozen men on the floor, bleeding in varying degrees, one of them Corporal Troughton, who had covered Hervey well but painfully. Corporal Perrot was already binding up his shoulder. He'd live; as would four of the Luddites—for the time being, at least. Another was stone dead, and four more were holding their hands so high they were touching the beams.

"Right, you bastards, let's have you all in the yard," growled Armstrong.

When they were gone, Bartle climbed down from the eaves. He dusted off his shoulders, then held up his pocketbook. "I have it all, sir."

Hervey sighed, with no little relief. "You'll both be very glad to get back to London, I'm sure!"

Wilks blew out the residue from his pistol pan. "Sir, I can't tell you how fine it was to smell powder smoke once again!"

CHAPTER 17

TO THE VICTOR

Mansfield, Mid-November

Three weeks passed in which there was not only a cessation of Luddite violence in the shire but also a remarkable disinclination for the age-old activities of the night such as poaching and housebreaking, for the belief throughout the county was that the authorities now had the ear to all unlawful activity. The magistrates and solid citizens of the borough were fulsome in their praise of Hervey's troop for the affair of the Crow's Nest, and sent them at once a quantity of beer and ham.

The *Nottingham Mercury* was no less appreciative, and lauded the regiment in several editions. "We may safely say," it proclaimed with lofty certainty, "that there cannot be a regiment in the service more efficient, nor more just in its doings . . . than His Majesty's Sixth Light Dragoons. Lieutenant Colonel the Earl of Towcester has demonstrated himself to be an officer of very singular abilities."

The report was taken up by *The Times,* too, so that Lord Towcester became, in the space of only two months, a name on the lips of London tattlers, and, some said, in Whitehall itself. Ezra Barrow even made a wager with his subalterns that his lordship would be promoted major general within the year. Hervey half hoped that it would be so, for they would then be rid of a commanding officer in whom there was not the slightest confidence outside the pages of the newspapers, and with others equally ill informed. And yet he could scarcely wish the man to be placed in a position where there would be greater opportunity for him to make mischief. In truth, he wished that Sir Francis Evans would exercise some influence at the Horse Guards and hasten Lord Towcester's advance to the half-pay list.

Predictably, Lord Towcester had raged when he had heard of the business at the Crow's Nest, and had only been pacified when he learned of Sir Francis Evans's hand in matters (although as the earl told Hervey pointedly, it was *he* who would make a report on his fitness for promotion, not the GOC). A few days after *The Times*'s report, Hervey was summoned to Nottingham to hear the results of the inquiry by the Excise commissioners into the events surrounding the French landing, which, in broad terms, exonerated him from all blame, but he was dismayed to learn later that the document had been with the lieutenant colonel for over a month.

Throughout this time, however, it was Henrietta who gave Hervey most cause for anxiety. In herself, she appeared well, but the news of Princess Charlotte's condition, which came by one means or another almost daily from London (once by letter in the princess's own hand), had put her in low spirits. On the third of November she had received word that the queen herself had expressed anxiety, for the birth of the royal infant was then a fortnight overdue, and there was yet no sign. Dr. Croft was steadfastly refusing any intervention, and the princess was becoming hourly more melancholy. Then, on the seventh, there was intelligence that Princess Charlotte was at last in labor—and Henrietta's spirits rallied. But on the tenth came the terrible news that Charlotte and her child were dead.

Hervey spent a despondent breakfast with Henrietta that morning. He had the greatest difficulty condoling with her to any appreciable effect, for a part of her sorrow was at the loss of an association which, though by no means ever close, was nonetheless a true one. Yet he also knew that there was an element of foreboding in her sorrow, and *that* he felt wholly powerless to ease. But he had to leave her temporarily, nevertheless, since Sir Abraham Cole had sent him a note the evening before, saying that there was business of which he would speak, and in seclusion, and that he would come with his chaise at ten.

The melancholy news from London was dampening Sir Abraham's spirits, too, as he and Hervey set off towards Welbeck next morning. Sir Abraham was of the decided opinion that it boded ill for the peace of the country, for with no infant heir to the throne on which the populace might dote, there was all too much opportunity for the Whigs—and even republicans—to exploit the ample shortcomings of the Prince Regent. He was sure that there would be trouble when it came to a coronation: the Princess Caroline was not going to be excluded easily, and might well become a figurehead for forces opposed to the regent. Hervey questioned whether the princess would take such a course, but Sir Abraham pronounced himself sure that she lacked the sense to realize, let alone resist, such exploitation. Hervey felt some need to speak for his erstwhile royal colonel, but then thought better, for her reputation was now such that any reasonable man could not but share Sir Abraham's opinion— albeit with the greatest sadness.

Sir Abraham said he was pleased beyond measure that the Luddite troubles seemed abated—finished, even—for throughout the North and Midlands the forces of the law were making inroads on the secretive organization. But he was unhappily of a mind that Luddite violence would soon be replaced by Reform violence, perhaps a more damaging thing than the sledgehammers of the machine breakers, for its objective was less material than political.

The day was sunny, a fine autumn morning for all that the news and prospects were grim. After a little way farther they stopped to drop the barouche's half hood, to continue with the senses open fully to the sights, the sounds, and the scents of the season in this, said Sir Abraham proudly, "the finest of the shires." In another half an hour they turned through the gates of Manvers Priory, a house about the same size as Sir Abraham's own, but with a larger park and a small lake within its grounds. Hervey had seen it before only at a distance, for it had not suffered attack nor threat of it, its occupant being an elderly dowager of the Dukeries. He was intrigued, therefore, as they pulled up to the front, and Sir Abraham bid him step down.

The house bore signs that the occupant was not at home, however: the windows were shuttered, the chimneys idle, and there was no footman to attend them.

"Lady Anne died three weeks ago, I'm sorry to say," Sir Abraham told him. "She was a good sort—knew her neighbors and village folk alike."

"It's a fair prospect, the lake especially. Do I suppose that you bring me here because you intend taking the lease?" Since Hervey had never met Lady Anne, there seemed no reason to express any particular regret at her passing.

Sir Abraham smiled. "You're ever sharp, Captain Hervey. Yes, I had a mind to negotiate for the lease."

"Then you'll not rebuild Clipstone? I thought that surveyors were already at work."

"Oh, yes. Indeed I shall rebuild Clipstone!"

"Then why should you want the lease on this house?"

Sir Abraham smiled again, took a flask from the door pocket, and offered it him. "Captain Hervey, command of the Sherwood Yeomanry falls vacant soon. The bench and the association are of one mind—that you should have it. And with command shall go the lease of Manvers Priory!"

Hervey had never been more astounded than by this proposition—not even the appointment to the duke's staff, nor the brevet and its promise of regimental promotion. He could scarcely make a sound, even of astonishment.

"And, Captain Hervey—how may I put this?—you would be handsomely salaried."

"Sir Abraham, I . . ."

"And there are other inducements, indeed. The living of Manvers Parva is vacant—a very presentable one, I'm told—and the tenant of Manvers Priory has the advowson. There are one or two pretty cottages with the estate, too."

"Sir Abraham, I confess I am exceedingly flattered, more than I can express . . . but I cannot think entirely clearly."

"Of course, Captain Hervey, of course!" said Sir Abraham. "This is scarcely a matter on which I would expect a decision from the *saddle,* so to speak. A week, shall we say?"

Hervey took his leave of Sir Abraham some distance from the grange, deciding that a walk might give him opportunity to assemble his thoughts and objections before sharing them with Henrietta.

Although the new appointment carried the rank of lieutenant colonel, it would hold no seniority within the army as a whole. He would have to sell out from the Sixth, of course. But perhaps if he went on half-pay instead he could rejoin the colors later, as major possibly? Or, if his seniority and means allowed it, as lieutenant colonel, although that rank would require a prodigious sum of money. But Sir Abraham had hinted that the yeomanry command would not leave him impecunious—quite the opposite, indeed—although the upkeep of Manvers Priory and the social obligations of a commanding officer of yeomanry would also make their demands. Then again, what prospects did he truly have with the Sixth? He stood on the wrong side of his commanding officer, and that would be enough to blight any hope of advancement. Yet how might he like leaving the regiment, perhaps for good, and those who had come to look upon him as more than just an officer? In the army, people came and went all the time. Nothing was permanent, and that, he supposed, was one of the strengths of the system, as well as one of its weaknesses. He needn't leave *everyone* behind, though. He could make Armstrong serjeant major and let him have one of the pretty cottages for his family, Collins could be promoted serjeant, and Johnson corporal. He might even be able to make Mr. Lincoln quartermaster. There was much more to this advancement than just his *own* fortunes.

Hervey thought of his father. Was this not the very solution to his problems with the archdeacon? Why should not the Reverend Thomas Hervey become rector of Manvers Parva, and find his ease in its extensive glebe and two thousand a year? Elizabeth would be content, as the countryside was pleasant and there seemed rather more opportunity here of her moving in county circles. Even Mrs. Strange could have employment in the parish school.

Henrietta, too, would have a house in which she might truly feel at home, not the mean little places they would otherwise have to take. Seeing her that night, asleep at the White Hart in Nottingham, he had come to realize how unkind was his transplanting of her from the elegance of Longleat to the soldier's camp. At Manvers Priory she would enjoy the company of her equals in the county, and, indeed, in the neighboring ones, for driving was a good deal easier than in Wiltshire. She and Elizabeth could see each other often again. Above all, she and he would see each other every day. They need hardly spend an evening, let alone a night, but in each other's company. And here she could bear their children in comfort and safety, and raise them healthily. If ever a death had been more instructive than the Princess Charlotte's and her child's, he did not know of it.

As Hervey walked into the grange yard his mind was made up, and his opinion was strengthened—in respect of his reasoning at least—by the report which greeted him.

"Hervey! Thunderously good news!" beamed Seton Canning, rushing over from the picket post. "Those rumors these past weeks: well, we're to see America after all!"

Hervey appeared perplexed.

"The regiment is being sent to Canada with two others—infantry. There's a great to-do about warship building on the lakes. We're wanted to make a show on the border!"

Private Johnson brought coffee into a sitting room at the grange, where Hervey and Henrietta were in earnest conversation.

"Thank you, Johnson. That will be all. I shall not be at watering parade. Ask Mr. Seton Canning to carry on, if you will."

"Right, sir." Johnson picked up his captain's cloak and shako and left without another word.

"No, Matthew," said Henrietta when the door was closed.

Hervey was astonished. It had not crossed his mind for one second that she might have any objection whatever. "But *why,* my love? Everything about this offer is so singularly attractive!"

"No, it is not. Not everything."

He was now thoroughly perplexed. "You have not seen the house, I grant you, but—"

"It is not the house, Matthew."

"Then what is it?"

She sighed. "You speak of Serjeant Armstrong: why should he be happy to take his ease in a cottage in Manvers Parva? It would be like taking a foxhound from last year's entry and putting a collar on it. And Corporal Collins, too: do you think he is so hungry for a serjeant's chevron that he would wish to join a regiment of catshooters, as you call them?"

Henrietta's forthrightness took him aback, as well as her evident grasp of military cant. She had rallied bravely from the morning's news—that much was clear.

"And what about *you*, Matthew? How should *you* like it? Do you mean to tell me that the prospect of trotting about Nottinghamshire for the next twenty years shall please you?"

"My darling, it is not *I* whom I think of. There is the happiness of . . ." He looked at the swelling at her skirts, slight though it still was.

She took his hand. "Matthew, dearest, if you are not happy then I can never be. And if you care to think on that you cannot but see that this business with the yeomanry would be a very sad affair indeed."

"But the orders for Canada?"

"Matthew, your troop has been abuzz with life since the news came! I have no doubt that you yourself are eager for it, too."

She smiled so warmly that he could not help but concede her point, though with an embarrassed sort of grin.

"But the *consequences*, my love: they scarcely bear thinking about."

"What consequences, Matthew?"

"That you and I shall be parted, and at the very worst of times!"

Henrietta's smile returned, accompanied by the familiar, disarming, little shake of the head. "Oh, no, my love. We shall not be parted. I have every mind to see Canada myself."

PART 3

THE AFFAIR AT NIAGARA

Treaty of Peace and Amity
between His Britannic Majesty and the United States of America

His Britannic Majesty and the United States of America desirous of terminating the war which has unhappily subsisted between the two Countries, and of restoring upon principles of perfect reciprocity, Peace, Friendship, and good Understanding between them . . . have agreed upon the following Articles.

ARTICLE THE FIRST

There shall be a firm and universal Peace between His Britannic Majesty and the United States, and between their respective Countries, Territories, Cities, Towns, and People of every degree without exception of places or persons. All hostilities both by sea and land shall cease as soon as this Treaty shall have been ratified by both parties as hereinafter mentioned. . . .

ARTICLE THE NINTH

The United States of America engages to put an end immediately after the Ratification of the present Treaty to hostilities with all the Tribes or Nations of Indians with whom they may be at war at the time of such Ratification, and forthwith to restore to such Tribes or Nations respectively all the possessions, rights, and privileges which they may have enjoyed or been entitled to in one thousand eight hundred and eleven previous to such hostilities. Provided always that such Tribes or Nations shall agree to desist from all hostilities against the United States of America, their Citizens, and Subjects upon the Ratification of the present Treaty being notified to such Tribes or Nations, and shall so desist accordingly. And His Britannic Majesty engages on his part to put an end immediately after Ratification of the present Treaty to hostilities with all the Tribes or Nations of Indians with whom He may be at war at the time of such Ratification, and forthwith to restore to such Tribes or Nations respectively all the possessions, rights, and privileges, which they may have enjoyed or been entitled to in one thousand eight hundred and eleven previous to such hostilities. Provided always that such Tribes or Nations shall agree to desist from all hostilities against His Britannic Majesty and His Subjects upon the Ratification of the present Treaty being notified to such Tribes or Nations, and shall so desist accordingly . . .

Done in triplicate at Ghent the twenty-fourth day of December, one thousand eight hundred and fourteen.

GAMBIER
HENRY GOULBURN
WILLIAM ADAMS
JOHN QUINCY ADAMS
J. A. BAYARD
H. CLAY
JON. RUSSELL
ALBERT GALLATIN

CHAPTER 18

REUNIONS

York
Upper Canada
12 January 1818

My dear Father,
You will have received by now, I trust, the brief note of our
safe arrival in Quebec one week past, and I pray that this letter, too, shall find you and Mama and Elizabeth in good
health. I can only add that I pray, also, for your peace and
tranquillity in respect of the disagreements with the diocese,
and I await news of the proceedings of the consistory court
with confidence that Justice shall in the end be done.

Of our own situation I am pleased to send you every good
report, and more fully than I was able in my last. The regiment (less one troop to form a depot at Hounslow) left
Liverpool on the 28th of November with all its horses, and so
well fitted were the transports that we lost naught but half a
dozen during the voyage. This was also occasioned by calm

seas throughout yet a very favorable wind which made for a
faster crossing than sometimes is made, so that we entered
the St. Lawrence River on the 2nd of January, and proceeded
under tow by steam barge (which I had never seen before) for
as far as the rapids above Montreal. There we were disem-
barked and two troops under the major proceeded to that
city where they are to reinforce the garrison. The remaining
three troops were transferred to Lake Ontario, and so to here
at the western part.

I shall not describe the difficulties we had on account of
the *severe* cold (though it is said that the winter this year is
much less severe than usual, else we should not have been
able to get so far up the river) but the men and horses bore it
unexpectedly well, perhaps because the air, though cold, is
very dry and there has been little wind. Above all, Henrietta
has suffered it without distress or complaint. We had good
quarters on the ship which brought us, and the two dozen
wives who accompany the regiment are treated with every
consideration by the agents. For much of the transfer to Lake
Ontario the ladies were taken by sledge and, covered with
furs, they had a very pleasant ride of it indeed! At first I
thought that Henrietta might remain in Montreal for her confinement, but, there being still two months, and she feeling in
hale condition, she has accompanied me here.

York is the most unlikely capital you ever saw. There are
scarce a thousand inhabitants, not counting military. It was
burned by the Americans five years ago and there is much
bitterness still at it. But it grows almost by the day, even in the
depths of winter. What is so very pleasing, though, is that the
lieutenant governor here (in Upper Canada, I mean) is Sir
Peregrine Maitland, who commanded the Guards at
Waterloo. He is the finest of men. And his wife is Lady Sarah
Lennox, an acquaintance of Henrietta's, and his aide-de-
camp of but two months is Charles Addinsel, whose reac-
quaintance from Peninsular days I never felt more pleased to
make. He was a good friend of d'Arcey Jessope's, of whom
you heard me speak much. So neither Henrietta nor I shall be
wanting in engaging company, it seems, no matter how hard a
winter it goes.

As to the military purpose for which we were hastened
here (I feel that I may say this without prejudice to safety) it
would appear that the alarm is past, and we may find ourselves altogether more agreeably employed than was supposed. . . .

Hervey put down his pen and read over the letter. What his father would
make of the vivid ink, he did not know. Perhaps he should have explained that his own had frozen solid on the last leg of the journey, broken the glass of the bottle, and then, when the baggage had been brought
inside, thawed into his unexpectedly absorbent pelisse coat. Private
Johnson said he could remove the ink without too much trouble, but
Hervey doubted it, and thought he would have to reconcile himself to
writing off a second coat in ten years. He'd see a pauper's grave yet, he
sighed.

He looked again at the last paragraph. It was not untrue; he need not
concern himself there. But it was so far from the whole truth that he worried it was more than he habitually allowed under the general principle
of not alarming his family (which had always made his letters from the
Peninsula read as if he had been little more than a spectator). Of course
there was no present danger of renewed fighting: that much was clear to
him in Quebec. This man Bagot, whom Lord Liverpool had sent to settle the question of warships on the Great Lakes, was, by all accounts, not
a man to misjudge things: it seemed that he had drawn the sting that remained of the late war with a new protocol. Hervey was looking forward
to meeting him at dinner at the lieutenant governor's that evening.

But the evening would not, of course, be unalloyed pleasure, for there
would also be the brooding presence of Lord Towcester. What a joy the
last two months had been, separated most of the time by a mile or more
of ocean in their respective transports. However, any hope that the sea air
had improved his lordship's disposition, in essentials, was dashed in
Quebec, where he had stomped about the governor general's apartments
in petulant rage, his desire for easy glory thwarted by the tidings of
peace. There, Hervey had wondered yet again if he should have accepted
Sir Abraham's handsome offer. In truth, he had wondered long about it
during the Atlantic passage, but so pleasant was the cruise that the offer
had faded greatly in its temptation by the time they reached Canada. But
all of Towcester's baseness had been laid bare again since their landfall,
at least to Hervey's eyes, and he could scarcely hope to avoid any more

trials of loyalty. And try as he might to see this country favorably (and there was much in its raw beauty that appealed) Hervey could not detach his feelings from those he supposed Henrietta must have. How, in heaven's name, might she be happy in this frontier of nature? He would love her with all the intensity a man could, but was that—in the spirit's sense—enough to keep the cold from her?

Oh, how he might look back now on the happy, unhurried intimacy of the crossing, and wish he had secured that state forever at Manvers Priory. Was his soldiery so essential a part of that happiness? Henrietta had thought it so, yes; but had he himself truly contemplated it— contemplated it *thoroughly*? He smiled again as the crossing came back to mind, the dinner at Christmas with all the officers, squeezed around the mess table, Henrietta full of laughter. And then the capering with the other ranks that evening. How she had seemed to enjoy both so much. That had been his second Christmas at sea, in three—and never one at home since Shrewsbury. Was this really to be his life forever? Not forever, of course, for even an officer of his age must know of his natural mortality. But was it to be the pattern for all of the life he so wanted for them both? How difficult he found it. How difficult when you loved someone as viscerally *and* cerebrally as he did—*and* when that love was soon to bear its first fruit.

The trouble was—and he knew it not even as deeply as in his heart of hearts—there was no appeasing a man like Towcester. The boil, as it were, was forced to come to some ghastly head, where the lance was all that was left. But might a running sore thereby follow? He could not be certain of success with the blade. Yes, the boil would come to a head, and he would surely have to take the lance to it. The last thing he could afford, however, was for that to occur too soon—while Henrietta still carried their child, for he knew full well that her mind was prey enough still to the doubts born of Princess Charlotte's sad confinement. He was no free agent, even in military matters, now that he had taken a wife.

"You are sure this evening will not fatigue you?"

"Not excessively," replied Henrietta. "Really, this baby is being so very good to me."

Truly, it was. There was a color about her face always, as if she were the girl again. It stirred him as much as had her blushes in those first, novel days of intimacy after their marriage. Her eyes seemed just that bit brighter, too, her voice that much richer. Her hair was a silky gloss—the stallion's coat, where before it might have been the gelding's. The fact of there being a baby, too, was almost imperceptible beneath her high-bodiced dress, though the swelling beneath the bodice must betoken it to anyone who knew her usual figure. Hervey put the fur cloak about her, fastened the front, and then put on his own cloak. "Very well, then, let us to the Maitlands."

The distance to the lieutenant governor's residence was nothing but a few furlongs, but the cold and the snow made even this a trial on foot, so they were taking a carriage heated by a warming pan. The scene was not unlike Horningsham when, every few years or so, the village was besieged by a hard winter. Or, rather, by a month of hard winter instead of the three or even four which came every year here. Snow lay deep over gardens and pasture, and high along the sides of houses, except for the trenchlike path cleared to door or stable. The houses, as in Horningsham, were too scattered to be of any support to each other: there was no network of clearance, therefore, and the notion of community (outside the walls of the fort itself) seemed smothered by this great white blanket. But community there was, thanks largely to the efforts of the garrison, who tirelessly cleared the snow from the main thoroughfares after each fall, making them passable to sled and wheel alike. But unlike Horningsham, there were oil lamps along the streets, and these were now lighting Hervey's and Henrietta's way to the Maitlands as well as might a full moon of a Wiltshire summer. The snow magnified the power of the little lamps, which in their homely flickers made the bitter outdoors seem so much less forbidding, and the two were received only a very few minutes later at Government House not greatly much chilled.

Henrietta had taken tea that very day with Lady Sarah Maitland, and so their conversation was resumed on the same terms of only a few hours before. Hervey had seen Captain Addinsel for a little while on their first evening, two days ago, but they had yet to have any real opportunity for discourse. First, though, he paid his respects to General Maitland, who chatted agreeably after their introduction. Their exchanges were brief, however, in consequence of the arrival of Lord Towcester, followed at once by the minister from the embassy in Washington—Charles Bagot—and his wife. This gave Addinsel the opportunity to take Hervey aside to meet the other dinner guests, one of whom he found immediately engaging.

As acting superintendent of the Upper Canada division, Major Barry

Lawrence wore the green facings—collar, cuffs, and lapels—of the Indian Department of British North America. He was a man of about Hervey's build, in his middle thirties, with a skin the color of new-tanned leather, and when he learned that Hervey was only lately returned from India, he began an interrogation designed to acquaint himself with any similarities in the native methods of organization and fighting. However, Hervey was eventually able to persuade him to volunteer details of the North American Indian, being, he argued, a rather more pertinent subject to time and place. The superintendent was able to say only a little, though, before dinner was announced, leaving Hervey obviously disappointed.

"Come to the department tomorrow, at ten, say, and we can resume," said Lawrence as they proceeded to the dining room. "I'm pleased you take an interest, for it is the most important business to be settled now that we have an agreement on naval matters."

They were fourteen at dinner, but the table was not large, and there was an intimacy to proceedings despite the formality of the seating arrangements. As a privy councillor, Mr. Charles Bagot, envoy-extraordinary and minister plenipotentiary to the United States of America, came before an earl in precedence, and so was seated on Sir Peregrine Maitland's right, with Lady Mary Bagot on his left. Across the table from her husband sat Lady Sarah Maitland, with Lord Towcester on her right. Henrietta was to the minister's right, and Hervey almost opposite. For the first courses Hervey chatted with Charles Addinsel, who sat adjacent at the end of the table, and then to the widow of a commanding officer of the New Brunswick Fencibles, who had remained in York when her late husband's regiment had returned east. From time to time he stole a glance at Henrietta. Once, she caught his look and held it several seconds, reddening about the neck in the way she did when they embraced. Her eyes promised him they would embrace again that evening, for Henrietta's ardor was in no degree diminished by her condition. Indeed, if anything it seemed intensified. And he himself was no less invigorated by it, for all the little blooms of fecundity—the swellings and ripeness—roused every instinct to be one with her.

By the time the sweet dishes were served, the conversation had become enlarged, or rather, the talk at the center of the table was being listened to attentively by the guests at the ends. Lady Sarah Maitland leaned forward, turning towards Hervey, and smiling very prettily said she understood that he, too, had been at the Battle of Waterloo, "and I wonder, did you see anything of my husband's guardsmen?"

The table fell silent. Hervey reddened deeply. Lady Sarah was the same age as Henrietta, and some fifteen years or so her husband's junior. Her inquiry was of a childlike innocence and pride, and not one which even modesty might resist. "I did indeed, ma'am," was the best Hervey could manage, however.

Sir Peregrine, who had hitherto borne a somewhat distant, patrician look, now softened, seeming to smile at the remembrance, even.

"Did you observe when the duke bid them stand up?" asked Lady Sarah.

"Yes, ma'am. We were not so very far on their left at that moment."

"Then tell me how it appeared, for I have heard several accounts," she pressed.

"Well, ma'am, it was towards the end of the day, as you will recall, and Bonaparte had become desperate and sent his Imperial Guards at our center. They marched towards where there was a gap in our line of infantry, with only a brigade of light cavalry seeming to stand between them and Brussels. And just as it seemed they would be able to take the ridge and drive on to that city, up stood a whole brigade of guardsmen which I swear I had not even seen until that moment, so perfectly still had they remained in the corn."

"It was an unusual drill movement," Sir Peregrine acknowledged.

"And then they swept the French back down the hill?" prompted Lady Sarah.

"Indeed, ma'am. It was the end. The Duke of Wellington gave the order for the whole line to advance."

Lady Sarah smiled adoringly at her husband.

"There was some very apt musketry from others at that moment, we should not forget," said Sir Peregrine. "The Sixth had a good gallop at the French hill, too, as I remember, Hervey?"

"Yes, sir."

"Who was commanding at that stage? Lord George Irvine was with the Prince of Orange, was he not?"

"Yes, he was, sir. I am afraid our major was killed and all our captains accounted for. The command had devolved upon me in the closing minutes."

Henrietta now bore the same look of admiration as the general's wife. But she had also seen the look on Lord Towcester's face—distaste, an intense envy, indeed.

"And Captain Hervey must have performed those duties very well," said Lady Mary Bagot to Sir Peregrine, though in a voice to be heard by the table as a whole, "because he was afterwards made aide-de-camp to my uncle."

This further revelation made Hervey redden once more. He had no idea of Lady Mary Bagot's kinship with the duke. Henrietta glanced at Lord Towcester again. His envy was so intense as to appear quite alarming to her.

"I confess to feeling humbled by the presence of *two* Waterloo men," declared Lady Mary's husband.

Hervey was amazed that a minister with plenipotentiary powers should express himself humbled in any way by a soldier, but he thought his sentiment genuine nevertheless.

Sir Peregrine was equally self-deprecating. "Oh, now, for my part at least, I would own that it was sheer circumstance, and infinitely to be preferred to the fighting that Pakenham's army had in the Mississippi at the time."

"Well, let us pray there is no recrudescence, on either front," conceded Bagot.

Lady Sarah Maitland made to rise, her chair eased by a footman. "Not *too* long, my dear," she said, fixing her husband with a smile that none might resist. "There can surely be little to detain you now that there is so universal a peace."

The men stood as she led the ladies to the drawing room.

When they were gone, the junior guests closed to the middle of the table, and the port was passed. Lord Towcester lit a cigar. "And what is your opinion of recrudescence here, Bagot? Do the Americans covet His Majesty's provinces still?"

The tone was the merest shade lofty, but enough to register with the minister plenipotentiary. "Well, Lord Towcester, 'covet' would imply to me that the United States laid claim to Canada and would not be at rest until that claim is granted," began Bagot. "I do not see it thus, though if it were possible to seize the provinces with impunity I should not doubt that the temptation would be too great." He lit a cigar, too, blowing smoke confidently towards the ceiling. "But the time is passed. They failed to take advantage of our distraction by Bonaparte, and they know they have not the strength to take on our fleet and army now. I have just finished negotiating the neutrality of the Great Lakes, indeed. They have given up any right of a naval presence on them, save a few vessels to protect their legitimate interests, in return for the same. Yet we could reinforce the lakes at any time from the Atlantic, with sufficient determination. And the *St. Lawrence*—a first-rate—is laid up in ordinary. Recommissioned, she would still outgun anything the Americans could put on Lake Ontario for at least a year."

"I heard they had something to meet her with in the *New Orleans?*" said Lord Towcester.

Bagot took another leisurely draw on his cigar. "A hundred and ten guns to seventy-four? Not, I think, good odds. And in any case, the *New Orleans* is still on the stocks."

Lord Towcester frowned. "And so you believe that the border may now be left unguarded?"

"I did not say that, Lord Towcester," replied Bagot, frowning equally. "I believe, though, that it permits a strategy over a long term of disengaging from a forward defense of the frontiers. The United States has, anyway, other priorities. It is the south and west which more naturally engages the people seeking new land. And in doing so they run into the native Indians and the Spanish. That will absorb the energies of government these next twenty years."

Sir Peregrine Maitland refilled his glass and passed the port to the superintendent of the Indian Department. "How say you, Lawrence?"

Barry Lawrence took the decanter and poured himself a glass, raising his eyebrows as if to say he was touching on something unfathomable. "Well, Sir Peregrine, I believe the Americans are about to begin a struggle that will take a generation and more to end."

Lord Towcester looked incredulous. "Do you mean to say that an assortment of savages will trouble an army which inflicted so much pain on our own?"

"I'm afraid I do, your lordship."

Lord Towcester huffed.

"And I very much fear that we in Canada may not escape the consequences. Have you heard of the affair at Niagara?"

Sir Peregrine was apparently none too keen to have it related. "Let us adjourn, gentlemen. These are weighty matters for an evening such as this, and Major Lawrence shall anyway have every opportunity these winter months to tell you of his concerns."

By now Hervey had formed a very agreeable opinion indeed of the superintendent, who was quite evidently a forthright man with a passion for his subject. Indeed, Lawrence put him in mind of the collector of Guntoor, and he wondered at the ability of the nation to produce men of aptness such as they, able so to immerse themselves in a society alien in every way, with danger and reward in wholly unequal proportions. "Shall you tell me of this affair tomorrow when we meet?" he whispered as they left the room.

The superintendent looked at him and raised an eyebrow. "Do you have a strong stomach?"

Major Lawrence's office was like no other Hervey had seen. Whereas the collector of Guntoor's had the appearance of a donnish study, the superintendent of the Indian department's was both museum of curiosities and military headquarters. One long wall was covered in shields and arrows, and in glass-topped cases there were silver bracelets, amber necklaces, and other finely worked pieces. On the wall behind his desk were feathered headdresses pinned flat. But on the other long wall were perhaps twenty maps rolled and tied, and on the table beneath, magnifying glasses, compasses, rulers, and measuring sticks.

"Coffee?" asked the superintendent, taking an enamel pot from the top of the stove.

"I thank you, yes," said Hervey, looking about the walls.

"It's not just decorative, either. Every feather has its meaning."

"And do you know of it?"

"Most, yes. And my field officers know what I do not. A lot of it is bygone stuff even to the Indians, though. They've been expert shots with musket and rifle for many years now. I'll tell you of the more extraordinary pieces another time, perhaps. I thought we might speak of your duties here. Your troop is to have the Niagara frontier, is it not?"

Hervey confirmed that it was so, although he had yet to have precise orders. General Rolt, the general officer commanding in Upper Canada, was still in Quebec meeting with the commander in chief. "And Lord Towcester has instructions not to embark on anything until his return."

Lawrence nodded. "Though if I were you, I should want to have a look at the river itself soon. It's the only place the Americans made any real showing in the war. Oh, they landed here in York and knocked the place about a good deal, but they didn't reinforce the landing. It was a halfhearted affair. The point about the Niagara River frontier is that it's a mere furlong and a bit across at its narrowest point. Have you studied the map, yet?"

"No," admitted Hervey. "We've yet to see one of the frontier. All I have is a very general one—Melish's *Seat of War,* which I was able to buy in but an hour in Quebec."

"A good start, though. It ought to give you a feeling for the size of the country." He pulled at one of the ribbons on his map wall, and down dropped an enlargement of the Melish print, with colored hatchings and additions in his own hand. "I've marked the general areas in which are the predominant tribes or nations of Indians." He indicated these with a feathered arrow. "The Indians you will see west of York, towards the Niagara frontier, are those of the Six Nations. I admire them a great deal; theirs is a confederacy that's endured for three hundred and fifty years."

"What's the basis of their confederation?" Hervey drew his chair up closer to the map.

"The language family. They are able to make themselves understood readily enough. You have heard of Hiawatha?"

Hervey had not. "Or else I forget."

"No matter. In the middle of the sixteenth century, as tradition has it, Hiawatha united five of the nations which lived in these northern parts— the Cayugas, Mohawks, Oneidas, Onondagas, and Senecas." He pointed to north and south of Lake Ontario. "The Iroquois, they are usually known as. And later they admitted the Tuscarora tribe—of the same family, so to speak. The original league was called 'the great peace,' but it was only a peace among the Iroquois themselves. To other nations they were immensely warlike. The Huron, the Erie, and others—they had all but been destroyed by the 1700s, and the Iroquois spread west to the Illinois River."

"How did they stand with regard to us?" asked Hervey, making notes.

"That is of the essence. In the middle of the last century we encouraged them to raid the French settlements, and they were a not insignificant factor in the final defeat of Montcalm. When it came to the revolution in America, however, the league split. The Oneida and part of the Tuscarora supported the colonists, the rest threw in with us. The Mohawks fought especially hard. When the war was finished, the loyal tribes were given land about these parts, chiefly on the Grand River, here at the junction of Upper and Lower Canada. The others were treated ill, duped by the Americans into selling their land, or given poorer country in exchange farther west."

"And so in the late war, I presume our Indians remained loyal?"

"Indeed. And not only in the sense of not taking up arms against us but of actually fighting for us. The Americans had continued to deal so ill with their Indians that we had capital support from tribes within the republic, too. The so-called backwoodsmen there murdered a great number of the Shawanese tribe and stole their land. The Shawanese had a very fine leader—Tecumseh: you have heard of him, perhaps?"

Again, Hervey had not.

"Oh, a great man—a *very* great man. I do not think I ever met his equal even in a red coat. He led the best light infantry you would ever see."

"Shall I meet him?"

Major Lawrence smiled. "He lacked Christian baptism, so it is unlikely."

"Ah. And was he killed in battle?"

The major sighed. "There's the rub with the Indians, for Tecumseh was killed fighting when those in red coats alongside him had taken to their heels. The same happened here at York, and worse at Niagara."

"This is the affair you spoke of last night?"

"Yes, and it exercises me a great deal at present, for the scalp lock of the chief who was killed at Niagara—at least, the Indians *believe* it to be his—was made a spectacle of only lately at Buffalo."

Hervey peered at the map.

"Here, across the river on Lake Erie—in the United States, that is."

"How did it happen?"

"Our general—Riall—had taken a force with several hundred Indians of the Mississauga tribe across the river and captured Fort Niagara, and he was making his way to Buffalo when the Americans counterattacked strongly. For some reason he'd conceived a mistrust of his Indians—perhaps because earlier they'd received emissaries from the nations fighting with the Americans. And when they promised they would stand he wouldn't believe them, and gave way, so that the weight of attack was unevenly borne by them."

"And this scalp lock was taken by the *American* Indians?"

"It were better that it had been so, but the Mississaugas believe that one of the Kentucky riflemen took it—with his teeth."

Hervey looked startled.

Lawrence smiled. "The Indians are commonly referred to as savages. But to my knowledge, they would only ever use a knife."

Hervey smiled with him. "That is indeed a comfort to know."

"Well, then, enough of these parlor stories for the time being. I have to say, though, the Kentucky men had their reasons, for they'd suffered many an outrage at home, though whose score on that account was the greatest is open to question. But I will own that the affair of the scalp lock at Niagara is exercising me. The Mississaugas are not of the old confederacy, but if they're unhappy with us then they might infect the Six Nations with their discontent."

Hervey made more notes.

Lawrence refilled both coffee cups, and took up his pointer again. "Let us leave Indian affairs for the time being. Let us return to geography—the Niagara River. It is important you know its features. . . ."

CHAPTER 19

TIME SPENT IN RECONNAISSANCE

Fort York, a Week Later

Hervey found the first week of their garrison uncommonly hard. Though the barracks in Fort York were well found—they had been rebuilt only four years earlier, having been twice burned—the cold outdoors went ill with both officers and dragoons, and parades were few. The horse lines were improvised but ample, with bracken for bedding and good hay in fair quantities, and troop horse and charger alike had coats as thick as Hervey could remember since Corunna. After a few days, voyageurs of the Hudson's Bay Company arrived with the regiment's winter clothing—infantry greatcoats of gray kersey, and the beef boots and fur caps which had been authorized for dismounted dress instead of the cloaks, hussar boots, and shakos which scarcely kept even an active man warm. A brisk trade was done in extra fur, too.

Henrietta had remained indoors for the most part. Lady Sarah Maitland had begged her to come and lodge at Government House, but she had steadfastly insisted on remaining with her husband in their cramped quarters in the fort, though after only a few days, through the generosity of the lieutenant governor's lady, they were furnished very comfortably—so comfortably, in fact, that with their traveling service, she was able to give two small dinner parties, and to receive Sarah Maitland daily in the morning or afternoon appropriately, and sometimes both. Even Ruth, Henrietta's lady's maid, complained only once in that time—when Private Johnson had left unguarded a pan of linseed on the kitchen range, and it had boiled over and run down the side and onto a pair of her mistress's shoes which stood there drying.

More than once Hervey had watched his wife as she read, or wrote, or busied herself with some little detail of their domestic arrangements, and marveled at her choosing to forgo the comfort of Manvers Priory for this. Had she known how difficult it would be? Would she now change her mind if it were possible? Never had he seen her look more contented, though. It humbled him, indeed. And he envied her the apparent contentment, for although he had accepted the inevitable cure of the lance in respect of Lord Towcester—to puncture the impostor, and express all the malice—he had reached no conclusions as to when or how. In truth, though his mind told him the lance was inevitable, his every instinct recoiled from it still.

A few days after the voyageurs had come, and with General Rolt still in Quebec, Sir Peregrine Maitland suggested to Lord Towcester that a reconnaissance along the Niagara frontier might be made to advantage. "For I think it would be no bad thing to trail your red cloaks along the border and give something for the Americans across the river to observe."

Lord Towcester agreed at once. It was unlikely of itself to secure him the Bath ribbon, which every Waterloo colonel was wearing, but it must be a beginning. And with but a single road, and guides, there could hardly be much opportunity of becoming lost, which had always been his anxiety on taking to the field before. Nevertheless, it took three full days of preparation by the adjutant before he felt himself ready to take the lead of the Niagara patrol—furnished, though it was, entirely by Hervey's troop.

The distance from York to Fort George, where the Niagara River entered Lake Ontario, was eighty-five miles. A little over half of it would be done by way of Dundas Street, the military road which ran from the St. Lawrence River just above Montreal, through York and on to London on the Thames River not far short of the Michigan border. At Burlington Bay, the westernmost point of Lake Ontario, they would leave the road and take a slower one along the southwest shore of the lake, crossing many streams, to the fort. It was, under clement conditions, with an overnight rest at the marching camp at Burlington, a journey of but two days, with a further day, then, to show along the Niagara River frontier to Fort Erie. Retracing their steps, it would be the same again home. A seven-day patrol with a day's lairage was nothing exceptional by Peninsular standards, but although no snow had fallen for a week, it was colder than when they had arrived. Hervey's principal concern was forage, and then their own rations. He had seen how fast a troop horse finished its hard feed in conditions like this (not *quite* like this, for the Astorgias had not been as cold, though they had been wet), and how a dragoon emptied his mess tin of beef and dumplings in half the usual time. He therefore decided on one bat-horse for every two troopers.

"I will not have my regiment turned into a commissary train, Captain Hervey!" Lord Towcester objected on being told of this.

To Hervey that chafed badly. If there were one thing of which he was certain it was the business of maintaining condition of men and horses in the field. It couldn't be book learned, only bought by true experience. "Your lordship, I was thinking of unencumbering the troop horses, else they will look like—"

"I will not be contradicted, Captain Hervey! General Maitland shall take the salute as the patrol leaves, and I intend its looking as crack as anything he ever saw at Waterloo. Do you understand, sir?"

Hervey did—all too well. But still there remained the question of feed and rations, for the quartermaster's art was the one that permitted the least flight of fancy. "Your lordship, how therefore do you wish the victuals to be transported?"

Lord Towcester was in thrusting form. "If needs be we shall live off the land!"

If the lieutenant colonel had said he expected them to be provisioned on the march by ravens, like the children of Israel, Hervey could hardly have been more shocked. His silence was not apparent to Lord Towcester, however, who was attending instead to the guest list for the regiment's first dinner in ten days' time. But in Towcester's vanity and inexperience, Hervey saw an opportunity to have his way, albeit deviously. "Your lordship, might I make a suggestion in order that General Maitland should see us at our best?"

Lord Towcester looked up. "By all means, Captain Hervey."

"If we send horses on ahead with winter stores and all the feed, we should then be able to parade in field dress and cloaks, without even a blanket roll on the saddles."

Lord Towcester nodded. "I shall consider it, Captain Hervey."

"Ride in cloaks only?" Serjeant Armstrong looked astonished.

"That is what I said," Hervey told him. "We shall propel ourselves briskly, and it will keep the weight down."

Armstrong looked unconvinced.

"The first stage is a good road," Hervey continued. "We ought to make the marching camp in eight hours."

"Not on this snow we won't. I rode out to the picket post this morning and it's balling worse than I ever saw. We might as well take the shoes off."

"It would be tempting if we knew what the ground would be like at Niagara, but it might be rocklike."

"Well, if that's the best you can do, sir—"

"I fear it is. Now, do I need to remind you that this patrol is your chance to display to the lieutenant colonel?"

Armstrong nodded. "Aye. The *last* chance."

"Then who shall we place in charge of the bat-horses?"

"Clarkson, I reckon."

Hervey thought for a while. "Would you make Clarkson next for serjeant?"

"In the troop? Yes. But given the choice I'd have Collins. Clarkson's good, and he'll be a bloody clewed-up serjeant major in his turn. But Collins's got the stamp of a Lincoln."

"Do you think so? I'm not saying I don't agree, but . . ."

"That's because Collins is the best corporal in the regiment, and because he seems every bit a corporal you wonder if he can be a serjeant. When he's a serjeant it'll be the same. I've always reckoned the best—NCOs *and* officers—strike you whatever rank they're in. I never did understand the idea that someone could be a lousy troop man but a good RSM or colonel. More coffee?"

Hervey held out his tin cup, contemplating Armstrong's proposition. If there were any other NCOs with such an opinion, he supposed they would never venture to give it. "You don't believe that, because there are different qualities needed to be a troop man from those of the commissary, you could do one well and the other badly?"

"I wasn't saying that, sir. I don't believe every good serjeant would make an RSM, or captain a colonel. But I do believe it goes the other way round. The best horses run well on any going."

Hervey smiled at the imagery. "In principle I think you may be wrong. But I confess that in practice all I've ever seen says you're right. I suspect Mr. Lincoln was a clewed-up corporal."

"You can bet on it. I wish he'd come back soon."

"We all say amen to that."

"But I grant you Clarkson runs Collins close, sir. Are you to fill the vacancy, then?"

Hervey sighed. "It's unfair on Clarkson if I manage to get Collins back and promote him. It's unfair, too, to try an exchange. They're both drawing pay of serjeant, as I understand it, so I thought I'd let things run a bit longer to see what turned up."

Armstrong smiled. "That's what Major Edmonds would have done. 'First whiff of black powder and all bets are off,' he always said."

Hervey frowned. "That doesn't say much for Clarkson's chances, then. There'll be no black powder here. And, do you know, I shall be glad of it, and so should you be. Fatherhood's not best an absentee state, I think."

"Bloody 'ell, sir. Who's been telling you that?"

"Nobody."

"You mean you thought of it yourself?"

Hervey raised his eyebrows.

"Sir, I'd be thinking about half-pay if I were you!"

"Oh, I don't know. I saw a pretty sort of crib being knocked up yesterday in the serjeants' lines."

Armstrong made an unconvincing huffing sound as he left the troop office.

In the modest but comfortable Hervey quarters, Henrietta was being stoical—as was Caithlin Armstrong in that corner of the barracks that served as the Armstrongs' quarters. This sort of thing—the Niagara patrol—was after all why the Sixth had come to the Canadas, although both wives had perhaps thought that winter quarters would allow them the months of their confinement united with their men.

" 'The captain's lady and Judy O'Grady!' " said Hervey, smiling proudly when Henrietta declared she was not in the least preoccupied by the prospect of his leaving her.

She looked at him, puzzled.

He frowned. It was easy to forget that it had been less than a year since she had been taken on strength, so to speak. Barrack-room wisdom took rather longer to acquire. " 'The captain's lady and Judy O'Grady are sisters under the skin.' It's one of the things the men say. Except they say the *colonel's* lady."

Henrietta did not tell him that a day had not passed without her imagining Princess Charlotte's terrible trial—and fate—and without wondering why she, Lady Henrietta Hervey, should expect to be spared when a royal princess, attended by the foremost obstetrician of the land, had fared no better in her labor than a beast of the field. She wondered if she would bear it well when her own trial came. The newspapers had made much of the princess's courage, of her bearing the agonies "with a Brunswick heart." Not for Charlotte the laudanum's ease. Did *she* have a heart as strong as a Brunswick? She feared not. Indeed, she knew it.

"Matthew, you will be close when the time comes, won't you?"

He knelt by her side and took her hand.

"Just at your duty in the fort," she explained, placing her other hand over his, "so that if . . . then I should feel I could bear it the better."

"Yes," he said, gently. "I don't imagine there'll be another patrol in months. When the time comes I shall remain in my office until you send for me."

He kissed her forehead, and then she kissed his lips.

"Matthew, if anything were to happen . . ."

She seemed to be searching for the words, but Hervey could not help because he was unsure of what exactly was her fear (she had said not a word to him about Princess Charlotte since they had set sail from England).

"If anything should happen to me . . ."

He saw at once, now, and put an arm around her. "My dear, I was not going to say anything of this, but our surgeon told me he would never have allowed the princess to go on as she did had he been in attendance."

Henrietta looked at him, perplexed.

He hesitated. "He would have delivered the child by section."

Well had he hesitated, and better had he said nothing at all. He cursed himself as the color drained from Henrietta's face like sand from a minute-glass.

"My darling, I—"

She gripped his hand hard. "Matthew, do you know what you say?"

He had thought he did. Now he was not sure.

"No woman survives that, Matthew!"

He couldn't understand. "The surgeon is a good man. Why would he have said that?"

Henrietta's distress took longer to subside than her husband expected, but subside it did, and they agreed that there would be no more talk of such things, and that they would rest confident in the will of God and the combined wisdom of the several doctors and birth attendants at her disposal. At dinner that evening she was as gay as she ever was, and later, in each other's arms, she told him she feared nothing as long as he was with her. Only the next day did he really comprehend the fright he had given her in speaking of a caesarian section, for when he confronted the surgeon with Henrietta's dismay, the Glasgow veteran of many a field amputation had rounded on him and cursed him for his ignorance, telling him it was only in the last decade that his profession had been able to perform a live section successfully, and that every woman knew it was but a desperate remedy to save the child only. "D'ye know naught about these things, man?" he had demanded. And Hervey had had to confess that there was indeed a void in his learning.

When the time came for the patrol to leave, Henrietta said her goodbyes nobly, bidding her husband a happy, even carefree, farewell. She had, after all, a good reserve of novels, she assured him, and the frequent company of Lady Sarah Maitland. And he in turn was content to believe that her anxiety had been of the moment only, exacerbated by his clumsy reassurance. And if he had been alarmed to know the truth, he would have been proud nevertheless to know how completely she had been taken on strength, how completely she now played the role of captain's lady—though not so much for the sake of the Judy O'Gradys but for the man she considered was her very life.

From an upstairs window when he was gone, Henrietta watched the half-troop parade for the lieutenant governor. Thirty-two dragoons and four officers—the lieutenant colonel, adjutant, Hervey, and Seton Canning—ranked past Sir Peregrine Maitland in their red cloaks as the trumpet major and four trumpeters blew the general salute. Red cloaks against the snow: confident, uncompromising contrast, just like Hervey himself. "Please God, deliver him," she prayed passionately, clutching her hands together. "Deliver him from evil and from himself."

Outside the gates Major Lawrence joined them, on a hardy-looking cob, together with two Cayuga Indians equally well mounted. The three were well wrapped in buckskin, fox, and beaver, their feet especially. Lawrence stared incredulously at the patrol. "Why in God's name are you not wearing winter warms, Hervey? When the sun goes you'll turn to blocks of ice."

"We're going to trot in a minute or so," replied Hervey.

"Then you'll be warmer while you do," Lawrence frowned. "But you can't trot the whole way to Burlington. And on this snow if you rush it you'll have falls. Four or five inches down there's ice like glass, and this fresh stuff will ball up, too."

"To tell the truth, my intention is to catch up the bat-horses."

"You'll be sorely pressed to do that: they left an hour ago!"

Hervey paused just long enough to judge his secret safe with the superintendent. "I told them they were to mark time at the first five-mile point."

Lawrence smiled. "That was wise as well as cunning. But I promise you you'll never make the same mistake of parting from your supply again after an hour of this in cloaks and boots!"

Hervey sighed. "That's what I was hoping," and he made a sort of knowing frown. "Why are you come, incidentally?"

"I've called a meeting of my field officers at Fort Erie. It seemed opportune."

"And the Indians are your escorts?"

Lawrence smiled indulgently. "I rather fancied they would do you well as scouts."

"Ah, yes, indeed. I'm very grateful. Shall I send two dragoons with them?"

"I think not. They'll be happier left alone." He nodded to the Indians.

The Cayugas sped off at once to take the far point. The Iroquois were not known as a horse nation, but that was not apparent as they put their ponies into a canter in a very few paces. And besides being able to warn early of anything that might hinder the patrol's progress, they would be excellent guides, it seemed, for in the dusting of snow, as Lawrence called it, which the dawn had brought, their tracks stood out plainly. Not that taking a false turn on Dundas Street seemed likely, since on either side was a formidable barrier of fir trees. Only here and there would they find a clearing for a dwelling house, or where timber had been cut for a more distant purpose.

Serjeant Armstrong had been let in on the bat-horse plan only late that morning, and he had obligingly continued to pretend he had no idea that

Hervey was acting other than with an entirely free hand. The bat-horses' tracks looked as fresh as the Cayugas', for there was no wind to drift the snow, and the sun was not strong enough to melt so much as one snowflake on a pine needle. But they were not the trailing lines of trotting horses, and certainly not the furrows of the Cayugas' hand gallop. Clarkson was doing his job—thank God.

Major Lawrence had fallen in beside the lieutenant colonel as the patrol set off, but he soon found him too taciturn to persist with, and so Hervey had his company again before not too long. And glad of it he would be, too, for otherwise Dundas Street was but cold monotony.

It was not long before they made the rendezvous with the bat-horses, however, and Lord Towcester's obvious relief was such that Hervey did not even bother with the lines he had rehearsed. They had ridden for little more than an hour, yet he knew they would soon have had men slipping into winter torpor. He had seen it once before, in the Astorgias. It was the easy way: they would stop fighting the cold, allow the numbness to come, and then a sleep they would not emerge from.

In that hour, too, they had not seen any living thing of the wild, nor even a trace of one. There would surely be no more talk of living off the land. Indeed, the lieutenant colonel now seemed content to let Hervey have command of the patrol in all its details, and did not object when he ordered horses to be led from time to time, even though he himself had made his objections to the practice known often enough.

The rest of the march to Fort George was as without incident as the country was without wildlife. An owl was heard in the night, and some birds briefly at first light. But the call of a wolf, which the men had hourly expected (and keenly so), did not come. The bivouac at Burlington was a hard one, and a wolf's call would have been some consolation, something of which to write home to thrill the humdrum, for little sleep was had by any. The campfires had seemed without heat, the rum without ability to warm beyond a few minutes. Resuming the march, if not actually a pleasure, had been a relief. Except that everywhere the forest enveloped them, the trees so heavy with snow that it seemed as if they were beneath the walls of some great white city. For miles there was nothing else to see. And the steamy breath of six dozen horses and men gave it an eeriness quite unlike anything Hervey had seen before—or, for that matter, Armstrong either.

But Fort George welcomed them generously. Its quartermaster was relieved to have an opportunity to break out the stores, for he had laid in provisions for twice the number of troops than would need them now the threat of hostilities seemed certain to be past. The patrol ate well on salt pork and buffalo, pickled *pomme blanche* and *compote,* and they slept well in the stove-heated barracks. Lord Towcester was entertained by the fort's commandant, and retired early, leaving Hervey to listen to one of Major Lawrence's field officers.

"The condition of the Six Nations between the Erie and the Huron is daily more distressing," said the lieutenant, an officer who had been so long seconded to the Indian department that he still referred to his own regiment as the Royal Americans. "It's the want of game, everywhere. Three of the hunting groups have already broken camp and moved to find other grounds, and they haven't had to do that in more than a generation."

"Why *is* there so little game?" asked Hervey. He understood this winter to be a not especially hard one.

"The winter's by no means the harshest," replied the lieutenant. "And that's puzzling the Six Nations, too. But there's no doubting the deer and the bear have gone—and the beaver above all. Some of the younger braves are saying it's the fault of the white man. They know he doesn't rob them or harry them as his cousin below the lakes does, but they reckon he upsets the balance of things in the wilderness."

"And do you think that resentment will turn against us?" Hervey sounded intrigued rather than anxious.

"Well," said the lieutenant, noting that Major Lawrence, too, was waiting intently on the reply. "I've heard talk again of the affair of the Niagara scalp lock, and how it spoke for the way the white man would abandon his Indian friends to save his own skin when the time came. The braves wonder how long it will be before the white man above and below the lakes makes common cause against them."

"Are there other voices?" said Major Lawrence, relighting his cigar.

"Yes, the elders are saying that spring will see the return of the deer, the bear, and the beaver. But again, the younger braves point out that, after the spring, and the summer, and the autumn, there will come another winter."

They sat late into the small hours talking of what it might come to.

They left Fort George at nine the next morning, red cloaks over winter warms. It must have been a good display to the American garrison across the river. Lord Towcester seemed content that it was, steadfastly refusing even to glance towards Fort Niagara, for such was his contempt for the American revolutionaries, as he insisted on calling them.

They made the heights of Queenston before eleven. They passed above the falls after midday, hearing more than they saw of the great cataract, though the winter flow was a trickle compared with the spring thaw, and took their ease for an hour in Chippeway, where reports of their progress brought out villagers bearing kettles and pots of boiling water even as they rode up. In the afternoon they passed through the rich settlements of the upper Niagara, and on down to Fort Erie, arriving a little before last light. Here the evening was much as the one before, with another of Major Lawrence's field officers confirming the troubling assessment of the Indians' condition, although he was not inclined to believe that the younger braves' blaming the white man would come to much once spring began to show.

Next morning, snow was falling as the troop mustered for the return march, and there was talk of staying at the fort until it stopped. But Lord Towcester saw no reason why they should not at least set out, for between Fort Erie and Chippeway there was shelter enough if the snow became heavier, and they could bivouac at any number of places if things came to the worst. He had matters pressing in plenty at York. Hervey was content enough with the condition of the troop after his morning inspection, and so they left by the road they had come on at a quarter to ten, the Cayuga scouts this time taking a much closer point since visibility was reduced.

Major Lawrence decided not to return with them, however. He intended taking the ferry across the river to Buffalo to meet with his counterpart there, to discover what policy the United States would be adopting towards their Indians in the spring. Rumors of inevitable displacements had already reached him in York from diplomatic sources in Montreal, and Mr. Bagot himself had thought that the settlers' inroads west of the Missouri would soon unravel Washington's resettlement policy.

They made the fifteen miles to Chippeway just after midday. The snow had stopped falling soon after they set off, and they had been able to maintain a brisk trot for a mile or so at a time. They made a brief halt at the village, where the people showed the same alacrity in hospitality as the day before, and the dragoons were again able to eat hot without the trouble of dismounting their own camp kettles.

Lord Towcester summoned Hervey to his side. "See here, there is no need at all of our spending another night at Fort George. I consider there to be no purpose in it, anyway. We can take this road here"—he indicated the line with a gloved finger, rather indistinctly—"along Lundy's Lane to begin with. There was some skirmish of cavalry in the war there, so it must be passable to the horse. We may then proceed to the road from Queenston to Burlington that runs atop the ridge, instead of skirting the lake. It will save us all of eight leagues, and a further night."

Hervey was not so sure. Indeed, he felt uneasy. If the lieutenant colonel wished to curtail the patrol, that was of course his prerogative, and he assumed that Lord Towcester possessed that discretion in Sir Peregrine's orders. But the distance by this direct route was, even at a rough calculation, not much short of forty-five miles. They had at best five hours of daylight left, though the moon and snow would make movement at night along a road relatively easy. But if the weather were to change again, the route could be treacherous. And the road through the forest to the Burlington ridge looked little better than a track.

"Do you think we should ask the Indians, your lordship?"

"Confound the Indians, Captain Hervey! Do you even know enough of their language? They'll do as they're damn well told!"

Lord Towcester was clearly in one of his peremptory moods, but Hervey felt bound to risk one more objection. "We might be benighted, though, sir, however well we do."

"In heaven's name, Captain Hervey! I heard tell at Fort George of a woman who went on *foot* this way during the war, and warned our men of an attack! You're not telling me you're afraid to take to the woods on a horse if a confounded woman can do it on her feet!"

Hervey had heard of Mrs. Secord's fearless journey. But she had walked from *Queenstown,* not Chippeway, and in the middle of summer. He thought it useless to point this out to Lord Towcester, however. "Very good, your lordship. I will tell the scouts," he said, wondering to himself if he could.

In fact, communicating with the scouts was not as difficult as Hervey expected. He was able to get them to comprehend his intentions easily enough in a mixture of English and simple sign language (the map, predictably, was of no use to the proceedings). They were evidently unhappy with the news—for three reasons, as far as he could make out. First, the road was difficult, with many ups and downs and streams to cross. Then they made signs indicating that night would fall on them, and finally something about passing through land which the Mississauga hunted. Hervey was only too relieved that they did not turn and walk away when he told them he intended taking the road anyway. But it was his first taste of an Indian's displeasure, even in that brief exchange, and it was not palatable.

He called Serjeant Armstrong aside and made a clean breast of things. "I'll not say anything to Mr. Seton Canning, but it's as well you know my apprehension. I daresay all will be well. We'll end up huddled in the forest after midnight when the moon sets, but that we can bear. And the Indians will be used to people riding through if there's a road cut, so they can't be all that troubled by our doing so. But I want NCOs' pistols primed all the same. No others, mind."

Armstrong nodded. "I was talking to them Indians last night. They're worried where all the game's going—all of them are. Some of the tribes are starving."

Hervey could only admire his serjeant's way with men. "Major Lawrence's officers have been telling me this as well."

"I suggest we take flints out of weapons, too—except the NCOs, I mean. If one of them greenheads' pistols goes off . . ."

Hervey nodded. "Aye. It doesn't bear thinking about."

In the event, the road was better than Hervey had imagined, but narrow. They rode in file rather than threes, though, and from time to time the files had to merge. But the snow hadn't settled so deep as on the road they had left, and it didn't ball in the hooves. They managed some good trots in the first ten miles. The Cayugas rode very close point, however, not once losing sight behind. They seemed distinctly less at ease than on the ride out, and not a word passed between them.

The forest impressed its silence on the dragoons, too. For the most part, the only sound was the occasional snort from their plodding troopers, or the jingling of a bridoon, or the chink of stirrups as the files came too close. Looking left or right into the forest, Hervey could not imagine the sound traveling more than a few yards in that mass of fir, beech, and elm. It looked impenetrable, thicker than anything he had seen in India, even. And all the time not a sight nor sound of another living thing, on the ground, in the trees, or overhead.

The Mississaugas came out of the forest like some sudden, mechanical change of scenery on a stage. There seemed no movement, only appearance—a dozen or so warriors at the same instant, in the same attitude, well wrapped in long moosehide coats, full hair to the shoulders, faces dyed red above the cheekbones. They stood, rifle in left hand, motionless and wholly impassive.

The Cayugas halted—*froze*. Lord Towcester drew his pistol, pulling back the hammer with his left hand. He lost his grip, grabbed as it fell, but missed. It hit the ground handle first, springing the hammer. The noise was like a cannon in the silence. He spun his horse round.

"Threes about! Threes about!" he shouted. But there was no room for even files to turn. He barged at Hervey and his trumpeter to make way.

Hervey was so startled, he grabbed his arm. "Sir, they've gone, they've gone."

Lord Towcester turned in the saddle. The Mississaugas had disappeared as suddenly as they had come. He was dumbstruck.

"We should trot on, sir," pressed Hervey. "Look, the scouts are doing the same!" He seized the lieutenant colonel's reins and pulled his horse into motion.

CHAPTER 20

ORDERS JUST RECEIVED

Fort York, Two Days Later

The quarter guard turned out as the patrol neared the gates. Twelve dragoons of the inlying picket brought their carbines to the present, and the corporal brought his saber to the carry. The trumpeters blew Attention, and orderlies stood ready to take the reins of the chargers.

The Earl of Towcester acknowledged the respects without halting. "Carry on, Captain Hervey," he said, barely audibly, his right leg already out of the stirrup. The lieutenant colonel's groom took in hand the big black gelding and, without a backward glance or another word, Lord Towcester strode away to his quarters, the adjutant a few paces behind him.

Hervey fronted to the patrol. "The commanding officer would wish me to express his appreciation of your exertions this past week. The conditions were trying and your conduct exemplary. There shall be a rum issue and stand-down of twenty-four hours from watch setting this evening. Fall out, Mr. Seton Canning. Carry on, please, Serjeant Armstrong."

"I'll see to stables, if you wish, Hervey," said Seton Canning as they dismounted.

"Thank you. Yes." How decent of his lieutenant to guess so much of his mind. Henrietta would have claimed him anyway, in her condition, but Canning was not to know how keenly Hervey wanted to relate to her Lord Towcester's infamous conduct. "I shan't be long. Just an hour, perhaps."

"As you please, Hervey. There's no need of haste on my account."

Haste or no, it did not take Hervey long to walk to his quarters, even in the two feet of new snow lying about the fort, which fatigue parties were already clearing into neat pathways. Smoke rising from the double chimney of his quarters promised a warm homecoming, but the fresh sleigh tracks outside suggested they would not be alone. He opened the door, expecting to find Lady Sarah Maitland, though it was early for calling.

"Hopwood? What are *you* doing here?"

Private Hopwood was carrying a basket of logs to the fire. "Corporal Collins sent me to mind the house, sir. Her ladyship was taken to General Maitland's this morning. She wasn't feeling well, sir."

Hervey's mouth fell open.

"I'm sure it's nothing serious, sir," Hopwood added quickly.

"Indeed? Did the surgeon say that?" asked Hervey, impatiently, replacing his shako and turning for the door.

"I didn't see him, sir. But I know that he's gone to the general's with her."

It was, of course, an obliging thing for a dragoon to want to allay his captain's anxiety, but so wholly uninformed an opinion was not of the least value to him. "Very well. I shall go there at once." But now he found himself wanting to make amends for his impatience by some display of ease. "And while I am gone, would you be so very good as to draw me a bath?"

As Hervey opened the door, a sleigh halted outside. A youngish woman in a black cloak stepped out. "Captain Hervey, sir?"

"Yes?"

"I am Janette, sir, Lady Sarah Maitland's maid. I am come to bring some things for your wife."

"Things? What things?"

The maid looked down awkwardly. "Ladies' things, sir."

Hervey fancied he knew the contents of their quarters well enough, but, as with Hopwood, he could not quite bring himself to disappoint someone so evidently intent on performing a good deed. "Very well. Do please go inside." He nearly said "*come* inside," but he had committed himself to stepping out at once for the Maitlands'.

"Thank you, sir. Shall you be going back to Government House?"

"I have not yet *been* there. I am only this minute returned to the town." He was tired, the business was beginning to fray, and all he could think about was getting to his wife.

"Oh!" the maid's manner changed at once.

"What is it? Why do you say that?"

"You don't know her ladyship is in labor, sir?"

Hervey's mouth fell open. "No, no—indeed I do not!"

His response alarmed her. "I think I had better get these things, then, sir."

"Yes, yes—of course! Tell me, is my wife . . ."

"I trust so, sir. I was given my orders by her ladyship—the general's lady, I mean—direct."

It took him a quarter of an hour to walk to Government House. He walked so fast in the end that he slipped and slid for much of the way. He took the salted steps of the lieutenant governor's residence two at a time, and pulled the bell rope.

"Ah, indeed, Captain Hervey, sir," replied the footman, stepping aside to let him enter.

The house was silent. "Is her ladyship at home?"

"Her ladyship is at home, sir. I will announce you."

The footman showed him to an anteroom. There Hervey recovered his breath and something of his composure, and tried to clear his mind in order to calculate the date again. But it still came out the same. They'd talked of the beginning of March, surely? There were a full six weeks to run. What was the danger in so early a labor? *Was* there any danger? Hadn't Daniel Coates said that a mare carried from forty weeks to more than a year, depending on whether she were a big shire or a pony? Was it the same with humans? Everyone spoke of nine months, but was it more for a bigger woman, and fewer for one more delicately made? Had Kitty Spence, the tiny Longleat seamstress, carried her little girl as long as Annie Patten had carried those rough twins of hers? Sturdy Annie, the Longleat dairymaid who used to pin fast his head in her huge bosom when he was a boy—surely she would have needed longer? How little he seemed to know. Why was Lady Sarah so long in coming? Why did *no* one come? What was amiss?

"Captain Hervey, forgive me!" Lady Sarah Maitland was come at last, smiling wide and confidently. "I had to put on another dress. Allow me to congratulate you on being the father of a most beautiful daughter!"

Hervey stood speechless.

"A *very* beautiful daughter. I never saw such eyes and hair!"

"And . . . And Henrietta?"

"Oh, she is fine, *fine*—very well indeed! A few minutes more and you shall be able to see her. My husband's physician and your regimental surgeon attended throughout, but they scarce had a thing to detain them."

He shook his head in a sort of disbelief.

"And I may tell you she bore it all with a most noble heart. *Dear* Henrietta. Oh, but I forget—some refreshment? How was your patrol? Was it very arduous? How is Lord Towcester?"

He didn't have to answer, for Henrietta's maid entered, smiling, too. "Your ladyship, sir." She curtsied to each. "Her ladyship is ready to receive Captain Hervey now."

"Thank you, Ruth." Hervey glanced eagerly at Sarah Maitland.

"Come, Captain Hervey." She led him to the stairs.

He had meant to ask how his wife was here, and to express the thanks due to the Maitlands for their unusual hospitality, but he found his tongue strangely tied. Sarah Maitland was saying something about his daughter being the first child to be born in York that year . . . or perhaps she said the first girl, or . . .

"Here, Captain Hervey. I shall leave you." She opened the door to a dressing room, and motioned to another.

He tidied his stock in a looking glass, checked that all his tunic buttons were fastened, then knocked softly on the door to the bedchamber.

"Come," came a male voice.

He opened the door gently.

"Matthew!"

There was pleasure and pride and relief all together in that single word. But how spent Henrietta sounded, too. Her hair lay on the pillow as it had that night at the Nottingham inn, and he knew again that he had laid privations in her way. She should by rights have been at Longleat, in the great rose bedchamber that had been hers since childhood.

"See, Matthew." She turned her eyes to the Maitlands' nurse.

He took her hand, and bent and kissed her forehead, but she made a little sound of protest, and he kissed her again, on the lips. The doctor nodded, and the nurse presented their swaddled issue, and Hervey stared with pride and wonder in equal measure. He saw what Sarah Maitland had told him, for there were the largest, bluest of eyes, and the most luxuriant shock of dark hair.

Henrietta squeezed his hand. "I'm sorry, my love, for you wanted a son truly very much."

Her voice was so tired that even just saying the words could not have been without effort. He was wholly at a loss to respond to anything so entirely selfless.

"We must decide on a name," she said, raising her head slightly to see better.

"My darling, I never so much as once uttered any thought that I wished for a boy. She is quite perfect. I would not have things any other way."

"Then sit with me a while, and let us speak of it, for I can't bear to think of her without a name."

Stables was done by the time he returned to the troop lines. Indeed, the orderly trumpeter was sounding first post for watch setting. Hervey complimented him as he passed the guard room. "A pretty sound for so cold a night, Martin!"

Private Martin saluted. "Thank you, sir. But a whole tone flat, I'm sorry to say." Martin took his music seriously. He did not quite have perfect pitch, but he had a good memory. "I'd warmed it by the stove for a quarter of an hour until its pitch were right, sir. Two minutes later and it's dropped a whole tone. I thought it'd freeze to my lips."

Even to Hervey, his mind so agreeably preoccupied as it was, the cold was uncommonly severe. "Has the guard commander shortened the duties, do you know?"

"He has, sir. To half."

"That's as well. Very good, Martin. I should begin warming your trumpet for *second* post if I were you!"

"Aye, sir! Good night, then, sir." Something, clearly, had put the captain in good spirits. He saluted again as Hervey turned for the troop office.

A sound man, Martin, said Hervey to himself. Meet to replace Susan Medwell. It seemed strange to think like that, perhaps, but there could be no other way. Once a man was struck off strength—no matter what the circumstances—it was a case of "soldier on" for those who remained. No one was irreplaceable. All else was mere sentiment. That, at least, was what Hervey had always tried to tell himself. Now, especially, must he do so since he bore the additional rank of father. He must soldier on, no matter how difficult his commanding officer made it. The Sixth were

strong enough to ride out a man like Towcester, were they not? His real
nature would soon become apparent to those in authority, and he would
be checked, surely, for wasn't that the way with the army?

He was surprised to see Major Lawrence in the troop office. "A word,
Hervey, if you please."

The troop orderly serjeant made to leave.

"Is Mr. Seton Canning in the lines, Corporal Sykes?" asked Hervey,
winding his hunter. It still seemed a mean instrument compared with the
one it had replaced, and every time he wound it now he felt the want of
his old friend's gay society most keenly. In d'Arcey Jessope he could have
confided happily, even if that delightful Coldstreamer's counsel had not
always been practical.

"He's in his quarters, sir. Shall I fetch him?"

"No. Have him informed that I shall do picket officer's rounds myself,
please."

"Very good, sir."

Lawrence scarcely waited for the door to close. "What in the name of
heaven happened at Niagara? There's all manner of rumor abroad on the
reservations."

Hervey poured himself coffee, took off his cape and shako, and sat
down. "One of the patrol's pistols discharged accidentally when a hunting party came out of the woods."

Lawrence frowned. "No, Hervey—that will never do! I never expected
such a thing from you of all men."

Hervey sighed. How easy it would be to tell him all, to pretend Major
Lawrence were d'Arcey Jessope. And what hard-edged counsel he would
have by return. Yes, it would be very easy. But Lawrence wasn't Jessope.
There was no basis to mutual trust—yet—other than instinct. They had
not campaigned together, they did not wear the same uniform. Hervey
had no right to discuss his commanding officer with Lawrence, no matter what the inducement. "I cannot think what you mean. That is the
substantive report," he said defiantly, though sadly.

"Well, to begin with, I never imagined I would hear you use the word
'accidental.' "

"Well, it was certainly not deliberate."

"Do not sport with me, sir! You know very well that the term is *negli-
gent* discharge!"

"That would be the term if we were talking of the Mutiny Act, yes. But
it doesn't render my report inaccurate."

Major Lawrence's powers of observation were not to be underestimated. "Hervey, whom are you shielding?"

That might well have been impertinent, but Hervey knew it was apt. He supposed the Cayugas had already told him. But much as he was tempted to confide, the circumstances made it impossible, for nothing he told the superintendent could be in confidence. "What does that matter, Lawrence? What is the greater problem?"

"The tribes are saying the white soldiers rode through their hunting land without thought for disturbing the little game there was, and even fired to frighten them away."

"We were on a road that appeared on a map."

It was the superintendent's turn to sigh. "The Cayugas say you are a brave man."

"Do they indeed? How would they know one way or the other?" Hervey managed an expression of innocence as much as puzzlement.

Lawrence narrowed his eyes. "They told me what they saw."

"You must have a care that they saw enough."

"Oh, I shall, Hervey; I shall. For it is my duty to apprise the lieutenant governor of all matters touching on the affairs of the Indian nations. And when he returns I shall give him account."

Hervey had not known Sir Peregrine was away. "Where is he gone?"

"To Quebec. And he shall be gone another fortnight, too. But on his return I must give him my assessment."

"Of course you must. And any report on our encounter with the Indians must properly come from Lord Towcester, not from me."

"So I should hope. Do you know when I might have it?"

Hervey was puzzled by the persistence. "Tomorrow, I should imagine. The day after, at the latest."

"Indeed, Captain Hervey?" smiled Lawrence. "How so?"

Hervey looked at him blankly.

"Lord Towcester set out for Quebec by sleigh this afternoon. Did you not know?"

After first parade next day—a pale affair with all those of the patrol stood-down—Seton Canning went to the troop office. "It was good of you to stand my picket for me last night, Hervey."

His captain smiled. "I had rather forgotten myself earlier. I didn't know it was so late."

"You have my hearty congratulations, at any rate, sir. St. Oswald has gone to find flowers to send to Government House."

Hervey smiled again. "I salute his gallantry—and even more his optimism, Canning, for where in heaven's name does he expect to find flowers here?"

"I asked him the same, but . . . I had intended coming to see you last night, you know."

"That was very good of you, but there was really no need—"

"No, Hervey, not about your good news, but rather about our misfortune."

"I don't follow."

Seton Canning took a deep breath. "Look here, sir: how long are we to suffer that man?"

Hervey quickened, but then gave him the benefit. "Which man?"

"Towcester, of course! He'll be the death of—"

"Mr. *Canning*!" Hervey's tone managed reprimand, surprise, and disappointment in one go.

"It's no good, Hervey. We can't pretend we didn't see what we saw. The man bolted!"

"That is not true, Canning!"

"Oh, Hervey! Have it that way if you will, but if you hadn't barred his way he would have fled!"

Hervey had known this might come. The last twelve hours had merely been an unexpected suspense. But it made it no easier. "Sit down, Harry."

Seton Canning took off his gloves and laid them in his lap with his forage cap. "Please don't speak of the necessity of loyalty, Hervey. I know full well what you might say on that account. I'm your lieutenant. Like it or not, the men look to me when . . . when they feel unease with . . ."

"With their captain?"

"No . . . not that; not that way. Surely you know what I mean?"

Hervey did. He might say, though, that that was the true price of a lieutenancy, not the cash sum which the agents demanded. But he had learned enough these past three years to know that that would sound like cant. "You will have to trust me, Harry. I can say no more."

"Of *course* I trust you, Hervey! The whole troop would follow you over those damned falls if you led them!"

It was only yesterday that Hervey had had the same sentiments for Joseph Edmonds and Edward Lankester. They, of course, would have known how to act. Major Edmonds would have taken the affair head-on. There would have been blood on the stable floor, so to speak, but the matter would have been resolved. Captain Lankester would have found an altogether different way—subtle, indirect—and would have succeeded with patrician ease. It was not by fear that Hervey shied from Edmonds's direct approach, or from distaste that he eschewed Lankester's indirect methods. It was just that he lacked the certainty for the first, and the craft for the second. And there was no other way. Yet his troop evidently expected him to find one. "If I have the troop's trust, why did you feel it necessary to speak thus, Harry?"

Seton Canning picked at imagined idle ends on his cap. "Perhaps I didn't trust myself."

Hervey sighed. Why did his lieutenant imagine himself alone in this? "We all have our doubts, Canning. All we can do in the end is hope for the grace to do our duty."

A week passed, a week of guards, drills, and fatigues—of nothing more, indeed, than a week at Hounslow would likely bring, except that a great number of the fatigues were as a consequence of the bitter chill, worse now than when they had arrived. They shoveled snow, cut firewood, and drew ice, as well as the hundred and one stable and cookhouse fatigues that detained so many of them, no matter where the station. It was hard labor. But it was no more than a homesteader thereabouts would be obliged to do. The Canadas were spoken of as a land of opportunity, but in the depths of winter it was first a question of survival. Yet on the whole the dragoons liked it. They fed well, the wet canteen of an evening was lively—the trappers passing through regaled them with extraordinary tales, as well as dispensing princely hospitality—and the parade hours were not long. In one sense, too, Hervey could not have imagined himself happier, except for the nagging question of his superior and the incident in the forest.

Hervey was not so proud that he ruled out talking of it with someone. The problem was, *who?* Lawrence had his own loyalties. Charles Addinsel was in Quebec with General Maitland, and anyway, as aide-de-camp his loyalties must be to his principal. The DAAG, he scarcely knew. He had even thought about Bagot, who was to return in a day or so from Sackett's Harbor, where he had been inspecting the *New Orleans*. Hervey had very much taken to him. Bagot was not more than ten years his senior, and his wife, as the duke's niece, would already have predisposed her husband to believe that his complaint would not be frivolous. Yet what should Bagot be expected to know of military particulars? As far as Hervey was aware, the man had never so much as worn a militia coat. And, besides the practical, how honorable was it to take the affairs of the regiment to one so wholly unconnected with it (less so even than Lawrence)? No, Mr. Bagot would not do. Which left only those who shared the roman VI. The adjutant? It was unthinkable. Seton Canning? Insupportable. Strickland was days away, as was the major. There was the chaplain, of course, the Reverend Mr. Esmond Shepherd, M.A. Oxon., who had been unable to obtain a living for himself, and had taken his bishop's advice instead to answer the call for military chaplains. He was a faithful man, he said Morning and Evening Prayer conscientiously, he preached unmemorably but aptly at divine worship on a Sunday, he visited the sick, dined unobtrusively with the officers, and was treated kindly by the ranks but otherwise generally ignored. Hervey had some regard for him. Even now the chaplain was preparing for the ministration of baptism that afternoon to their infant. And yet Mr. Shepherd could offer him no more advice, surely, than that he must do his duty according to his conscience. Doing one's duty was never as difficult as some supposed it to be. The difficulty lay always in determining what *was* that duty.

The one man whose advice would be a tempered affair of good sense and sound military judgment was Armstrong. And yet Hervey could not bring himself to ask it for two reasons. Armstrong's standing in the regiment was high, yet the merest whiff of perfidy—even if by association only—would have the lieutenant colonel exact a terrible price from him. Secondly (and it was the mark of a shrewdness which would have been wanting even a year ago), if Hervey were indeed to take command of the regiment at some early stage, he did not wish to have an Armstrong who had somehow been involved with that process. It was an antique suspicion, the same, indeed, that had dogged the Praetorians. But he was sure his classicals served him well in this regard.

He had told Henrietta, of course. She had laughed, and said that at least he would be able to make the decisions for himself if the commanding officer insisted on taking to the rear. He had remonstrated with her, but she had not been in a mood for the woes of the Sixth. Why, indeed, should she be? Even though she had formerly insisted that he tell her all, she had her child at her breast, had she not?

And now there was baptism to be done in another half an hour, and Henrietta was in some distress, for she had become so big about the bust that her coat would not fasten well. Ruth was working some small miracle with pins and thread, while the nurse—seconded from the Maitlands'—stood ready with the sleeping infant. Mr. Shepherd had made the concession that the ministration need not be of a Sunday, on account of the availability of the godparents or those by proxy, but he had made no concession to the weather, and therefore the place, which was why they were now preparing for another sally into the bitter cold.

Once at the church, though, they were glad of the weather, for they might have been at Horningsham, so peaceful was it. The incumbent, Dr. Strachan, who had lately distinguished himself during the occupation of the town by the enemy's forces, conducted the service in the warm and gentle tones of Aberdeen. This was much to Hervey's and Henrietta's satisfaction, for the drier and remoter tones of Oxford, had Mr. Shepherd officiated throughout rather than merely delivering a short homily, would only have made things seem more chill.

The godparents or their proxies stood eager for their duty. Henrietta had known *her* duty in this regard, and was well pleased with the choice. John Keble had been her husband's choice of godfather for many months. He had been canvassed early, and had responded in the way that perhaps only he, of all their acquaintances, might. It was true that Henrietta would not have chosen him herself, but in the case of there being a son, the second godfather was to have been William Devonshire (and in the case of a daughter it could not matter a great deal anyway). Her husband was content—*that* was the important thing—and Seton Canning was standing impeccable proxy for Mr. Keble. As for the godmothers, Henrietta's first intent had been bitterly thwarted by Princess Charlotte's death (indeed, her thought to call her daughter the same now seemed less appealing). The second godmother had long been arranged: Lady Camilla Cavendish, who would serve as well as William Devonshire would to a son. Lady Mary Bagot stood proxy. And in place of Princess Charlotte, Henrietta had asked Sarah Maitland. A Lennox, even one who had made an improvident match (all society knew the Duke of Richmond's opinion of his daughter's choice), would always be an apt supporter.

And so, the prayers and promises done, the godparents certified, as they were required by the Prayer Book, that "the Child may well endure it," Dr. Strachan dipped his charge "discreetly and warily" into the water, and declared "Georgiana Charlotte Sarah Elizabeth, I baptize thee in the Name of the Father, and of the Son, and of the Holy Ghost. Amen."

———

Afterwards they sat down to a dinner which would not have dishonored Longleat. The Maitlands' chef had at his call fish of the first quality, goose both wild and fattened, and all the ice he could ever wish for to prepare his confections. And Hervey had laid in Champagne, hock, burgundy, and good tawny before they had left England. The hour was very late, the cigars were making the air thick, and Hervey had not thought once in three hours of his disagreeable commanding officer, when a note from Major Lawrence was handed to him. It read "Please be so good as to come to my office the very first thing tomorrow so that I may apprise you of orders just received from Quebec."

"No reply, Johnson," he said, taking a long draw on his cigar.

Johnson retired silently with the tray like a seasoned footman.

Hervey sighed to himself: *orders just received.* This was his life, and the interludes of domesticity were always going to be hostage to the Horse Guards' will. But now, of all times, he thought himself deserving of a *little* peace.

"Hervey, there are times, let me tell you, when I wonder if our masters in London do not believe that America is any more a foreign part than . . . well, Wales!"

Hervey smiled halfheartedly. He had had little sleep that night; he had even arrived at the Indian office before Major Lawrence. He felt himself in no position to judge the superintendent's proposition, besides which, he was not entirely sure to which masters in London he referred.

"I would have said Ireland rather than Wales," continued Lawrence. "But I do believe there is a greater readiness to see the native condition of that place than there is here."

It was a moot point, and ordinarily Hervey would have liked to debate it.

"It's the same in every department, Hervey. The War Office never fails to misunderstand the nature of the country. The Admiralty's no better, mind. D'you know that when the War of 1812 began, they sent out great coppers to the shipyards here for the men-o'-war on the lakes to store water in?"

Hervey's blank response was evidence that Lawrence's point had escaped him.

"They're the largest sweetwater lakes in the world, Hervey!"

"Oh, yes, of course."

"It's no shame that *you* do not twig the matter, but one might expect more of their lordships. And now the foreign secretary instructs," Lawrence read from a sheet of paper "that we 'render every assistance to the forces of the United States in the suppression of the Indian resistance on their western frontier'!"

Hervey thought for a moment, puzzled by the vehemence of the superintendent's opposition. "Is that so wholly bad?"

"Hervey, did you hear *anything* I said when last we spoke? Our relations with the Indians in Upper Canada have on the whole been happy—the result of prudent policies. But of late the relations have been tried by any number of little things. If we take a hand against the nations in the United States—whether they be enemies of the Canada nations or no—there are bound to be consequences, ructions." He raked the stove vigorously to let the wood ash fall and the flames to have more updraft. "Since the affair at Niagara—the *two* affairs at Niagara, I might add, now that your commanding officer has entered the lists—the Indians do not trust us as before. The Six Nations, especially, believe we will sell them cheap at some time in the future. This is the very worst thing we could be doing. And it comes from ill-advised folk in London with not a notion of the frontier—or, indeed, a care."

The lament of a field officer that London did not know or care was not new to him. He had heard it in many the same measure in the Peninsula, and lately in India. But Lawrence's tone was unusually strident. "I don't really understand why the United States should *need* our help, anyway," Hervey replied, shaking his head. "Let's be frank: their army worsted ours at New Orleans."

"Ah," nodded Lawrence, as if what he was going to say would entirely prove his contention. "Their army consists now of infantry, artillery, and engineers. They have no cavalry."

"What?" said Hervey, unable to conceive such a thing was possible. "You mean none at all?"

"No, none at all. They stood 'em all down two years ago, as soon as the war was ended." Rattled though he was, Lawrence could still manage a smile: "Dear stuff, cavalry!"

"The want is evidently *costing* them dear at present. And is that what we are to do? Send them cavalry?"

"Yes, that is what they've asked for. To Detroit, to be precise."

"Where is that?"

Lawrence pointed on the map.

"But that's two hundred miles, by the look of it."

"A little more, although the road is good. But at this time of year the going will be hard, to say the least. Now, look, the DAAG agreed to let me tell you of the situation and mission in general terms, and then he will discuss with you whatever detail you feel is unsettled. He's having a copy of the commander in chief's orders made, detailing the limits of your intervention—which, I am sorry to say, do not seem great."

Hervey nodded. "Very well. Who are these Indians who give the Americans so much trouble?"

Lawrence put more wood into the stove. "You recall what I said before about the disparate treatment of the nations by ourselves and the Americans?"

"Yes, in broad terms."

"The Shawanese are one of their trickiest problems in this respect. They're a Tennessee and Ohio nation, and they fought the colonists there tooth and claw. Then the authorities made various deals with them, and served them very ill indeed, and now they're pretty well rootless. They broke up into any number of groups last century. Some moved to the Carolinas, some west, some northeast. But one of the groups was with Tecumseh, and they were dealt with very sorely by the Americans just a year before the war began—at a place called Tippecanoe River. They broke up their settlements while the braves were away. The name's enough to make a Shawanese boil now. It seems they're implacably opposed to any further treating with the American Indian department." Lawrence paused to light a cheroot.

Hervey was already taking notes. "How warlike a tribe are they? In nature, I mean."

The superintendent took a long draw, and sighed. "Well, who knows? The guts may have been knocked out of them these past three or four years. But I'll say this: the Shawanese were consistently the most warlike in first opposing white settlement. I think they're a very embittered nation, now—not given to parley. And any embittered Indian can be a fearsome warrior. There's a group trying to move up into Michigan, perhaps across the border, even. The Shawanese are Algonkians, not Iroquois, but since the war they've felt they had more in common than held them apart. I believe the Six Nations would allow them space. We're not talking of many hundreds, after all."

Hervey listened for another half hour, making copious notes, taking down suggestions, asking any and every detail. By the end he was reassured that he had a picture that would serve him well, though he suspected that ultimately his orders would hardly permit much discretion. It was a great comfort to know that the superintendent himself would come with him to Detroit, even if only for a few days.

Henrietta bore the news as well as she had that of Hervey's patrol to Niagara, although here was a mission of perhaps months rather than a week. She said, very assuredly, that as soon as it was apt she would travel to Detroit to be with him. How Caithlin Armstrong received the news Hervey did not know. It troubled him to be putting husband and wife asunder at such a time, and he had even thought of leaving Serjeant Armstrong at Fort York in charge of rear details. But that would have been irregular, and Armstrong would never have had it anyway.

Hervey's orders specified not fewer than fifty sabers, and that taxed the troop sorely, what with sickness and general duties, but he managed to draft something that would serve. He gave over the orders to Seton Canning the next morning, and then took two days alone with his wife and daughter while the troop made ready. He imagined, too, that he would know by the end of this brief furlough what was to be done respecting Lord Towcester—what *he*, Hervey, must do, for it was clear now that nothing would happen except by his own hand. And throughout he prayed that the lieutenant colonel would not return before they left for Detroit.

Only the second prayer seemed to be answered. Lord Towcester was detained in Quebec, and there was peace about Fort York. But Hervey had been unable to see *any* proper course respecting the lieutenant colonel's fitness for command. Do something he must, however, and so in the last hour of his furlough he had taken pen and paper, and written his submission as fully as he was able.

He now read his submission aloud to Henrietta, and to his surprise, she thought it well. He read her the letter once more so that there could be no mistaking his intention.

"Matthew, it will be well, I tell you. General Rolt is by all accounts a sensible man. He will know that a subordinate officer would not make such complaint without the gravest cause."

Hervey nodded.

"I do wish you would let me speak to Sarah Maitland, though. She would—"

"No," said Hervey, gently but emphatically. "There must be no cause for Lord Towcester to claim that anyone is scheming against him. General Rolt would very properly sympathize with him if he were persuaded that there had been scheming."

"As you wish, my love," she smiled. And then she took his hand and kissed his cheek. "Shall you look in the nursery once more before you go?"

Their daughter was sleeping. The eyes were bluer and bigger, and the hair more abundant still. The child had the look of the mother, and Hervey could scarcely comprehend it. He could only feel it, deep in his vitals—the force, the obligation, that was paternity.

CHAPTER 21

THE FINISHER

Fort Detroit, Michigan Territory, February 27

Never had Hervey found a mission so simple in conception and yet so difficult in execution. And it was Nature that accounted for both. The hundred fifty miles of country between Detroit and Lake Michigan was easy going—for the most part empty plain, broken occasionally by low-lying hills, the rivers running straight, either to Lake Michigan itself or east to the Erie—and the snow betrayed the tracks of anything that moved. However, the snow fell so often that a guileful enemy, if such the Shawanese could be called, had only to lay up until the sky told him that snow would soon fall again, and then continue his evasion secure in the knowledge that his tracks were being covered. And the Shawanese could read the sky, it seemed, for Hervey and his troop had not seen a single brave—nor even an infirm old squaw—in a fortnight of patrolling the line of the Raisin and Grand rivers.

He put down his pen, and began to read over his letter to Henrietta.

My darling wife,
Yours to me of the day after our parting is now at hand, my
having returned only this very morning from a tour of the

country. Your sentiments I return in all their measure. I am so very content, and principally because you declare yourself to be so. I, too, pray that we may be reunited soon, and I am so very glad that you say you will come here as soon as I send word. Fort Detroit, and the town of that name, is an agreeable settlement, and you would be comfortable there. The Americans are hospitable, if somewhat brusque in their manners, and my quarters are adequate. Or you might stay instead at Fort Malden on the Canadian side of the river, for there is a ferry by which our lines of communication run from Fort Brownstown, where the troop is quartered, and on to York. I am brought to Detroit, some twenty miles or so north of there, because the American general's flag flies here. If you believe yourself to be strong enough for the journey, then the rear details may arrange an escort for you, for there is frequent traffic on account of the dispatches &c. I am glad you have found a wet nurse with whom to leave our daughter, though the weather is warming so rapidly now that in another month I am sure it would be not unwise to have her brought, too.

I have seen a great many wild creatures here, whereas we saw none before. There is moose and elk, and quite easy to catch, since they tire easily in the snow, and can be driven into deep drifts where they stick fast. We do not shoot them since the noise would give away our presence to the Shawanese. I have seen fox and raccoon, and, I think, porcupine, but our guides say they take to winter quarters, so perhaps it was something else. We have seen black bears, several times. We are not able to get near, for they take off surprisingly fast at our approach, but they stand much bigger than I imagined. And—at last—we have heard wolves, and so many of the dragoons are now content. Indeed, we hear wolves almost every night. Sometimes they are a very discordant noise indeed, when they all just seem to howl for no reason but to proclaim they are there, but from time to time a single, far distant wolf calling is a very melancholy sound indeed. I am sure you will love to see all that Nature displays here.

In all respects we are well. Seton Canning and St. Oswald are greatly enjoying their liberty, and it is very good for St.

Oswald especially to have this chance of long patrols of his own. Serjeant Armstrong awaits his news with surprising want of ease. I never saw him so agitated! If this duty continues as uneventfully, then I shall send him back to York for a few days. I should also tell you, by the way, that Gilbert seems made for this weather. He can trot with so high an action that snow as deep as his hocks hardly detains him. And at a hundred yards he is invisible!

But the news I am least pleased with—and which you must, by now, have yourself heard—is that Joynson is gone back to England an invalid. Besides being sorry for him in his unhealth, I fear my letter, with its enclosure for General Rolt, will not have reached him before he left. Indeed, I cannot see how it possibly could. And so I am left now with no alternative but to request an interview with the general as soon as he is come back from Quebec, though when I shall be able to return to York I have no idea. I chide myself that I should have acted earlier—in England, indeed—but in truth I cannot see how before this affair of his at Niagara I had any evidence to go on that would stand scrutiny. What one thinks of as being of overwhelming import in the regiment suddenly sounds thin skillee indeed in a general's headquarters. And even the Niagara business is not beyond refute. I do so regret, now, the courtesy of writing first to the major, but every bit of me as a soldier said I must. It is a very dreadful thing to have done, to complain of one's commanding officer, and I can only suppose that I was trying not to compound my delinquency by submitting the complaint through the major. For the moment, therefore, I can do no more than submit my request for an interview with the general, and trust to God that he is a fairminded man.

And so, with these presents I must conclude, for there is a rider about to leave with dispatches, and I do so wish you—and now our daughter—to have this expression of love and admiration, as well as assurances that it leaves me well and as content as I might be in the circumstances of our separation.

Your ever loving husband,
Matthew Hervey

Brigadier General Sam Power was a man whom Hervey knew at once to be just the sort of officer whose generalship he would enjoy. His family were farmers from the west of the territory, and he had enlisted in the Michigan Legionary Corps on its formation in 1805, serving first with the rifle and then with the cavalry company. In 1808, when the regular army was enlarged, he went to the new military academy at West Point in New York State, and was subsequently commissioned into the Second Infantry. He had served with Zachary Taylor on the Wabash, Winfield Scott at Niagara, and Andrew Jackson at New Orleans, and he was not yet thirty-five. His blue staff uniform put Hervey in mind of Captain Peto, except that where at first meeting Peto had been guarded, distant, almost hostile, Power was open, warm, and thoroughly engaging.

"Captain Hervey. I am so glad we meet, sir. And sorry for its being two whole weeks after coming to my country. Sit you down!"

A vigorous handshake reinforced the welcome, and coffee, and apple-jack from the Power family's farm, sealed it. "It's a great privilege for me to have a troop of His Majesty's dragoons at my disposal, Captain Hervey. Congress must be ruing their paring. But it is a good thing for our armies to be cooperating, at long last."

Hervey said it was his privilege, too, but hoped it could be one without bloodshed.

"I'm not happy with these Indian wars myself, Captain Hervey. I regret very much some of the excesses of my countrymen. Some of the nations have a right to feel aggrieved. Yet the settlement of this land is not something that any can now set their face against. That is the reality. From now on it should be the proper management of that inevitable fact—the westward progress of the frontier. I only wish we were managing it as well as you are in Canada." General Power offered him a cigar, and lit one himself.

Hervey lit his and made appreciative noises.

The general smiled with satisfaction. "Yes, best Havana. We had them brought from just across the water when I was in New Orleans, if you follow."

Hervey did, but would not dwell on the notion. "And so the Shawanese, sir?"

Power sighed. "The Shawanese. Goddamn it, they can be as awkward as a bent nail. You know they believe the Creator is a woman? The Finisher as they call her. Well, they have a new prophet, related to

Tecumseh, and he claims the Finisher has prepared a land of milk and honey for them near their brothers the Ojibwa and their cousins of the Six Nations. That means northern Michigan—and Ontario, for that matter. The trouble is, the department's lost track of the main group altogether. They're not even sure they've left the Indiana territory. If they're making north on the western side of the lake, past Fort Dearborn"—he pointed to the map again—"there are too few troops to hand to track them, let alone turn them back, and then they could come into the territory from the north—not easy, of course, but perhaps a sight easier than trying to run a line of blue in the south."

"What do you propose, then, sir?"

General Power poured more coffee, and relit his cigar. "I don't have you indefinitely: that's a strong consideration. But as the thaw comes on, the rivers won't be easy for the Shawanese to cross. I reckon two infantry companies could picket the gap between the Maxanic and the Raisin, and then if we cover the fords once in twenty-four hours we'd pick up a crossing. They'd never do it in less, not with the spring melts. And their ponies are grass fed, so you shouldn't have much trouble catching them on corn."

"We're consuming that corn at a fair rate, sir."

"Yes, I know. My quartermaster general's working on it."

Hervey thanked him. "Presumably the Shawanese can't just wade anywhere?"

"Indeed, no. They can't all swim, and they won't want to cross too close to the lakes for fear of running into folk, or of not leaving themselves room to maneuver if they're discovered. I should like you to keep up your patrols along the Grand River for the time being, but be ready to move up to the Maxanic in strength. That just gives space to close with them before the country begins to open up." The general pointed on the map how they might have the run of northern Michigan. "I've taken several dozen Winnebago scouts onto the payroll, and I'm confident they'll come up with something. The point is, if we can confront them in strength—overwhelming strength—they mightn't draw a bowstring at all."

Hervey said he would apprise Fort York of the intention in his next dispatch.

General Power nodded. "I'm told your colonel is to visit, by the way?"

Hervey's spirits fell. "I was not aware of it, sir," but he thought that sounded a little curt, and tried to seem more eager. "But I imagine he would wish to. He's been in Quebec these past weeks."

"The Earl of . . . *Towcester* is it?"

Hervey put his pronunciation to right.

"I should be very happy to receive him with full honors here—if he would like that."

"I believe he would regard that highly, sir."

CHAPTER 22

BITTER COLD

The Maxanic River, Three Weeks Later

Fires burned all about A Troop's camp. They had buffalo hide blankets and fir frond beds, but still Hervey was cold. Nor was it a cold that bit at the extremities only but one which rendered him sleepless and unaccountably fearful. He needed this sleep, for he had been in the saddle for the best part of three days since the alarm. How like the exercise on Chobham Common it had seemed when he had told his officers and NCOs of his design, and how different the reality was—the cold, and an enemy who thought in so alien a way, and who fought not as soldiers but as men desperate to preserve their very being. Here, on the shallow snow-covered hills of southern Michigan—a place he could only imagine might be pleasant without its white shroud—he felt for the first time an uncertainty in the outcome, for he could not take the initiative and he had never met his adversary before.

He felt the want of Serjeant Armstrong keenly, too. Armstrong, now also the father of a fine, healthy daughter, remained at Brownstown, from where the troop's supplies, intelligence, and orders came. Hervey would have trusted no other for the task, but he was paying the price. At that witching hour of night, when the wolf called—menacing now, where first it had been novel and diverting—Armstrong would have been about the place, cursing, sparing no one, just waiting for a dragoon to complain of the cold or use it as an excuse for some dereliction. In the end it was so much easier to be afraid of Serjeant Armstrong than something altogether unknown.

The Winnebago scouts had soon repaid their investment. They had told General Power that the Shawanese would pass around the headwaters of the Maxanic, and then of the Raisin, when the full moon next shone. It was now the night before that moon, but the sky was overcast and the dark was like the first quarter's. The thaw had begun a week before, making the crossings treacherous and narrowing the Shawanese's options, but three days ago there had been a sudden relapse into deep winter, with heavy falls of snow and then a fall of the glass so great that the surface of the snow was now frozen as one continuous sheet. Horses were losing condition rapidly. Their heads were frost-covered, their breath freezing even as it left the nostrils. Fetlocks became chafed or clean cut with every step through the ice crust, and a red trail had often marked their progress of late.

Hervey forced himself from his bed to begin a tour of the sentries. It would test all his skill in hiding his own dejection in this godforsaken wilderness.

At Brownstown, Henrietta slept little better, not for want of warmth or security but because she had hoped so very much to see her husband that day. The ferry and sleigh ride from Fort Malden that morning had been pleasant, a pleasure she was not expecting to have again for some weeks. But, on arriving at Fort Brownstown, she had encountered Lord Towcester, and his mood had been extraordinarily malevolent—the reason for which she could only guess. He had ordered her to return to York at once, and, she recorded in her journal, in terms that overstepped any mark of a gentleman. When she had made to protest, he had pointed out that she was in military quarters and would hear him in silence.

He had even disbarred to her the ferry to Fort Malden, since he required it for his own purposes, he said. "You must take a sleigh to Detroit, madam," he had told her, "and wait on your husband in that place, or else cross there and wait at Malden. Either way, you shall not consume military supplies for another day more in this fort!"

Henrietta's suspicions as to the cause of the earl's ill humor, if correct, indicated that her initiative in writing to the Duke of Huntingdon had been speedier in its consequences than she had imagined. But she hadn't the initiative here, and she knew she had little option but to submit to the lieutenant colonel's will. She regretted its ill effects with Serjeant Armstrong, however. He had immediately declared that he would escort her himself to Detroit, but when Lord Towcester found out, it sent him into a rage. He accused Armstrong of failing to comprehend where his duty lay, and of loyalties inimical to the well-being of the regiment. Armstrong had argued, forcefully, that his captain had told him that the whole of Michigan south of Detroit was to be regarded as hostile until such time that they had apprehended or turned back the Shawanese.

"Stuff and nonsense, Serjeant!" Lord Towcester had roared. "I have myself just come from Detroit. Did I then pass through hostile country? Bah! It had all the appearance of Surrey!"

Serjeant Armstrong pressed his case. "Your lordship, they were my orders. And the intelligence is come from the highest level. The Americans have spies with the Indians. I don't think—"

"*Spies*, Serjeant Armstrong? Renegade Indians who'd sell anything for the price of a tot! And '*orders*' you call them? From Americans? Tush, sir! One more word and I'll have your stripes!"

At this, even the adjutant had looked uneasy. Armstrong had seen the futility of further argument, however, and had knuckled his forehead instead. And so all he had been able to do by way of seeing Henrietta decently back to Detroit was detail three troopers and Lance Corporal Atyeo to escort the sleigh, and threaten them to secrecy and a start before first light so that Lord Towcester would not learn of it in time to countermand the instructions.

Henrietta stared into the darkness of her chamber, resigned to being sent away but wishing—praying—that her husband might somehow come to her before the day did.

Just after six there came a knock. Henrietta had woken a few minutes before. Indeed, she had slept only very fitfully. She rose, put on her cloak, for the fire's embers were giving off little heat now, turned up the oil lamp, and opened the door. A dragoon stood with a tray covered by a white cloth.

"The serjeant said to bring you this, ma'am," he whispered.

Henrietta's spirits could hardly have been lower, but she smiled at him warmly, for she could see his unease. "Serjeant Armstrong is very good." She opened the door wide to allow the dragoon to pass.

He put the tray on the table and removed the cloth. Steam rose from the spout of a coffeepot. "The serjeant said to tell you, ma'am, that it's chocolate, not coffee."

Henrietta smiled again; Armstrong must have been very resourceful to find her favorite here. "What is your name?" she asked the dragoon.

"Stancliff, ma'am."

"Well, thank you, Private Stancliff, and please convey my thanks to Serjeant Armstrong, too. Do you think I might have a little hot water later?"

"Yes, ma'am, of course, ma'am. And the serjeant says to tell you we'll be leaving at seven, ma'am, if that's all right with you."

"Yes, that will do very well for me. You are coming, too?"

"Yes, ma'am. Corporal Atyeo's in charge, and there'll be Painter and Morris as well."

Henrietta did not know them, but they sounded true enough men.

When Private Stancliff had gone, Henrietta sipped the chocolate and held aside the curtains to look out into the yard below. She hoped still to see her husband—just long enough for them to bid each other farewell, even—but there was no sign of him yet. It was dark, and all she could make out by the flickering torches was her sleigh, the little, long-coated horse standing patiently between the shafts, its breath white in the cold air. She shivered, a little afraid now.

At seven, with half an hour still to go before first light, Serjeant Armstrong saw off the sleigh and its escort. "Take this with you, ma'am," he said, giving Henrietta her husband's repeating carbine. "If so much as a footpad comes anywhere near you, Atyeo and his men'll see to them, don't you worry. But . . ."

"Yes, I know, Serjeant Armstrong." Henrietta squeezed his hand and smiled at him. "Much better to have something of one's own in case they don't notice."

"Aye, ma'am. Something like that! Just point it in the air and keep pulling the trigger. It'd frighten a lion!"

"I'm sure it would," she said, finding herself trying to reassure *him*. "My husband has shown me it. And again, thank you so very much for what you tried to . . . for arranging this. And many, *many* congratulations on the birth of your *beautiful* daughter. You will be enchanted when you see her."

Armstrong turned very red. "Thank you, ma'am. I never thought I'd long to see anyone so much as I do that lass and her bairn!"

She leaned across and kissed his forehead. "Good-bye," she whispered. "I hope to see you again very soon."

An hour later, unable to bear it any longer, Serjeant Armstrong took his horse and galloped after the sleigh.

At ten o'clock, two hours after first light, Hervey received word from his easternmost vidette that a party of at least twenty Shawanese had crossed the headwaters of the Raisin and were making for the lakeside road.

"But that makes no sense at all," said Seton Canning. "Why expose themselves at the part most likely to be patrolled?"

Hervey cursed to himself. "Because it *isn't* the most likely to be patrolled. And they know it! Who'd patrol the last road the Indians would dare use?"

"Do you think they're trying to draw us away from here, so that the slower ones can pass through?"

"Possibly. But a party of Shawanese braves on the Detroit road makes us look damned stupid to say the least. They killed one of the trappers who saw them. They'll make mischief, right enough."

"What do you want to do?"

"No one will be using the Detroit road: that much we know. The general said they would close it as soon as there was word that the Shawanese were on the move. So the best we can do is send a division direct to Detroit across country and expect to intercept the party as they strike northwest before the town. Not even Shawanese possessed would ride straight for the fort!"

"Do you want me to take the division?"

"If you please. And you'd better send someone to inform Brownstown, and detach a man to Detroit when you get within safe distance. Good luck, Harry!"

The sleigh horse stumbled and slid to a walk as they began to descend the slope to the stream crossing, a wooden bridge distinguishable only by the snow-covered rails, three feet high. Corporal Atyeo walked his horse across to prove it in the prescribed fashion, and then signaled on his party. As he lowered his hand an arrow struck him in the neck, and he fell like a sack from the saddle. At once the troopers reached for their carbines and closed on the sleigh, the driver already crouching low on the board. Two arrows struck Private Stancliff in the back, knocking every bit of wind from him. He fell without a sound. Morris and Painter were good shots and fair swordsmen, but could see no target for their marksmanship. Henrietta crouched in the well of the sleigh, gripping the carbine tight, numb with terror.

"Let's go!" called Morris to the driver, now cowering between the traces. A flight of three arrows struck home, and Morris, the Norfolk farmer's boy, fell crying.

Henrietta saw him fall. She crawled from the sleigh to his side and pulled him to her.

"Oh, miss, miss . . ." he sobbed.

Tears ran down her cheeks as she shook with cold and fright.

Private Painter slid from the saddle to crouch by them, carbine at the aim. If he were frightened, he didn't show it. "Crawl to the sledge, ma'am. We can fight 'em off from there. They won't want to close with us."

Henrietta did as she was told, for Morris was dead. Painter prized his carbine from his hand and took off his pouch belt, then crawled to Henrietta's side. "Don't worry, ma'am. I've never missed so much as a hare."

But Private Painter did not have a repeating carbine, and was able to fire only once in the sudden rush of Shawanese. He knelt to aim. One brave fell clutching his chest, but before the dragoon could so much as bite the top off the next cartridge, a Hudson's Bay tomahawk split open his chest like a spatchcock. Henrietta fought hard not to faint.

The warriors, heads shaven but for topknots, cheeks stippled red with war paint, seized the troop horses. One brave pulled the driver from under the traces, pushed him to his knees and hacked his head from his shoulders as if he were butchering a sheep. Another, taller than the rest, and wearing a gold nose ring, took his scalping knife and knelt by Corporal Atyeo's lifeless body. He grasped the long fair hair with his left hand—so special a prize. He cut the scalp with two deft slices—one with and one against the sun—then loosened the skin with the point of the knife, and pulled with his feet against Atyeo's shoulders until the scalp came away with a sucking sound.

Henrietta had already hid her eyes, but her sobs came all the more.

It was the sight of Atyeo's scalp that raised Armstrong's blood to the boil as he bore down the slope screaming murder at them. "Fight me! Fight me! you bloody bastards, you bloody heathen, coward bastards! Fight me, any one of you!"

The Shawanese were stunned.

Armstrong leaped from his mare still at full tilt. The point of his saber went clean through Atyeo's defiler. He stood and roared his challenge the more. "Fight *me*—any of you!"

One brave launched at him with a tomahawk, but Armstrong merely sidestepped and took off the man's hand with a deft slice. "That's it! That's it! Come on, you savages—one by one. There's a different cut for every bastard of you!"

But he didn't see the warrior crouching behind. The tomahawk struck at that defiant head and stopped the tirade abruptly. Henrietta's frantic sobbing sounded ever louder in the sudden silence.

A brave who wore two eagle feathers at his throat, and carried a rifle, walked towards the sleigh and pulled Henrietta from under it. She had the carbine in her hand still, though he made no attempt to take it. She pulled her arm free—he did not grip it hard. He took several steps back, as if to admire his prize. She leveled the carbine and squeezed the trigger. The recoil snapped her wrist like a twig, and the rifle flew from her hands. She screamed in pain, turned and ran back towards the bridge, sobbing wildly. A warrior trotted his pony to bar her way. She scrambled down the bank to cross below, but the ice broke as she took the first step. She plunged up to her shoulders, the shock silencing her. Still she fought. She seized at the reeds on the bank, and somehow managed to drag herself out, watched silently the while by the Shawanese. Then the cold began to numb, where first it had bitten. What little strength was left was leaving her, and she knew it.

She began to sob uncontrollably. "Oh, my baby, my baby! Oh, Matthew! Matthew! Please God! Please God!"

She was on her knees before the warriors. It was snowing again, and bitterly, bitterly cold.

"Please, please!" she cried. If only the Indian would spare her, she could drive the sleigh the last few miles to safety—for all the cold, and her dousing, and her broken wrist. She knew she could do it. She *must* do it—for her baby, for Matthew.

The warrior with two feathers cradled his rifle in the crook of his arm, and fired. The sleigh horse fell dead in the traces. He turned and motioned the braves to follow, and the Shawanese rode off taking the other horses with them.

CHAPTER 23

RECKONINGS

Fort Brownstown, Next Day

Seton Canning spoke very softly. "And that is as much as we could make out, Hervey. Those dragoons must have fought like lions for her."

Hervey nodded slowly, using every ounce of his strength to keep his composure. He wanted to give way, but duty bound him tight even now. "What an end. What a terrible, terrible end." His voice cracked tellingly.

Seton Canning watched him anxiously, unable to find any word to help.

"And Henrietta—she ? . . ."

"Hervey, I am sure she was not . . . *touched* by any of them. She lay under a buffalo hide, huddled up to the horse. There was no fear in her eyes. She even looked—I can hardly say this—*peaceful,* almost. But she'd been soaked from head to foot. That much was clear. Whether she had tried to hide by the river I just don't know. The snow had covered all the tracks."

Hervey stayed silent for a full minute. "Thank you, Harry. Thank you for . . . I think I should like to be left to myself for now, if you please."

Seton Canning rose, but Hervey had one more thought. "Corporal Collins is trying to track the war party, you say?"

The lieutenant shook his head. "It's not a case of *trying*, Hervey. Collins won't give up till he's got every one of them with a noose round their neck."

Hervey nodded again. "The rest of the Shawanese we backed away easily enough when you'd left. They were a sorry sight. The Indian department men could scarcely believe it." It seemed to make it more incredible still that Henrietta should have died this way.

"A few days' cold and . . ."

"Yes, Harry. Nature doesn't seem to spare her own, even."

"Sir?"

"No matter."

Left alone, there was nothing to stand between Hervey and his darkest thoughts. Every instance that he might have averted Henrietta's death, every occasion that Lord Towcester's conduct had given him just cause to protest to higher authority—and there had been many if only he had possessed the resolve to do so—paraded before him like ranked troops at a review. Even the vision of Sir Abraham Cole and Manvers Priory, where yet they might have been enjoying their wedded bliss, loomed like some infernal specter. He buried his head in his hands at the sudden vision of a crib on the fine lawn of that gentle mansion. How might their daughter ever forgive him when she learned the truth?

There was a knock, and the surgeon came in. "Good morning, Hervey. I'm so very very sorry. I can give you something, later—if you want to sleep, that is."

"Thank you, Ritchie. Perhaps I'll be glad of it then, but not at the moment."

"Aye . . . aye. Whenever you're ready."

"Is there any more news?"

The surgeon sighed. "No. No sign of consciousness yet. But he'll live, I'm pretty certain of it. Any man that can survive this long will live. That shako is a hell of a fine thing. It took the force from the blow, and it's as well that it broke his skull, for that's what put Armstrong out as if he were dead."

"But how did he survive the cold then, when . . ."

"Henrietta was soaked to the skin, so Canning told me. She was only minutes from death as soon as that happened, unless someone could have helped her. Armstrong? Well . . ."

"Enough said, Ritchie. Thank you. Let's just pray that Armstrong re-covers his faculties."

"Aye, let's pray that. Well, I'd better get back to see that he's still breathing properly. I'm so very sorry, Hervey." He put a hand on his shoulder. "You know . . . that is . . . the cold is not so fearsome a death as others. Henrietta would have slipped into a peaceful sleep. She . . ."

Hervey gave the surgeon what thankful smile he could manage, and sank back in his chair as the door closed. The clock struck the quarter and then the half hour, and many were his visions of Henrietta in that time—happy visions of childhood, courtship, and wedding day, shared perhaps by others; and there were more intimate ones, too, of which he alone could know.

At length he buttoned up his tunic, rose, and left the room.

"His lordship will see you now, Hervey," said the adjutant, in a voice dis-tinctly subdued.

The commanding officer's temporary quarters were only a dozen yards from where Hervey had been alone with his thoughts, but they might have been a league away. He put on his shako and said he was ready. The adjutant opened the door, and both entered.

Lord Towcester nodded to acknowledge Hervey's salute. "You'd bet-ter sit down, in the circumstances, Captain Hervey."

"I should rather stand, if you please, your lordship."

The lieutenant colonel looked a little taken aback. "Very well. Then let me express my deepest regrets at your very sorry news."

Hervey ignored the sentiments. "Your lordship, there is one thing which puzzles me. Why was my wife leaving the fort, and by that road?"

"Captain Hervey, I hardly think this is the time or—"

"I am sorry, your lordship, but I very much consider that it is. My wife had come here to see me—there is no ordinance against that—and the road she was on had been closed by order of the Americans and myself." Hervey's manner was cold, insistent, but respectful still.

Lord Towcester's eyes showed no more warmth than they had ever done. His mouth had closed to a slit, and his words began to come with a hiss. "Was I expected to know that, sir?"

"But why did you send her away?" Hervey's anger was now only barely concealed.

"Did I say that I had, sir?"

"Do you deny it?" Still Hervey kept his anger just in check, though Lord Towcester could not know how hard he struggled.

"Captain Hervey, your tone is becoming impertinent!"

Hervey's tone was still as cold as the air outside, and seemingly as calm. "Why did you send my wife away, sir?"

Lord Towcester huffed. "Because, sir, she had taken to meddling!"

"I *beg* your lordship's pardon?" The contempt was undisguised.

"It seems that she had written to the Duke of Huntingdon, raking over dead coals."

"I consider your sending her away improper. And I need hardly add that if you had not done so she would be alive at this minute."

"*What!*"

"Even if you did not know the road were closed, I consider that it was a reckless thing to have done, and I shall make my complaint to General Rolt."

"You impertinent devil!" roared Towcester. "Mr. Dauntsey, you will take this officer's sword!"

The adjutant stood openmouthed. "My lord! Captain Hervey has just suffered the most wretched bereavement!"

"That is no excuse for insubordination! Take his sword, sir!"

"There will be no need of that," rasped Hervey. "I shall send in my papers this very day. But I shall also lay before the major general my complaints, including your late conduct at Niagara, and certain other matters of which I have been made aware."

"How *dare* you, Captain Hervey! *What* conduct? *What* matters?"

"You will discover, your lordship. But I believe I may say that it were better that your lordship placed a pistol to his head!" He saluted slowly and turned on his heel.

Lord Towcester struck the table in so great a rage that the veneer splintered. "Stay where you are, sir! I have not finished with you! Mr. Dauntsey, arrest that officer!"

But the adjutant made no move.

Back in his quarters, Hervey took the letter from his pocket. He had had it now for no longer than he had known the worst, and his sister's neat round hand was a comfort, even if, as he supposed, it bore ill news. But what ill news could possibly compound his grief? Elizabeth's earnest face was before him now, and there was solace in it. Without doubt there was solace.

Horningsham
10 December 1817

My dearest Matthew,

I bring you news that you will scarcely be able to believe. Our
father has been made archdeacon and a canon of the cathedral! I cannot begin to explain how this all came about, for up
until only a very few days ago we were certain that he was to
be deprived of the living here. But the bishop deems that the
offenses of which he stood accused, and which charges were
to have been heard by the consistory, were all occasioned by
misunderstanding. The old archdeacon has been translated
to Ely, where he is made dean, and the bishop, it seems, believed it only right that Father, whose nerves have suffered so
very ill these past months, should have the preferment in his
stead. And so he is now *Archdeacon of Sarum,* and by the
time this letter reaches you he will have been installed, and so
you may write to him thus.

Mama is restored to all her former spirits. She even says
she hopes the old archdeacon will have a perpetual chill in
the Ely fens! And now that there is peace and ease in the vicarage I myself shall go to Warwickshire, to Lord John
Howard's people, for his sister is to give a ball. I do not think
you met her. She came to Bath last winter when her brother
took a house there for the season, and I like her very much.

I pray that this finds both you and Henrietta in excellent
health and spirits. By my reckoning, this shall reach you not
many weeks, or even days, before the birth of my nephew—or
shall it be niece? I long to hear of that news, which I do *pray*
you will hasten to us here by the speediest of means!

And so I shall end, for it pleases me more than I can say to
write to you a letter with such happy content at last, and I do
not wish to dilute its happiness with common tattle. God is
very good to us!

Your ever affectionate sister,
Elizabeth

Hervey folded the letter carefully and put it back into his pocket. He
would write to Elizabeth, and at the same time to Lord and Lady Bath, to

say that he had lost his wife—that *he* had lost his wife. He did not know how he would find the words, however, nor even the courage.

But for one letter he was certain he could find both words and courage in ample measure. He went to the desk, took out pens and paper, sat upright in the chair and looked out of the window. Despite the bitter cold, his dragoons were going about their business as best they could, for in the army, life must always go on, and with as little interruption as might be. Hervey dipped his pen in the inkwell, and began to write his report to the major general.

Turn the page for excerpts from
Allan Mallinson's first two novels
featuring Matthew Hervey

A CLOSE RUN THING

and

HONORABLE COMPANY

A CLOSE RUN THING

After what seemed an age, but which the adjutant's journal would record as one quarter hour only, the sound of Mercer's troop returning broke the silence—the thud of hooves pounding on soft ground, the clatter of running gear and, above it all, the jingle of harness. The six gun teams galloped straight through the gap between Vivian's and Vandeleur's brigades onto the forward slope and deployed in two sections, the faster way of coming into action than by the usual three divisions. As they did so a thunderous fire erupted far over to the right.

"I think it has begun in earnest, then," Hervey said to his trumpeter coolly. "Eleven-thirty, by my reckoning."

But before the man could make any reply the French battery opened up, ripple fire so that the gunners could better observe their fall of shot and correct. The rounds went high, but one gun at least needed to make no corrections, its shell slamming into the ground and exploding five yards in front of Edmonds. His horse, a fine black mare bought the previous summer at Banbridge, and Edmonds's pride and joy, was thrown screaming onto her back, legs flaying frantically for several seconds before falling still. The major lay motionless by her side, his body riddled with splinters, his neck broken.

The Sixth let out a groan the like of which Hervey had never heard. One trooper close by threw up noisily; another fell out of the saddle in a dead faint. He himself was frozen with uncommon horror.

"Mr. Hervey, take command of the squadron, please," he heard Lankester saying as the captain rode forward to assume Edmonds's place. RSM Lincoln and the major's trumpeter, himself bleeding from the lacerations of a dozen splinters, were already dismounting to carry their commanding officer to the rear. Lankester had to think quicker than ever before, as, with dismay, he perceived that his first order in command might be to retire—as shameful to him as it was perilous to the unity of the line. The French gunners, with the range thus established, would now be loading solid shot rather than shell, or even double loading both. In open order the roundshot would go through each of the four ranks like a hot knife through butter, but they were at least drawn up in line of squadrons (by Vivian's prudence, or the need to show a wide front?—he could not know which). Was there enough time, even, to go threes-about to get behind the crest? But then, if the French corrected high, there might just be . . . Lankester had it! *"Dismount!"* he shouted.

No reviewing officer could have faulted the steadiness with which the Sixth executed that command. It was as if they saw Edmonds himself observing the movement, and they rendered it precisely as required in the 1801 manual, as he would have wanted it. In open order they did not need to make ready. Taking the time from the man in front, each trooper threw a lock of his horse's mane into the left hand, at the same time quitting the right stirrup and placing the forefinger and thumb of the right hand on the pommel of the saddle. Then a pause before the second motion. Bearing on the left stirrup, assisted by the right hand, each man brought the right leg clear over the cantle, many a trooper repeating to himself the orders his roughrider had barked at him so many times in training: "In this position the body is to be kept perfectly upright, the shoulders well back, the breast out, the belly in, without constraint, the back hollow, the thighs and legs together, and the head turned to the front over the left shoulder!" The third motion brought the right leg to the ground and the left leg from the stirrup. Scarcely had the left foot touched the ground than the four guns fired in unison. Three round-shots whistled just above head height to go bouncing harmlessly down the reverse slope. The fourth slammed into one of Mercer's guns, now unlimbered and being aligned with the hand spikes. It turned the big nine-pounder over as if a toy, crushing the layer beneath the barrel. He screamed so loudly that Mercer's own fire order could scarcely be heard.

"Shell, one thousand, three degrees!" he called through a speaking trumpet, while the ammunition numbers ran forward to the stricken gun. The other layers worked as calmly as if at drill on Woolwich marshes, calculating the angle of the forward slope with the plumb line in order to offset the three-degree elevation on the tangent sight. But Hervey heard

the range—one thousand yards—with surprise, and hurriedly pulled out his field sketch.

"No, sir!" he called to the astonished artillery captain as he dropped his reins and sprinted toward him. "I have *paced* it. Eight hundred!"

Mercer turned with a look like thunder, but Hervey's confidence was unshakable. "Truly, sir, I have *paced* it; it is no more than eight hundred yards—that slope is deceptive."

Mercer's profession was not about being deceived by slopes—sixteen years an artillery officer, most of them on active service, and this boy from a cavalry regiment was correcting his fire orders in front of his troop! The layers stared at him, frozen for an instant. Yet something in Hervey's manner was so compelling that, for the first time since leaving Woolwich, Mercer accepted a correction. "By heavens, boy, you had better be right!" he shouted menacingly. "*Eight hundred,* two degrees, two guns ranging!"

Number One Section's lead gun fired, followed by the second section's. Hervey watched with admiration, but anxiously, as the crews worked with mechanical exactness. The ventsmen had their leather-stalled thumbs over the touchholes in an instant to prevent the ingress of air (blowback from smoldering powder was ever the risk) while the number sevens swabbed the barrels with sponge staves. Both shells arched faithfully across the valley to strike their target squarely. The first exploded between two of the guns, felling most of the gun numbers. The other set light to an ammunition limber, and the secondary explosions at once threw the remainder of the battery into confusion. Mercer confirmed the settings as the number eights were loading the bagged charges and their fixed projectiles. The number sevens turned round their staves and rammed home the charges with the solid end. The ventsmen stuck prickers down the touchholes and primed them with quills of gunpowder, the lead-gun numbers struggling to reposition and re-lay their pieces after the violent recoil.

"*Fire!*" shouted Mercer. The gunner layers ignited the primers with portfires, and the four remaining nine-pounders belched their explosive shells at the horse battery. Twenty seconds it had taken, by Hervey's reckoning—faster even than a rifleman might reload!

They wrought a woeful havoc, too, the French gunners who were not yet casualties of the ranging salvo cut down almost to a man by the splintering metal. Cheering erupted from the ranks of the Sixth, but Mercer's work was not finished. "Number One, shell, carry on! Remainder, three rounds shot, three degrees, *fire!*" he called, adding the extra degree's elevation for the heavier roundshot. Having killed the gunners, he intended completing the battery's destruction. It was as much vengeance as military necessity: the French might have killed the Sixth's commanding officer, but they had also killed three of Mercer's gunners and destroyed one of his guns.

In two more minutes the gleaming French cannon and limbers were a wreck of shattered wood and twisted metal, the drivers having decided on prudence rather than on bringing their teams forward with shell continuing its ruinous work.

"Stop! Cease loading!" ordered Mercer, and his gunners began making safe again, sponging barrels and returning charges to the limbers, while the captain, grim faced, turned and rode up to Hervey's squadron.

"Well done, sir. Hervey, is it not?" he asked, raising his hat.

"It is, sir," said Hervey, returning the salute and wondering how it might be that Captain Cavalié Mercer should know his name.

"If we had fired at one thousand yards, the rounds would have fallen unobserved beyond the ridge. The French had our range and would have fired off three salvos before we could have corrected onto them. I think they would have broken us," said Mercer gravely, before adding with a sigh: "That is why Adye's *Pocket Gunner* condemns contra-battery fire."

"Except where the infantry are suffering more than the enemy's," Hervey added on an impulse.

"Upon my word! A cavalryman who has read the artillery manual. I thought you read only French novels," replied Mercer without the trace of a smile, and he reined about and trotted away to lead his troop out of action.

Hervey now looked about for the RSM, praying that there might be news that Edmonds would somehow live, though knowing there could not be. Had he but died *gloriously,* sword in hand, going for the enemy. Not *this* way, unceremoniously, with the opening shot. Even though Hervey had seen men beheaded by shot, or disemboweled by shell splinter, Edmonds's death was still . . . *unseemly*.

Lankester called him over. "Hervey," he began, with a shake of the head, "I have not time to begin to express to you my regard, for there is immediate business to be about. You are not the senior lieutenant, but Strickland is new to us and, besides, I do not wish to take him away from Third Squadron at this time. So you will keep First Squadron for as long as we are in action this day. But remember this: First has always been the directing squadron, and to reorder that now would be imprudent. It will come to action soon enough, and when we go forward keep the pace steady, or else the supports will take off and there'll be the very devil of a mess."

"Yes, sir," replied Hervey resolutely.

Lankester smiled. "You will do your duty well enough, Matthew."

But it did not come to action as promptly as Lankester had expected. Midday passed with the noise of battle continuing to their right but still nothing of consequence to their front. Hervey sat motionless before his squadron. It was not the first time he had seen clear air between himself and the enemy, but hitherto behind him had been no more than a picket, a half troop at most. He wished profoundly, however, that the circumstances had been different—that in front of him, two horses' length, and to his left, there might have been Edmonds. He raised a hand to wipe away the moistness in his eyes. "Mr. Canning!" he bellowed.

Cornet Seton Canning closed up from A Troop and saluted. "Sir?"

"Mr. Canning, if we are to advance, you will keep the pace steady and remain within strict support distance, do you understand? There must be no bunching or running on to B and in this heavy going it will not be easy. I do not wish to be bumped!"

"I shall do my best, sir; you may depend upon it," he replied eagerly.

"I know you will," said Hervey encouragingly; and then, as if they were at some field day, he began examining his cornet's understanding of the battle. "Canning, why do you suppose that battery came into action against us?"

"To test our strength, sir?"

"Perhaps, yes. But what did it achieve?"

"Nothing, sir, in the larger scheme of things."

"Are you sure?"

"Well . . . I . . ."

"Let me put it to you that it has told the French two things. First, that they cannot tempt us from this flank too easily; and, second, that the duke will send guns here if we are threatened."

"I see, sir. But to what use would the French put that intelligence?"

"How do you suppose Bonaparte will fight this battle? He would not risk manoeuvring against this flank with the Prussians close enough to take him in *his* flank as he did so. And he is too much of a general to attempt a frontal assault."

"So he will manoeuvre against our right?" suggested Canning.

"That is what *I* should do, having first tried to tempt the duke to reinforce elsewhere along his line at the expense of that flank. So do you now think there might have been purpose in that battery's otherwise imponderable action?"

"Yes, sir," replied Canning, in evident awe of his senior's grasp of strategy. Yet not long after Cornet Canning's admiring response, at about one o'clock, there began a series of events which astonished them both—astonished them all. A cannonade like the crack of doom erupted from the massed batteries in the French center, so loud that it made the horses start even on this distant flank. Nero all but threw his rider, who had dropped the reins to record some detail in his sketchbook. Though Hervey could not see the guns because of the lay of the land and the smoke now drifting across the valley—nor, indeed, any fall of shot—he concluded somehow that the cannonade was directed on the center of the line. To what purpose, however, he could not immediately discern. Canning, too, thought they must be directed at the very place they had bivouacked. "Why do they pound the center, sir? Do they expect the duke will reinforce it?"

"That could be so, yes, but it is now so late in the day that Bonaparte is chancing much by doing so. It will be telling with what he follows, for it is the very devil of a hard pounding."

"Will not all the infantry in the center be carried away by shot?" asked Canning incredulously.

"If they were to stand in its way, yes," replied Hervey, "but the duke will have disposed them on the reverse of the slope. They will be sorely plagued there, but by no means as ill as if on the for'ard."

Canning nodded, feeling foolish for not having come to that conclusion for himself. But the cannonading continued longer than ever Hervey had supposed likely—for a full half hour or more. And the sound of the guns carried to Brussels, where the doors and windows shook, and to Antwerp. And even across the Channel to Kent, where two days later, before news of the battle reached England, the *Kentish Gazette* would report that "a heavy and incessant firing was heard from this coast on Sunday evening in the direction of Dunkirk."

"Hervey, how will the French attack?" asked Canning at length.

Hervey at first confessed himself puzzled. "Yet if they *do* assault the center they must first break up the duke's line, for the musketry of those battalions would be too great for advancing infantry to withstand. He may suppose, of course, that his artillery has shaken our infantry so badly that they will not stand. Bonaparte has, too, a fairish quantity of heavy cavalry, and if these move against the center, then the brigades will have to form square, thereby reducing the number of muskets that can be brought to bear. He must support them with horse batteries, of course, or our own cavalry and artillery would frustrate him. But if he followed up at once with infantry in large numbers he might gain the crest."

"And what should *we* do then?"

"Our orders are to stay in this place," replied Hervey cautiously. "And, indeed, if we abandon it, the French might very well take advantage and turn our flank, though I still cannot see how they dare risk doing so with the Prussians so close."

"Where *are* the Prussians, then, sir?" asked Canning ingenuously.

"We may be sure they are making best speed toward us, Canning. Do not be afeard of that."

"But, sir, if the French were about to gain the crest in the center, what would be the good of our remaining here? Surely—"

"Canning, your shrewdness does you credit, for that is the very question on which the battle might turn. And that is why we have generals."

"I see, sir," replied the cornet, reassured, while Hervey merely lapsed into thoughtful silence.

A quarter of an hour passed. Little could they make of what was happening in the center because of the dense clouds of smoke drifting across the valley. But then, between the thunderous volleys, there came a different sound: cheering, shouting, drums, and soon, quite distinctly, although almost a mile away, cries of *"Vive l'empereur!"* And as the cannonading fell away the distinctive beat of the drums could be made out: *rum-dum, rum-dum, rummadum dummadum, dum, dum.*

"What is that, Hervey?" asked Canning with a look of alarm.

"It is called the *pas de charge*," he replied ominously, peering through his telescope, though still the powder smoke was too thick to see whence the drumming came. And then the smoke cleared enough for there to be no doubt. "See there, Canning! *That* is how the French will attack—nay, *do* attack!"

Canning put his own telescope to his eye and gasped. "But—"

"But what?" said Hervey briskly.

"But they come in great columns, like Greek phalanxes. And the cavalry—I can see lancers and cuirassiers—they are on the flanks. You said they must first make our infantry form square!"

"Then, if our center is intact, they will pay dearly. How fast can our infantry volley?"

"I confess I do not know, sir, for I have never seen them," Canning replied sheepishly.

"Twice in a minute. And they do so in two ranks only, instead of three, unlike every other army in the field: hence the duke can dispose of such a long line. How many do you count in those French columns?"

"I cannot rightly see, for there are so many. . . ."

Hervey peered even more intently through his telescope as the clouds of smoke cleared, the massed battery having halted its bombardment. "Well, Canning, unless I am very much mistaken those are not battalion but divisional columns. They will be even more susceptible to fire."

Canning continued to study them. "But there seem to be hundreds so tight packed that—"

"That ball and case would ravage them. Aye, indeed, and our infantry will enfilade them, too. In those French divisions there are probably eight battalions—six hundred men to a battalion. They'll front two hundred, twenty-five ranks deep or more."

"But why . . . ?"

"Suppose yourself for a moment to be standing in the path of one of those columns. Might you not be intimidated?"

"Yes, sir, I fancy that I might."

"Well, that is how Bonaparte has swept so many from the field these past years. I tell you, Canning, it takes nerves of steel to stand your ground before such a machine!"

Hervey and Canning (every man in the Sixth, indeed) now watched with a mixture of exhilaration and dread as three divisional columns—all of fourteen thousand men—marched up the slope, astride the Brussels high road, toward the strongest part of the duke's line, while a fourth veered toward Papelotte farm and the Nassauers below. Hervey could not at first believe it—a frontal assault, no manoeuvre, and this from the greatest proponent of that art in Europe! He felt somehow cheated that in their first direct encounter with Bonaparte they faced the tactics of the battering ram.

HONORABLE COMPANY

There was, thankfully, a moon—enough to permit Hervey's little force to leave Chintalpore along the road to Jhansikote at a brisk trot. Four kos, nearly ten miles—they could be there by midnight. And then what? Three or so hours to think of something.

At the front of the column rode Hervey and Locke, the jemadar and two sowars riding point half a furlong ahead. Behind them were six paired ranks of lancers, then the galloper gun, and then four more pairs. And at the rear was Johnson, his carbine primed and ready to fire at the slightest sign of riot (Selden had said that the sowars could be trusted, but Johnson was there to reinforce that trust). Hervey was content he could at least rely on his mount, for Jessye had more spring in her trot than he had felt in many weeks. How quickly she had regained her strength—faithful, honest mare. And he had his rifled carbine, the percussion lock which had saved his life at Waterloo—probably the only one at the battle, and the only one in India, for sure.

They hardly spoke, for Locke had no idea how they might subdue two thousand mutinous sepoys, and Hervey was absorbed in that very question. He could find no practical help in what he had said earlier to the rajah, that nothing could be done without good and early intelligence, and that it was with artillery that war was made. All he had by way of intelligence was that there were two thousand armed, mutinous sepoys at Jhansikote readying to march at dawn. As for artillery, his amounted to one galloper gun that could throw a four-pound shot perhaps a thousand yards. Bold action in all circumstances, demanded Peto's treatise—the moral effect of surprise. Surprise, indeed, was the only thing they might have in this affair.

They made good progress to begin with, but the jemadar warned them that a mile or so before Jhansikote the road narrowed and passed through thick jungle. Here would be a picket, for certain. But the picket evidently was expecting no trouble since a fire gave away both its presence and disposition—fortified as it was by the tree felled across the road.

Hervey's troop stopped well short. He dismounted and advanced cautiously until he could hear the fire crackling, peering through the darkness with his telescope—as much an aid at night for seeing close up as it was by day for distance. He could see no one his side of the tree. It was impossible to know how many were on the other, but he didn't imagine there would be many, since all they would be expected to do was raise the alarm rather than fight any lengthy action. However, they were within half a mile of Jhansikote, and shots would carry that far, even muffled by the forest. He could not risk an assault head-on. Back he stalked to the troop to tell Locke and the jemadar that they would have to approach through the forest and take the picket with the sword from a flank.

The jemadar looked alarmed. "Sowars not like go in forest, sahib," he stammered.

He knew some English: that much would be useful. Hervey might have owned to a dislike for it too, but instead spoke to him briskly in Urdu.

"Sahib!" snapped the jemadar when he was done, saluting and turning back to look for his dafadar.

"What did you say to him?" asked Locke.

"I told him they would have more to fear from me than the jungle."

Locke sighed. "They're more likely to die with *you*, that's for sure! Shall we go left or right?"

"It seems the same to me. Shall we toss a rupee for it?" he replied lightly.

"For heaven's sake, man!"

"Very well. Which side is the moon?"

Locke glanced skyward. "The left."

"In that case we attack from the right," said Hervey.

Locke said nothing for a moment, and then he could conceal his puzzlement no longer. "Why then from the right?"

"Because, as Hindoos, they will sleep facing the moon, and we shall therefore have the advantage of them."

Locke could not but admire Hervey's acquisition of such useful knowledge in the short time they had been in the country. "Very well, then," he whispered, "right it is!"

The jemadar returned with his dafadar and fifteen troopers, leaving the rest as horse holders. The NCO looked a good man, a Rajpoot, thought Hervey—the high cheekbones and supreme confidence. Private Johnson came up, but Hervey said he was to stay to keep an eye on the horse holders. Johnson took Jessye from him and started for the rear, for once without protest, though the muttering beneath his breath was all that Hervey needed to be reassured that his groom had not lost any of his former spirits. The remainder drew their sabers slowly and silently, and then, in single file, led by Hervey, they slipped into the forest.

The moon was still good to them. They were able to see the road—now little more than a track—and keep parallel with it as they edged cautiously through the unearthly darkness. There was more undergrowth than where he had spent the earlier part of the day, for the road allowed in light, and with that came growth on the floor itself. It was not enough to slow their progress greatly: anxiety to keep silence was what checked them. That and the dread of what lurked in the blackness. He shivered at the thought of the hamadryads.

It took more than a half hour to cover the three hundred yards to where the tree lay across the road. They had slowed to the snail's pace as they neared it, for although the fire was an excellent beacon, and they were able to align themselves well, the undergrowth, the dead leaves on the forest floor especially, made for noise. Hervey stopped as he came level with the picket, only twenty yards into the jungle, and motioned half a dozen of the sowars to pass him so that he would be in the center of the line as they broke from the forest edge. Five more minutes and they were ready. Something rustled on the ground not a yard in front. He froze, expecting any second to feel the creature's strike, or to hear a sowar shriek—or the picket to sound alarm. But there was nothing. Only the heavy silence of the jungle. He waited a full five minutes more and then motioned the line to advance. His heart pounded so hard he swore he could hear it.

The sepoy sentry at the tree, seeing them rush in, had only a second's horror before the dafadar's tulwar cut his head clean from his shoulders. After that it was easy. Simply a business of dispatching the remainder in their sleep—eleven in all. Not one let out so much as a cry. It was a brisk, bloody business—over in less than a minute.

As they searched the dead, Hervey looked into the faces of the sowars who had just slaughtered their fellows. Whatever he saw he could not fathom, but one thing at least—they were more determined faces than before. Even the jemadar looked more resolute. "Good work!" said Hervey; "Well done, Jemadar sahib, well done!"

The jemadar's self-esteem grew visibly. It *was* good work—swift death to the enemy and no blood of their own shed.

"More men are flattered into courage than are bullied out of cowardice," said Hervey to Locke as they sheathed their swords.

Locke seemed pensive. "Hervey, you said they would be sleeping with their faces to the moon. They were sleeping the other way."

Hervey smiled. "I don't play brag, my dear Locke: perhaps I should! How in heaven's name was I to know which way they would be sleeping?" He turned to the jemadar. "And now we must get that gun over this tree, Jemadar sahib!"

Locke was still shaking his head even as Hervey gave the orders for the gun dafadar.

The jemadar assembled his NCOs, and there were words, increasingly heated, none of which Hervey could understand. In their haste to be away, the dafadar had not brought the tools to enable them to disassemble the piece and lift it—barrel, trail, and wheels.

"Jesus, nothing's easy!" swore Locke. "We could build a ramp and then haul it over, I suppose."

"It would take too long," said Hervey. "Jemadar sahib, the dafadar will have to jump with the gun."

The jemadar relayed the instruction but the dafadar replied with much shaking of the head. "He says the horse does not jump, sahib."

"Nonsense!" said Hervey. "*All* horses jump—perfectly naturally!"

"I do not think the dafadar will be able to do so, sahib," replied the jemadar skeptically.

Hervey sighed. "Very well, let *me* try."

Locke voiced his disquiet, too, but what alternative was there? said Hervey: "We can't take all night building a ramp. The worst that can happen is that we'll end up with the horse and gun straddling the tree, and then we shall just have to cut it from between the shafts. There is, at least, plenty of moon!"

He went up to the gun horse. "He pulls to the left always, sahib," said the dafadar, helping Hervey to shorten the stirrup leathers when he had mounted.

That was more the pity, thought Hervey, for he would need his right arm to drive him at the tree with the flat of his sword: all he could do was put him at his fence with so much speed that he would have no time to think about running out. The horse was a big country-bred; Hervey thought it strange the dafadar had never jumped him. Was it really possible that he could *not* jump?

"Does tha want me to give thee a lead?" chirped Johnson out of the gloom.

That was exactly what Hervey was about to ask the jemadar to do. But Johnson he could wholly rely on. *And* Jessye—the covert hack so much derided by his fellow officers when he had first joined the Sixth. "Take her, then," he said; "keep me close up behind, but we've got to hit the tree at a pace!"

A minute or so later they were ready and Hervey signaled the off. Johnson put Jessye into a canter in a few strides and Hervey was surprised by how the gun horse was able to match her. He didn't need his sword until they were a dozen strides from the tree, and even then it looked unnecessary, for the gelding was chasing her strongly. The teak barrier was plain to see in the moonlight—that much was a mercy—and Jessye cleared it easily. Hervey gave the gun horse his head and slapped his quarters with his sword for all he was worth, feeling the beginning of a pull to the left.

He jumped. He jumped big! Hervey felt the gun lift behind him, praying that the shafts wouldn't break from the harness. The gun horse landed square but on his off fore, throwing Hervey's balance and almost tipping him out of the saddle. But he recovered just quick enough to get both legs firm on as the gun bounced hard on the ground, the horse stumbling perilously for several strides, needing every bit of Hervey's leg to pick him up. It was a full fifty yards before he was able to bring him to the halt.

The acclamation that followed was too loud for his liking, but Hervey was pleased enough with his success to let it pass. The dafadar proffered his embarrassed apologies but Hervey made light of it. "Only serve your gun bravely when the time comes," he replied—and the NCO returned a look that assured him on that, at least, he could count.

The remainder of the troop led their horses into the forest, round the tree, and remounted the other side. Hervey decided they must now walk rather than trot, for he could not risk the noise as they neared the objective. Nevertheless, it was not many minutes before they were at the forest edge a quarter of a mile from the walls of Jhansikote. They dismounted once more, and Hervey, Locke, and the jemadar went forward. The moon seemed even stronger now, but there was concealment enough in the shadow pools at the foot of the trees, and Hervey could soon see the white walls of the cantonment with perfect clarity through his telescope. They brought to mind the chalk cliffs that had welcomed him home, and the Sixth, two years before—and looked every bit as daunting to scale. Between the forest edge and the walls there was nothing—no scrub for cover, no nullah along which they might crawl. And this nothing was bathed in moonlight so bright that even a crouching figure would throw a shadow for any sharp-eyed sentry to see. Hervey was growing more dismayed, for the moon was still high and could not possibly set before dawn. "How might a frigate take on a first-rate? For that's how it seems to me!" he whispered to Locke.

Locke grimaced: it was unthinkable. "She would have to lay alongside her before the big ship's guns were run out, that's for sure. And I dare say she would have to board her before she could beat to quarters. But what ship of the line would allow any other to do that? We need a *ruse de guerre!*"

"Just so," sighed Hervey, trying hard, but in vain, to think by what subterfuge they could cross the ground unseen—let alone gain the walls. He kept peering through his telescope for some clue.

A minute or more later and he saw what first he had failed to see. The merest glow, from a sentry's fire at the foot of the walls, revealed it. He had located the great gates easily enough in his first sweep of the telescope—immense teak barricades solid enough to withstand a whole battery of galloper guns. They stood out in the solid whiteness of the walls—Nelson style—like the gunports of a man-of-war. And he had supposed them closed. Why, indeed, would they not be? Yet, why *should* they be? After all, the mutineers had a picket out, and the only troops loyal to the rajah were days away across the Godavari. He cursed himself for not seeing before. As he peered ever more intently through his telescope his heart began to race, for as his eyes became accustomed to the pools of darkness, and he gained a more accurate sense of perspective, he saw that the sentry's fire was *inside* the gates! He snapped his 'scope closed.

"What is it?" said Locke.

"The gates are *open:* they are *wide* open!" he replied, smiling broadly.

Locke was not immediately reassured that they were delivered of their difficulty. "And your plan, therefore?"

"To attack—*at once!*"

"You mean . . . to ride straight at the gates?"

"Just so! *Through* the gates!" said Hervey without hesitating.

"Ride straight into the cantonment?"

"Yes."

Locke paused a moment, in case he had missed some obvious key to victory. "And when we are inside—what then?"

"We fight."

Locke made himself pause again, certain that some vital element had escaped his understanding. Soon he realized it had not. "Hervey, that's suicide; it's beyond a forlorn hope, even!"

Hervey smiled again. "Racker! *Wollt du ewig leben?*"

Locke began to laugh, and had to cover his mouth lest the noise carry.

"Matthew Hervey, it is *you* who is the rascal! Frederick the Great indeed! He was cursing a whole regiment of guards, as well you know! You mean us to gallop into their lines and just fight?"

"That's what a boarding party would do, is it not? It would clamber aboard and *fight*. It wouldn't have a plan!"

Henry Locke had to agree it was so.

"Well, then, I wish you to take charge of the gun. I'll have the jemadar with me. He is not the stoutest of hearts but I believe he would wish to be one, and that in my experience is often good enough. The dafadar's a good man, and there is Johnson."

"What have we to fear, then?" replied Locke, clapping Hervey on the shoulder.

"And we shall have surprise," he added with uncommon assurance.

It did not take long for the jemadar to relay the orders, for there were few to relay. They consisted of, in essence, galloping straight for the gates (the risk that they might be swung shut at their approach meant speed took precedence over stealth), bringing the gun into action against the armory and magazine, and firing the barrack houses. "We shall have to fight for our lives, Jemadar sahib," Hervey had warned, and the jemadar's face had been filled with dread. Yet he spoke firmly to his men, referring several times to Hervey as "son of Wellesley sahib," and that they were about to relive the great deeds of Assaye. At the close of the peroration the dafadar raised a clenched fist and swore a blood-chilling oath (there was no mistaking the meaning), and the sowars likewise.

Locke reported the gun primed, with a wad to keep the charge in place as they galloped: it would take but seconds to load the bagged grape (he adhered strictly to the naval term). "I'll take at least a dozen of the murderous heathens with that first round—and we have nineteen more, and ten roundshot!"

Hervey, buoyed by the audacity, drew his saber. He had already loaded both carbine and pistol, but it was with steel that he expected they would first come to close quarters with the mutineers. When he had sheathed that same sword after Waterloo, he had somehow imagined that he might never again draw it on the battlefield—and, for sure, never in so distant a place. It had accounted for many men, had never let him down—Sheffield steel and always kept sharp. Before Waterloo they had sharpened *both* edges, fearing the cuirasses of the French heavies could only be run through with the point. He hadn't liked it since it spoiled the saber's balance, and more than one trooper cut his horse's ears, or even his own arm, recovering it from a slice. He had let the concave edge blunt soon after; he had no doubts he could run his point through any mutineer *this* morning. In any case, pointing was what a lancer did: a light dragoon fought with cut and slice. He smiled to himself: his first time in action with the lance on his side. But he didn't care to calculate the odds on being able to give an account of it later.

Johnson brought Jessye up. Hervey rubbed the little mare's muzzle with the palm of his hand, blew into her nose—as he had done every time before mounting since he had first backed her a dozen or so years before—then sprang into the saddle with sword still in hand. The troop formed in a column of twos, the galloper gun in the middle, and the jemadar, with his trumpeter, took post just to Hervey's rear. Johnson closed to his side on his Arab (still napping as much as on the approach march), and for once Hervey did not order him to the rear, for he knew he would protest loudly—and, ultimately, disobey. He looked over his shoulder one more time, and then waved his sword aloft: "Charge!" he shouted.

And the lieutenant of marines said quietly, "Here goes the last of the Lockes of Locke-hall."